D0033437

Love in another time, another place.

UNIVERSAL PRAISE FOR ANNE AVERY

FOR *FAR STAR:*

"Impressively textured and filled with haunting poignancy, this emotionally powerful love story is another significant step forward for futuristic romance!"

—*Romantic Times*

AND FOR *A DISTANT STAR:*

"*A Distant Star* sweeps the reader into strange and wonderful worlds filled with high adventure and love. This is my kind of futuristic romance!"

—Kathleen Morgan, author of *Firestar*

"*A Distant Star* is a must read for all futuristic romance fans...Anne Avery has a bright future in this genre."

—*Affaire de Coeur*

Love in another time, another place.

"Ms. Avery opens wonderfully imaginative new horizons on the leading edge of romance!"

—Romantic Times

BREATHLESS...

Tarl had no intention of letting her go. It was too sweet, too wonderfully delicious to feel her moving against him, regardless of her intent. She was warm and real and very, very female against his maleness. The heavy robe she wore was merely a tantalizing reminder of the beauty of her naked body, of the softness of her breasts and skin that he remembered so distinctly and in such amazing detail.

"I—I'm sorry," he said at last, ashamed suddenly to meet her eyes. His hands dropped to his sides and he stepped back, away from her. "I didn't mean...That is..."

Marna, too, was fighting for breath. Even in the dark he could see her lips were parted and her eyes wide and black and achingly alive. She swallowed, licked her lips, and said, "I don't know whether to hate you more for kissing me in the first place...or for stopping once you started."

Other *Love Spell* Books by Anne Avery:
A DISTANT STAR
ALL'S FAIR
ENCHANTED CROSSINGS
FAR STAR

HIDDEN Heart

ANNE AVERY

LOVE SPELL  NEW YORK CITY

LOVE SPELL®

July 1996

Published by

Dorchester Publishing Co., Inc.
276 Fifth Avenue
New York, NY 10001

Printed in the United States of America.

HIDDEN

Heart

Chapter One

If he got killed because of this little adventure, Tarl swore he would never forgive himself.

With a sudden, angry burst of speed, he vaulted the bushes clustered along one side of the night-shrouded building in front of him and dove into the even darker shadows of a walkway running between the building and the shrubbery.

Tarl slowed to a walk, relieved at the silence and the enfolding dark. His heart hammered painfully in his chest. His lungs labored to drag in air. Three weeks of indolence were proving more detrimental than he'd expected.

Unfortunately, the five men from Internal Security who had pursued him so intently over the past half hour showed no signs of slowing down. If they'd been reasonable, rational men like him, they would have given up long ago.

Tarl grunted in disapproval. He didn't think very highly of unreasonable, irrational people. Especially if they seemed as determined to cause him severe bodily harm as these men did.

When they'd found Tarl slinking through the shadows of the disreputable back streets of Diloran Central, they had opted for the shoot first, ask questions later approach to public relations. In Tarl's opinion, that sort of attitude was distinctly unproductive—not to say downright difficult to live with.

He hated to think what the men would have done if they'd known about the cache of government arms now slowly disintegrating under the acid bath he'd carefully poured over it.

An energy beam hit the building wall only millimeters from Tarl's head, showering him in tiny chips of plascrete. The wall glowed in the dark.

Tarl swore and ducked, then dived behind the protection of a nearby tree trunk. If the energy beam had hit him, he'd be dead by now. The patrol was shooting to kill.

Not a nice thing to do to the man who would soon be the leader of the entire planet . . . assuming he lived long enough.

With great care, Tarl peered around the tree. Nothing. At least, nothing that he could see in the dark. He couldn't hear anything except the faint rustle of leaves in the night breeze. Whoever had shot at him wasn't moving; until he did, Tarl had no chance of spotting him among the lush gardens surrounding the buildings of the main government complex—the gardens he'd counted on to cover his return to his personal quarters.

Tarl studied what little he could see of the nearby buildings through the heavy foliage. The columned glass-and-plascrete edifices, so beautifully airy and open by day, stood shrouded in shadows by night, virtually untouched by the dim illumination of hidden lights. The building he was aiming for, the palace of the Controllor of Diloran that had been home to his family for generations, lay several hundred meters farther on, out of sight and, right now, clearly out of reach.

He frowned, not at all happy with the looming possibility

of being caught outside his quarters at this hour of the night while dressed in stark black clothes undeniably intended for activities of which the official government in general—and his uncle in particular—would not approve. Of course, if he were dead, the difficulties of explaining his actions would be considerably lessened. However, Tarl didn't find that option overly appealing.

He glared at the faint glow that still lingered on the wall. When he'd left Diloran thirteen years earlier, Internal Security had possessed short-range stunners. Now standard equipment included projectile rifles and longer-range energy guns like the one that had almost killed him. The change was a poor commentary on the course of Diloran politics under his beloved uncle's control.

Another shot from the energy gun served as an effective reminder that his uncle's methods of government weren't his primary concern at the moment. Tarl crouched lower, then scuttled into the heavy undergrowth. At least the bushes and densely planted flower beds provided a more effective cover to his retreat than the open streets he'd navigated earlier. But only so long as he didn't make any noise.

Not an easy achievement, Tarl soon realized. Either he'd been a lot smaller when he was a boy and trying to elude his irate parents and tutors, or the bushes themselves had grown considerably over the past fifteen years. By the time he'd skirted the first building, the muscles of his arms, thighs, and belly trembled with the effort of making himself as small as possible. To make matters worse, he wasn't having nearly as much fun as he'd had all those years ago.

A sharp cry warned him he'd been discovered. Tarl swore and burst from the confining bushes, almost grateful for the physical release. Halfway across the open area, he realized he'd taken the wrong tack entirely.

Three of his five pursuers were after him again. He had no idea where the other two might be. Ahead. Behind. To the side. It didn't matter. He had no choice but to keep going.

Suddenly, the fourth man lunged at him out of the darker shadows to the right, with the fifth man right behind.

Tarl caught the dull glint of the men's weapons before he dodged to the left, into the blackness of an alleyway that ran between trees so old and massive that they shut out all light. Overarching branches created a tunnel that sucked him deeper into the darkness. The path, heaved by the ancient roots that twisted beneath the surface, grabbed at his feet in the dark, threatening to trip him.

Instead of slowing, Tarl redoubled his efforts, unable to repress a smirk of triumph despite his gasps for air. He knew where he was now.

Almost without thought, he counted. One. Two. Three. The seventh tree, there on the right. The grass muffled the sounds of his footsteps. He slowed abruptly, turned on the ball of his foot, and leapt for the broad, low-hanging branch that had so often served him on his youthful expeditions.

He almost missed. The half-forgotten childhood memories that told Tarl where the branch was forgot to remind him he was a child no longer, and considerably taller than he'd once been. He hit the branch with his elbow, hard, then had to scramble for a firm grip. As he swung up into the leafy cavern above him, Tarl promised himself a good, solid round of cursing at the pain shooting from his abused elbow. But not now.

Right now he'd have to be satisfied with hearing his hunters thundering by beneath him, swearing and stumbling and staggering over the uneven ground. He grinned. Pity he didn't have a bag of ice water like the one he'd once dropped on a persistent tutor who'd been cleverer than most at figuring out his tricks. The men were gone quickly, swallowed up, still cursing, in the distant depths of the alleyway.

With a fond smile for his long-ago transgressions, Tarl climbed higher into the tree, then carefully maneuvered his way along another branch that provided access to the top of a tall wall. The wall surrounded the private gardens of the palace guest quarters, which would provide a way back to the palace itself and his own comfortable quarters.

A minute's search revealed the depredations of some inconsiderate gardener—the gnarly vine Tarl had once used to climb down was gone. The drop to the garden itself was too great, even for a grown man. That left him no choice but to work his way along the top of the wall—no easy task in the dark—until he found an equally sturdy tree inside the garden, which provided a way down.

Unlike the ground outside the garden wall, the grass inside was as flat and carefully trimmed as a carpet. The night air stood still, heavy with the mingled scents of flowers that must be massed in beds on all sides, but which now lay hidden in the encompassing darkness. Tarl breathed deeply, savoring the delicate sweetness, letting his heartbeat slow and his muscles relax.

The guards might eventually figure out where he'd gone. Or they might not. In any case, he ought to have enough time to find an open window or door that would give him access to the guest rooms. As a boy, Tarl had often found that visitors headed to evening functions neglected to lock the windows and garden doors to their rooms. Such negligence had proved useful on more than one occasion when his regular line of retreat was blocked. Once inside the guest quarters, it was a relatively simple matter to reach the subterranean service tunnels that led to the palace.

Moving carefully so as not to fall in any flower beds, Tarl headed toward the building that was no more than a black, shapeless mass at the far side of the garden. As he got closer, the changing angle allowed a hint of light from beyond the trees to creep through. The light reflected dully off the dark rectangles of doors and the broad panes of glass belonging to each of the six-sided ground-floor chambers jutting out from the bulk of the building like so many large, elegant boxes. These were the quarters reserved for the favored guests—and the most easily accessible.

Tarl tried the first door, then the second, the third, and all the windows in between. Locked, every one. He could finagle his way past a lock, but a window or door obligingly left open required much less effort. He kept trying.

The third chamber from the end provided what he sought. The windows stood open, dark and gaping without the warmth of an interior light to soften their stark flatness. The room's occupant was gone, then. Or asleep. Tarl crept to the base of the nearest window and paused, straining to catch any sound from inside, however faint. Nothing. The room was empty and his way clear.

He could see better at this end of the garden, where it was unprotected by the massive trees that surrounded the farther end. Here, too, underwater lights in a lily pool half hidden among the flowers and shrubbery contributed their own vague luminescence, softening the dark. It was a simple matter to find a purchase for hands and feet as he hoisted himself over the sill and into the room beyond.

Tarl was five steps into the room before he realized that it wasn't vacant after all. As his senses registered a human presence standing in front of the farthest window, Tarl spun around, preparing to vault back out the way he'd come.

A soft but undeniably commanding voice stopped him where he stood. "I will kill you before you're halfway out that window."

Tarl froze. A woman. He grinned and relaxed ever so slightly. Maybe his luck hadn't gone bad, after all. He'd met few women he couldn't convince to see things his way—certainly none who possessed a voice as sweetly tempting as hers. Her threat just added spice to the exchange.

He turned back slowly, taking care to wipe any hint of a

grin from his face. It wasn't wise to let even the gentlest of the sex think you didn't take their threats seriously.

Tarl wasn't sure if it was the sight of her that did it, or the sight of the weapon she held, but his throat squeezed shut and the muscles of his stomach and diaphragm tensed so suddenly that it hurt.

The weapon she held was unmistakable, even in the dark. The small disruptor would be silent and far more effective than even the laser rifle the Internal Security patrol had used against him. He'd be dead before he knew she'd fired.

As for her . . .

Tarl choked, fighting to get his lungs working and his pulse under control.

She was magnificent. A vision of erotic dreams clothed in pale light and shadow and nothing more.

She was also stark naked.

Except for her hair. Could you call a woman naked if she was only partially visible through a midnight-black cloud of curly hair that fell free over her shoulders and breasts and down below her hips? Hair that caught the hint of light from the window behind her and transformed it, turning it into an enticingly sensual aura around her that revealed the feminine outlines of her body even as it concealed the intimate, alluring secrets of her womanhood?

His eyes roamed over what he could see of the soft curve of shoulder and breast and hip. The long, clean line from hip to knee to . . .

Well, he couldn't see her feet in the dark. Only those tantalizing curves, those taunting hints of beauty, of . . .

Of sex, he wanted to say. No. Sexuality. And passion.

Certainly passion. Or was that just his own physical reaction?

Tarl shook his head, trying to drive out the tormenting images flooding his mind.

Her hold on the disruptor hadn't wavered by so much as a heartbeat. Whoever this unknown guest was, she was accustomed to holding a disruptor. He'd bet she was accustomed to using it, too.

After due consideration, Tarl raised his hands. Slowly. "I didn't realize anyone was in."

"No?"

"No. I was just . . . passing through, so to speak."

Tarl assumed his most engaging smile. The effort was wasted. She probably couldn't see his expression any better than he could see hers. If she could, then he'd have to assume she didn't think much of engaging smiles. Pity.

He tried again. "I didn't mean to bother you. I'll just—"

"You'll stay right where you are."

The hand holding the disruptor came up a fraction, just enough so his head, rather than his heart, was the target. Not that it would make any difference, of course.

Not to be outdone, Tarl raised his hands a little higher, too.

"What are you doing here?" she demanded, her voice as coolly steady as if she were asking his choice of wine at dinner.

"As I told you, just passing through."

"I wasn't aware the Controllor's guest quarters were commonly used as a public thoroughfare."

"Well, not commonly, no. The thing is . . ."

Tarl started to lower his hands and take a friendly step forward, but the slight tensing of her body, the barely perceptible tightening of her grip on the disruptor, convinced him otherwise.

"The thing is," he continued, hands back at shoulder height, palms out, "I got lost. My quarters are in the palace, but I went out for walk and . . . got lost." He shrugged. "I didn't relish the idea of just knocking at the front door, so I thought I could find a way back without troubling anyone. You know how it is."

His light, slightly teasing tone didn't work. She hadn't moved.

Tarl frowned. Given the circumstances, it wasn't right that she should be so cool and unruffled. Granted, she held the disruptor, but he was a stranger, a male, and an intruder. He was clothed and she most certainly was not. He was bigger than she was, stronger, and probably faster.

None of those considerations appeared to have occurred to her for she stood, still and calm, like a statue of the virgin goddess sculpted of light and dark and the cool night air, as unconcerned by her nakedness or her vulnerability as if she were surrounded by a dozen armed guards.

Tarl's frown deepened. Was that it? Were there guards outside the door, armed and ready to burst in at her slightest cry? Then why the disruptor? And why hadn't she called for help, even if she didn't appear to need any?

She wasn't likely to offer any explanation, so it might behoove him to supply one that would satisfy her, instead. He was growing decidedly uncomfortable with that disruptor pointed at him so unwaveringly.

"All right," he admitted. "I wasn't lost. I was out with a woman whose friends—mmm, disapprove."

"Dressed in what looks like a Galactic Marine's night battle dress?"

Tarl winced. Talk of the clothes he was wearing could be more damaging than any rumors that he'd been outside the palace in the first place. "You have to admit I blend well with the shadows."

"Why were you sneaking into my room? There's no one here but my father, my maid, and me." The words were scarcely out of her mouth before she stiffened with the realization that she'd made a serious mistake. "And our guards," she added hastily.

No guards, then. That was some comfort, at least. And it was nice to know she wasn't quite as calm or as accustomed to confrontations like this as she appeared. She wouldn't have blundered so badly, otherwise. Not that he was going to make the mistake of letting her know that *he* knew she was virtually defenseless.

Except for the disruptor, Tarl reminded himself. Even in her surprise at the slip of her tongue, her hand hadn't wobbled. Not even a little.

''My rooms are in the palace,'' he said, letting just the tiniest hint of a wheedle creep into his voice, ''but that's so closely guarded I thought it would be easier to try the service tunnels beneath this building, instead. I didn't hear any sound from your room, so I figured it was empty and—''

His recital of half truths was broken off by the distant buzzing of a bell, immediately followed by the thunder of fists hammering on the outer door of the building. Tarl tensed, his attention divided between the disruptor and the sounds of angry, righteous men balked of their quarry. The patrol had clearly given up their fruitless pursuit outside and were determined to search for him elsewhere, starting with the first building near where they'd lost him. Eventually their tempers would cool and they'd realize that disturbing the Controllor-Regent's guests could not, by any stretch of the imagination, be considered a career enhancing move. Right now, however, they were too enraged to think of anything but capturing him as quickly as possible, regardless of protocol.

''Well, I think I'll be going now,'' Tarl said lightly. He lowered his hands and backed up slowly, one careful step at a time, toward the window through which he'd entered.

His captor watched him take one step, then two, then glanced toward the door of her chamber, listening to the continued hammering on the main door and the sound of servants scurrying to answer before the Controller's distinguished guests should be disturbed. Her head dipped slightly and Tarl thought he could see her eyes half close as she concentrated, trying to sort out the sounds. When he took the third step, her head snapped back up, eyes wide open and firmly fixed on him.

"I didn't say you could go."

Tarl shrugged helplessly. He couldn't afford to wait for her permission much longer. He took another cautious step backward, then another.

"Who are they?" she demanded, her attention torn between his stealthy retreat and the noise outside the room. The hammering ceased abruptly, to be immediately followed by angry voices. "What do they want with you?"

"They're Internal Security," Tarl said. He ignored her second question and posed one of his own. "Do you really want them to find me here? Under the circumstances?" He nodded slightly in her direction—more specific references to her state of undress were surely unnecessary. "I could easily claim you invited me. By the time they sorted it out . . ."

Tarl took another half step back, keeping his weight on the balls of his feet, ready to whirl and dive out the window as soon as he was close enough.

"You haven't answered my question. What do they want with *you?*"

The irate question was interrupted by an angry shout of protest from outside in the hallway, followed by the scuffle of feet as the Internal Security patrol forced their way into the building over the objections of the defending servants. Only an occasional word came through clearly in the confusion, but those few were enough.

"Criminal . . . followed . . . associating with the Tevah . . . Traitor!"

Tarl's captor had turned slightly toward the door, straining to catch the jumbled, muffled conversation from the corridor. At mention of the Tevah, the secret society that common gossip said was working toward the overthrow of the Diloran government, her head snapped back toward him.

"You're a member of the Tevah?"

"Me?"

From along the corridor came the sounds of doors being thrown open, of irate protests and even angrier demands from the patrol for the servants to get out of their way.

Too late to flee. They'd catch him in the garden before he could get back up that tree and over the wall. All they had to do was turn on the external lights so they could see clearly enough to shoot. This time around, they'd be very sure not to miss.

He'd always held by the belief that a wise man knew when there was no fighting the inevitable. Tarl let his hands drop to his sides, forced his muscles to relax. The patrol wouldn't kill him if he didn't try to fight or run away. He had no doubt he'd get as rough a handling as they could manage while they took him into custody, however.

Once his identity was established, he'd be set free, but by then it would be too late. The carefully crafted persona he'd worked so hard to assume over the last few weeks would be utterly destroyed, and he would be forced to confront his uncle and his uncle's supporters in the government before he was ready.

Well, this whole, crazy charade was becoming a bore, anyway. Maybe he should be grateful for the excuse to get the brewing confrontation over and done with.

"Take off your shirt."

The hissed command startled Tarl out of his thoughts. He blinked, then stared at the woman in front of him. It took a moment for his brain to register the fact that she was no longer pointing the disruptor at him, but had turned its barrel toward the door, instead.

"I beg your pardon?"

"Take off your shirt. And your boots, too." She wasn't paying attention to him or his befuddled state, however, because she was already halfway across the room. Before Tarl could say anything, she was fumbling with the complex electronic and mechanical locks at the door. He could hear the snick and clip of metal against metal, even if he couldn't see her clearly.

"What are you doing?" Tarl demanded, too loudly.

"Be quiet, you fool." She hesitated. Tarl had the impression that she ran her hands over the lock system, then tugged at the door itself, but he couldn't be sure in the dark. "Just do as I say. Then get in bed. The far side. Under the covers."

She took a second to wave imperiously toward the broad, heavily curtained bed that filled one corner of the room, then bent and pressed her ear to the door as if straining to hear more clearly.

This was crazy. Had she locked or unlocked the outside door? If she'd locked it, why had it been unlocked before? He couldn't think of an explanation for her unlocking it, unless she thought it was easier—and safer—to explain a man in her bed than a man cowering under it.

Not that he had the luxury of worrying, anyway. The sounds outside the room were getting louder and coming uncomfortably closer.

With a slight hiss of exasperation, Tarl tugged off his shirt and flung it over the far side of the bed, out of sight. There was no time to worry about his boots. He ripped back the heavy covers on the bed, then slid in, boots and all.

It didn't take a full second for him to realize the boots were a mistake. They were big and clumsy and they caught on the sheets, making it difficult for him to slide to the far side of the bed. Tarl was pulling at the covers, kicking at the sheets, and swearing ferociously under his breath when his captor, disruptor still firmly clasped in her hand, lifted the edge of the covers and slid in beside him.

Tarl had thought he was prepared for it. But the reality of a warm, curvaceous, and totally naked female body in the bed beside him was unsettling, to say the least. That he could scarcely see her in the shadowed depths of the curtained bed only made the matter more enticing. So what if she found the task of hiding her disrupter in the folds of the bed curtains more appealing than exploring his masculine charms? Given a chance, he could change her priorities.

Before he could say anything, she tugged at the covers, pulling them out of his hands, then slid closer. Tarl's head was swimming, his body automatically responding to the possibilities inherent in the situation, when she put her hand against his side and shoved.

"Eeyah! Your hands are cold!"

"Move, you idiot. Do you want them to find you?"

"Well, you didn't have to—"

She snorted in disgust and shoved harder. "I should have shot you when I had the chance. Move!"

Tarl moved. Or tried to. The sheets tangled around his boots didn't seem in favor of the idea, however. He kicked harder, which only managed to pull the sheets free and let a cool whoosh of air under the covers.

"I told you to take off your boots!"

"There wasn't time!" Tarl protested, digging both elbows into the mattress and dragging himself bodily to the side. Sheets and covers came with him, jerked free at the end by his thrashing. It would be a whole lot easier if he could see what he was doing, if he could just stop for a minute to get untangled.

"There would have been time if you'd done what I told you when—"

Whatever else she might have said was cut short by the sudden hammering of a fist on her door.

The hammering signaled an attack, so far as Tarl was concerned. Before he had a chance to react to the shouted demand for entrance, she fell on him.

Or, rather, she pounced. One minute Tarl was fighting to straighten the covers, the next minute he couldn't think, and he certainly couldn't fight, because her warm, full breasts were crushed against his chest, her hands were cupped about his face, and her lips were pressed to his in a kiss that, to his dizzied senses, seemed as real and passionate and demanding as any kiss he'd ever experienced.

Tarl gulped, blinked, and flailed helplessly at the air before his instincts finally took over the battle his rational mind was losing. He breathed deeply. That pressed his chest firmly against hers. Instead of helplessly batting at the air, he wrapped his arms around her and drew her even more tightly against him. Instead of wasting the opportunity on gulping and gaping, Tarl let his open mouth soften, welcoming her touch, her lips, her warmth.

By the time the Internal Security patrol broke into the room, Tarl could scarcely remember who they were or what was going on. Involuntarily, he tightened his hold around his partner, shaken and ashamed that he could have forgotten so easily.

Not that he had much time for contemplating his failings. With a squeal of indignation, the woman in Tarl's arms pushed herself into a sitting position, shoving off from his chest with such decisive energy that she knocked the wind out of him and made him gasp.

''Who are you?'' she demanded, turning to face the open doorway at the same time she slid back in the bed, closer to him.

Tarl blinked and swallowed hard. She was so close, her bare bottom was pressed tight against his side, warm and round and firm, yet—

''What do you want? What are you doing in my room?'' With each question, her voice rose higher, became more breathless and helplessly fluttery. Suddenly, as though she'd just remembered her nakedness, she gasped and grabbed for the tumbled covers, dragging the edges up to cover her breasts.

At least, that was what Tarl assumed she was doing. He couldn't see anything because in grabbing the covers, she'd rocked back until the small of her back was only inches from his face, and the wild, curly mass of her hair covered his head, effectively blinding him. The faint scent of sweet herbs that lingered on her skin and in her hair, mingled with her own human, feminine warmth, almost overcame whatever pitiful remnant of his wits he still possessed.

He breathed deeply, struggling for control, only to be further disconcerted when she jerked the brocaded coverlet off him—and almost succeeded in dragging everything else with it. Tarl gulped and grabbed for the sheet and remaining covers, then slid deeper into the shadows cast by the heavy curtains. Even in the dark and the confusion, and with the added distraction of a naked woman to addle their brains, the patrol might sense something amiss if they discovered he'd worn his pants and boots to bed.

"Your pardon, lady," one of the patrol members managed to choke out at last. "We're looking for a man, a—"

She shrieked. Even Tarl flinched, and pressed himself flatter against the bed. "A man? A man!" She grabbed the pillow beside her and flung it at the intruders with clumsy force. "Get out!" she shouted. "Get out!"

Abandoning the coverlet, she jerked the second pillow out from under Tarl's head. Thus armed, she bounded out of bed and charged the five heavily armed men standing in the open doorway.

Chapter Two

Tarl watched the unequal battle from the safety of the shadowed, tumbled recesses of the heavily curtained bed. Once the first blow landed, he could see that the end was a foregone conclusion.

"You break into *my* room . . ." The pillow made a loud *thwump!* when it hit. "Looking for a man!" *Fwump!* "Here!"

The second man she aimed for ducked. The pillow struck the man behind him full in the face. She swung back and hit the first man again.

"How dare you insult me!" Her first target staggered back into the arms of a fellow member of the patrol. Her hair swirled about her in the light pouring in from the hallway, alternately hiding, then revealing, her breasts and belly and long, long legs. "You misbegotten offspring of a desert goat! You foul—"

"Lady! *Kiria!*" The one man she hadn't yet managed to hit—two of his comrades had taken the brunt of a blow intended for him—raised his hands in supplication. ''We're from Internal Security, Kiria. We're not accusing you of anything. We're looking for a suspected criminal and spy.''

''In *my* room?''

''We thought—''

''You don't appear to have thought at all!'' She hoisted the pillow and prepared to swing again, but this time her adversaries were ready.

One man grabbed her wrists. A second jerked the pillow out of her hands, then nervously retreated to a safe vantage point with the pillow firmly clutched against his midriff. Two more tried to slink out the door, only to find their way blocked by the press of wide-eyed, anxious servants in the corridor outside. From the men's expressions, Tarl guessed the five were starting to realize they'd seriously overstepped their bounds by forcing their way into the government guest quarters and upsetting at least one of the honored guests.

Despite the loss of her weapon and heedless of her eye-catching state of undress, the honored guest in question didn't hesitate to pursue her advantage. ''Not only do you *not* appear to have thought, I have serious doubts you are capable of *any* activity which might require intelligence.''

''Kiria, if you—''

''If you were capable of thinking,'' she continued relentlessly, moving forward one step and driving the men back two, ''you would have realized that I—I!—Marna of Jiandu, daughter of Eileak, Elder of the Zeyn—could not be guilty of harboring a criminal.''

Tarl almost jerked upright, out of the shadows. A finely honed instinct for self-preservation was the only thing that prevented him from betraying himself in his shock at her pronouncement.

Of all the rooms he might have broken into, he'd managed to choose the one belonging to a woman whose father was the leader of the oldest, proudest, and most fiercely xenophobic of all the Old Families on Diloran—the leader who had requested a special audience with Marott Grisaan and his nephew, Tarl, the newly returned heir to the controllorship of Diloran, in the expressed hope of ending some of the tensions that had existed for so long between the Zeyn and the rest of the inhabitants of the planet; the leader who could create enormous problems for everyone if he left Government Palace enraged and offended.

Tarl's timing couldn't have been worse if he'd tried.

Clearly, the men from Internal Security felt much the same about their own intrusion.

"Kiria, we—"

"Our duty requires—"

Marna of Jiandu, however, wasn't about to wait for any apologies. She ignored their attempts at explanation and forged ahead, her voice rising higher and growing louder with every word she spoke.

"You would have realized that I, a guest of the Controllor-Regent of Diloran, would not appreciate having my privacy disturbed—and in such an ill-mannered way, too!" She took another step forward. The five took another two steps back, which left them jammed in the open doorway, incapable of going anywhere at all.

One, however, had enough presence of mind—or sheer perversity, Tarl wasn't sure which—to try to peer past her, into the darkness behind her that hid the bed—and him. "If you would permit us to search—"

"Permit you to search! Search my quarters, you mean? How dare you even *suggest* such a thing?"

Nothing remained of the cold, implacable woman who had greeted Tarl with a disruptor firmly clutched in her hand. Even unclothed and unarmed, Marna of Jiandu was all fire and feminine fury, magnificent and intimidatingly passionate. Tarl couldn't help wonder which persona was more natural to her and which she'd assumed.

"You may be sure the Controllor-Regent will hear of this insult to me, and to the Zeyn," Marna continued, unchecked.

She pointed imperiously to one of the servants cowering in the corridor. "You! Take these men's names and service numbers. Immediately! Then give them to my servant. I will deal with all this tomorrow morning. And get these men out of my room. *Now!*"

Tarl, safely ensconced in the vast, comfortable bed, couldn't help grinning as both servants and patrol hastened to obey her command, creating even more confusion in the process. A loud, solidly built woman, who insisted on forcing her way into the room while the patrol fought to get out, managed to complicate matters further.

"Get out of my way!" she roared, thumping one retreating patrol member on the shoulder when he didn't move fast enough to suit her. "Disturb the Kiria Marna, will you? Out. Out!" With more thumps and punches and not a few grunts of satisfaction when a blow landed squarely on its target, the woman shouldered her way through the melee and into the room.

At sight of her mistress, unclothed and standing in the light pouring into the room from the corridor, the woman stopped short, astounded. "Kiria Marna! What is the meaning of this!"

Before Marna had a chance to reply, the woman awkwardly whirled around, shoved the last patrol member into the hallway, and firmly slammed the door on him, plunging the room back into darkness.

"Such shame!" she muttered angrily, oblivious of the dark. "A fight on your first night here! And after all you were taught! What will your father say? I've a good mind to tell him about this, too!"

As his eyes adapted to the dark again, Tarl saw the older woman turn toward the bed, head cocked to one side as if listening for a sound that would reveal what she could not see. She moved a bit closer. Tarl caught the faint scrape of her foot dragging along the floor.

"Where are the lights, Kiria?" she demanded.

"I don't know. I haven't figured out how to work them yet." Marna's response held a trace of resentment at the unexpected exposure of her ignorance. At least it explained the door locks.

The older woman stopped and fumbled in the folds of her gown, then abruptly held up a small glow-light that fit snugly in the palm of her hand. It didn't give much light, but it was enough to reveal Tarl caught in the tangle of sheets like a fish in a net. He blinked and raised his hand to shield his face, but nothing could have shielded him from the serving woman's indignation.

"So! There *is* a man here!" Heedless of her crippled foot, she stalked toward the bed with all the grim determination of a general advancing against the enemy, the glow-light held aloft like a banner of war. "Who are you? You're not of the Zeyn. What are you doing here? Are you this criminal they were chasing?"

Tarl kept his hand in front of his face even as he leaned into the shadows, away from the dim light and the threatening scowl of the outraged serving woman.

"I—um, I—" He faltered, torn between embarrassment at being caught in so undignified a position and the equally strong urge to laugh. Laughter, he knew, would seal his fate, yet he could feel it bubbling inside him, waiting for a chance to burst out. The whole situation was absurd—and undeniably entertaining.

Marna, who had crossed the room in her servant's wake, saved him by grabbing the light and setting it aside, where it illuminated her and her maid, but left him in the shadows. Tarl let his hand drop, relieved. He didn't try to slide out the other side of the bed as he'd originally planned, however. He'd had more than enough experience with protective servants to know that escape was futile.

"Well? What do you have to say for yourself?" the older woman demanded.

"Sesha, please." Marna tugged on her serving woman's

sleeve. ''Don't embarrass us.''

''Embarrass you! Is that possible? I never dreamed I'd see such a sight! You—a woman of the Zeyn and daughter of the Elder, brawling with common trash like any—any—''

''Cavern fighter?''

Sesha tilted her chin upward with an indignant sniff. ''The title's too kind, but I'd be ashamed to speak more plainly.''

''He was running from the patrol,'' Marna said reasonably, as though that explained it all. ''They said he belonged to the Tevah.''

''Humpf!'' Sesha crossed her arms across her chest and glared at Marna, then at Tarl.

Tarl couldn't help it. He flinched. He'd had his own Sesha as a boy, a stout, equally redoubtable nursemaid whom no one could intimidate, and he remembered all too clearly how much *she'd* disapproved of his numerous transgressions.

''It's all a mistake,'' he said in as coaxingly contrite a tone of voice as he could muster. ''I was—''

''He was just leaving, Sesha,'' Marna cut in firmly. Her voice dropped and became softer, younger somehow. ''Promise me you won't tell Father about this, Sesha. Please?''

Sesha snorted, then crossed her arms even more firmly across her chest. ''I'll say nothing of finding a man in your bed. But to find you without a stitch of clothing on, and tomorrow just hours away . . . Ashamed! That's what you should be. The sands of your mother would freeze where they are if they knew.''

Marna laughed. The muscles in Tarl's stomach and groin tightened involuntarily at the sound. There was something disarmingly honest and unfeigned about that laugh, something appealingly at odds with the various roles she'd assumed since he'd first crawled through her window—was it really only a few minutes ago?

''You don't believe that any more than I do. And Father

wouldn't mind if it weren't for everything else. Here,'' she added, bending to snatch up a robe that had fallen from the bed to the floor. ''If I cover myself, will you promise not to tell Father?''

Sesha showed no signs of relenting.

''You know I'm perfectly free to do as I please, Sesha,'' Marna said, very soft, very serious. ''At least until tomorrow. We don't need to bother my father with anything until then, and after . . . well, after tomorrow, it won't much matter, will it?''

It was the last argument that seemed the most persuasive.

''You've got your robe all twisted 'round,'' Sesha grumbled, unbending sufficiently to help her mistress into the garment. ''There. Like this.''

Tarl watched in regret as Marna's graceful nude form disappeared into the heavy folds of the robe. A sudden, sharp memory of how her body had felt pressed against his, of how warm and soft she was, of how deliciously tempting the smell and touch and taste of her had been, flooded his senses. He flushed, and was grateful for the enshrouding shadows.

The minute Marna finished knotting her sash, she wrapped her hands around Sesha's arm and drew her away from the bed. ''Go back to sleep, Sesha,'' she pleaded. ''I'll take care of everything here. You know I will. And besides, there'll be a servant in the hallway waiting to give you the names of those men who broke into my room. I don't want to lose that.''

''Animals!'' Sesha snapped, diverted.

''Exactly,'' Marna said, leading her toward the door.

Instead of following meekly, Sesha turned back to glare at Tarl. ''He's to leave. Immediately.''

''Of course.''

''And he's not to come back.''

''Of course not.'' Marna opened the door, taking care that no one outside would be able to spot Tarl.

"I mean it, Kiria." In the brighter light that poured in from the hall, Sesha's eyebrows appeared to have slid halfway down her nose, so severe was her frown.

"I know you do." Marna opened the door wider. "Good night, Sesha."

"You'll lock the door?"

"The minute you're gone."

"Promise?"

Marna shoved her insistent serving woman out the door. "I promise."

"If you'd locked the door properly the first time, this wouldn't have happened. Think of tomorrow—"

Whatever else Sesha might have had to say was cut short when Marna abruptly shoved the door shut behind her, then struggled with the locks until she was sure that some, at least, were engaged.

Safe now from further intrusions, Tarl carefully untangled himself from the bedclothes, then fumbled around on the far side of the bed, searching for his abandoned shirt. By the time he'd retrieved his shirt and regained his feet, Marna was standing beside the bed, watching him in the dull half-light cast by the glow-light she'd set aside.

Once again, she held the disruptor in her hands, and once again she pointed it squarely at him.

At sight of the weapon, Tarl froze. He hadn't noticed her retrieve it from its hiding place.

"I see," he said, very softly.

"No, I don't think you do."

The ice was back in her voice. The crazy banshee of the pillow fight was gone. The pampered young woman who'd so easily placated her outraged servant might never have existed.

Tarl shrugged, bemused by her mercurial behavior. "All right, I don't. How about explaining it to me?"

"I'm afraid I don't have the time or the interest. But I'd be more than happy to escort you out the window . . . and out of my life. Right now."

"Would you mind if I got dressed first?"

She opened her mouth, clearly irritated by his flippancy, then closed it without saying a word. Her lips thinned until they were nothing more than a dark slash across her face, but she didn't object. With a sharp flick of the hand that held the disruptor, she motioned him to get dressed.

Tarl had had his fair share of experience at dressing in the dark. He'd even had some practice while in the company of a woman whose bed he'd shared. But he'd never yet attempted it when that same woman was pointing a disruptor at his middle. He found the experience humiliating, absurd, and distinctly unnerving, all at the same time.

As he shoved his arms into the sleeves, then tugged the soft black fabric over his head, he was uncomfortably aware of an odd tightness and expectant tingling in that portion of his anatomy below his ribs and above his belt, the part that would be the first to feel the effects of the disruptor should Marna of Jiandu suddenly decide to shoot him. The last time he'd felt so foolish and so vulnerable was when the tribe of aboriginals on Biack Prime had held him, bound and gagged, while they debated the respective merits of broiling him for that night's dinner or pickling him for future consumption.

Fortunately, Marna wasn't a cannibal and didn't seem inclined to shoot. Then again, she also didn't seem inclined to drop the disruptor and give him another of those kisses of which he'd had such a brief and tantalizing taste.

Between one concern and the other, Tarl found the task of pulling on his shirt rather more difficult than usual. The top of his head popped out of the collar, but the edge of the cloth caught on the bridge of his nose and the top of one ear. That left him half blinded and helplessly waving his arms in the air while he struggled to shove his hands out the ends of sleeves that seemed to be growing longer by the second.

''Mmrphf,'' Tarl said, thrashing about.

''Idiot,'' Marna said, stepping closer to tug down one sleeve. ''You got it turned inside out.'' With one quick, efficient jerk, she freed his hand.

Tarl used the liberated hand to pull the shirt over his head, then hold on to the recalcitrant garment while he forced his other hand out the end of the second sleeve.

He felt—and undoubtedly looked—a complete and utter fool.

The situation called for immediate action to restore his battered reputation.

Now that he was in control of all his limbs, and Marna was so enticingly close, Tarl decided the best course of action was to do what he'd been thinking about doing for some time—ever since she'd landed on him in bed, in fact.

He grabbed her, wrapping her in his arms and pulling her close against him so he could claim another kiss. He opted to ignore the tip of the disruptor, which she immediately planted against his side.

''You're not going to shoot me now,'' he said softly, his lips only centimeters from hers. ''How would you explain the body?''

''Mmrphf,'' Marna said. She couldn't say anything more definite because Tarl had covered her mouth with his and was resolutely trying to coax a response from her.

It wasn't easy. She tensed in his arms, straining to break free of his hold on her. She shoved against his chest, heedless of the disruptor she still held or the fact that, by virtue of their embrace, it was now pointed directly at his chin. She wriggled. She squirmed. She even tried kicking him, but bare feet were of little avail against his booted shins.

Eventually, she gave in.

She had to. Tarl had no intention of letting her go. It was

too sweet, too wonderfully delicious to feel her moving against him, regardless of her intent. She was warm and real and very, very female against his maleness. The heavy robe she wore was merely a tantalizing reminder of the beauty of her naked body, of the softness of her breasts and skin that he remembered so distinctly and in such amazing detail. Her hair, feather light, poured over his hands in a thousand curly, silky tendrils that generated a delicious tingling on his skin and along his nerves.

He felt light-headed—hot, dizzy, and hungry for more.

And he couldn't have any more. Tarl knew that, knew he shouldn't have taken as much as he had.

The kiss that began as a teasing relief to the tension that had gripped him ever since the first patrol spotted him in the city had flared into something far more dangerous than he'd anticipated. It would be safer to fling himself on the mercy of Internal Security than risk delving deeper into the sweet promise of Marna of Jiandu.

Reluctantly, Tarl slid his hands from her back to her sides, softened the pressure of his lips against hers, then, even more reluctantly, pushed her away from him.

He took a deep breath, startled to realize that his heart was racing and his lungs laboring for air. His hands trembled ever so slightly. He had to dig his fingers into the heavy fabric of Marna's robe to still their betraying quiver.

It took a moment for his whirling senses to quiet sufficiently so he could focus on the face before him and discern the dim outline of her features, half hidden in the tumbled mass of her hair.

"I—I'm sorry," he said at last, ashamed, suddenly, to meet her eyes. His hands dropped to his sides and he stepped back, away from her. "I didn't mean . . . That is . . ."

Marna, too, was fighting for breath. Even in the dark he could see that her lips were parted and her eyes wide and black and achingly alive. She swallowed, licked her lips, and said, "I don't know whether to hate you more for kissing me in the first place . . . or for stopping once you started."

Tarl jerked, startled by the unexpected admission. What kind of woman was this that she dared such a confession, and under such conditions? He'd expected her to slap him, threaten him, call for help—anything but acknowledge the charged awareness that had sparked between them.

For the first time in his life, he, Tarl Grisaan, heir to the controllorship of the planet Diloran, battle-hardened and much-decorated lieutenant of the Galactic Marines, adventurer, lover, jokester, and impostor, felt totally incapable of dealing with the situation confronting him.

Under the circumstances, retreat was the only option.

Ignominious retreat, at that, but Tarl wasn't up to trying to preserve his dignity.

He took an awkward step backward, then another. "I think it's time I was going," he said, his voice tight. He turned abruptly and fled.

He was halfway out the window when Marna caught up with him.

"Wait!" she snapped, grabbing him by the back of his shirt.

Tarl froze. The ice was back in her voice. Without letting go his grip on the window edge, he slowly twisted around.

Her eyes glittered dark and threatening in the pale light from the garden outside. The collar of her robe gaped, exposing the shadowed curve of one soft breast, yet even that garment's heavy folds couldn't hide the tension that gripped her slender body.

"If you ever speak of this—to *anyone*—I will have your head for it. Do you understand?" she demanded, leaning closer so he could see the threat in her expression.

Tarl felt his lips stretch in a relieved grin. Threats, outrage, and indignation were infinitely easier to deal with than the naked honesty she'd offered him a moment before.

"I wouldn't dream of sharing you—with *anyone,*" he assured her, and was surprised to realize there was more than a drop of truth in that statement. "Well, I'd best be going. If you'd just release me . . . ?"

Her brows lowered in a frown even as her fingers tightened their grip on his shirt. "You said you were using the service tunnels."

"I don't think it would be wise to venture out into the hall right now. But thanks for your help. You make a delightful bed companion."

Marna gave a sharp, angry hiss and let go of his shirt—undoubtedly with the intention of hitting him. Tarl didn't wait long enough to find out. He swung out the window and silently dropped to the ground below.

"Good night," he whispered, and gave her a mocking salute. "Sweet dreams."

Before she had a chance to respond, he darted back into the shadows at the far side of the garden, safely out of sight of any eyes other than hers that might be watching.

It cost him an effort of will, but Tarl didn't look back until he'd regained the top of the wall where he'd started.

There was nothing to see behind him except the dark bulk of the building and the dead, flat blackness of window after window after window. From the tree-shrouded vantage of the wall, he couldn't even tell which windows were hers, let alone see if she was watching him.

Tarl tightened his grip on the branch just above his head. It was a shame he'd never be able to follow up on tonight's meeting.

But perhaps that was for the best.

With a small, regretful shake of his head, Tarl swung off the wall and into the massive old tree on the other side. At the moment, he wasn't sure what he wanted. Not sure at all.

The stranger disappeared into the dark as quickly and quietly as he'd come. Marna watched the shadows, straining to catch one last glimpse of him, but he was gone. Nothing moved in the night outside her window. Nothing moved in the darkness within.

Heedless of the disruptor she still held, Marna drew the heavy robe more tightly about her.

She couldn't possibly be wishing he'd stayed. It was absurd. Impossible.

Yet she did.

Her lips still burned with the heat of his kisses. Her body ached with the longing he had stirred to life with such unthinking ease.

Whoever he was, he had been rude, cocky, presumptuous . . . and undeniably attractive, even in the dark. Or maybe it was the dark that had lent such potency to his masculine appeal. The dark and her own relief at finding a distraction, however brief, from thoughts of what lay before her.

A vague breeze drifted through the open window, heavy with moisture and the cloyingly sweet scents of the garden outside her room. Marna shivered at the unfamiliar brush of cool, damp air across her skin.

With sudden resolution, she dragged the window closed and pulled down the heavy shades that would shut out the night . . . and the coming morning. Nothing could shut out the doubts that had crept back in along with the night air.

Marna's hands clenched involuntarily. She started as her fingers curled tightly around her disruptor.

Like all children of the Zeyn, she'd long ago learned how to handle the weapon. The deserts of Diloran could be deadly, and no one was allowed out of the caverns unless he or she was armed.

She'd originally come to the window in hope of spotting a few of the stars she knew so well from the nighttime sky at home and had picked up the disruptor without thinking. In its familiarity it had seemed a comforting anchor, tangible proof of who and what she was, confirmation of why she was here. She'd wanted to have something solid to hold as counterweight to the uncertainties that surrounded her.

Now the weapon was merely an ugly reminder of what she wanted to ignore, for this one night, at least. Tomorrow would come soon enough.

Marna turned, intent on forgetting her troublesome thoughts, only to find her eye caught by a small, graceful chair placed to one side of the window. In its fragility, its decorative uselessness, it was totally unlike anything that could be found in the sprawling network of desert caves and caverns that were home to her people.

The opulent room bore little resemblance to the somber caverns she knew, where the only furnishings were brightly colored cushions and the walls and floors were nothing more than dark gray stone shot through with minerals and fragments of crystals that caught the light, stone whose beauty came as much from its comfortable familiarity as its naturally stark simplicity.

In the desert, an interior space as vast as this would have been filled with twenty people working or taking their ease, all gossiping and arguing and laughing, secure in the comfortable camaraderie that was the heart of their daily life. Yet here she was the room's sole occupant. All the finery, all the furniture, all the luxurious trappings were for her alone for as long as she required them.

There was nothing, absolutely nothing, in the room that resembled any part of the world she knew—except the dark.

She found the thought appalling. Never had she felt so lost, or so very much alone.

Marna shivered. Only when she started to hug herself in an effort to repress the shivers did she realize that she still held her disruptor.

For an instant she stared at the weapon; then, with sudden decision, she crossed to the one thing in all the room that was hers, a carved chest that had been set on the floor at one side, out of the way. The chest was old and worn and ugly. It had been her mother's, and her mother's mother's before that. Besides her clothes and her disruptor, it was all she had brought with her, all she had to remind her of the home she'd left behind.

Without stopping to question her actions, Marna knelt and opened the chest, placed the disruptor on top of the clothes that filled it, then closed the heavy lid with a snap. She should forget all this, stop thinking and go to bed. She was tired—exhausted, really—worn out by expectation, nervous excitement, and a day that had been far longer than usual and far more difficult than she'd anticipated.

Yet just as she'd clung to the disruptor earlier, she clung to the old chest now. Its rough, worn surface, pitted with age and heavy use, was comfortingly familiar beneath her hands. It and its contents were a part of her life, the only things she truly owned. The only things she'd ever owned.

The thought made her blink. Her gaze dropped and she stared at the chest, as if seeing it for the first time.

The only thing she owned.

It had never seemed important before, because no one of the Zeyn, not even her father, owned more than his weapons, a few changes of clothes, and a chest in which to keep them. No one had need of anything more, for everything else—the food they ate, the tools they used, the beds they slept in, the caverns in which they lived—belonged to the Family. Everything.

Although she'd been taught that other cultures, decadent cultures such as the one in which she now found herself, put more store in owning things, Marna had never fully realized what that implied. Until now.

In the name of her people, her father and the Zeyn Elders had given her an urgent assignment that she had accepted despite her doubts. The task had seemed so necessary, so eminently manageable when she was safe within the caves, secure among the people she'd known all her life. But here in this huge, echoing room, alone in the dark, the task before her seemed neither necessary nor manageable. It seemed . . . impossible.

Everything was so different from what she'd expected, despite her training. So many things about Diloran's most important city, Diloran Central, had shocked her. Awed her, if she was honest. The crowds of people filling the streets and the moving walkways. The overwhelming green of trees and grass and flowers. And the water! Ponds and pools and fountains everywhere she looked.

Marna shook her head sharply and forced herself to stand, willing away such unsettling thoughts. She shut off the small glow-light, stripped off her robe, then crossed the room to the bed, grateful for the enshrouding dark. In the dark, at least, the room and the furnishings around her were mere shadows she could ignore. Shadows she could forget . . . for a little while, anyway . . . if she tried.

But even the dark gave no protection against the urgent, sensual memories that rose at the first touch of the sheets and the faint trace of a man's scent which wafted from them.

Involuntarily, Marna tensed and the skin at the back of her neck prickled with the sense that someone was standing right behind her, silent in the dark. She was blind, yet she could see him; alone, yet she could feel him, *taste* him. He was there, as real and vital and unnerving as if he still lay waiting for her, a dark, tempting shadow between the mounded sheets.

No, that wasn't right. He hadn't been waiting for her, only hiding, running from . . . from . . . she didn't know from what. It didn't matter. She wouldn't have turned him over to Marott Grisaan's Internal Security, whatever his crime.

Marna shook her head, trying to drive out the jumbled memories; she tensed her body, trying to force out the tormenting heat that had risen, unbidden, in her veins.

There was no one here. No one. She was alone in the dark.

And that was worse.

With resolute force, she dragged back the heavy covers and slid between the sheets, heedless of the bed's disordered state. A tug here, a pull there, and it would be fine. Not until she lay back did she remember that she'd used both pillows in her assault on the security patrol.

For an instant she considered getting up to retrieve the one she'd thrown, then decided it didn't matter. She could do without.

It wasn't so simple a matter to arrange the covers, however. She tugged and squirmed and wriggled, then barely choked back an exclamation of disgust when her toes encountered a small lump of something cold and damp. It took a second for her to realize that the lump was nothing more than a piece of compacted earth scraped off the stranger's boots in his thrashing about.

Marna sighed at the thought and abandoned the attempt to straighten the bed coverings. Instead, she burrowed into the vast depths of the bed, creating a warm, safe hole, and, her head pillowed on her arm, gave herself to sleep.

But sleep wouldn't come.

The silken sheets brushed against her nipples, reminding her of how soft the hair on his chest had been—fine and curly, wonderfully teasing against her skin.

She shivered, ever so slightly, and remembered how warm he'd been, how solid and comfortingly masculine.

She licked her lips, and felt again the shape of his mouth, the sharp edge of his teeth, the eagerness of his tongue. She hadn't meant to kiss him, but in the excitement of the moment, somehow her lips had brushed against his and . . . No, that wasn't right.

She rolled over, trying to get away from the memory, and realized there was nothing to stop her. She was alone in the vast bed. Alone in the room.

And the morning was hours away.

Marna barely managed to choke back the sob that rose in her throat. The stranger, whoever he was, was gone, and tomorrow it would all begin in earnest.

Alone, she curled in on herself and shut her eyes against the dark and the echoing emptiness.

Chapter Three

"What do you think?" Tarl asked, turning his head slightly and lifting his chin in order to get the full effect of his magnificence in the mirror. "I especially like this new wig. Blond curls are so much more striking than short brown hair, don't you agree?"

A wizened old man seated nearby, his body bent under the weight of an enormous hump on his back, closed his eyes as if in pain. If Joeffrey Baland had been a babe in arms, Tarl would have diagnosed his former tutor's problem as a severe case of gas. But Joeffrey was no babe and his reaction was not due to gas.

Tarl set the hand mirror back on his dressing table and stood abruptly. "You're right. I do very well as a blond, but lavender is simply *not* my color."

With his long robes rustling and swirling about him, Tarl minced across the room to where several garishly colored robes had been carelessly tossed on the edge of his vast bed. With an exclamation of delight, he snatched a robe from the pile and whirled back to confront his friend.

"This will work much better, don't you think?"

Joeffrey grimaced. "Why must you indulge in this nonsense? My people have swept this suite for spy devices twice a day, every day, since you arrived. There's absolutely nothing here."

"Tsk," Tarl chided, throwing the robe down on the bed while he slipped out of its objectionable predecessor. "For someone with so many brains, you can be exceedingly dense, my friend. I've told you. If I'm to maintain this 'pose,' as you call it, I have to make sure it's a part of me. I must become so accustomed to walking and talking and thinking in character that I never risk stepping out of it."

He slipped the new robe on, then turned to admire himself in the full-length mirrors that lined the wall opposite. "Besides, the silk in these robes is a lot more pleasant against the skin than whatever abomination it is they use for field dress in the Galactic Marines."

Joeffrey snorted in disgust. His gnarled hands tightened on the cane he leaned on to support his misshapen upper body. "This from the man who has spent the last thirteen years of his life in rough territory assignments for the Galactic Marines. Sometimes I think you're certifiably crazy."

Tarl's grin widened as he winked at his friend. "You're right. I *am* rather surprised I didn't trade a life in the Marines for all this long ago."

With the forced calm of a parent whose patience with a fractious child is wearing thin, Joeffrey said, "I know I suggested you make people think you're still the frail creature you were when your uncle kicked you off the planet at fifteen—excuse me," he amended sarcastically, "sent you away for your health. Marott's not above having you killed if he thinks you're a threat to his power. But why go to this ridiculous extreme?"

"Extreme?" Tarl demanded, feigning indignation. "I'll

have you know these clothes are considered the height of fashion.''

''By men who are ten years younger than you and have nothing better to do with their time than parade around like fools. You're twenty-eight years old, man!'' Joeffrey pounded his cane on the floor for emphasis. ''Don't you think it's time you stopped treating life as if it were some game created for your personal entertainment?''

''If I really thought that, Joeffrey,'' Tarl replied sharply, ''I wouldn't be here in the first place. I never asked to be born a Grisaan. Just because one meddling busybody named Yerlaf Grisaan managed to keep the people on this planet from killing each other three hundred years ago doesn't mean his descendants should be condemned to stick around and solve everyone's problems forever. It's about time the inhabitants of Diloran took a little responsibility for their own lives, instead of putting the load on my family's shoulders.''

''So why did you agree to come back? When I tracked you down on Regulus to tell you about all the troubles your uncle has created, why didn't you just tell me you weren't interested?''

Tarl shrugged, unwilling to meet the sharply knowing look in his old friend's eye. How could he explain his motivations to Joeffrey when he still wasn't sure himself what they were?

He didn't want to become Controllor of Diloran. Even though eleven generations of his family had occupied the supreme position of power on the planet, he was absolutely sure that he did *not* want to become the twelfth.

In the years since his uncle, Marott Grisaan, had exiled him from Diloran, ostensibly for the sake of his health, Tarl had found his own way in life. For a thin, sickly child such as he'd been, his assignment to the Galactic Marines had been a blatant attempt to get him killed in a socially acceptable way. Yet instead of dying, Tarl had thrived. The work of opening new worlds and maintaining peace on settled ones had been hard, dangerous, and eminently satisfying. He'd risen to the rank of Lieutenant, a position he was proud of because he'd earned it, not inherited it. Not once had he considered leaving the Marines, or known any regrets for the privileged life he'd left behind.

Yet when Joeffrey Baland, Tarl's former tutor and a respected advisor to both Tarl's father and uncle, had tracked him down at that barren outpost on Regulus and demanded he return to Diloran, Tarl hadn't needed much convincing. Joeffrey's recitation of his uncle's abuses of power had stirred Tarl's anger and his sense of justice. He couldn't say no since he knew that he, through his refusal to return to Diloran, was partly responsible for having let his uncle remain in power for so long.

Too late had it occurred to him that his return might create expectations he couldn't fulfill, that those who preferred tradition might pressure him to assume the position that was "rightfully" his by inheritance. The Controllorship had been given into his uncle's keeping during Tarl's minority, but that minority had ended years before. Now Joeffrey and the constantly quarreling leaders he'd brought together in the subversive group they called the Tevah expected Tarl to help them remove his uncle from power.

The trouble was, their expectations didn't stop there. Tarl knew they expected him to take on the responsibilities of Controllor of Diloran and take care of the world's problems, just as his father had before him, and his father's father before that, and so on in a line stretching back to old Yerlaf, who couldn't keep his nose in his own business.

He wouldn't admit it to Joeffrey, but Tarl knew the outrageous role of fop and fool that he'd adopted was more than a ploy to keep his uncle from feeling threatened. It was a way to keep himself safe from the importunities of people who preferred to put their world into one man's safekeeping rather than assume responsibility for its management themselves. It was a way to keep himself from being sucked into a life he didn't want by centuries of traditions he'd rejected long ago.

Tarl shrugged once more, then smiled sweetly. "Why did I come back? Come now. You know how persuasive you can be when you want. And even you wouldn't have expected me to turn down this comfortable little gig just so I could stay on that hellish outpost, would you?"

Joeffrey's frown deepened to a scowl. On his homely, wrinkled face, the scowl was a terrible thing to behold. "You *know* you couldn't have refused if you'd wanted. Your sense of duty runs far too deep, whether you're willing to admit it or not. But—"

Tarl twirled in front of the mirror, admiring himself, but Joeffrey was not to be deterred.

"But I don't understand this crazy game you're playing. Who's going to take you seriously when you look and act like a fool?"

"You don't approve of Marine black, either, but without it, I don't think I'd have had the edifying experience of watching my uncle's men shipping arms to subversives undermining three of the most important Old Families on Diloran."

Joeffrey snorted in triumph. "So it *was* you! The Internal Security report this morning carried an item about a suspected criminal having destroyed a cache of government weapons in the Korale district last night. He was followed onto the grounds of the palace, but disappeared."

Tarl smothered an polite yawn. "Really?"

"I told you not to get involved!"

It was really rather amazing, Tarl reflected, just how much vehemence his old tutor could get into his voice without ever raising it above a normal speaking level. "I didn't."

"You're telling me it wasn't you that Security chased last night?"

"Oh, it was me, all right. I couldn't just let that shipment go out to those troublemakers my beloved uncle is supporting, now could I?" When Joeffrey didn't respond, Tarl added, "I have to confess, I was rather surprised it was so easy. You would have thought Marott would require his people to be more . . . discreet in their operations."

Joeffrey snorted again. "Your uncle respects no one, most especially not those who oppose him. And he can get away with it because three hundred years of history have led us to expect that the power of the Controllor will be wielded wisely and justly, for the good of all."

"You see my point? About the inhabitants of Diloran needing to take a little responsibility for their own lives?"

If he did, Joeffrey chose to ignore it. "I told you about those shipments, anyway. Why did you risk your neck just so you could destroy them yourself?"

Tarl shrugged. "Being told isn't the same as seeing, and seeing isn't the same as acting. If the people in your Tevah would act, rather than quarrel with each other, I might not have *had* to destroy that shipment myself. Besides, I rather enjoyed the chance to get a little exercise. You wouldn't begrudge me a little exercise, would you?"

Joeffrey glared rather than dignify that question with a reply.

The corner of Tarl's mouth twitched, but he decided not to pursue the issue. Instead, he pranced across to the dressing table and rummaged in an overflowing jewel box. "Now where did I . . . ? Oh! Here it is."

He pulled out a heavily enameled earring distinguished by a surprising number of pendant drops and held it up to the side of his face. He beamed in satisfaction. "Yes, that will do nicely."

While Joeffrey watched in silent disapprobation, Tarl fastened his robe, then tied an eye-popping yellow sash around his middle. The front of the robe's full skirt he left open to the bottom edge of the sash, revealing long, well-shaped legs encased in dark blue leggings. The formal slippers on his feet boasted embroidered beadwork that flashed in the light with every step he took. The enameled earring, which he carefully hooked over the edge of his left ear, added the final, necessary note of garish but fashionable color to the total ensemble.

Tarl stepped back from the mirror and preened. "Perfect! You know, Joeffrey, I'm really grateful I let you talk me into coming back to Diloran. If it hadn't been for you, I never would have discovered I have such a flair for Diloran high fashion."

Goaded past endurance, Joeffrey grabbed the mirror Tarl had left on the dressing table and flung it at his former pupil with all the force he could muster. Tarl easily caught the mirror backhanded, then negligently set it down with a laugh.

"Let's go. We're already stylishly late, and I can't wait to see what dear Uncle Marott thinks about my latest ensemble."

The vast Hall of the Public was packed with citizens who had come for the monthy audience and to gawk at the newly returned heir to the controllorship.

Marott Grisaan, an impressive man clothed in severely tailored garments, stood in front of the enormous judge's bench where the Controllor and his senior advisors always sat during formal audiences, balefully watching Tarl's advance.

"Do you think we are here for our own pleasure?" he demanded hotly as Tarl glided up the broad stone steps to him. "Do you think we have nothing better to do than wait for you to arrive?"

"Now, Uncle," Tarl said soothingly. "You shouldn't get in such a temper. It can't be good for your health." He frowned and carefully brushed a minuscule speck of lint off his uncle's sleeve. "Especially at your age."

Marott Grisaan's face darkened in fury, and only the restraining hand of an advisor prevented him from launching himself at his nephew.

This close to his uncle, Tarl was struck, not for the first time, by how much they looked alike. There in that lean face, now twisted into a dozen sharp angles by rage, Tarl saw himself at fifty. Hard, cynical perhaps, but not unhandsome. They shared the same close-cropped, dark brown hair and brown eyes, the same pale skin, the same spare, lean-muscled frame. Even their hands, long and slender, seemed cast from the same mold. It was like looking at a picture of what he might become if he couldn't escape Diloran and all the demands driving him.

Even as a child, Tarl had been aware of his uncle's craving for the position of power that chance had given first to his father, then to him. How ironic that he'd never wanted what Marott Grisaan desired with all his heart and soul. How different life would have been—for all of them—if fate had been more rational in its dispensations!

But fate was seldom rational, and however little he'd wanted to return to Diloran, Tarl knew he could not have ignored the long list of charges that Joeffrey Baland had leveled with such unemotional precision against Marott Grisaan.

Repression. Abuse of power. Greed, not for money, but for the even greater power that money could buy. Stirring up animosity among the various groups on Diloran. Deliberately playing the powerful, antagonistic Old Families against each other, thus ensuring that their resources and energies were wasted in quarreling among themselves rather than turned to more constructive uses—or against Marott.

Unfortunately, Tarl wasn't so sure the same charges couldn't have been laid, although not on so grand a scale, against his own father. As the influence of the Grisaan family had become more entrenched with the years, the obsessive need to hold on to that influence had swelled and grown stronger in Marott Grisaan and in Tarl's father, Melcor Grisaan. The only surprise, to Tarl, was that so little of the obsession showed in the face of the man before him.

"I'm sorry, Uncle," Tarl said at last, forcing a faint, dishonest note of contrition into his voice. "I didn't mean to be so late." He paused; then, because it wouldn't serve his purposes to appear too concerned about his uncle's feelings, he added innocently, "You know how difficult it can be getting dressed in the morning. Would you believe, I had to try on *three* different robes before I found one that suited!"

The last comment destroyed whatever good might have been gained by his apology, but rather than erupt once more in rage, Marott Grisaan turned aside, clearly disgusted with his nephew's affected ways. He gestured toward a pair of chairs set at the far side of the dais. "You'll sit there," he said. "And Joeffrey will sit beside you to give you the background of the cases under discussion. Keep your mouth shut for a change and don't indulge in any of your silly, prating nonsense. Not today."

Without another word, he took his place in the high-backed chair behind the bench. Obviously relieved, the senior advisors immediately took their designated positions in the less impressive chairs arrayed on either side of his. Lower ranked advisors and officials seated themselves in the row of chairs at the back of the dais. The monthly formal audience of the Controllor-Regent of Diloran, Marott Grisaan, was about to begin.

As the crowd in the Hall stilled expectantly, Tarl caught his uncle glancing over at him. He couldn't read the cold, still expression on his uncle's face, but had no trouble interpreting the implicit threat behind it. With deliberate care, he crossed one leg over the other and made a point of carefully settling the full skirts of his robe around him.

The first two hours of the audience were given over to the

grievances and complaints that could not be resolved within the Families themselves. The monthly audiences were a tradition started by Tarl's ancestor, Yerlaf, and despite their shortcomings continued to be a respected venue for working out problems among the citizens of Diloran.

As the proceedings droned on and the noise level inside the vast Hall rose sufficiently to cover their conversation, Joeffrey stopped trying to discuss the cases themselves. He swung his heavy, misshapen head around so he could peer at Tarl.

"You see this Hall, Tarl?" he demanded. "You see the people that fill it? They are here, rather than out slitting each other's throats, because your ancestors created a system of government that works, in spite of its human failings and the Diloran people's constant quarreling."

Tarl refused to rise to the bait, but that didn't deter Joeffrey.

"Your father was a weak leader, Tarl. Your uncle is corrupt and power-mad. But before them, your family provided wise, sound leadership that carried this planet, with all its Families and factions and discords, through three hundred years of peace. The people want you back. They *need* you. You can't refuse them. You can't deny your destiny. I *know* you."

Tarl's fingers tightened around the arm of his chair. Even that carved wood, worn smooth by the generations who had sat where he sat now, was a reminder of the weight of history that Joeffrey wanted to lay on his shoulders. He shook his head.

"No, Joeffrey. This world's changed in three hundred years. It's time the people of Diloran learned to work together on their own. It's long past time my family was forgotten."

He shifted angrily in his chair, wishing he could leave, knowing he could not. He'd agreed to do what he could to help the Tevah remove Marott Grisaan from office, but he would go no further—not even for Joeffrey, who had been more of a father to him than his own father had ever dreamed of being.

Tarl turned back, ready to continue the argument, but his eye caught someone in the crowd watching him, clearly puzzled by his abrupt behavior. He'd fallen out of character, and his change of manner was beginning to attract attention.

With an effort, he got his temper under control, then languidly extended one slippered foot for Joeffrey's admiration. "What do you think of the beadwork on these slippers, Joeffrey? Not too garish, is it? All those colors had me worried, but—"

Joeffrey snorted in disgust. With an awkward heave, he rose to his feet, keeping one hand on the arm of the chair to steady himself until he was sure of his balance. His other hand wrapped around his cane like a claw. "If you won't listen to sense, I won't listen to nonsense. I'm leaving. But you think about what I've said," he added, poking the end of his cane at Tarl, "and be warned that I'm going to say it again."

With that, he shuffled away, heedless of the convention that no one on the dais was allowed to leave until the audience was ended. Joeffrey Baland had turned his powerful intellect to the service of the people of Diloran, but he wasn't above using the excuse of his deformity to his advantage whenever it suited him.

Tarl grimaced as he watched his old mentor depart. He'd made his stand clear long before he ever set foot back on Diloran, but Joeffrey was as stubborn as he was brilliant, and he had long ago decided that Tarl would be one of the greatest of the Controllors of Diloran. He didn't intend to let Tarl prove him wrong, regardless of what Tarl felt about the matter.

Since he had no convenient excuse to escape the audience,

Tarl gloomily settled into his chair and let his gaze roam over the crowd.

The Hall of the Public, a vast, gracefully beautiful edifice built more than three hundred years earlier, was designed to hold three thousand people with ease. Usually less than half that number attended the formal audiences. Today, the Hall was packed. Every seat in the banks of seating arrayed along the walls and at the far end was taken. The vast open floor was jammed with a milling crowd of visitors, dignitaries, low-level government officials, and the merely curious. Large monitors and individual listening posts allowed even those farthest from the dais to hear and see everything that happened, but from the steady murmur of background conversation, Tarl suspected that more people were interested in talking and exchanging gossip than in listening to the proceedings themselves. And when they weren't talking among themselves, Tarl had the uncomfortable feeling they were studying him.

It was to be expected. He'd known it would happen, but he didn't like it. Each time he caught a covert glance in his direction, each time he turned to find some stranger studying him, eyes squinched in speculative assessment, Tarl felt his gut churn with the same helpless, angry resentment he'd felt with every droning lecture about his duty as a Grisaan that he'd endured as a boy—and that he still received from Joeffrey at every opportunity.

Tarl's fingers curled into his palm, drawing up the fabric of his robe and crushing it in the vise of his fist. For an instant, he stared at his hand and the crumpled ball of fabric he held, then slowly forced his fingers to relax and his hand to open.

The audience dragged on. Nothing about the proceedings had changed from the audiences Tarl had endured while his father was still alive. His wig itched, his earring pinched, and he quickly became as thoroughly bored as he ever remembered being.

The last petition was handled with such dispatch that Tarl suspected his uncle had tired of the formalities, as well. He watched enviously as people on the main floor took advantage of the moment to slip out of the Hall while attendants set up a second dais for Eileak of Zeyn, who was to address the gathering. Tarl could only hope that Marna would put in an appearance with her father. He deserved the chance to see her again, even if only from a distance, as compensation for having suffered through the audience thus far.

It didn't take long for the attendants to finish with the preparations and for the Hall to refill with the expectant public. At a signal from one of the officials near the main doors, Marott Grisaan rose and came around to the front of the bench, where he took up a commanding stance appropriate to the Controllor-Regent. Several days earlier, a nervous aide had asked Tarl if he wanted to stand beside his uncle during the ceremony and had obviously been relieved when Tarl declined the honor. Marott would not have appreciated being upstaged, and it suited Tarl to remain comfortably ignored in the background as much as possible—for now, at least.

After a quick glance around the Hall, Marott Grisaan nodded to the guards at the main doors, which were immediately swung wide. With solemn dignity, the procession commenced.

A dozen Zeyn officials and guards, indistinguishable in their traditional dull-gold robes, led the way and quickly took up positions at either side of the dais. Behind them, walking alone to emphasize his importance, came Eileak, Elder of the Zeyn, garbed in the same heavy, hooded robe the rest of his people wore.

Tarl scarcely noticed. His attention was fixed on the proud, black-haired woman behind Eileak. His breath caught in his throat and his hands tightened around the arms of his chair as he leaned forward to watch her.

Neither his eyes nor his memory had played him false.

Marna of Jiandu was as beautiful as he remembered.

Instead of falling about her in a cloud of curls, her hair had been braided, then woven into an intricate coif. Beneath that night-black crown her features seemed impossibly delicate, her eyes enormous dark pools in which a man might easily drown. The only hint of nervousness was betrayed by the slight flush beneath her dusky skin, and even that might have been his imagination, the product of the hot red blood that suddenly surged through his own veins at the sight of her.

Tarl tried, and failed, to see in this stately queen the naked, pillow-wielding wench who had so recklessly flung herself into a brawl with armed men the night before. He had no trouble imagining what it would be like to free her from her encompassing garments, to unweave those heavy braids so her hair once again floated about her shoulders and breasts and hips. No trouble at all.

Tarl abruptly crossed his legs and tugged the edges of his robe over his lap.

Three deep breaths helped a little. So did counting to ten in Graustakian. But the benefits of those strategies lasted only so long as he kept his eyes off Marna of Jiandu. And that, Tarl was quickly learning, was something he wasn't able to manage for very long.

She stood on the dias beside her father, head high, hands calmly clasped in front of her, as Eileak launched into a long-winded peroration. Tarl didn't have the foggiest notion what her father was saying, any more than he'd understood his uncle's official greeting. It didn't matter, because if he couldn't undress her, all he wanted to do was sit and watch Marna of Jiandu.

If it hadn't been for the sudden murmur of surprise that rippled through the assembled crowd, Tarl might not have caught anything that Eileak of Zeyn was saying.

That would have been a mistake, for it seemed Eileak was talking about him.

"... and so, with the return of the young son of the noble house of Grisaan, with the return of he who, from his birth, was destined to lead the people of Diloran, we rejoice." Eileak raised his hands and his voice grew louder, stronger. "We rejoice. We sing our songs of welcome and of thanksgiving. We look to the future and dream of a peace like that which his noble ancestor, Yerlaf Grisaan, brought to all Diloran three hundred years ago."

Eileak paused and looked about him, obviously judging his audience. He needn't have worried. Three thousand faces were fixed on him, trying to guess the purpose of this impassioned oration.

He slowly lowered his hands to his sides, then continued, "We dream of peace. But we also work for that same peace, so that it may have life outside our dreams. And to that end, I am here to offer my daughter, Marna of Jiandu, as lawful companion to Tarl Grisaan, heir to the Controllorship of Diloran."

Chapter Four

Tarl choked and almost fell off his chair.

His uncle looked like some war monument carved from stone, every muscle frozen into eternal rigidity. But looks could be deceiving. Tarl's instincts told him that Marott Grisaan's brain was whirling madly, trying to decipher the motives behind this outlandish proposal—or, more likely, trying to decide if an alliance with the Zeyn, even through his nephew, was more likely to hurt or hinder his bid for eventual possession of the Controllorship.

With great care, Tarl planted himself firmly in his seat and tugged his gaudy robe into place. He had to give Eileak credit. That crafty desert dweller had contrived to make it impossible for any Grisaan to reject his offer. They couldn't risk the repercussions of a public insult to the Elder of the oldest of the Old Families on Diloran. And at the moment, Tarl couldn't think of any insult greater than publicly rejecting the offer of a political and sexual liaison with Eileak's daughter.

Evidently Marott Grisaan had arrived at the same conclusion. Whatever misgivings he had would have to wait for later consideration. Right now, he couldn't afford to let the silence continue, and he knew it.

"Respected Elder," he said, speaking slowly and letting his voice echo in the vast, silent Hall. "I am honored . . . my *nephew* is honored by this proposal. It is a young man's dream to have as his companion a woman as beautiful and, I have no doubt, as wise and gentle as your daughter, Marna of Jiandu. To know that she is the daughter of the honored Elder of the Zeyn, to know that she represents all that is noble in her ancient people, must make the thought of joining with her all the sweeter. On behalf of myself, on behalf of the people of Diloran, and most especially on behalf of my beloved nephew, Tarl, I thank you . . . and I accept."

Tarl could only be grateful for his uncle's florid posturing. The irritation it generated managed to get his brain working again. Unfortunately, his brain wasn't providing any useful ideas for escaping the trap he could see yawning before him. Once tied to Marna of Jiandu, the possibilities of his ever escaping the controllorship of Diloran and the overwhelming load of responsibilities that came with the position dwindled to virtually nothing.

Not that Marna wasn't a temptation. Even now, Tarl couldn't help responding to her calm dignity and quiet pride. But no woman, no matter how temptingly beautiful, was worth getting trapped in a life he'd never wanted. Not even Marna.

For the moment, however, his options were extremely limited. He could either put a good face on the mess and go out there in front of all these people, accepting her as his pledged companion, or . . .

Tarl frowned. The only "or" he could think of was fainting dead away and being carried out of the Hall feet first. Even now, dressed in a wig and tight hose and the most tasteless robe he'd ever worn, Tarl didn't think he was quite up to the repercussions of *that.*

Which meant—

"Come, nephew," his uncle said, letting the words roll out with pompous emphasis. "Greet Marna of Jiandu."

She hadn't thought it would be this bad. Even in her worst imaginings, she hadn't thought it would be *nearly* this bad.

Marna forced her hands to stop shredding her dinner cloth beneath the table. She didn't look up when a servant deftly took away her untouched plate of roast gashiya in wine sauce, and another servant just as deftly placed sautéed vegetables and delicate spirals of what she thought might be smoked petan in front of her.

To her shame, she felt no desire to eat, regardless of the generosity of the servings or the quality of the meal. If she were to be so wasteful among her own people, she would be publicly scolded and denied permission to attend the following meal, regardless of how hungry she might become. Just looking at all this food, knowing that no one would criticize her for wasted delicacies that might have fed five people, told her she didn't belong in this strange, decadent world and never would.

As if fretting about the food was the real issue.

Tarl Grisaan's presence at her side had made the past hour one of the most excruciatingly long, unpleasant penances of her entire life.

When she'd agreed to her father's and the Zeyn Elders' request that she undertake the task they'd presented, Marna had accepted the risks and the hardships. But she'd been thinking more in terms of a survival test, with life and death in the balance, than in terms of the provoking, if not downright embarrassing, encounters that now threatened to be her daily lot.

Granted, if everything went as planned she would eventually be rid of Tarl Grisaan, but in the interim she would be forced to spend her time with an idiot who just happened to be heir to the most powerful and influential position in all of Diloran. And what honor could there be in vanquishing an idiot?

She couldn't bear even one more glance at him. If she was forced to look at that disgusting froth of blond curls and garish silk that passed for a man again, she'd be sorely tempted to fling her plate and all its contents into his face.

Bad enough that she couldn't eradicate the memory of him in the Hall. All through her father's speech and Marott Grisaan's pompous reply, she'd surreptitiously scanned the faces of the people on the dais opposite, trying to identify the man to whom she was to be pledged. She'd identified two or three young men she thought might possibly be him. What she hadn't expected was to see a slender, priggish popinjay dressed in the most outlandish robe she'd ever seen carefully pick his way down the dais steps and through the crowd toward her—but only after he'd adjusted his curls, straightened his sash, and made sure his robe hung properly!

It had taken every drop of self-control she possessed not to turn and run right then.

How could this have happened? Surely someone must have known that the heir to the Controllorship was . . . was . . .

"*Do* try the petan," her newly pledged companion suggested. "It's absolutely wonderful. *Really.*"

Marna flinched. Even his voice was annoying. It grated on her ear with the same exquisite awfulness of nails across shale.

"Or would you prefer some of these billa nuts?" he continued, oblivious to her shudder of distaste. "My uncle imports them specially."

Marna stared at the long, delicately sculpted hand that held the proffered bowl of nuts. His skin was pale and fine, as if he'd never ventured out in the sun or worked at anything more strenuous than passing gilt bowls or lifting crystal goblets.

"You don't like nuts?" The delicate hand gracefully replaced the bowl of nuts and picked up a small glass plate of sweetmeats. "Then how about some of these . . . um, well, I don't know what they are, but they're very good, anyway."

Something in his voice, some odd, new note of—was it understanding? sympathy?—made Marna look up in spite of her earlier resolution not to.

She found herself looking into the warmest, gentlest pair of brown eyes she'd ever seen. She blinked, and looked again.

Whatever else she might find to disparage in Tarl Grisaan, Marna decided she liked his eyes. There was warmth in them—warmth, a trace of humor, and, perhaps, understanding. They weren't the most beautiful color she'd ever seen. They were brown, plain and simple. The lashes that fringed them weren't inordinately thick or long or in any other way unusual. His brows were a lighter shade of brown, slightly tinged with red, providing an odd contrast to his blond hair.

He smiled slightly, the faintest of upward curls at the corners of his mouth. His eyes glowed.

Yes, there was definitely understanding. And he *had* been kind to her maid earlier, making sure Sesha had an opportunity to eat and a comfortable place to sit so she could ease her crippled leg. Maybe if she could just think of his eyes and his small kindnesses, she could forget or ignore everything else about him.

"You don't eat sweets, either? Then I'm afraid I've nothing left to offer." He glanced down at her plate. "If the food is not to your liking, you can send for something else, you know."

Marna straightened at that, suddenly aware she'd let her guard down. "I'm not hungry," she said, rather more sharply than she'd intended. As an awkward afterthought, she added, "Thank you."

"Then ask them to put some aside for later. Just have them deliver it to your room."

"For later? But the meal is being served now."

"But you're not hungry now."

"Yes, but . . ." Marna let the thought die. Set aside food to eat when she pleased? What an absurd, self-centered notion! She'd never be allowed to do that if she were in the caverns. It would cause too many problems for the managers of the kitchens and would be seen as pure selfishness on her part. She ate when everyone else ate, or she went hungry. That's the way it was—for everyone.

A sudden, sharp longing to be home, safe and among people she knew, stabbed through her. Marna dropped her gaze to her plate, fighting against the emotion. If only this were as easy as challenging a stranger who'd broken into her room!

The thought of the dark stranger reminded her of his laughter, his confidence, the hardness of his lean body. It reminded her of his kisses. And that stirred an uncomfortable heat in her veins she'd just as soon not suffer.

"Personally," her companion continued in a thoughtful, if slightly affected drawl, "I've never liked petan, smoked or otherwise. Doesn't matter how rare it is. I'd pay *not* to eat it, if I had a choice. Such a bore."

The last was uttered in a tone exactly suited to the spoiled, self-centered fool his appearance declared him to be. With a rush, all her dislike for the man came flooding back, driving out the disturbing thoughts of the stranger and his kisses. Imagine being so unreasonable as to reject good food! At least she knew she was guilty of inexcusable waste in not eating what had been set before her. To sneer at such bounty, especially at what others considered a delicacy, was unforgivable.

"I suppose you're accustomed to dining like this all the time," she said tartly, meeting his gaze defiantly.

He laughed at that, and once more her dislike of him receded before the irresistible warmth in his eyes. "I don't think you'd believe me if I told you some of the meals I've had over the years," he said. The corner of his mouth twitched once more at some thought he obviously found entertaining.

Marna's chin came up. Was he laughing at her? At her lack of sophistication? "I suppose you find a meal as grand as this one rather boring."

This time one brown eyebrow quirked upward along with the corner of his mouth. "I did until you decided to talk to me."

To Marna's dismay, she felt her cheeks grow warm under his amused scrutiny. Worse, she had a suspicion he was enjoying himself in an exchange of which he seemed to be getting decidedly the better. Was this what her tutors had called flirting? The odd, masculine behavior they'd told her was to be expected from a decadent male with neither Family nor good manners? Yet was someone who looked and talked like Tarl Grisaan even *capable* of flirting?

"What do you think of Diloran Central so far?" he asked with a disconcerting change of conversational direction.

She hesitated only a moment. At least talking eased the tension that had gripped her for the past hour. "You waste water." If he was going to laugh at her, she wasn't going to feel any compunction about giving an honest, direct answer, no matter how ill-mannered such behavior might be. "And the people on the street are very rude. I watched them pass each other without a word of greeting."

"But they don't know each other."

"Does that mean they don't need to acknowledge the others' presence?"

He appeared to give that some thought. "No, I don't suppose it does."

"And your buildings. All that empty space. Why build things you don't need?"

"What do you mean?" To Marna's surprise, he honestly seemed to want to know.

"Well . . ." she hesitated, unwilling to mention her oversized quarters, which might easily have housed a dozen Zeyn. It seemed too personal, too . . . intimate, to speak of such things as private spaces. Especially now, and with this man beside her.

"There's this room, for instance." She turned to sweep the vast dining area with a frown. "There are—what? three hundred people here now? Four hundred? Yet rather than use your Hall of the Public, which could easily have served everyone here, you have created another big room. Why?"

"Why not?"

Marna bristled, but a glance at his expression told her he'd asked the question in all seriousness. A fleeting thought struck her that this was an odd conversation to hold with a man who appeared to worry more about his curls and clothes than he did about more important things, but the thought disappeared in her relief at being able to vent some of her frustrations with this strange world in which she now found herself.

"Why not? You waste energy and materials and time building it, and for what? A dinner every now and then?"

"Actually, my uncle holds a few formal breakfasts and luncheons here, as well."

"That's not what I meant!"

Again that disturbing, intriguing little twitch at the corner of his mouth. "No?"

"No." Marna only just stopped herself from an ill-mannered snort of disgust. "Among my people, a cavern this size would be used for meals, for meetings and story telling, for . . . oh! for a dozen things. It would never be wasted as you waste this room.''

He lifted his head to study the elegant, formal room before them, giving Marna a clear view of his profile. Strange. There was no hint of softness in that thin, sharp nose or the jutting chin and angled jaw. Nothing about the way he held his head seemed effeminate or overly mannered, yet those absurd golden curls and that nightmarish robe spoke of someone who, by the standards of her people, could scarcely be considered a man. She dropped her gaze just as he swung back to her, unwilling for him to see the puzzlement and disdain that warred within her.

''You think it's wasted space.''

It wasn't a question, really, but Marna could hear something in his voice that spoke of a dozen questions he'd left unspoken. ''Of course.''

''Yet it is beautiful. A grand setting for honored guests such as your father and yourself. A setting that enhances the pleasure of the meal . . . and the company.''

It was the thoughtful, patient note she heard in his words, rather than the words themselves, that induced her to study the room about her once again. It took a moment for her to see what he meant.

It *was* a beautiful room, with a soaring ceiling painted the faintest shade of sun-drenched blue and graceful columns of polished gray-green stone that arched out above and around them like the sheltering branches of ancient trees. One wall was made of glittering mirrors, the other of glass that opened onto a garden where hidden lights created a wonderland of dazzling fountains and secret shadows, reflected back again in the mirrored wall. Yet somehow, despite its size and grandeur, the room contrived to be a space that welcomed the people it enclosed and provided a backdrop to, rather than an intimidating presence around, the human commerce within its walls.

In spite of herself, Marna found her eyes growing wide and her heart quickening in response to the beauty she'd never noticed before, the beauty she might never have noticed had not Tarl Grisaan brought it to her attention.

"Well? It *is* a beautiful room, is it not?" he said softly, as though afraid to break the spell that held her.

It was a polite query, not a taunt, yet Marna stiffened, resentful that she should so easily have been placed at a disadvantage. "Beauty is not an essential in life, and if creating it means wasting resources, then it is best forgotten."

The words were out of her mouth before she realized they were a direct quote from one of the most influential Elders after her father, an old man named Yethan who was one of those who railed constantly against any threat to Zeyn tradition. It was strange to hear herself repeating his words, for she'd often argued, sometimes vehemently, against his narrow views and grim outlook.

Her answer evidently caught Tarl by surprise as well, for he said nothing, merely stared at her, his mouth slightly pursed, a frown caught between his eyebrows.

"Well?" she demanded when she could no longer endure his perusal. "Don't you agree?"

After a long moment, he shook his head, once, in negation. "No, I don't."

"But how can you justify—"

"Why should I have to justify beauty? Isn't it enough that it exists?" He, too, studied the room a second time. "Beauty is the greatest thing this city has to offer," he said after a moment, then added, a trifle sadly, "It may well be the *only* thing it has to offer."

He didn't look at her, but at the room, when he said it, as if he were speaking more to himself than to her. For the first time since he'd come prancing up to her in the Hall of the Public, Marna could detect no trace of affectation in his words or his manner.

Before she could question the change in him or think of anything to say in response, he shook his head, as if shaking out the thoughts that troubled him. When he spoke again, his tone of voice was as prissily affected as before, and Marna could only wonder if she'd imagined that sad, thoughtful note she'd heard a moment earlier.

"We're being sadly philosophical tonight. Not the best tone for a dinner that ought to be a celebration. Come, let's talk of more pleasant subjects."

It was Marna's turn to purse her lips and frown. "Such as?"

He shrugged and gave a soft little laugh that was just barely this side of a titter. "I don't know. How about . . . you?"

Marna jumped. "Me? There's nothing to tell of interest about me." She hesitated. "How about *you?* Did not my father tell me that you had spent recent years in the Galactic Marines?" She tried, and failed, to keep a trace of skepticism out of her question. What Marine would ever claim beauty existed for its own sake? Or wear an earring?

This time there was no mistake. He definitely tittered. "Oh, lets not talk about *that.* It was so . . . *boring.*"

"The Galactic Marines were boring?"

"All that paperwork. It was *such* a trial." He fidgeted with the eating utensils at the side of his plate, as if the mere thought of the Marines alarmed him. "I just *couldn't* accept an assignment to some of those awful places I read about in the reports."

"But I thought you had to go wherever they sent you?"

"Not if you're assigned to the Central Headquarters Staff." He beamed, clearly relieved that he, at least, had managed to obtain an assignment that brought neither honor nor glory in its wake. "And the *clothes!*" He smoothed the cloth of his sleeve admiringly. "Those dreadful uniforms aren't in the *least* bit stylish."

"No, they're not." What else could she say in response

to a statement like that? Marna's estimation of Tarl Grisaan, which had been slowly creeping up in spite of her determination to despise him, plummeted once more.

Whatever he might have said in reply was lost in the stir of the crowd when Marott Grisaan, as host, rose to indicate that the dinner had ended. Marna was startled to see that at least one, if not two courses had come and gone in the interim. A delicate crystal bowl filled to the brim with costly stewed quaa'va sat, untouched, in front of her. She'd never even noticed the servants putting it there.

She rose to her feet with more haste than grace, grateful for the opportunity to escape. Tarl was faster.

"You must let me escort you to your father," he said, then added, "I *insist,*" when she started to object.

He took her hand in his with an arch playfulness that Marna found distinctly distasteful. She couldn't pull free of his grasp—not when so many people were watching them.

Head high, face carefully expressionless, Marna of Jiandu permitted herself to be led from the table she and Tarl had occupied in lonely splendor at one end of the hall to the table her father had shared with Marott Grisaan at the other. To her chagrin, instead of regally sweeping through the crowd as befitted the heir to the Controllorship of Diloran, Tarl minced and pranced and stopped a dozen times to politely let others pass in front of them, heedless of the respect that was due his rank—and hers.

By the time they reached the Controllor-Regent and her father, Marna's cheeks were burning with suppressed rage and humiliation.

Only later, when she was safely in her chamber, alone, did it dawn on her that Tarl Grisaan's hand had been unexpectedly cool and hard beneath her fingers and that he had resisted her attempts to pull free of his grasp with a sure strength that was as unobtrusive as it was irresistible.

He'd thought hell had been the nine months he'd spent in the swamps of Saltos III.

He'd been wrong.

Hell was spending an hour and a half beside one of the most temptingly delectable women he'd ever met, and either prattling on like a fool or maintaining a conversation that threatened to be as disturbing to his good sense as her presence was to his senses.

Breathing heavily, Tarl forced himself through another agonizing sequence of kre'at'su exercises, hoping the intense physical effort would counteract the potent effect she'd had on him, knowing it wouldn't.

Marna of Jiandu had dropped into his life with all the devastating power of a neural bomb, setting his nerve endings tingling with her very nearness, freezing them with her haughty disdain.

He'd found it amusing to land in her bed last night. It was *not* amusing to think of being forced into a long-term commitment to her that would, inevitably, limit his freedom to act and trap him in the life he'd spent too many years trying to escape.

Yet despite an hour's vigorous exercise and another hour's even more vigorous thought before that, Tarl couldn't see any way out of the net being drawn up around him.

He came to the end of the kre'at'su sequence and dropped, panting and sweating, to the floor.

Part of the trouble was, he hadn't the slightest idea what she thought about the situation to which her father had committed her.

When he'd first faced her, there in the Hall, he'd been startled to find himself gazing into the coldest, flattest, most unemotional eyes he'd ever seen. He'd thought Marna of Jiandu disconcertingly cold and unemotional when she'd been facing him with a disruptor in her hand, but he'd been wrong. This was cold. Cold deep enough to freeze a man's soul.

Then he'd watched her at the formal dinner, seen the resolute way she kept her eyes on her plate and only toyed with the exotic foods presented to her, and he'd wondered just how much that cold demeanor had been a protective device, a way to keep her heart from feeling the pain of a political alliance she probably wanted no more than he. Once, and then only fleetingly, he'd thought he'd seen her lower lip quiver. But that small, betraying spasm had come and gone so swiftly he wasn't sure if he'd really seen it, after all.

Even knowing it would be wiser to keep her at a distance, he'd found himself trying to work his way beneath that veneer of ice. He had asked her what she thought of his city, and she had responded with a quiet, but scathingly perceptive denunciation that barely managed to conceal her longing for her own safe, familiar world. Her comments on the formal dining hall had been just by her standards, yet when he'd pointed out the beauty of the place, she'd responded with a sensitivity that was clearly innate.

Tarl sighed and shoved to his feet. Trying to find the real Marna of Jiandu amidst all the conflicting revelations of her character was like trying to find a single flower in a garden filled with flowers, half of which possessed wickedly sharp thorns. It couldn't be done. At least, not by him. And he didn't want to try.

If only there were some way he could convince her to abandon the idea of becoming his companion.

There wasn't. He might woo a stone statue with equal chance of success. Marna of Jiandu wouldn't be susceptible to the blandishments of Tarl Grisaan, fop and fool, no matter what he had to say.

At the thought, Tarl froze, remembering last night.

Marna might not listen to Tarl Grisaan, but she'd been unexpectedly willing to risk her good name, at the very least, to protect an unknown fugitive.

With a sudden burst of energy, Tarl crossed to his dressing room.

Maybe it *was* possible to woo a statue, after all.

Chapter Five

The gardens lay still and shadowed, far quieter than they'd been the night before when he'd had Internal Security hot on his trail.

Tarl slipped out of the protective screen of bushes, satisfied there was no one around to observe his movements. The nice thing about living in the Palace of the Controllor was that security was much looser inside the walls that surrounded the vast complex of buildings than it was outside. The bureaucrats in Internal Security clearly operated under the comfortable assumption that no one inside was likely to be engaged in nefarious activities at this or any other time of night.

Tarl heartily approved of mistaken assumptions—if they worked to his advantage.

Keeping to the deepest shadows, he slowly worked his way toward the guest quarters. The familiar dark alley of ancient trees was gloomily empty; the tufted grass swallowed any sound he might have made. Coming from this direction, the opposite of last night, he looked for the eleventh tree on the left. He was up and over the wall, then back down into the garden in a matter of seconds.

As before, there were no lights showing in any of the windows. He'd taken care earlier in the day to learn that Eileak of Zeyn's quarters where at the farthest end, separated from his daughter's by the room of the serving maid, Sesha, and that of Eileak's manservant. The rest of the rooms were empty since the remainder of Eileak's followers had been housed in comfortable, but less elegant accommodations farther from the central palace. It was an eminently convenient arrangement for a man bent on a clandestine tryst.

Marna's window stood open. Just like the night before, no sound came from the room beyond. This time, however, Tarl decided not to venture farther without taking the elementary precaution of alerting her to his presence. She might be tempted to use her disruptor the second time around, just for the practice. He bent and scooped up a few small beads of gravel from the flower bed, then carefully tossed them, one after the other, at the window.

By the second handful, Tarl was debating the wisdom of crawling through the window unannounced when Marna's head suddenly appeared in the opening.

To his disappointment, she was fully clothed in a robe with long sleeves and a collar that came all the way up the base of her throat. But her hair was down, drifting about her face as soft as a shadow. That was something, at any rate.

"Who—?" The instant she recognized him, her tone changed from puzzlement to irritation. "What do you want?" she demanded, low enough so only he could hear her.

"I want to talk to you."

"But I don't want to talk to you."

"Just for a moment."

"You caused enough problems last night," she hissed, clearly irritated by his request. "I'm not interest in brawling tonight."

"I didn't bring any friends this time. Honest."

Although the last word was spoken with a soulful plaintiveness calculated to warm the heart of even the coldest female, it didn't work with Marna. She drew in her head and started to pull the window closed behind her.

Desperate, Tarl launched himself at the opening. He caught her by surprise as he tumbled over the sill and into the room in an inelegant sprawl.

His method of entry might have caught her by surprise, but by the time Tarl had rolled back up into a crouch, Marna had her disruptor pointing straight at a spot right between his eyes.

"What do you do? Sleep with that thing?" he demanded plaintively. This wasn't quite the way he'd envisioned beginning the conversation.

"I said I didn't want visitors."

"Actually, that's not quite what you *said*." Tarl shoved to his feet, but she was prepared for him. She backed away, just far enough so she'd have time to shoot him if he jumped her.

"That's what I meant and you know it."

"You should be more accurate."

"My aim with a disruptor is quite accurate. Would you like to test me on it?"

Tarl held his hands out to his side, palms up. "No, I wouldn't. I'm quite willing to take your word for it. But that's not why I came."

Marna hesitated for a moment, then shrugged in irritation and lowered the disruptor. "So why *did* you come?"

"I—" Tarl began confidently enough, but instantly found he couldn't go any further.

It had seemed such a simple proposition when he was still in his room, dizzy from exercise. Talk to her. Convince her it wasn't in her best interest or her people's to pledge herself as companion to Tarl Grisaan. Simple.

Now, he wondered if he was crazy. Who was he—a nameless criminal, so far as Marna was concerned—to tell her, the daughter of Eileak of Zeyn, what to do? She might as easily shoot him where he stood as listen to such ravings.

Tarl cleared his throat and tried again. "I wanted to tell you not to throw yourself away on that fool, Grisaan."

She tensed. The disruptor came up once more. "What do you know about the matter?"

"Not much," Tarl admitted, wishing he could see her clearly. "But I *do* know you're not the kind of woman who would be happy being bound to him, heir to the controllorship or no."

She shifted her weight on her feet, as if his words had thrown her ever so slightly off balance. "How do you know about that?"

"I was there. In the Hall of the Public. I heard your father offer you as companion."

Marna cocked her head to one side, suspicious. Her eyes never left his face. "I didn't see you there."

"Maybe you missed a few faces in all those thousands." He paused, to give his words more impact, then added, "At least you couldn't miss *him* in a crowd. Not in a robe like the one he had on today." He'd have to have been blind not to see her flinch at his words.

"Clothes are not important."

"Do you think he'd agree? I'll bet he's spent more on all his fancy robes and earrings and glittery shoes than you've spent on clothes in your entire life."

Marna straightened, wrapped both hands around her disruptor, and drew a bead on his heart. "I won't listen to this. Get out of my room. Now!"

Tarl's shoulders slumped in relief. By the strain he could hear in Marna's voice, by the way she physically fought against confronting a truth she didn't want to acknowledge, he'd found the confirmation he'd needed.

Marna of Jiandu was as unhappy as he was about being pledged as companion to him.

And if she was unhappy, then there was a chance, a very small chance, that he could convince her to abandon a scheme that her father, or perhaps her father and the other Elders of the Zeyn, had concocted. A scheme she had accepted because she had to, because it was her duty.

Better than anyone, he understood the onerous claims of duty. Heedless of the disruptor pointed at him so steadily, Tarl cautiously crossed the space dividing them, removed the weapon from Marna's hands, and set it aside.

"Let me help you," he said gently. "No one has the right to force you against your will, no matter how important the cause."

She looked up at him then, but her hands stayed frozen in front of her, as if she no longer knew what to do with them.

"You don't understand," she said.

Even in the dark, Tarl could see her lips pinch shut against all the other things she wanted to say and couldn't. Something within him snapped at that.

He'd spent years fighting against the never-ending demands that duty and honor and responsibility could make on him, and he hadn't won the battle yet. His presence here on Diloran was proof of that.

Marna of Jiandu was only just learning there was a battle to be fought; she hadn't yet found any hope of winning it. If he did nothing else, Tarl vowed, he would give her that hope. No matter what.

"I understand," he said, his voice low to hide the jumbled emotions that trembled on the tip of his tongue, waiting for the release he dared not give them.

Without thinking, he gently brushed the unruly curtain of hair away from her face, then let his fingers trail through the midnight strands that were as light and softly clinging as spider silk. "I *do* understand, Marna. Better than anyone. Believe me."

There were a hundred other things he ought to say, but Tarl suddenly found he couldn't say them. He knew he ought to let her go. Instead, he shoved his fingers deeper into her hair, feeling the weight of it fold around his hands as he traced the curve of her skull, letting his fingers trail downward until his palm pressed against the side of her throat and he could feel the thudding heat of her blood beneath the skin.

He'd only meant to comfort her, but somehow the simple gesture had been transformed into a tormentingly sensual exploration that invited him onward. He let the side of his thumb brush over her earlobe, then trace the delicate ridge of the helix, up and around and back down the curve of her ear. He was conscious of the sudden speeding up of his own heart and blood in response, and for one brief, mad moment he wondered what would happen if he let himself explore farther.

Her hand abruptly came up to capture his. "Don't," she said, but instead of pulling his hand away, she laced her fingers into his, pressed her palm to the back of his hand, and held him there against her.

"I don't even know your name," she said, and there was as much wonder in her voice as there was uncertainty.

"Toff." The name was out before he realized it, a childhood nickname from a time when he hadn't yet faced the future that others had planned for him. He didn't know why it came so easily now. He hadn't thought of it in years. "It's Toff."

"Toff." She dropped her gaze and Tarl sensed rather than saw her frown. "It's a strange name."

His fingers tightened their hold on her. "Yes, I suppose it is."

"Toff." She nodded, as if confirming something to herself, then tugged his hand away, but without releasing her hold on him. "You just don't understand."

Tarl twisted his hand in hers so that they clung, palm to palm, fingers woven tightly together as if denying the dark night that still divided them. With his other hand, he gently forced her chin up until she was looking at him once again. "You don't have to go through with this if you don't want to, Marna. You *don't.* No one can make you."

She shook her head. Tarl could hear the soft brush of her hair across her shoulders and back. The faint sound was more than enough to rouse an urgent, distracting heat deep in his belly.

"I have to. For my people."

It was Tarl's turn to frown. With an effort, he forced his thoughts away from the heat flaring within him. "For your people? How can your being pledged to Tarl Grisaan help your people? He's not Controller yet, you know. If his uncle has anything to say about the matter, he won't survive long enough, anyway. What benefit can there possibly be for your people if you're companion to a dead man?"

Tarl wasn't sure if it was his words, or the angry insistence in his voice, but Marna sucked in her breath with a hiss and jerked back, away from him.

"Don't say that!" she cried. "What do you know of the matter, anyway? You who come sneaking in windows like a thief in the night? I don't even know you. Why should I listen to anything you say? Why?"

Because I'm telling you everything you're afraid to tell yourself, Tarl wanted to shout. Because you don't want this insane life that others are choosing for you. Because . . .

He had a dozen reasons why she should listen to him. A hundred. And he didn't give her one. Not now. It was enough to have made her admit, even if only to herself, that she wanted nothing of the political machinations into which others were dragging her. That admission was the first and most important step in getting free. The other steps would be no less important, but none would be as hard as this first confrontation between heart and mind. He knew. He just wished he could tell her.

Instead, he said, "You should listen to me because I'm telling you the same things you're telling yourself."

"No! That's not true!" She was close to shouting, heedless that she might attract attention neither of them wanted.

"It is. You know it is." Tarl might have said more, but some small, still rational voice at the back of his mind told him he'd said too much already. Instead, he took a deep breath and forced his hands to drop to his sides; then he slowly backed up to the open window.

She remained where he'd left her, watching him, her body strung so tight with the anger and doubt and denial his words had roused that the tension radiated from her.

"Think about it, Marna of Jiandu," he said softly. "That's all I ask. Just think about it." With that, he slipped through the window and dropped to the ground.

Once there, however, he found it wasn't as easy to slip back into the shadows as it had been the night before. Despite the risk that someone might see him, Tarl turned back, wondering if she would be at the window. She wasn't. The opening above him was empty and dark, with no trace of life behind it.

He ought to leave. He'd had a long night last night and come too close to being captured for comfort. Today had been just as long and filled with far too many unsettling events. Tomorrow promised to be even longer. Getting a good night's sleep would be a reasonable, sensible course of action.

Yet still he hesitated. He took one step back, then another, his gaze still fixed on that dark window above him. One last glimpse of her. That's all he wanted. Some small indication that she hadn't entirely rejected him or his warning.

A bare moment before he was ready to concede defeat and slip away, Marna leaned out the window. She seemed little more than a shadowed face floating in the darkness, her black hair and dark robe almost invisible in the night, but her whispered words carried clearly on the still air.

"You'll take care?"

Absurd to give so much power to such simple words, but Tarl felt his body grow suddenly lighter, as if her concern had lifted a weight from him he hadn't realized he was carrying. He couldn't help grinning, even in the dark.

"Of course!" He retreated another step, but this time there was a bounce in his step that hadn't been there a moment before. "I'll be back, you know!"

That admission caught him by surprise. He hadn't meant to say that. He hadn't had any intention of returning. Yet even as he spoke, Tarl knew he wouldn't have retracted his words even if he could. He *would* be back. Whether it was wise or not, he knew he couldn't stay away.

Marna's only answer was a hissed, "Don't be a fool!"

Tarl didn't bother to respond—it was far too late for warnings, even if he'd cared to heed them. Instead, he saluted her, just as he had the night before, then turned and ducked into the shadows.

This time, however, he looked back often as he made his way toward the far end of the garden. And every time he turned to look, Marna was still at the window, watching for him in the night.

As Tarl dropped out of the old tree into the pitch-black alleyway, he found he couldn't repress a small, self-mocking smile. He'd just given Marna the first of a long series of lectures on the rights of the individual that he'd recited to himself for his own benefit for years.

If he still couldn't practice what he preached, even after all this time, how did he think Marna was going to manage? Wasn't his presence on Diloran clear proof that he couldn't put aside the claims of duty any more than she could?

He could have remained on Regulus if he'd really wanted

to. He could have written a statement of abdication or whatever the proper term was for a man who was willing to abandon an inherited position he'd never assumed. He could have laughed in Joeffrey's face and gone on about his life and let his uncle work out the legal niceties of his non-appearance.

There had to be any number of ways he could have avoided returning to Diloran, yet here he was, playing the role of a fool, plotting with rebels, and trying to get out of a forced pledge of companionship that would tie him into his traditional role more firmly than ever.

Perhaps Joeffrey was right and he was certifiably crazy.

After all, he hadn't spotted the holes in his tutor's arguments and plans until he'd actually gotten back to Diloran. Only then had that wily old man admitted that, as a means of getting Tarl safely back on the planet, he'd convinced Marott Grisaan of the need to bring his nephew back, not to kill him right off, as Tarl had thought, but to show the world how inept Tarl Grisaan was—and *then* kill him.

Joeffrey had convinced Marott that the first approach might have left some residents grumbling and wondering about Marott Grisaan's right to be Controller of Diloran. The other led everyone to think that no matter how much they might dislike him, Marott was a better choice as leader than his nephew would ever have been.

That revelation had led to another.

Tarl had always known that his uncle could have had him killed any number of times, both before and after he'd been admitted to the Marines. He'd just figured Marott had been content to leave him alone so long as Tarl returned the favor. That misperception might have cost him his life if Joeffrey hadn't been systematically fooling the Controllor-Regent with false reports of Tarl's bumbling incompetence as a file clerk for the Galactic Marines.

Not until then had Tarl realized the kind of double life

Joeffrey had been living all those years, juggling his schemes and his lies and his half-truths, trying to control the worst of Marott Grisaan's excesses while keeping the controllorship alive as a respected institution—all in the hope that one day he, Tarl, would return to Diloran to take up the position for which he'd been trained from birth.

What a shame Joeffrey had never believed him when, even as a boy, Tarl had sworn that he wanted no part of his inheritance, that he wanted to make his own life in his own way, free of history and the obligations bequeathed by his ancestors.

Yet despite all his protestations of independence, he obviously hadn't managed to escape the demands of duty and responsibility anymore than Marna had. If he had, he wouldn't be here now, hunched into the deepest shadows in a night-shrouded, tree-lined alleyway, wondering what to do next.

Tarl sighed and leaned against the age-roughened trunk of the tree beside him, listening to the silence. What madness had prompted him to come? Marna wasn't going to turn aside from the course that had been set for her, and no prompting from a furtive stranger was going to induce her to try.

Just the thought of her was enough to generate an uncomfortable heat in his blood, yet he'd be a fool to press the matter. She couldn't refuse her people's demands anymore than he'd been able to reject Joeffrey's demands on him. The towering garden wall that divided them now was no greater than the wall of conflicting loyalties and expectations that divided them in life, and nothing would change that in the short time left before the Tevah had ousted his uncle and he was free to leave Diloran.

With sudden decision, Tarl shoved away from the tree. He ought to go to bed, but he was far too restless to sleep. The memory of Marna, of her hair sifting across his skin and the warmth of her beneath his hand, would be enough to keep him half-witted for hours.

If he was going to be half-witted, he might as well make the most of the situation and indulge in a little night-time exploration of his uncle's weapons caches. An unaccompanied jaunt into the central part of the city at this time of night ought to provide all the ammunition Joeffrey needed for a rousing sermon on the virtues of common sense and caution. It wouldn't do for his friend to grow listless for want of an argument to keep his blood stirred up.

And who knew? Maybe he could run into another Internal Security patrol that would provide the excuse he needed to jump back into Marna of Jiandu's bed.

At the thought, Tarl grinned. He could always hope.

"I can't go through with this!" Marna kept her back straight and her head high as she confronted her father. She didn't have much chance of winning the argument, but she'd have no chance at all if she resorted to pleading. "You saw him. There is no honor in fighting against a man who is scarcely a man!"

Eileak of Zeyn gave a small grunt that might have been an indication of assent, or disgust, or both. In the bright morning sunlight streaming through the windows of his private chambers, he looked unnaturally tired and tense. Life in Diloran Central didn't seem to agree with him anymore than it did with her.

"You were originally intended for the uncle. You know that," he said sternly. "But now that the heir has returned, *he* is the one you are best pledged to, regardless of whether he is a man or not. Our plans need not be greatly altered, one way or the other. It only adds one more small task to your assignment."

Marna choked at thought of the "one small task." "I can't believe that the only way to ensure the downfall of the Grisaans is for me to be pledged as the young one's companion. Surely there are other—"

"Enough!" Her father slammed the edge of his right hand against the palm of his left, as sharply as though he were cutting off her objections with an ax. "We have discussed this before and I will not discuss it again. The Elders have decided. It is your duty to do what you are told, without asking questions and without demanding to know why. Are you not of the Zeyn?"

When Marna nodded, mute yet stubborn, he continued, "Well, then, be a Zeyn!"

He hesitated; then his voice dropped and his hard, black eyes softened. "I would not have chosen such a companion for you, but it is only for a short time, after all, my daughter. It is not as if you were bound to him, obligated to mate and bear young. That, truly, would be unacceptable. But as pledged companion, you can see more, hear more, *do* more than anyone else to obtain the information we need."

He smiled gently and brought his hand up to touch her cheek. "You are so like your mother. Proud. Willful. But intelligent and brave, as well. I know you will do what is required of you, what is best for our people, just as she would have."

Marna smiled sadly. It had been a long time since he'd last spoken of her mother, who had died in a hunting accident fifteen years earlier. She knew her father loved her, but his duties as Elder and his responsibilities as leader of the Zeyn had always taken priority. Always.

Eileak's eyes darkened and grew stern once more. His hand knotted into a fist. "You will need your intelligence and courage. These Grisaans are slowly destroying us, killing us with their stranglehold on our trade and their support of these decadent Families who encroach on our territories, defile our sands, destroy our world."

Inwardly, Marna sighed. Her father was once more caught in an old anger that had grown over the years until it nearly consumed him. He would do anything to protect the traditions and lands of his people, and he'd long ago decided it was the power and the enmity of the Grisaans that lay at the heart of the changes threatening the Zeyn, from inside as well as from without. Nothing could convince him otherwise.

"If the Grisaans are destroyed," Eileak continued grimly, "then we will have greater freedom to act as we think best for our people. And *you* are the one who will destroy them."

Marna's heart sank as she watched her father's mouth twist in a feral smile. The Elders agreed with him. She hadn't prevailed against them in the caverns, and she would not prevail here. Her duty now was to obey, no matter how distasteful the task.

"Now, go to this Tarl Grisaan," Eileak continued. "Become his friend. Make him take you on a tour of his decadent city as he promised you last night. Make him want you."

Her father smiled again, slowly, in hungry anticipation of what lay ahead. "Get to know him and his uncle well, so that your destruction of them will be that much more complete."

Chilled to her core, Marna bowed silently with the courteous respect due her father and the Elder of the Zeyn, and turned to go. She was halfway to the outer door of his chamber when he spoke again.

"Speak to your maid," he said harshly. "I saw her sitting last night. Eating!"

Marna's hands clenched at the contempt in his voice. To him, Sesha was a servant, a cripple and therefore a parasite on the Zeyn, good only for menial work that no one who was whole and fit would ever stoop to perform. He had never understood Marna's passionate loyalty to a woman who was almost a second mother to her, and he never would.

"It was Kiri Grisaan who invited Sesha to sit, Father. He saw that her bad leg would pain her if she were forced to stand for so long. He was the one who ordered the Palace servants to offer her food."

Eileak grunted. He couldn't argue against an act by the man to whom his daughter was pledged, no matter how much he would have liked to. "Well, see that she is not so obvious the next time, do you hear? I will not have her bringing shame on our people by her behavior. Bad enough that she should exist at all, without her displaying her infirmity to everyone!"

"Yes, Father." She would not mention the matter to Sesha, but her father didn't have to know that.

When her father remained silent, Marna slipped out of the room as quietly as she could, unwilling to attract his attention again.

And then she went in search of someone who could lead her to Tarl Grisaan. Her father had said she was to demand a tour of the city, and demand a tour she would. He'd never said she had to like it.

Chapter Six

It was midday before Tarl Grisaan's attendants finally admitted Marna to the area of his personal quarters where he received his visitors each day. She'd tried four different times that morning to see him, and each time she'd been politely but firmly turned away with profuse apologies that Kiri Grisaan was not yet receiving visitors.

Since these repeated rejections came on top of her father's lecture and a sleepless night torn between the doubts that a stranger's words had stirred within her and the even more unsettling physical need he'd roused without even trying, she wasn't in any mood to be either patient or understanding.

By the time she was finally allowed past the door by the obsequious attendants, Marna found she could barely control an anger that had started out, hours earlier, as mere irritation.

Tarl Grisaan might be heir to the controllorship, but he had a great deal to learn about courtesy! During her morning's wait it had occurred to her that if he'd taken up his duties as controllor when he'd reached the age of nineteen, as he should have, she might never have been forced to enter into this detestable scheme in the first place. By the time she'd crossed the antechamber and swept through the double doors into his main room, Marna was prepared to be thoroughly difficult.

She wasn't ten steps inside the room, however, when she was brought up short at the sight of Tarl, somewhat more tastefully though no less richly dressed in a pale pink robe over scarlet hose, meekly seated in a massive carved chair at the far end of the room while an old, hunchbacked cripple lectured him roundly.

"You have not been attending, Kiri Grisaan!" the old man ranted, bobbing his oversized bald head up and down for emphasis. "I tell you that supplies, government supplies, are being stolen and you smile nicely and ask if we can't order more. I tell you that more supplies—arms, this time!—were destroyed by saboteurs last night, and you say that you did not sleep well! As if your sleeping well were my concern!"

The old man laboriously stumped over to a vast carved table, picked up a sheaf of documents from a dozen disorderly piles of documents stacked there, and stumped back to Tarl, who had taken advantage of the break in the lecturing to check the state of his manicure.

An attendant posted near the door was clearly struggling not to reveal her shock at the undignified proceedings.

"Here!" the old man snorted, coming to a clumsy halt in front of his unrepentant audience of one. "I have prepared another economic analysis which you must, absolutely *must,* read. A report on the economic ties among the Old Families and the central government. Do you understand?" To lend emphasis to his demands, he thumped Tarl soundly on the top of the head with the sheaf of papers before irritably waving them under his nose.

Tarl yawned and took the documents, more, Marna thought, to protect his exquisitely curled blond hair than because of any real interest in the documents themselves. "Are these going to be as boring as all the other analyses you wanted me to read?"

"Boring!" The old man snorted again and swung around in disgust, as if looking for an escape from the obdurate stupidity of his pupil. His massive, twisted hump and misshapen spine made his every movement horribly awkward, as painful to watch as it must have been for him to endure.

"Boring!" He swung back. "Just read it. And read the rest I gave you, as well. I'll have more for you tomorrow. There's much you've left to learn, and no time in which to learn it."

Tarl looked up at that, as if to protest the threat of more work, and spotted Marna. He grinned and straightened out of his negligent slouch, obviously relieved to find a ready excuse to escape more bullying. With unbecoming haste, he tucked Joeffrey's papers behind him.

"Kiria!" he said. "Welcome! You couldn't have come at a better time!"

Something in his voice made Marna hesitate for an instant, as some half-formed memory flitted past her conscious mind. But just for an instant. Then Tarl giggled and whatever memory he'd stirred disappeared as quickly as rain in the desert.

"I have been trying to see you, Kiri Grisaan," she said with dignity, unwilling to make a show of her anger in front of strangers, and one of them a cripple. She tried hard not to look at the old man, but his was too powerful a presence to ignore for long. "I tried four times to get past your attendants earlier, but each time they refused me admittance."

The old man *humpffed* in disgust. "Clearly you do not yet know of our distinguished leader's sleeping habits, Kiria."

Marna's head came up at that.

Tarl giggled again, but managed to stifle at least part of

that repulsive sound by coyly pressing his fingertips to his lips. "What Joeffrey means is that I don't sleep well at night, so I often linger in bed in the morning."

"Linger! Malinger, if you ask me!" Joeffrey retorted. "He was a lazy student as a boy, and he's no better now he's grown."

Appalled and fascinated, all at the same time, Marna stared at the old man's ugly, distorted features, at the dry, age-splotched skin stretched tight over his bald pate and the wispy fringe of yellowish-white hair that did nothing to hide the fact that his left ear was set slightly higher on his skull than the right. Never in all her life had she seen such a twisted, deformed mockery of a human being. If the Sands were kind, she never would again. The thought of his pain, and the burden he must be to those around him, made her stomach lurch uncomfortably. At least Sesha could walk without assistance and serve other, more able-bodied inhabitants of the caverns. Of what benefit could this man possibly be?

"Permit me to present you to each other," Tarl said, rising to his feet and shaking out the skirts of his robe with delicate grace. "I have a feeling you'll find you have a great deal in common, starting with your opinions of me."

He gave a lazy, self-mocking twist of his wrist as he gestured to Joeffrey with his left hand. "Marna of Jiandu, permit me to present my former tutor, now my uncle's senior economic advisor, Joeffrey Baland. Joeffrey," he added, indicating Marna with his right hand, "meet Marna of Jiandu, daughter of Eileak of the Zeyn and, as of yesterday, my pledged companion."

"Kiria Marna," Joeffrey Baland said politely, giving her a courtly bow.

Marna nodded, too shocked to be capable of speech. This wretched creature was Joeffrey Baland? How was that possible? Even her father spoke of him with respect, but now, to find the man was a stunted cripple . . . !

"Well, I see I may as well abandon my efforts at education for the rest of the morning," Joeffrey said sharply, turning his attention back to Tarl. "If I weren't a foolish old man, I'd abandon the effort altogether, but I won't give up hope yet. If you'd just read—"

"Yes, yes. I promise." Tarl gestured to the attendant by the door to bring the cane she held. He took the cane from her and handed it to his disgruntled instructor. "Here, Joeffrey. Same time tomorrow?"

"*Humpff,*" Joeffrey said again, thumping the cane on the floor. "As well spend my time singing to a herd of goats as try to teach you economics, but, yes, I'll be here tomorrow, same time."

"Good! Good! I'll be ready," Tarl said heartily. "Until then!"

He stood and watched as Joeffrey slowly made his way across the room, muttering angrily to himself and punctuating his thoughts by thumping his cane on the floor as he went. The attendant respectfully followed after the old man, clearly relieved to escape. Only after the woman had closed the doors behind them did Tarl turn his attention back to Marna.

"Well, what was it you wished to discuss with me?" he said, beaming as if nothing would bring him greater satisfaction than an intimate chat with her.

Marna frowned, angry and disgusted and unsure if those emotions were directed more at him and his wretched tutor or at herself. She hadn't meant to speak, had meant to ignore the situation entirely, but the words burst out before she could stop them. "How can that be Joeffrey Baland? He's a cripple! Hunchbacked and lame and—and ugly!"

She might as well have physically attacked him. Tarl's mouth hardened and his eyes—those soft, gentle brown eyes that had seemed so understanding at the dinner last night—

flashed with sudden anger. He straightened slowly, until every muscle in his body must have stretched to its limit. "That's right. Why don't you add that he's old, as well, just to cover every possible point?"

Clearly he'd meant to ignore her reaction to Joeffrey Baland, but her outburst had made that impossible. Now he was prepared to take her head-on. Gone was any hint of softness or simpering foolishness. The man who stood before her was unmistakably riled, but Marna was too upset to heed the signs.

"How can you permit someone like—like *that* to occupy a position of such importance?" she demanded. "Senior economic advisor? Surely you don't think me so gullible that I'll accept such a preposterous claim?"

"You have no right to accept or deny anything. Joeffrey Baland is what he is, the most brilliant economist on Diloran. Isn't that enough?"

"But . . . but he's *lame.*" Marna waved her arms helplessly, unable to find words to explain herself, irritated that this silly, pink-robed fool who worried about his manicure should indulge in self-righteous anger at her expense. What had induced his people to forget the needs of the community to such an extent that they would permit an individual like Joeffrey Baland to exist?

"I don't understand your objections," Tarl said at last, clearly struggling to regain his self-control. "After all, your maid is lame."

"My maid? Sesha? But she was injured in a rock slide, after she'd gained the right to leave the caverns. That's why she's a maid. She wasn't *born* crippled." By what right did he compare her beloved Sesha's situation with this Joeffrey Baland's?

"And that makes all the difference?"

Marna flinched at the scorn in his voice. How could she explain the principles of communal protection, including the preservation of resources for the use of those who could productively contribute to the community, to a man who clearly wouldn't understand them anyway?

"Of course it does," she said at last, struggling to keep her voice steady. "A crippled babe would take far more from the community than it could ever give back, but an adult who has already been trained . . ." She shrugged. "That's another matter entirely."

"Of *course* it is," he said, scornfully parroting her words. He breathed in deeply through his nose and turned away from her, his shoulders rigid with anger. For several seconds he glared at the far wall without speaking, his back so straight and stiff he might have been a stone carving rather than a living human being; then he took another deep breath, sighed, and turned back to face her, his features carefully schooled into expressionless calm.

"I didn't mean to quarrel with you," he said at last, extending his right hand, palm up, in a gesture of mingled apology and forgiveness. "I'm sorry."

Marna frowned, then reluctantly laid her hand in his. She didn't owe him any apology—it was, after all, his own people's socially destructive policies that were the issue, not her objections to them—but there was nothing to be gained by continuing their argument. She had more important concerns to discuss than his senseless defense of a cripple. "Of course."

A muscle in his cheek twitched in response to her curt reply, but that was all. His fingers closed around hers with the barest minimum of pressure required by good manners; then he released her hand and stepped back. "What was it you wished to see me about?"

At the polite reminder of her four wasted visits earlier that morning, Marna's anger threatened a resurgence, but she sternly stamped it down. Her father had said she should make the man her friend before she made him her companion. She hadn't begun very well and it would behoove her to regain lost ground as quickly as possible.

In a more even tone, she said, "Last night, just before we parted, you offered to show me around your city if I wished."

"I remember."

"I would like to see Diloran Central. It would be . . ." She hesitated, half choking on the words, but managed to get them out at last. "It would be a great pleasure if you could accompany me."

Tarl bowed, ever so slightly, his face still coolly expressionless. "It would be an honor for me, certainly. When would you like to go?"

"Now would be convenient."

He jerked upright at that, clearly startled. "Now?" All his nervous fussiness returned with a rush. He tugged at the glittering monstrosity that hung on his ear. "I'm hardly dressed for—But I'd be delighted," he added quickly, obviously sensing her surge of irritation at his foolishness. "Now would be absolutely perfect."

Now was *not* absolutely perfect, Tarl thought. He didn't appreciate her haughty dignity or her uncalled-for attack on Joeffrey. The Zeyn were known for their intolerance of physical or mental disabilities. He didn't care. The extraordinarily harsh conditions under which they'd established their society hundreds of years ago might have made such an attitude necessary at one time, but the need for such rigid adherence to that code had long since disappeared. Too bad the social stigma hadn't disappeared with it.

To cover his anger, Tarl turned away to retrieve the papers he'd abandoned on his chair when she came in.

At first glance, this particular sheaf of papers looked like any dull bureaucratic report, but it contained highly classified information on the shipment of arms to dissidents across Diloran—shipments that were being made through the "generosity" of his uncle, who hoped to undermine the political stability of the more influential Old Families and thus strengthen his own political position.

Joeffrey had taken advantage of Marott Grisaan's orders that he "do whatever was necessary with that damned idiot nephew of mine" to reestablish their old relationship of tutor and student. It had proved to be an effective way of surreptitiously passing the economic, political, and military information Tarl needed to understand what was going on throughout Diloran. While palace gossips tittered over Joeffrey's growing frustration with his hopeless pupil, Tarl was absorbing information that would help him in his work with the Tevah and their efforts to bring down Marott Grisaan.

The reports were relatively easy to hide in the mass of papers that Joeffrey brought him daily because the old man was famous—infamous was a better word—for his preference for printed rather than computerized reports. The rest of the camouflaging reports and publications ended up being piled higher and higher on the table. No one would ever notice if the towering piles didn't include *everything* Joeffrey had showered on him over the last few weeks.

The only weak point in the strategy was the time between Joeffrey handing him the documents and his reading, then destroying them. Since he wouldn't have a chance to review this latest report immediately, as he usually did, Tarl decided he'd bury it in the untidy stack on the table, then take Marna for this city tour she was demanding.

Tarl straightened, the papers in his left hand, and was just turning back to face Marna when Marott Grisaan strode into the room unannounced.

This was the perfect culmination to his morning, Tarl decided sourly, taking in his uncle's forbidding scowl and aggressive stride. No doubt the fates considered it just repayment for his having indulged in the illicit expedition last night.

"Uncle!" he exclaimed, beaming. "How *nice* of you to drop in!" He extended his right hand in greeting, but took care to keep the papers in his left half hidden in the long folds of his robe. "What brings you here?"

Marott Grisaan ignored his nephew's outstretched hand. "I came—" Whatever he was going to say was cut short when he caught sight of Marna.

Tarl watched, amused, as his uncle's anger vanished instantly, to be replaced by a suave charm that must have required years of practice to perfect.

"Kiria Marna," Marott said, crossing to her and extending his hand with graceful aplomb.

Instead of taking his hand, Marna nodded and neatly tucked her hands inside her full sleeves. Either bad manners were catching, or suave charm didn't impress her. Charm, like flattery, flirting, and most of the other social insincerities, wasn't much appreciated by Zeyn women, who were as capable of surviving in the cruel Diloran desert as any man.

"I have come to request that Kiri Tarl show me your city as he promised," Marna said now, meeting Marott's irritation with cool aplomb. "Perhaps you would like to accompany us, Kiri Grisaan?"

Taking advantage of Marott's momentary distraction, Tarl dumped Joeffrey's papers on top of the jumbled stacks of paper already on the table. He'd have to bury them in the mess later. In the meantime, he could only hope Marott wasn't too inquisitive. Tarl casually propped himself on the arm of his chair, at just the right angle so Marott wouldn't be facing the table, and pretended to be fascinated by the conversation.

"I'm afraid I have too much work to join you," Marott said, easily brushing away Marna's suggestion that he accompany them. "You two go right ahead and enjoy yourselves. It will be an excellent opportunity for you to get to know one another." Despite his years of practice at hiding his feelings, Marott couldn't quite disguise his relief at having an excuse to avoid the excursion.

Tarl had to admit to a twinge of envy. He wished *he* had a good excuse. The prospect of spending hours in a skimmer alone with Marna of Jiandu was . . . He wasn't sure what it was, and it didn't bear thinking about.

"As long as you're here, however," Marott continued, "I would like to discuss this matter of your pledge of companionship with Tarl. Your father . . ." He hesitated, then cleared his throat uncomfortably. "Your father caught me by surprise, I'm afraid."

And that had been Eileak of Zeyn's plan all along, Tarl knew. Not that Marott Grisaan needed to be told that.

As Marott politely listed some of the issues of protocol that needed to be clarified and resolved, Tarl watched Marna, searching her calm features for some hint of what she was thinking.

She had to have known that her father intended to ensure she was pledged as companion by offering her in a *very* public forum, where the pledge could not be rejected without risk of political embarrassment, at the very least, or open declarations of war, at the worst. But was she an innocent pawn, or an active player in a dangerous political game?

And what was Eileak of Zeyn's purpose, anyway? Even Joeffrey's carefully constructed network for information gathering had not foreseen this move by the Zeyn, the only Old Family not represented in the Tevah.

His thoughts were interrupted by Marott Grisaan saying heartily, "Well, I really don't need to bother you with all these details. I'm sure your father and I and our assistants can work it out to everyone's satisfaction."

He turned back to Tarl, his features suddenly set in stern lines of disapproval. From the way Marott's eyes flashed, Tarl suspected that his uncle wouldn't have settled for anything so tame as mere disapproval if Marna hadn't been present.

"The reason I came, Tarl, is to tell you that I am receiving an increasing number of complaints that you have been—shall we say, annoying?—members of my staff with your constant flood of questions and ill-informed opinions. This has to stop. Immediately. Despite my need for him, I have assigned Joeffrey to tutor you so that you can catch up after your years of absence. I will *not* have you annoying anyone else, is that understood? Their time is far too precious to waste."

Tarl pouted, just a little. "But all Joeffrey does is give me *tons* of boring reading. Don't you think it would be better if I sat in on *your* meetings, uncle? Saw things from close up, so to speak?"

Tarl had thought to divert his uncle, but he'd been wrong. Marott frowned, as if struck by a sudden, rather unpleasant thought, and glanced at the table and its pile of printed material. Was it his imagination, Tarl wondered, or did Marott look just the tiniest bit suspicious?

"May I see this boring reading?" Marott asked, ignoring Tarl's question altogether. Without waiting for permission, he moved toward the table and the jumbled pile of documents and reports.

To Tarl, it seemed as if his uncle was heading straight for the crumpled sheaf of papers he'd just tossed on top of everything, right where it would be easy to spot.

His heart skipped a beat.

Hunchbacked, ugly old Joeffrey Baland was Marott Grisaan's most trusted advisor. He was also his most dangerous enemy and the driving force behind the Tevah's efforts to oust Marott and return Diloran to a more just rule. Joeffrey's effectiveness as leader of the Tevah would be destroyed and his life put at risk if Marott Grisaan ever saw some of the information the old advisor was passing Tarl on a daily basis.

Tarl bounded to his feet and headed after his uncle.

He reached the table just a step behind Marott Grisaan. "All that's so *dull,* Uncle," he complained, petulantly slapping at an especially thick wad of printed material. "Do *you* have to read all this? What's the use of being Controllor if all you do is spend your time being bored?''

Marott didn't waste time answering. He picked up the one document Tarl didn't want him to touch.

Tarl grabbed one of Joeffrey's beloved economic analyses and fanned it under his uncle's nose. ''Look at this one, uncle. Numbers. Just a whole bunch of numbers. How do you expect me to make any sense out of all that?''

To Marna, who had come up behind them, Tarl's objections sounded more like childish whining than rational protests. On the other hand, she had to admit that the heaps of papers in front of them were intimidating. She moved closer to the table, trying to catch titles or scraps of information in the jumble that might prove of interest to the Elders.

Marott Grisaan had picked up a crumpled sheaf of papers lying on top of the pile, but before he could glance at them, his nephew rudely stretched in front of him to grab another bundle buried halfway down a particularly tall and unsteady stack.

''And have you seen this one, Uncle?'' Tarl demanded, awkwardly tugging at the bundle he wanted without bothering to remove anything on top of it. ''It's a ridiculous— Oh, my! Oh, no! Catch that, Uncle. No! That one! *That* one!''

The last was added in a screech, but screeching was useless against the disaster Tarl Grisaan had set in motion.

As Marna watched, open-mouthed and wide-eyed, the stack Tarl had been burrowing into slowly tipped to one side, then collapsed. Its collapse triggered the immediate disintegration of the stack beside it, then the next stack over. Rather than helping matters, Tarl flailed about wildly, knocking over two stacks to every one he managed to rescue, then toppling the stack he'd just rescued when he twisted to grab at another.

Papers, bound documents, loose memoranda, economic pamphlets, and more cascaded off the table and onto the floor around Marott Grisaan.

The Controllor-Regent dropped the papers he held and jumped back, but not quickly enough. His feet, along with the papers he'd dropped, were buried in an avalanche of written material, only to be buried deeper still when Tarl managed to bump the last remaining stack with his elbow when he swung around to survey the damage he'd done.

For a moment, there was nothing but silence in the room.

Appalled, Marna stared at the floor. Or, rather, she stared at the spot where the floor had been before it was covered a half meter deep with papers.

She raised her eyes to stare at Marott Grisaan, who stood amidst the wreckage, rigid with mingled disbelief and anger.

And then she stared at her pledged companion, half sprawled across the table, one leg awkwardly waving in midair as he tried to regain his balance, arms outstretched to hold down the three or four papers that hadn't yet found their way to the floor. Tarl shifted slightly, just enough so he could stare at his uncle. He blinked, opened his mouth, then closed it without saying anything.

With great care, Marott pulled one leg out of the debris, then the other. He tugged his uniform into place and said, very distinctly, "If Joeffrey has given you this material to read, then you will read it. *All* of it. If you're busy with this, I can at least be sure you will not be annoying my staff. I trust you understand?"

Tarl nodded dumbly.

Without another word, Marott Grisaan turned and stalked from the room.

As soon as the outer door closed behind his uncle, Tarl Grisaan shoved off the table and back to his feet. He only knocked one paper off this time, but that might have been because there were so few left to dislodge.

Marna watched as he blankly surveyed the disaster he'd created, then raised his eyes to stare back at her. The fitted waist of his robe was hiked up around his ribs, revealing an glimpse of unexpectedly hard, flat belly over the top of scarlet leggings. His earring was twisted around at a decidedly rakish angle on his ear, but his elaborate blond curls were still neatly in place, exquisite in their perfection.

Tarl Grisaan, heir to the Controllorship of Diloran, closed his mouth, cleared his throat, and said, "How about that tour of the city now?"

Now, however, proved to be a half hour later, after Tarl had flustered five of his six attendants, disturbed the guards, and caused one of the palace servants to break out in a nervous sweat in response to his constantly changing orders. By the time Tarl finally led her through the labyrinthine palace hallways toward a side entrance, where a driver and skimmer would be waiting for them, Marna was heartily regretting having suggested the expedition in the first place, no matter what her father had said.

When Tarl waved a servant aside so he could hold a door for her, she glanced up as she passed him, trying to find some trace of the sympathetic man with whom she'd shared that disturbing, strangely intriguing conversation of the night before. Nothing she could see in his delicately featured face, in the silly curls or the garish earring, gave any hint that such a man had ever existed.

To Marna's surprise, Sesha was waiting for them at the shuttle.

"I sent someone to make sure she came along," Tarl said airily, as if he made a point of including servants in every city tour he took.

Selfishly, Marna couldn't help feeling relieved that she wouldn't be alone in the skimmer with Tarl, but a quick glance at Sesha's wrinkled, weather-beaten face showed that the older woman didn't appreciate the invitation.

Tarl held the door of the skimmer for Marna, but made no effort to help her in. When he turned to Sesha, however, he extended his hand to her as if he was accustomed to such gestures. "Watch that first step," he warned. "It will trip you up every time."

Sesha blinked, then stiffened. Her hands locked together in front of her so tightly that her knuckles stood out white, even under the dark, wrinkled skin.

Among the Zeyn, it was considered polite to ignore a crippled servant on the grounds that they wouldn't wish to be reminded of their deformity or their lower status. Tarl was not only *not* ignoring her, he was making matters worse by offering to help.

"You'll have a better view if you take the seat beside Kiria Marna," he said, smiling. The smile illuminated his face and made his brown eyes twinkle appealingly. "You may as well get as comfortable as you can, right at the start. There's a lot to see."

Flustered, Sesha took a step forward, then froze, clearly embarrassed by her awkward gait and the way her foot, forced into an unnatural position by her twisted hip and leg, dragged on the ground behind her.

From her seat in the skimmer, Marna watched, shocked into immobility by a sympathetic awareness of the humiliation Sesha had to be suffering at having her deformity pointed out like this. Her hands balled into fists in her lap as she desperately tried to decide if she would help matters, or embarrass Sesha even further, by interfering.

Tarl settled the matter by saying genially, and without his usual air of foolishness, "Come, now. Did someone warn you about my reputation as a guide? I'd be hurt to think you didn't want to give me a chance, at least!"

Faced with a choice between accepting Tarl Grisaan's help or insulting him, Sesha reluctantly opted for the help. Which she needed. The skimmer's high step would have been awkward for her to manage otherwise.

Once Sesha was settled in the seat beside Marna, Tarl climbed into the skimmer and settled into his seat.

"My!" he said. "Isn't this nice. I told the driver to give us a general overview, so to speak, then drop us off near Merchants Row. There's this absolutely *marvelous* jeweler's shop that you just *have* to see!"

Chapter Seven

So long as they remained in the skimmer, the tour of Diloran Central was fascinating and eye-opening. To her surprise, Marna found she even enjoyed Tarl's running commentary on the sights, no matter how unpleasantly his voice grated. He'd been off the planet for years, but he remembered his history and exhibited an unexpected understanding of the city and its people, an almost empathic comprehension of what was important to them, that made the dry recitation of facts and figures far more human.

Marna's pleasure in the tour vanished the minute they left the skimmer and ventured out into the crowded, noisy street that ran by the base of the steps and escalators leading up to the famous Merchants Row that Tarl insisted they see.

Tarl got out first, then turned to offer his hand to her. Marna chose to ignore him, and so stepped out into the path of a young man mounted on some kind of motorized wheel. He shouted an obscenity at her, then zipped around her in a flash of bright purple top and garish green leggings, and disappeared into the crowds.

Tarl grabbed her arm to steady her, but Marna shook him off, angered and humiliated at having so quickly been made to appear a fool in public.

"I'm all right!" she snapped, tugging her robes back into place.

"You're sure?" The worried frown on Tarl's face only irritated her further. Since when did a daughter of the Zeyn need a fool to protect her, regardless of where she was?

"I'm all *right,* I tell you! I simply didn't expect such appalling behavior, even here. Help Sesha if you want to help someone, not me."

Tarl meekly obeyed while Marna angrily scanned the crowd around them, alert for anyone like purple-and-green who might run into the older woman. With her crippled leg, Sesha wouldn't stand much chance against one of the local barbarians.

Her vigilance wasn't required. The crowd had already changed its flow to move around them. Marna caught more than one irritated glance tossed their way, but no sign of imminent attack.

"We go this way." Tarl indicated the broad stairs and crowded escalators that led upward to what, from this angle, looked like a park built on a shelf of land high above the busy streets around them. "The jeweler is five sections farther on, but I thought you'd like to see some of the shops and the buildings along the way. If we don't use the moving walkways, we can take our time and enjoy the sights."

He turned toward the nearest escalator. Marna started to follow him, then stopped as she suddenly realized she'd never used an escalator before, never even seen one except in pictures. She didn't care to reveal her ignorance to strangers, or to Tarl. Head high, she wheeled and took the stairs beside her in a rush, sweeping upward without a glance to either side, heedless of the people around her.

Her rush carried her well beyond the top of the stairs, on into the vast plaza that lay ahead of her, until the wonder of what she was seeing brought Marna up short, frozen in shock at this first glimpse of the most famous sector in Diloran's greatest city. She'd seen it hundreds of times in the classroom computers in the caverns, heard tales of it a hundred times more, but never until now had she realized how overwhelming the real thing could be.

Here, in the space of a few city sections, stood the first great buildings created by those who had settled Diloran centuries before. By using the traditional architecture of their individual home worlds, those first settlers had constructed monuments to the lives they'd left behind. They'd also created practical structures that represented their hope for the future for which they'd sacrificed so much.

Marna slowly turned on one heel, awed by the soaring spires on one great building, amused by the squat practicality of another, puzzled by the complex decorations on the next.

So many disparate structures crowded so close together should have formed a jumbled nightmare. Instead, they were breathtaking in their beauty and diversity.

Captivated by the fantasy that beckoned on all sides, Marna took a few hesitant steps forward only to stop again, overwhelmed by the implications of what she was seeing.

Never, until now, had she understood what those classroom modules had been trying to tell her about this sector and its role in representing the people of Diloran. Only now did it trouble her that one, and only one, of the Old Families was not represented by a building along Merchants Row.

According to her tutors, the Zeyn disdained such artificiality and ostentatious display. The Zeyn were people of nature, she'd been told, over and over again. The Zeyn took what nature offered and lived in harmony with it; they didn't try to turn it into something else entirely.

It had all made perfectly good sense when she'd been safe

in the caverns among her people. Out here, in the middle of it all, she suddenly regretted that the Zeyn were not a part of this overwhelming marvel.

"Magnificent, isn't it?"

Marna jumped, startled to find Tarl Grisaan suddenly standing beside her. She'd forgotten he existed.

Embarrassed to be caught gawking, Marna almost snapped out a sharp reply, but he wasn't even looking at her. His gaze was fixed on the buildings around them. He looked as foolish as ever, but a slight, surprisingly sensual smile softened his mouth.

"You know, after being away for so long, I'd forgotten how impressive all this is," he said. "The people of Diloran can be proud of this place. It's a monument to their past, but it's also a testament to their future." He frowned as he said that, then added, "At least, I hope it is."

Tarl laughed. It came out as more of an inane squeak. "No matter. We'd best get started if we want to see anything. There are *so* many wonderful shops here. Why, just the other day—"

It was the squeak that did it. Marna didn't care if her father had said she was supposed to make Tarl Grisaan her friend. She didn't care if her rudeness brought unpleasant repercussions in its wake. She couldn't bear a dissertation on shopping right now, no matter what.

Head high, Marna marched into the crowd, determined not to accept help from her escort and not to give way to anyone.

Her resolution didn't last long. The residents of Diloran Central appeared never to have had a lesson in public courtesy. Instead of keeping to the left and making way for others behind them who might be moving faster, they charged about in any direction that suited them, at whatever pace suited them, heedless of anyone they might inconvenience along the way.

Without intending it, Marna quickly became separated from the others.

For an instant, she considered waiting for Tarl to catch up with her, but the thought of acknowledging any sort of dependence on him rankled. He'd told her where they were going. How could she possibly get lost?

Sternly shoving aside the doubts that insisted on nagging at her, Marna plunged ahead, only to be brought up short by a brute of a man blithely walking his pet lierax. The tiny, six-legged creature seemed an incongruous companion for a man of his sort, but then pets were never allowed in the caverns.

Right after him came a peddler noisily offering some sort of gadgets for sale, then an old woman whose sharp cries and sharper elbows opened a path for her faster than good manners might have managed.

Marna turned to watch the woman's progress, amazed that such behavior should be tolerated, only to run into a gaggle of schoolchildren sweeping across the walkway like a flock of squawking, half-witted fleyia. She stumbled, but her indignant protests were wasted. The children were gone before the words were out of her mouth.

It didn't take long for Marna to realize that her usual rapid pace worked only if she was willing to weave and dodge her way through the crowds. Whenever she tried to move in a straight line, she invariably found herself running into someone or tripping over someone else. She could maintain her chosen course if she slowed down, but she had to stop frequently to avoid the speeders, who would have run over her otherwise.

Frustrated, Marna stopped dead, right in the middle of the walkway. Other than a few individuals inclined to grumble irritably at her choice of location, no one paid her any heed. Not one person greeted her. No one nodded, or in any way indicated any awareness of her existence other than by altering their path so as not to bump into her. Even the windows set in the buildings on either side seemed part of the general indifference, reflecting the passing multitude in an ever-changing display of indistinguishable, sun-blurred images, like something out of the nightmares Marna had suffered as a child.

Marna breathed deeply, fighting for control. After all, except for the chaos that reigned here, the street was little different from the main tunnels that connected the principal caverns at home. She was used to people around her, for Sands' sake! Lots of people.

The trouble was, she didn't know how to deal with this press of humanity racing by with no more interest in her than if she'd been a rock.

Marna's stomach heaved suddenly, and her mouth went dry. Her legs trembled and threatened to collapse under her.

Desperate, Marna locked her hands together and squeezed hard, digging her nails into her palms and hunching her shoulders against the fear that threatened to paralyze her.

This was absurd, she told herself wildly. She knew it was. No one was threatening her. Her life wasn't in any danger. She wasn't injured or incapacitated in any other way.

Sensible arguments, and not one of them helped.

Marna had never felt so lost, not even at the age of thirteen, when she'd been taken deep into the desert and left to find her way back as proof that she was an adult.

Hundreds of people were moving past her, yet not one of them was a friend. She wasn't even sure they'd notice if she collapsed at their feet. So far as these passing strangers were concerned, she was faceless, nameless, and virtually invisible. And nobody cared.

Then she saw Tarl. He came striding toward her through the crowd, his expression grim, his brow creased in a worried frown, as heedless of the passersby as they had been of her.

Gaudy earring, blond curls, and all, he looked absolutely wonderful, a familiar face in a sea of strangers that had threatened to swallow her whole.

He was at her side before she had a chance to take a step. His eyes flashed, dark and comforting, and his mouth softened in relief at finding her. For a moment, Marna had the insane impression that he was going to take her in his arms. And for an equally brief, insane moment, she very much hoped he would.

He didn't. Instead, he smiled and gently touched her sleeve. "For a while, there, I thought you were going to abandon us," he said. "I'm glad you decided not to."

It might have been the aftermath of her irrational fear, or the comfort of his presence in the faceless crowd, but something in his touch and voice roused a quick flare of heat in her that was as potent as it was unexpected.

That brought Marna back to reality with a snap. "I wasn't abandoning you," she said, hastily retreating into her dignity. "I'm simply not accustomed to walking so slowly, or to dealing with such ill-mannered crowds."

He grinned at that, a broad, boyish grin that lit his face the way the sun lit the desert on a bright spring morning. "If you think *these* crowds are bad, you should see the ones on—That is . . . er . . ." His smile disappeared at the same rate his words trailed off, until he was left with nothing but an uncomfortable grimace for his efforts.

He shifted his shoulders under his robe in a motion that didn't quite qualify as a shrug. "They can be irritating, can't they?"

Marna wasn't quite sure how he managed it, but with that incompetent little shrug, the flashing-eyed man who had so easily cleaved a way through the crowds was once more an affected, silly fool in an absurd pink robe and scarlet leggings.

She didn't have a chance to wonder if she was hallucinating again, because she suddenly spotted Sesha plowing through the crowd toward them, panting with her valiant effort to keep up despite her crippled leg.

Marna bit her lip in a sudden flush of shame. She'd been so unsettled by the magnificence of the buildings and upset by the rush around her that she hadn't stopped to think how much more difficult walking through these crowds would be for Sesha.

"Are you all right, Sesha?" she demanded, pushing past Tarl.

"Of course I am." Sesha drew herself up straighter in spite of the strain the movement would put on her hip and leg. "I'm just not used to these crowds, that's all."

Those proud words were a patent lie, for when Tarl offered the older woman his arm, she took it without hesitation. Marna couldn't remember when she'd ever seen Sesha cling to anyone for support, yet the older woman's hands were curled, white-knuckled, around Tarl's forearm.

And when did you ever see anyone offer their support, to Sesha or any other cripple, in the caverns? The silent rebuke that rose in her mind caught Marna by surprise.

The answer came, just as silent, but no less condemning. *Never. Not ever.*

"She managed just fine. I know, because I didn't leave her until we spotted you, no matter how much she complained about my company." Tarl looked straight at Marna as he spoke. Nothing in his expression, his words, or his tone indicated he was chastising her for her neglect of her maid, but there was no doubt in Marna's mind that that was exactly what he was doing.

"In fact," he added, glancing down approvingly at the older woman beside him, "I wouldn't mind having her make a path for me, now and again. She scared at least ten people into some manners, and I swear I even caught one apology!"

"More than one was needed! But it wouldn't have been so difficult if you'd listened to me and gone after Kiria

Marna as you should have.'' Sesha uncurled her hands from around Tarl's arm, but kept her weight carefully balanced on her good leg. It was a trick Marna had seen her use when her crippled leg was hurting, or she was tired. ''Shall we go, then? We're as ill-mannered as the rest, standing in the middle of the way talking when people are trying to get by.''

This time Marna meekly fell into step beside Tarl. She couldn't help noting that he chose a pace that comfortably accommodated Sesha's halting gait without giving any indication that he noticed her discomfort.

Even with Tarl beside her and Sesha, who was insisting on propriety, properly behind her, Marna found herself longing to escape from the press of people around them. If only she could retreat to her beloved desert; to that vast, stark world that swept to the horizon as if there were no end to it!

Yet even as that thought formed, Marna knew her world had altered too much since she'd boarded the shuttle two days earlier for her ever to find the same sense of security she'd once known. There *was* an end to the desert, after all. She'd seen it from the shuttle, seen the limitless sands reach their limits and disappear in the encroaching green of a different world entirely.

This world, she thought, looking around her in shuddering distaste. This noisy, noisome, unmannerly world where life seemed a distorted reflection of everything she'd known, everything she'd always taken for granted.

Did Sesha feel the same way? Marna wondered as she waited while the older woman clumsily negotiated a series of awkwardly constructed steps. Not that it mattered. Sesha had been told to accompany Marna, just as she'd been assigned to serve the family of Eileak ever since an accident almost twenty years earlier had left her with a crushed hip and leg and no hope of a future except as an attendant to others. She hadn't had any say in the matter and never would.

For the first time in her life, Marna wondered how Sesha felt about the subservient role that life and ill chance had thrust on her. She'd been a hunter, an honored position among the Zeyn, and now she was a servant, doing the work reserved for cripples and the unfit who could never venture outside the caverns alone.

Marna couldn't help thinking of another cripple she'd met that morning. An ugly hunchback who could scarcely stand and found walking far more difficult than Sesha, yet who somehow had risen to become senior economic advisor to the Controllor-Regent of Diloran.

Had Joeffrey Baland been of the Zeyn, he would never have been allowed to live.

The thought made Marna flinch, just as the memory of his crooked body made her stomach churn unpleasantly. And yet . . .

Tarl's hearty cry of, "Here we are at last!" broke in to grant her welcome relief from her thoughts. She looked up to find him watching her, his dark eyes shadowed with a speculative regard that made her wonder if he were somehow capable of reading her mind.

Then he turned and the sun caught the stones of his earring, reminding her of what the desert taught—that it was easy to be fooled by the shadows and lights and unfamiliar contours of an unknown land, and that an explorer had to proceed warily or risk being lost forever.

"Well, what do you think of this, then?" Tarl picked up the delicate curve of sculpted gold and held it to Marna's ear, knowing the act would tempt him as much as it would irritate her, but unable to resist nonetheless.

When she'd first demanded he follow through on his offer to show her the city, he'd thought an afternoon spent listening to his droning disquisition on the history, economics, and social and political structure of Diloran Central—enhanced with pure fabrication, should his memory fail him at any essential point—would go a long way toward convincing her of the need to break her pledge to him. He'd added a visit to this jeweler's shop on the grounds that, in this case, Marna of Jiandu couldn't have too much of a bad thing.

But then she'd broken from them at the entrance to Merchants Row, charging into the crowd with an angry, agitated determination that had no purpose, so far as he could see, beyond the motion itself, as if she sought to escape something deep within her own heart and soul. At first he'd let her go, thinking she simply needed a moment to herself after everything she'd experienced over the past two days. When she hadn't returned, he'd gone in search of her, and the longer he'd searched without finding her, the more he'd tasted the sharp bile of a rising panic.

She was a child of the desert, after all. She could survive for days alone in a wilderness of sand, but the heart of her world was the close, communal life of the caverns, where ties of kinship and responsibility bound everyone to one another. Nothing in her past would have prepared her for the crowded streets of the city where the mad, impersonal urgency could so easily overwhelm even the hardiest of city dwellers.

He'd been right to worry.

It hadn't been hard to spot her, standing frozen in the middle of the surging crowd like a solitary rock battered by the raging sea around it, her eyes wide with shock and hands knotted so tightly together that the bones stood out in ridges.

He'd felt ashamed then. Ashamed that he'd tried to make her situation so much more unpleasant than it already was, knowing it was really her father and the Elders of the Zeyn who drove her. Ashamed that he hadn't stopped to remember the doubts in her voice last night when she'd said, "you don't *understand.*" He'd understood then. He should have understood now.

The shame hadn't lasted long. Marna's silent denial of her fear and her quickness in retreating behind her cold, proud dignity served as reminders that he couldn't let his sympathy get in the way of what, in the long run, was best for both of them.

So he had retreated, too, hiding behind a fatuous grin and a blond wig and, now, an assumed fascination with the jeweled rings and earrings and brooches laid out in their trays beside him. He'd already picked out more than a dozen gaudy pairs for her with no success, but this simple gold set was different. He'd chosen it because its exquisite beauty matched hers, and because he couldn't resist.

"The gold will go wonderfully with your hair and skin," he said, catching the light with the delicate earring he held beside her face. He knew Marna had to see that brief flash in the mirror he'd forced into her hands, see the way the intricately embossed metal contrasted so perfectly with her black hair and dusky skin.

If she did, she gave no hint of pleasure in the sight. She simply sat, back rigidly straight, head high, and stared into the mirror she held up in front of her as he'd instructed. Tarl could feel the angry tension thrumming in her, her body proof against his touch as she was proof against his silly blandishments.

"You don't like it?" he asked, pouting.

When she didn't respond, he tossed the earring into an untidy heap of costly discards, then poked through the contents of another tray until he found an extravagant pair that appealed to the devil in him. She would absolutely, categorically, unequivocally despise them. "What about these?"

Without waiting for her response, Tarl deftly slipped one of the pair over the curve of her right ear, settling the intricate concoction of curlicued metal and semi-precious stones against the heavy mass of her braided hair. He slipped the second earring over his left ear; then, before she could react, he put his arm around her shoulder to draw her close and pressed his cheek against hers. With his free hand, he shifted the position in which she held the mirror so he could see them both in its polished surface.

The earrings were the most atrociously awful he'd found so far.

"Perfect." Tarl beamed and tilted the mirror to study the effect from a slightly different angle. Her cheek was warm silk against his, and he could smell the lingering fragrance of the herbal soap she'd used that morning.

He'd be a fool to let himself dwell on such distracting sensations, yet he couldn't repress the surge of heat that suddenly raced through his veins. Even her scarcely repressed fury at his outrageous behavior wasn't enough to dampen his reaction.

"Yours would go beautifully with that embroidered over-robe you wore in the Hall," he cooed, "and mine just matches a delightful lavender robe I've got. We'd make a lovely pair, don't you agree?"

Marna jerked away from him, then angrily tore her earring off to fling it back in its tray. "No, I do not! I don't want earrings. I don't want brooches. I don't want any jewelry at all! I've already told you, I do not wear jewelry. It is not the way of the Zeyn."

Tarl sat up straight in his chair and drew his chin into his chest in affronted dignity. The corners of his mouth drooped in a disappointed frown. "I thought you'd like a small gift. Now that we're pledged—"

"We're pledged, no more than that." She was panting from anger and some deeper, more unsettling emotion Tarl couldn't decipher, which had spread a dark rose stain across her cheeks and put fire into her midnight eyes. "I've spent the past half hour waiting while you played with these silly trinkets, but now I've had enough. I wish to return to the palace. Immediately.''

Marna's fingers tightened around the hand mirror she still held, as if it were a hammer and she was prepared to forcefully apply it to the top of his head if he proved difficult. Her breast rose and fell beneath her robe, taunting him with vivid memories of how she'd looked when he'd first found her, clothed in nothing but the night and her beautiful, unbound hair.

Tarl turned to Sesha, seeking support. He'd taken care to charm her right off by pulling up a chair and insisting, over her objections, that she sit down and be comfortable.

His efforts had clearly been wasted. Sesha was studying him with a puzzled, disapproving expression that rivaled Marna's for its lack of encouragement.

The shop attendant, far too wise to get involved, maintained the same polite, noncommittal expression she'd worn since they'd first walked into the shop. No help, then. He was on his own.

''Certainly we'll go back, if you wish,'' he said, and realized, suddenly, that it was his own reluctance to return to that luxurious prison which made him drag his feet now.

He'd played out his farce this afternoon, and if the hostility so visible in Marna's face was any indication, he'd played it well. A few more days of this and she would be gone, no matter the scandal that would follow her withdrawing her pledge to him as companion or the failure of whatever plot had prompted the pledge in the first place.

It was what he wanted, what *had* to be, and yet he found the prospect overwhelmingly depressing.

''We'll go, then. Our driver will be waiting for us around the corner.'' Marna's eyebrows shot up indignantly before he could add, ''You can't see Merchants Row unless you walk, but there's no need to go back that same way.'' Even though he was facing Marna and thus turned away from Sesha, he could hear her soft sigh of relief.

The shop attendant had the street door open before anyone else was out of their chairs. Marna went first, her head bent and eyes firmly fixed on the floor, her movements stiff with the anger that still held her in its grip. Sesha followed, then Tarl. The minute he spotted the skimmer and could be sure Marna and Sesha would be safe, Tarl muttered a quick excuse and turned back to the shop.

The startled attendant glanced up from the disordered trays she was rearranging to give him a small, hopeful smile. Tarl gave her his most engaging grin in return, then swiftly fished out that last, thoroughly outrageous pair of earrings. He started to hand them to her, but stopped when his eye caught the glint of the simple gold earrings he'd chosen not to provoke Marna, but because they suited her.

He hesitated, his hand hovering over the discarded pair. The Zeyn didn't wear jewelry. It was the reason he'd brought her here in the first place, knowing it would annoy her. She wouldn't appreciate so expensive and frivolous a gift. She wouldn't wear them if she had them.

All sensible, rational arguments, but there was nothing rational about the effect she had on him. If they were both forced to play a game that neither wanted, there ought to be some small pleasures in it. He would enjoy giving her the earrings. Whether she wore them or not, he'd at least be able to imagine how they'd look, half hidden in her hair, bright light against her shadowed skin. That alone made them worth the price.

With sudden decision, Tarl retrieved the golden earrings, then handed both pairs to the attendant.

Perhaps he'd give Marna the garish monstrosities, as well. A gift in honor of their pledge. The corner of his mouth twitched and he had to press his lips tightly together to keep from laughing out loud at the thought. Now *that* would be a gift she'd remember!

To Marna's dismay, once they were in the skimmer, Tarl picked up his lecture on the history of Diloran Central exactly where he'd left off earlier. Neither her cold silence nor her lowering frown dissuaded him from recounting whatever trivial item he could remember that he hadn't already mentioned. Marna suspected that a substantial percentage of his anecdotes were manufactured for the occasion, but she was too tired and far too confused to object.

For the first time in her life, she longed for silence and a space all to herself where she could think without fear of interruption by anyone. She longed for her room, the same room that only two days earlier had seemed so impossibly big and cold and empty.

All it had taken was one fleeting touch to tip her into a confusion of memory and physical sensation that still had her reeling. For one mad moment, when Tarl had carelessly brushed aside a loose strand of her hair to hold the golden earring against her cheek, she'd thought the night had come again and a quiet, dangerous man of shadows had returned to claim what he had not taken the night before.

Mad. Truly mad. That's what she had to be to let a simple touch unsettle her to such a degree.

Worse, it wasn't just the memory of a stranger that had so unsettled her. It was her own inability to sort imagination from reality. In that instant when the world had tilted slightly off center, she'd been convinced that Tarl was Toff, that fool and fighter had incomprehensibly become one, and that everything, absolutely everything, would somehow be resolved without the need for . . . for what she'd been sent to do.

And that was absurd.

Wasn't it?

She stared at Tarl and wondered. Was it?

He was still chattering. Abruptly he leaned forward, elbows tucked into his sides, and ducked his head so he could peer out the window at some great, tall building they were passing. He looked like a child, caught in the excitement of the passing scene.

What had she seen in him, sensed in him, that would make her think of the stranger who had twice crept into her room in the dark of night? He had none of the easy grace, none of the lean-muscled power or quiet self-confidence of the man who called himself Toff.

And yet it could be so.

A muscled body was easily disguised under full robes. Short, dark hair disappeared under a wig. Intelligence and a strong character could be hidden behind a fussy manner and an earring. And hadn't she, more than once, caught glimpses of someone else peering out of Tarl Grisaan's dark eyes? At the dinner last night, and again on Merchants Row when he'd parted the crowds to come to her?

She'd never seen that much of her night visitor, really—just a black-garbed form half-hidden in the dark, nothing more. Her body remembered hard muscles, sensitive hands, and a welcoming mouth, but his features were a blur, indistinct and impossible to recall.

She couldn't tell from the voice. One man spoke in whispers and low murmurs, the other with prim precision. One man used his words sparingly, the other chattered incessantly. One—

Marna clasped her hands tightly together, shoved them into her lap, and stared down at them uncertainly. She'd long ago stopped listening to Tarl's monologue. Now she saw only her hands, heard only the questions without answers that went racing around and around in her head.

Was Tarl Grisaan her unknown stranger? Was he the one the Security patrol had accused of being a criminal? Was he the only man she'd ever met who was capable of making her blood burn for the touch of him and her mouth ache for his kisses?

It was a mad idea. Mad.

And she knew why she had thought it.

Because she was beginning to question things she'd never questioned before.

Because she didn't want to believe that she could be pledged as companion to a man like the one who sat across from her now, endlessly droning on.

Because she didn't want to kill Tarl Grisaan.

Chapter Eight

The ride back to the Palace was one of the longest Tarl had ever endured. His brief burst of good humor in the jeweler's had long ago vanished under the strain of sitting directly across from Marna in the cramped skimmer, close enough to touch her if he just stretched out his hand, so close he could feel the tension and uncertainty in her now. His endless stream of chatter was the only protection he had against the concern, sympathy, and downright lust assailing him, and even that was proving less effective than he'd hoped.

Life was unfair. He'd always known it, but right now it seemed a great deal more unfair than usual. If it weren't for the abominable sense of duty and responsibility that had been ground into him as a child, he wouldn't be here right now. If he weren't here, Marna wouldn't be suffering through the shock of facing a culture that was totally foreign to her and forced into a relationship she clearly didn't want. And if Marna weren't here, then he wouldn't be enduring the uncomfortable stirrings in his loins that had made it necessary for him to keep his legs crossed for the past fifteen minutes.

The foolish masquerade that had started out as an entertaining farce, a way of mocking those who wanted him to be someone and something he wasn't, was quickly becoming a galling penance. More than anything else in the world right now, he wanted to stop acting the fool. He wanted to take Marna in his arms and kiss away the strain that was darkening her eyes and keeping her withdrawn and silent. He wanted—

Tarl forced the thought away. He wanted a lot of things, and right now, all of those things were impossibly out of reach. The world was closing in, whether he wanted it to or not. The only effective weapon he had to protect himself and, in an odd way, Marna, too, was this silly charade he was playing. And play it he would, until they were both free to follow their own paths in life rather than the paths that someone else had chosen for them.

Marott Grisaan's equerry met them at the side door, as fussily nervous as he'd been the day before in the Hall of the Public. His sharp little chin stuck out at an aggressive angle as he said, "His Excellency wishes to see you. Both of you," he added primly, nodding at Marna. "If you would be so kind . . ."

He bowed and gestured for them to follow him, making it clear that it didn't matter if they were kind or not. Marott Grisaan wanted to see them, and see them he would.

Ignoring both the equerry's impatience and Marna's protest, Sesha refused to budge until she'd straightened her mistress's robes and elaborately braided coif. The firm set of her mouth made it clear that no one was going to distract her from her responsibilities, regardless of his rank or the urgency of his demands.

Since it wouldn't do his image any good to have his pledged companion pay more attention to her appearance than he did, Tarl took advantage of the momentary distraction to straighten the skirts of his own robe and check his blond curls in the reflective surface of a window. His efforts drew a disapproving frown from Marna.

At least he needn't wonder about the topic his uncle wanted to discuss. Eileak of Zeyn's sly maneuver had overset a number of plans, including his uncle's, and Marott wasn't one to accept anyone's interference with his schemes.

In the past, the formal, public offer of companionship had always been the culmination of a process of negotiation and due deliberation conducted at great length behind the scenes. By simply appearing at the formal audience to offer his daughter as companion, Eileak had neatly and very conveniently sidestepped all that frustrating rigmarole—and put himself in a position of influence he could not have gained any other way, even in his role as Elder of one of the Old Families.

Tarl wished he knew what devious plan lay behind Eileak's offer. He'd already asked Joeffrey if there was any way out of this commitment. The answer had been an unequivocal, and very much unwelcome, no.

A few more weeks. That was all he had to endure before the Tevah was ready to move against his uncle. A few more weeks and he'd be free of Diloran forever. The words were a litany keeping time with the echoing beat of their footsteps in the wide corridors of the Palace.

Tarl couldn't resist the temptation to glance at Marna. The distaste he'd seen in her reflected image was gone, replaced by an expression of polite coolness that was far more unsettling. She was like the constantly shifting waters of a pond, seemingly transparent, yet never the same from one moment to the next. He found it impossible to judge the depths of her, no matter how hard he looked.

Who *was* Marna of Jiandu, Tarl wondered, and what did she think of her present situation? What did she think of him?

He didn't have time to wonder, because they'd arrived in front of the impressive double doors that led from the public waiting area into the antechamber, which in turn led to the Controllor's secretary's office, which led, at last, into the formal office of the Controllor himself, or in this case, the Controllor-Regent. Marott had taken over the office within hours of Tarl's father's death, and Tarl knew his uncle had no intention of giving it up to anyone.

The guards at the outer doors immediately jumped to open them, which raised a flurry of motion among the people who had been waiting outside, probably for hours. Any opening of the portals was apt to be their chance to get in to see the great man himself, and no one was willing to risk losing an opportunity because of being too slow.

In the spirit of ensuring his future as heir—or, more accurately, ensuring that he *had* no future as heir—Tarl beamed fatuously upon all and sundry, including the petitioners hoping for a personal audience, the bureaucrats awaiting an opportunity to talk to the Controllor-Regent, and the various hangers-on who were lounging about in expectation of something interesting happening. He offered the guards a smile of excessive good cheer and condescension, but they were too well-trained to react and kept their eyes glued straight ahead and their expressions suitably stern. Tarl noted a disapproving scowl or two among those in the lobby, however, so his efforts weren't totally wasted.

Not that he had much time for noticing things, for the equerry, clearly relieved at having completed his mission, swept them through the antechamber and the secretary's office and on into the formal office without missing a step. He abandoned them in the middle of a vast, sculpted rug that covered the floor between the office entrance and the equally impressive desk placed in front of the windows on the opposite side of the room.

Tarl scarcely noticed the man's departure or the sound of the massive doors shutting behind him. His attention was fixed on the two men in front of them.

It didn't look promising. Marott Grisaan sat behind the desk watching them with the unblinking intensity of a bird of prey, his lean figure clad in a carefully tailored uniform that emphasized his air of power and deadly self-assurance.

At first glance, Eileak of Zeyn seemed far less threatening in the traditional dull-gold robes of his people that flowed around him like the sands of his desert home, softening and hiding the lines of his body. Yet one glance at his weather-beaten face was enough to dispel the impression of softness forever. Eileak of Zeyn was a man as hard and unyielding as the desert he ruled, and only a fool would risk crossing him.

Two different men from very different backgrounds, but they might have been twins if the somber cast of their features and the humorless glitter in their dark eyes was any guide. Eileak had turned at their entrance, shifting in his chair so that he could see them more easily, but that was the only concession either of them made to Marna's and Tarl's presence.

Tarl couldn't help wondering what the atmosphere between the two men was like before they were interrupted. A trace of cold antipathy still lingered in the air of the sunny room, as unmistakable as the acrid odor of a smoldering fire.

His uncle was enough a politician to feign an amiability he was undoubtedly far from feeling. He rose from his chair and came across the room to greet them.

"Kiria Marna," he said, bowing slightly. "I trust my nephew proved an adequate host for your tour of the city?"

Tarl glanced at Marna, then suddenly discovered an intense interest in the sleeve of his robe. It was amazing how many bits of fluff could collect on his clothes if he wasn't careful.

"Kiri Grisaan was most . . . informative," Marna said stiffly. It was impossible to tell if her stiffness was due to her feelings about the afternoon or her dislike of his uncle, but after a second glance, Tarl decided he wouldn't make the effort to find out.

"Good. Good." Marott clearly opted for noncommittal enthusiasm—an excellent choice, under the circumstances, Tarl thought.

"Come, sit here," Marott added, drawing Marna to a chair placed at one side of the vast desk. "Your father and I have been discussing some of those small points of concern I mentioned this morning, and we wanted to inform you of our decision as soon as possible."

Although he hadn't been included in the invitation, Tarl trailed negligently after them. When his uncle made no effort to offer him a chair, he propped his hip on one end of the desk and busied himself arranging the skirts of his long robe in careful, graceful folds. The desk was an uncomfortable seat, but it provided an excellent vantage point from which to study everyone's reactions—and annoy them all indiscriminately. Judging from the stiff smile on his uncle's lips and the icy scorn in Eileak's eyes, he was off to a good start on the latter.

Marott chose not to say anything, but he made a point of swinging wide around Tarl on his way back to his chair, as if he was afraid that foolishness might be contagious.

Once settled, he glanced from Marna to Tarl and back again, cleared his throat, and said, "The honored Elder of the Zeyn has presented a . . . proposal which I at first resisted. On reflection, however, and taking into consideration the various issues involved, I have decided to accede to Kiri Eileak's wishes."

He hesitated, opened his mouth as if to say more, shut it again, and frowned, ever so slightly. In the end, Marott decided to dump the burden of explanation on his visitor's shoulders. "Perhaps it would be best if you explained the situation, Kiri," he said, turning to the silent Eileak.

The Elder of the Zeyn clearly didn't grant much importance to the niceties of political discussion. His brows came together in a frown that barely escaped being a scowl as he turned his disapproving gaze on Tarl. Without preamble, he said, "The ceremony of binding as companion between you and my daughter will proceed immediately."

Tarl jerked upright, shocked by the blunt pronouncement. At the edge of his vision he was aware of Marna, rigidly erect, staring at her father as if he were some strange being she'd never before encountered. Somewhere along the line someone had forgotten to include her in their plotting.

"I have been called home on affairs of great urgency," Eileak continued, totally unmoved by Marna's reaction to his decree. "Before I go, I wish to ensure that my daughter is properly situated."

Properly situated! Tarl barely kept from choking on his disgust and anger. Eileak of Zeyn might as well have been discussing the arrangement of furniture in a room as his daughter's future. The cold-blooded callousness of the man's attitude turned Tarl's stomach.

"Oh, surely not so *soon,* Kiri!" he protested with a nerve-grating titter. "After the surprise of the pledge, you know, and all the changes, and coming back home just a few weeks ago—why, I've scarcely unpacked, and there's—"

Eileak's head came up and his nostrils flared, as though he'd just caught a whiff of something disagreeable.

"—still so much to do," Tarl continued. "I'm sure Kiria Marna feels exactly the same way I do. After all, she's—"

"The ceremony of binding will be *today,*" Eileak insisted coldly, clearly struggling to keep a hold on his temper.

Tarl pressed harder, hoping against hope that even Eileak, determined as he was, would shrink from binding his daughter to a man who showed all the signs of being an idiot. "But there's still so much that has to be done before the ceremony! Guests to invite, banquets to plan, clothes to be bought. You just haven't *thought* about it, Kiri! Why, I don't see how we could possibly have anything ready before—''

''No banquets! No guests! No clothes!'' Eileak's voice grew louder and harsher with each item that was not to be considered in the ceremony. ''I have no time for such foolishness, and my daughter doesn't need it. You will—''

''No banquets? No new clothes? But think about *me!*'' Tarl pressed his hand to his heart in a theatrical gesture of despair. For a moment, he worried he'd gone too far, but the three before him didn't seem to doubt anything about him except his sanity. ''I've just returned to my home world. You can't possibly *imagine* how many things my uncle and Joeffrey have been insisting I learn. Just remembering the names of everyone gives me a headache! And to be bound as companion so soon . . . It's impossible. Simply impossible!''

From the expression on her face, Marna would back out now if she had any choice in the matter. Apparently she didn't, because instead of renouncing her pledge as companion, she stared at him with an expression that admirably blended disgust and horror. The thought of what she must be suffering, knowing she was to be bound to such an extravagant fool, almost made Tarl drop his assumed role. Almost, but not quite.

Marott Grisaan wasn't in much better shape than Marna. He was rigid with mingled shame and fury. If he could have managed the deed with impunity, Tarl was pretty sure his uncle would have murdered him right then and there.

Eileak, on the other hand, clearly wasn't about to let disgust, contempt, or anything else get in the way of the goal he'd set himself.

''Enough!'' he roared, rising to his feet. ''It is agreed, and that is all that matters. Your complaints are nothing but useless wind. They annoy me, but they will not make me change my mind.''

Tarl sniffed and pouted and hoped none of his own very

real anger or his growing desperation showed through. It was one thing to be pledged to Marna of Jiandu, quite another to be officially bound to her. A ceremony of binding was for life, regardless of the circumstances under which it was contracted.

There *was* a way out, of course—*if* he was willing to risk the inevitable consequences. All he had to do was refuse to agree to Eileak's demands.

Tarl wasn't willing to risk it. If he refused, the affront to Zeyn dignity would be seen as sufficient grounds for formal protests, at the very least. The leaders of the Old Families would be forced to choose sides, whether they wanted to or not. The inevitable disruption of the fragile political situation on Diloran could well lead to war between the various factions.

Was that what Eileak really wanted? Tarl wondered. For him to refuse so the Zeyn could profit from the resulting conflicts?

Tarl squelched the thought even as it occurred to him. The Zeyn wouldn't shy from a fight, but they were too independent to seek any advantage through that kind of political manipulation. There would be no honor in it, regardless of the political or economic gains they might achieve.

So many "couldn'ts." He couldn't refuse. He couldn't change Eileak's mind. He couldn't even demand more time until the ceremony of binding could be organized properly. Once pledged, it was the woman who decreed when the ceremony of binding would take place, and Marna would undoubtedly follow her father's lead, regardless of her own feelings.

Tarl's heart sank into his toes. He didn't want to be bound to Marna of Jiandu or to Diloran and its problems, yet his personal wants seemed pitifully unimportant when weighed against the possible repercussions of his refusing.

The only acceptable course of action was to go along—for now, at least. Eileak had him trapped, but that didn't mean he was trapped forever. Who knew what the future held? If worst came to even worse, once his uncle was out of office he could stage his own death. That approach would cause a few headaches with the Galactic Marines, but it would leave Marna an honorable widow rather than an outraged and insulted representative of the Zeyn.

Tarl opened his mouth to speak, then closed it as Marna, head high and body trembling with the power of the emotions warring within her, rose to her feet. She stared at her father for a long, long minute without speaking, as if the intensity of her feelings would be sufficient to sway him from the decision he'd made and now wanted to force on her.

When Eileak remained silent, she spoke.

"I have come to this place at your bidding," she said, her voice vibrating with restrained passion. "I accepted the tasks you gave me, and I will carry them out to the best of my ability, as is my duty. But I will not be bound to a man I do not know. Not so soon. Not like this. Not until *I* am ready for it. Do you understand, father? *I will not be bound to Tarl Grisaan!*"

The sun had only recently set when her father's servant, Kevar, knocked at Marna's door. "His Excellency requests your presence in his chambers, Kiria," the man said, bowing respectfully.

"Demands it, you mean," Marna replied tartly as she strode past him. Four long hours of being confined to her quarters at her father's command had fed her anger and strengthened her resolve until now Marna was prepared to fight all the Elders of the Zeyn rather than be formally bound to Tarl Grisaan.

Resistance hadn't been nearly so easy in the Controllor-Regent's office. Her first reaction to her father's unexpected demand had been shocked surprise that he would use the same tactics against her that he'd used against Tarl and Marott Grisaan. Her second had been an anguished realization that, like the Grisaans, she would be forced by tradition and honor to accept his deliberately public decree, whether she wanted to or not.

Yet just when she'd been about to give in, she'd heard a voice in her mind—a man's voice, so low it was almost a whisper, vibrating with the urgency of his message. *No one has the right to force you against your will,* the voice had said. *No matter how important the cause.*

With a rush of sensual memory as startlingly real and powerful as anything she'd ever experienced, Marna had felt as if the dark stranger were suddenly there beside her, his body warm and strong and alive against hers, his strength a gift to bolster hers.

No one has the right. . . .

It was his words and the memory of his voice that had given her the courage to refuse her father there in Marott Grisaan's office. It was the memory of *him* that had helped her endure the four long hours of enforced solitude afterward.

Alone in her room, Marna had struggled with a hundred new doubts that her father's actions and the day's experiences had added to her already heaping store of uncertainties. She'd never wanted to leave the desert. Even knowing how her people had suffered under the unjust politics of Tarl Grisaan's father and uncle, she'd never wanted to take up the fight her father sought to force on her.

Yet none of her protests or arguments were strong enough to stand against the claims of duty and the Elders' endless litany that there could be no relief from the Grisaans' persecution of the Zeyn until the Grisaans themselves were eliminated, that the best way to accomplish that objective was to get close enough to destroy them both, and that she, the daughter of Eileak of the Zeyn, was the only one among them who would ever have a chance of getting that close.

It was a source of shame to Marna that she'd ignored the strict Zeyn code of honor by undertaking the task the Elders had asked of her, but once she'd weighed her sacrifice against the greater good of the Zeyn, she'd decided that her people came first, regardless of her own feelings in the matter.

Of one thing Marna was certain, however. She had never, ever agreed to become bound companion to Tarl Grisaan.

Being pledged to him was one thing, since it required no greater emotional or physical intimacy between them than the social activities they'd already endured.

Being bound to him was something else entirely.

Once bound to Tarl Grisaan, she would be unable to refuse his presence *or* his bed, no matter how little she desired either.

Even for her people, she could not—*would* not—accept the soul-deep shame of betraying a man with whom she had made love, no matter how unwillingly she might have done so.

No one has the right. . . .

For four hours she'd paced her room, endlessly repeating the stranger's words until they were engraved in her brain, a talisman against the forces of tradition and accustomed obedience that argued for her surrender. And with each step Marna had taken, it seemed the stranger who had called himself Toff was there beside her, walking with her, back and forth. As the sun had faded and the night drawn in, she'd found herself reaching into the shadows, as if she could touch him, there in the dark.

I understand, he'd said, and Marna had taken comfort from knowing, somehow, that he really had.

That understanding would have to be her support now, for

she had no expectations that the past four hours would have eased her father's determination by even the slightest degree. If anything, he was probably angrier now than he'd been in Marott Grisaan's office earlier.

Head high, her expression as impassive as she could make it, Marna sailed through the door of her father's chamber.

Chapter Nine

Marna's demonstration of resolve was wasted—her father had chosen not to turn on the lights in his chamber. The vast, echoing room's only illumination was a glow-light set in the center of the table at which her father sat.

For an instant, Marna wondered fleetingly if the lights weren't on because Eileak hadn't yet learned how they were controlled and was unwilling to admit his ignorance.

She pushed the thought aside as quickly as it had come, but it left her uncomfortable. Until this afternoon, she'd never dreamed of doubting her father's abilities or his judgment. She didn't want to start adding to her already troublesome burden of doubts now.

The glow-light cast the usually harsh lines of her father's face into even more intimidating planes of light and dark, highlighting the underside of his jaw, the sharp point of his nose, and the line of his brow while leaving the rest in shadow. His eyes, sunk deep in their sockets, glittered as black as night, unblinking in their angry assessment of her and her defiance.

Marna came to a stop in front of the table and bowed, as was required. "Father. I have come as you requested."

He snorted. "Am I to feel honored that you now obey my commands? Or is it just that you wish to flaunt your new-found independence in my face?"

Marna blinked at the bitter anger in his voice. Before her hands could ball into fists, she buried them in the full sleeves of her robe.

When she didn't reply, Eileak snarled, "How dare you defy me like that? Shame my honor in front of strangers? Refuse to accept my guidance?"

Her father ranted on without giving Marna a chance to respond. His reproaches hit her with all the sting of wind-driven sand, making her flinch and duck her head against their fury.

She'd never felt his anger like this, never before tried to defy him, yet she wasn't ready to retreat, either. Four hours of solitude and anguished thought had guaranteed that.

The moment her father paused to gather breath, Marna's own angry words tumbled out unchecked.

"How dare you try to force me into something I never agreed to?" she demanded. "How dare you shame *my* honor? Isn't it enough that you want to turn me into a spy and assassin, without insisting I become bound companion to the very man you would have me destroy? Is *this* the way of the Zeyn? Is *this* the way you honor *me?*"

Her father sat on the other side of the table, unmoving and unmoved by her vehemence.

"I cannot explain my reasons to you," Eileak said at last, harshly. "I *will* not explain them to you. I am Elder of the Zeyn, as well as your father. I expect you to obey me as would any of our people."

"And I am an adult, with all the rights of an adult," Marna shot back just as harshly. "Have you forgotten that?

You cannot force me into anything, for any reason."

"Think of our people—"

"I *am* thinking of our people! I am thinking of the shame I would bring on them if I were to accept the life commitment of bound companion, only to betray it by carrying out your commands. I am thinking of the traditions that villify the dishonorable deeds you ask of me. I—"

Marna caught herself up short before her anger carried her away with it. Hidden in the fullness of her sleeves, her fingers dug hard into the muscles of her forearms. "There are—*must* be—other ways for us to fight free of the Grisaans' control without stooping so low," she added at last, more calmly but no less passionately.

Her father shook his head, as unyielding as hard rock in a storm. "I have said you do not understand. There are things—decisions—I cannot share with you. Secrets I cannot reveal. I should not have to," he added, more sharply than before. "Your duty to me and to our people should be enough."

He was right, Marna thought. It *should* be enough. She was of the Zeyn, and she was his daughter, and that should be more than enough.

It *had* been this morning. Now, it no longer was. Too much had happened in the hours that bridged the then and the now for it ever to be enough again.

"Father," she said, desperately fighting for calm and the words to explain her troubling doubts, "this afternoon, in the city, I visited Merchants Row. I saw the buildings there—so many different buildings, but not one that was ours. We don't even—"

"The Zeyn have no need for such things!"

"We are the only ones not represented there! The only ones of all the people on Diloran!"

Her father didn't deign to reply.

Marna plunged ahead anyway, anxious to explain the vague ideas that had taken root in her mind during the afternoon and that had grown in those long hours alone in her room.

"If we had been more a part of Diloran affairs, perhaps we would never have arrived at . . . at *this.*" In her agitation, Marna tugged her hands out of her sleeves and waved them in front of her as if she could grab the word she wanted out of thin air. "It all seemed so simple, back in the caverns, but it doesn't seem—"

"Enough!" Eileak thumped the table with his fist for emphasis and rose to his feet. For a moment, he glared at Marna as if he had never seen her before and did not like what he saw now. "If your disobedience and the shame it casts on my honor are of no importance to you, then so be it. I cannot force you into the ceremony of bonding, and I will not try."

He paused for the space of a heartbeat, just long enough for Marna's stomach to twist inside her as if she were suddenly dangling above an abyss, before adding, "But I will not let you retreat from the task you have been given. You are sworn to it, before me and the other Elders. You cannot refuse if you have any hope of ever returning home. Do you understand?"

Marna stared at him in shock. Her own father, threatening to cast her out of the caverns if she didn't do what he demanded of her? She opened her mouth, but her father gave her no chance to protest.

"Do you understand?"

By his rigid stance and the proud, angry set of his head, Marna knew that her father would not yield, no matter how many new arguments she presented, or how many alternatives she proposed. He loved her, but his greatest allegiance and his deepest love had always been reserved for the people he led. He would not countenance anything or anyone that stood in the way of what he perceived as being for the good of the Zeyn, not even his only daughter.

For a moment, the resolve Marna had nurtured so carefully

in the silence of her room faltered. It was one thing to risk her father's anger and her own honor, quite another to risk being cast out by her people, barred from the desert and the caverns that were her home and thrust into a world where she did not belong. All the doubts and worries she'd struggled against once more rose up to plague her, but this time they came girded with the potent threat of exile to strengthen them—and weaken her.

She might have yielded, then, if it weren't for the words she'd repeated over and over in the silence of her room: *No one has the right. . . .*

Suddenly, Marna could feel the dark stranger's hands upon her shoulders, feel his warmth and strength and the passionate belief that was in him. It was all the support she needed, all the support she would have, for her father would never understand, no matter how vehemently she argued her position.

"I understand, Father," she said at last, with difficulty. It was neither a commitment to what she'd begun, nor an admission of defeat. It was an acknowledgment that, yes, she understood the price she would pay if she did not carry through on her vow to destroy Tarl and Marott Grisaan.

And who knew? Perhaps she would never have to act. She'd been told to expect days, possibly weeks, of delay before she received the final order. Anything was possible in that time.

Drawing on what scraps of dignity she still possessed, she bowed slightly, as courtesy required when leaving a senior person's presence. "With your permission, Father?"

Eileak nodded curtly, dismissing her.

Marna was at the door when he spoke her name. Willing herself not to reveal her weakness, she turned to find him watching her.

It might have been the dim light, or her imagination, but she could have sworn she saw uncertainty and worry in his face. He started to move around the table toward her, his hand slightly raised as though he were going to extend it to her, but he stopped in mid-stride. For an instant, his fingers trembled, ever so slightly; then he curled them tight into his palm and let his hand fall back at his side.

"I will return to the desert tomorrow," he said after a moment's hesitation.

"So soon?" Marna couldn't prevent her dismay from showing in her voice. She hadn't expected him to leave. Not yet, anyway. She didn't *want* him to leave when there were still so many questions and so much anger between them.

"There are matters that must be attended to immediately. I hadn't planned . . ." His voice died away, as though he wasn't sure he could trust himself to say more.

When Marna didn't respond, Eileak cleared his throat uncomfortably, then added, more gently this time, "You will be all right, here with Sesha?"

Marna nodded. She didn't trust her own voice to speak.

"Good." Eileak nodded, too, as if to himself. "That's good. I know . . ." Once more he hesitated. "I know I can depend on you, Marna. After all, you are of the Zeyn . . . and you are my daughter."

Marna tried to swallow, and failed. Her fingers curled around a fold of her robe, so tightly that she could feel the bite of her nails, even through the heavy fabric. She wanted to go to him, wanted to have him wrap his arms around her and comfort her, just as he had when she was a small child, but she didn't move from her place by the door. Her father rarely let down his guard enough to reveal his emotions, and he never left it down long enough to let anyone, even her, slip through.

He didn't this time, either.

An instant later, whatever hint of emotion she'd detected was gone as if it had never been. He was once more the stern, unyielding leader of his people as he added, "There is nothing more. Make sure the door is firmly shut behind you and tell Kevar, who should be waiting outside, that I do not wish to be disturbed until I call for him. Do you understand?''

A slight inclination of her head was all the response Marna was capable of giving. It was all the acknowledgment Eileak wanted. He had turned away from her before she was even out the door.

Marna relayed her father's message to the silent man waiting in the hallway, then quickly turned away, before her voice broke and she gave in to the pain inside her.

She had almost reached her own chambers when the hot tears began to burn her eyes. Heedless of their sting, she fumbled with the lock on her door and, once inside, fumbled again in trying to close it. The dark washed over her like a welcome benediction as she slumped against the solid door and let the tears flow, too shaken to move.

''Are you all right?''

At first, Marna thought she'd imagined that soft voice from the shadows. She straightened and angrily dashed the tears from her cheeks with the backs of her hands. There was no one here. The room was locked, the windows shut, just as they had been when she left.

''Marna, are you all right?''

A lean, broad-shouldered shadow detached itself from the darkness surrounding her bed and came toward her, shocking her out of the emotional daze that had held her.

''How did you get in here?'' she demanded, pressing back against the door behind her. ''I locked the windows before I left.''

''You shut them.'' She could hear the smile in his voice. ''You aren't any better at window locks than you were with door locks that first time I dropped in.''

He was a dark, vital, almost invisible presence, so close she could feel the heat of his body and hear the scarcely perceptible rustle of his clothing as he moved. He leaned around her to test the lock. She could feel his arm brush against the sleeve of her robe. A faint scent of musk and man clung to him, teasing her senses.

"You're getting better," he said softly, leaning closer still. His breath was warm against her cheek. "It seems you've mastered the art of locking doors, at any rate."

She couldn't see his face. He was nothing but a black mass against the dark, yet Marna could have sworn he smiled. Of all the things she didn't want, she did not want him here, and she most certainly did not want to have to deal with his teasing humor.

Before she could slide away from him, he bent to brush a kiss across her lips. His mouth was warm and hard against hers, tempting, even now. Marna turned her head and shoved against his chest, trying to push him back.

Too late. His lips grazed her cheek, just where her tears had traced their way from eyelid to chin. He stiffened, but instead of leaving her, he delicately flicked his tongue across her skin, tasting the salty wetness.

Marna froze, torn between shame that he had discovered her tears and a sudden, aching desire to have him hold her and kiss away her fears. Beneath her hands, his chest felt solid and warm and oddly reassuring. It would be so easy, so very, very easy, for him to take her in his arms and comfort her, if only he would. If only she could find the courage to ask him.

Instead, she shoved harder, and this time she succeeded in pushing him away from her. She kept her back to the door and her hands up, ready to fend him off should he move closer.

"Why are you here?" she demanded. "Didn't your visit last night give you enough opportunity to meddle in my life?"

Even in the dark she could see him flinch, as though she'd struck him.

"Is that what you thought I was doing?"

"Weren't you?"

Suddenly, Marna wanted to lash out and hit something. To hit *him*.

His words and the memory of his presence had carried her through the past few hours, but they hadn't been enough to protect her against the fearsome threat of being barred from her home and her people forever. To find him waiting for her in the dark like this was a mockery as cruel and hurtful as any she had ever known.

Instead of hitting him, Marna shoved past him and strode across the room to the dim gray rectangles where the faint light from the garden shown through the windows. In her anger and confusion, her tears had started to fall again, but this time she let them course unchecked down her face.

With clumsy haste, she fumbled with the latches on a window, just as she had with the lock on the door. Her fingers were awkward and unresponsive to her demands, she was all but blind from her welling tears and the dark, but still she tried to work the locks free and throw open the window. She wanted him and his words out of her room and out of her life, wanted them gone with a desperate, clamoring urgency that allowed no room for thought or patience or rationality.

"Marna. Marna!" He was behind her now, his arms around her, his hands on hers as he tried to stop her mad, scrambling efforts. "Stop it, do you hear me? Stop it!"

With a gasp that was half sob, Marna knocked his arm away, then turned back to the latch. Too late. He wasn't blinded by tears or shaken by emotions he couldn't control. In one easy motion he wrapped his arms around her, pinning her arms to her sides as he drew her back against his chest and away from the window.

She wanted to fight him, wanted to break loose from his grip and fling herself at the window, but he was too strong, far stronger than his lean frame had led her to expect. And in that strength was a comfort almost great enough to challenge the pain inside her.

With a small, choked cry, she gave up and slumped back against him. She curled her hands over his forearms where they crossed her breast, suddenly grateful for his warmth and his strength and the simple fact that he was here with her, now, when she needed someone to cling to.

His hold on her relaxed, ever so slightly, but he made no move to let her go. Instead, he bent his head until his cheek pressed against her braids and his lips grazed the top of her ear. "Whatever it is," he murmured soothingly, "it will be all right."

Marna shook her head. "No it won't," she whispered, half choking on the words. "It won't ever be right again."

Her world and everything in it had tilted out of its orbit and it couldn't be put right, no matter how much she wanted it to. It wasn't his fault. It wasn't hers. It wasn't her father's, or the Elders', or anyone else's. It simply *was,* and she would have to learn to live with that, no matter how little she liked it.

Marna breathed deeply, forcing the air into her lungs and heart and blood. She could feel her chest expand, feel the way his arms shifted, ever so slightly, with the movement. Before he could pull away, she tightened her grip on him, wanting him not to let go. Not wanting to let him go. Not yet.

His broad shoulders sheltered hers; his body served as a protective wall at her back, solid and secure, curved to match the curve of hers, its outlines blurred but not softened by the heavy folds of her robe. The black cloth of his shirt was cool under her fingers, but still she could feel his heat and the lean, corded muscles beneath his skin.

A tear dropped from her chin to splash on her hand. The second fell on his sleeve. Marna sniffed and slid her hand across the wet spot, trying to rub it out without letting go. She shouldn't have wasted her effort.

"It's all right." His breath was warm against the curve of her ear, tantalizing. "It's all right to cry, too."

Marna blinked back the threatening tears and dropped her head, embarrassed by her body's instant response to that soft brush of air.

Two days ago—yesterday, even—she'd pointed a disruptor at the man she now clung to. Two days ago she would have shot him without hesitation. Now, she cried and was grateful for his warmth and his comforting touch.

"Why are you here?" she asked at last, her voice barely above a whisper, her eyes still stinging and wet with unshed tears.

"Why not?"

Marna stiffened at the teasing note in his words and voice, but he immediately drew her tighter against him.

"I'm sorry. I didn't mean . . . I shouldn't have said that."

"Do you always laugh at things? Make a joke of them?"

This time it was his turn to hesitate. Marna could feel his chest expand as he took a deep breath of his own.

"Laughing is so much easier, don't you think?" he said at last. He barely spoke above a whisper, yet there was an unexpected note of strain in his voice, as though it had cost him an effort to speak lightly.

"Easier than what?"

His arms tightened around her. He was holding her so close against him that Marna could scarcely breath.

"Easier than taking it all seriously. Life. This place. Duty." He cut his words off sharply, as though he found saying them somehow distasteful. "That's what you're doing, isn't it? Taking it seriously?"

What could she say to that? With sudden resolution, Marna twisted around in his arms, pressing her hands against his chest and arching away from him in the hope of getting a glimpse, at least, of his features. The light from the garden wasn't much, but it ought to be enough . . .

He must have read her mind, for though he eased his hold on her, he kept his hands on her shoulders. Just when she might have spied the shadowed outlines of his face, he turned and drew her around with him so it was she who was revealed instead.

For a moment, he said nothing; then his grip on her shoulders tightened and he said, very low and soft, "Is it so very bad, then?"

Marna stiffened, shaken once more by his gentleness. "What concern is it of yours?"

"None, I suppose."

"And how can you say such things, anyway? Aren't you of the Tevah? How can you belong and not care?"

It was his turn to stiffen. "What makes you think I'm with the Tevah?"

"The guards that first night. They said the man they were chasing belonged to the Tevah. And who else would be dressed in black and hiding in the dark? Especially here, inside the palace walls?"

When he still didn't speak, she asked, very softly, "Or aren't you sure?"

"Sure of what?"

"Of whether you belong."

Marna had intended her question to be slightly mocking, but he evidently didn't take it that way. Something in her words had struck a chord in him, dredged up a memory, perhaps, that now held him in its grasp.

Though she couldn't see his features, Marna sensed he was looking over her head, staring at something only he could see hidden in the shadows behind her. Slowly, as if unaware of what he did, he slid his hands down her arms, then up again, then down once more in a sensuous sweep that stirred a tingling heat along her skin and in her veins.

It didn't mean anything, Marna assured herself, trying to suppress her involuntary response to his touch. He just needed the human contact as much as she had a few minutes earlier.

When the silence stretched unbearably, she gently touched his cheek. His skin was warm, slightly roughened by the first, faint stubble of beard.

"Toff?" The name felt awkward on her tongue, absurdly childish, but she knew no other.

He stirred at that, as though her voice and the touch of her hand had brought him back from somewhere far away. With a soft sigh, he let out the breath he'd been holding, then turned his head to brush a soft kiss on her fingertips.

"Do you know," he said in a voice grown suddenly rough and uncertain, "I'm not really sure."

"Of what?"

"Of whether or not I really belong to the Tevah. If I belong here, in the palace. Or on Diloran. I'm not sure—" He cut his words off abruptly, as though he were afraid of saying them aloud. After a moment's hesitation, he said, very low, "I'm not sure I belong . . . anywhere."

Marna frowned. "Everyone belongs *somewhere.*"

"Do they?"

When she didn't answer, his grip on her arm tightened and his head came down, as if he were studying her face in the faint light, seeking some answer he thought she possessed. "Do they?" he demanded.

"How can they exist if they don't?" The question wasn't for him, it was for her. How would she survive if she were exiled from her beloved desert, her people, the caverns that had been her life and her refuge—her *world*—since the day she was born?

No! She would *not* think of failure. She didn't dare.

She would *not* listen to anything he might say. His words had led her to this in the first place.

With a fierceness that surprised her and startled him, Marna tore herself from his arms and backed away.

He made no move to follow her, just stood, a midnight shadow against the window.

When she didn't speak, he said softly, "Marna?"

Nothing more. Just her name, and in that name a world of questions she could never answer, a world of promises neither of them could ever keep.

"Go," she said. "Go and never come back."

There were, suddenly, other words she wanted to say. Words she wanted to shout, because shouting would make it so much easier, so much more real. *Don't tempt me. Don't torment me. Don't touch me. Don't . . .*

Tears welled in her eyes.

Don't leave me.

Shock exploded through her. Then disbelief. Then anger. The tears burned away in its heat.

What was she thinking? She was no weakling. She was of the Zeyn! Her father had shaken her with his sudden demands, threatened her with exile, but none of it mattered because she would accomplish the task she was sworn to. She had to, for her sake. For the sake of her people.

He hesitated, as if he sensed, even if he could not hear, the unspoken words that trembled in the dark between them. "Marna, I—"

"Did you hear me? You don't belong here. I should have turned you over to the Internal Security guards that first night."

He moved a step closer, then stopped. "You could have, but you didn't."

"I won't make the same mistake twice."

He didn't respond to that. He didn't move, either. He just stood watching her in the dim light that traced her features for him, but left his buried in shadow.

The silence stretched, and in that silence Marna could hear the ghostly echoes of the words that had given her the courage to stand against her father's demands. *No one has the right. . . .*

He'd been right, but that wasn't why she'd clung to the memory of him throughout the four long hours of isolation and doubt that she'd endured earlier.

That first night, when he'd kissed her and set her on fire with wanting him, she'd told him the truth, that she didn't know whether to hate him more for kissing her . . . or for stopping once he'd started. She wanted him to know the truth now, as well.

"You *have* to go," she said, fighting to keep her voice steady. "I don't want you to go, but what I want doesn't matter. The only thing that matters is that my people need me and you . . ." She stopped, swallowing hard to ease the constriction in her throat. "You make me forget why I'm here. So I ask you, please, just go."

He took so long to answer, Marna thought he wasn't going to respond at all. "We're alike, Marna, you and I. You know that, don't you?"

"It doesn't matter. I am pledged to Tarl Grisaan and you . . ."

"And I?"

"And you make me forget that fact."

Her words shook him in a way that sheer physical violence couldn't have. He drew his breath in with a startled hiss and staggered back, just as though she'd hit him.

Marna smiled, a grim, hard, sad little smile. "Do you understand now? I want you to go and I don't ever want you to come back. For my sake. Because I . . ."

"Yes?"

"Because I can't bear it."

He nodded, then. She could see the dark shadow that was his head go up and down, once, twice, three times, and with each nod he seemed to shrink a little, as if he'd lost some small part of himself with her words.

"All right," he said at last.

"You promise never to come back?"

"Yes." Reluctantly.

He lifted his arm as if he wanted to touch her, but let it fall again at his side. Without a word, he turned back to the window she'd clawed open.

Before he could take another step, Marna grabbed the back of his shirt, just as she had that first night, and pulled him back to her. Before he could even gasp, she was in his arms and pulling his head down to meet hers.

The world stopped. Time stopped. The moon stood still in the sky and the breeze froze in the open window.

The only thing left in all creation was the heat and hunger of his mouth on hers, the strength of his lean body and the aching fire of hers.

And then the kiss ended and he pulled back—or maybe she pulled away from him, Marna couldn't be sure. It didn't matter anyway. The cool night breeze once more flowed between them, dividing them with its soft caress. Time moved on, and with it all the rest of the world of which they were a part, whether he believed it or not.

He sighed, very soft and low—or maybe she did. That didn't matter, either. She didn't look when he slipped away, and she didn't bother to close the window behind him.

He was gone and she had his promise that he wouldn't return.

She was once more all alone in a vast, strange, echoing room where she did not belong and never would. But this time she didn't cry. She simply stood with her head high, arms wrapped tightly around her, and stared into the darkness around her, fighting not to remember.

Chapter Ten

The afternoon meeting with the representatives of the Sea Rangers Union broke up early, much to Tarl's relief. He suspected that his continual fidgeting with his wig during the Union representative's presentation might have had something to do with the meeting's premature end, but he didn't want to claim all the credit. Marott Grisaan's constant scowl had been a great deal more daunting to everyone concerned, and far more difficult to ignore.

Tarl remained discreetly to the side as the Union delegates and his uncle, closely followed by the advisors, analysts, and other hangers-on who had packed the room, marched off to more meetings—or other, less honorable diversions. He was delighted to note that there was an unmistakable wary tension in his uncle's movements that hadn't been there a month ago.

At Tarl's insistence and, in several cases, under his direction, the Tevah during the past three weeks had staged a variety of attacks against vulnerable economic, political, and military points within Marott Grisaan's empire. Every one of those attacks had proven far more effective than anyone had dreamed possible. It was quickly becoming apparent that there were far more fissures and fractures in Marott's political edifice than anyone had realized, and the far-flung members of the Tevah's network were extraordinarily adept at taking advantage of every one of them.

To Tarl's immense frustration, however, a majority of the Tevah leaders had decided their success was directly attributable to his leadership, with the result that they'd not only refused to permit him to be directly involved in any further activities that involved a risk of injury, but they'd also declared their support for him as the lawful Controllor of Diloran.

In a sense, their reactions were nothing more than history repeating itself. Every member of the Tevah leadership represented a different political or economic faction of the wider Diloran society. Three hundred years earlier, the leaders of those same factions had yielded control of the Diloran central government to Tarl's ancestor, Yerlaf Grisaan, on the premise that it was preferable to accept one ruler who was beholden to no one than to deal with the complicated and often conflicting rights and demands of the Old Families, the independent states, and every other group with enough power to influence Diloran affairs.

By insisting that Tarl was the rightful Controllor now, the members of the Tevah had opted for the same path of least resistance their ancestors had chosen. By living up to his pledge of helping the Tevah oust his uncle from power, Tarl had made his eventual escape from the bonds of his inheritance even more difficult.

The idea of staging his death, which had originally occurred to him as a way out of his pledge to Marna, was rapidly gaining appeal as a neat, effective, all-around-wonderful problem-solving technique for things like insistent former tutors and determined rebel leaders, as well. Tarl was beginning to fear that dying was the only way he was going to have a life of his own.

The reception area emptied rapidly, leaving Tarl in sole possession of the echoing space. Restless, he crossed to the vast wall of windows at the far side of the area and glared out at the exquisitely tended gardens and the throng of people on the walks, trying to decide what to do next.

Maybe he shouldn't have been quite so obnoxious earlier. At least in the meeting he could amuse himself by seeing just how outrageous he could be without attracting public censure from his uncle. Now he didn't even have that diversion, which left him with nothing else he had to do and nowhere else he had to be for the next couple of hours.

He didn't like inactivity. Never had. But worse than threatening him with boredom, his present lack of occupation left him too much time to dwell on a subject that had occupied his thoughts far more than he liked lately—namely, Marna of Jiandu.

As though he'd conjured her just by the power of his thoughts, Tarl suddenly spotted Marna making her way along one of the crowded garden paths. In spite of the uncountable number of vows he'd made to ignore her existence, he eagerly bent forward and pressed his hands against the window, trying to get a better view. He could see her dark hair bound up in its usual intricate arrangement of braids, her long robe, her . . .

Tarl grunted and angrily pushed away from the window. It wasn't Marna after all. Even though the woman was still too far away for him to distinguish her features, he could tell she lacked Marna's grace and proud dignity. Nothing about her hinted at the hidden fires that made Marna such a dangerous temptation. In fact, if he thought about it, he could probably spot ten dozen differences, not one of which would succeed in making him stop thinking of Marna.

Angry with himself, Tarl crossed his arms over his chest,

leaned back against a supporting column, and scowled at the blank wall opposite.

Three weeks. A few days more than that, actually, since Marna had walked into his life—or he'd fallen into hers, he wasn't sure which. Twenty-some days, and with each one his fascination with the daughter of Eileak of Zeyn grew greater—and even more impossible to acknowledge.

He was either crazy to let her unsettle him as easily as she had, or she was related to the mythical Ramorian Spellcasters who had the power to entrap men with their spells.

Crazy or bewitched. It all depended on how you looked at it, Tarl supposed.

If he'd had his way, he wouldn't be looking at it at all. He'd be back where Joeffrey had found him on Regulus, that freezing ball of ice and killing winds that the Galactic Marines called a strategic outpost. He'd be fighting the Fashil and trying to keep from dying of hypothermia and having a hell of a lot better time than he was having here amidst the beauty and the luxurious comforts of Diloran Central.

Unfortunately, he wasn't getting his way with much of anything.

Not with the Tevah, not with Joeffrey, and certainly not with Marna. She treated him with cool courtesy and kept him at a distance—not so great a distance as to start tongues wagging, but more than enough to frustrate him—completely unaware, so far as Tarl could tell, of the effect she was having on him.

And she was definitely having an effect. A disconcerting, temperature-raising, insomnia-generating effect that Tarl had not the slightest idea how to counter.

It might not have been so bad if he could have amused himself and relieved the tension between them by slipping into her quarters at night and stealing a few more of those rich, sweet kisses he'd already claimed. But he'd given his word that he wouldn't disturb her again, and little as he liked it, he'd stand by it, regardless of his personal suffering.

Joeffrey Baland's servant interrupted Tarl's silent grumblings. "Kiri Baland wishes to speak with you," the man said, bowing politely. "As soon as it may be convenient for you."

Tarl shoved away from the column he'd been using for support, grateful for the interruption. "You mean he wants me there five minutes ago."

The corner of the man's mouth twitched, ever so slightly. It was the only admission he could properly make, but Tarl knew the signs well enough. Joeffrey Baland would never be so patient as to wait on Tarl's convenience—or anyone else's.

Tarl used both hands to settle his wig firmly on his head. The gesture was as close as he could come right now to girding his loins. "Very well. Where is he?"

"At the Belcor fountain, Kiri, taking his afternoon cup of kava there, as he often does. He said to tell you that he would order extra kava and a cup for you."

Tarl couldn't help snorting in amusement. It wouldn't occur to Joeffrey to wonder if Tarl would come. His old tutor had too many years of experience in ordering people around to waste time worrying about his former pupil refusing a summons now.

As promised, Joeffrey was seated in his motorized cart at the farthest of the many carved stone tables placed near the fountain. Also as promised, there was a large pot and two cups on the table. One of the cups was already filled with the dark, flavorful kava that Joeffrey preferred.

"Took you long enough," he muttered when Tarl dropped into the chair across from him. It wasn't easy to make out his words over the roar and splash of the fountain, which was one of the reasons the old man had long ago established the custom of taking his afternoon refreshment here.

Tarl grinned. "I didn't want to muss my hair by running."

Joeffrey managed to restrain his comment to an expressive, "Hmmph!" Without asking, he lifted the pot and poured some of the dark, steaming kava into the second cup. "Drink this. It might put some sense into your head."

Tarl's grin widened, but disappeared in a grimace after his first sip of the bitter brew. "Phew! Are you sure you should be drinking it this strong?"

"It's good for you. Gets your brain cells working."

"Kills them off, you mean." Tarl put down his cup and met his old tutor's assessing gaze with a direct one of his own. "But you didn't bring me out here to discuss the health benefits of kava, did you?"

Joeffrey took a sip from his own cup, then set the cup down and curled his gnarled hands about the kava-warmed porcelain. Instead of answering Tarl's question, he asked one of his own. "Has your pledged companion ever said anything that would give you a hint of why she's here?"

"Marna?" Tarl couldn't hide the surprise in his voice. This wasn't what he'd expected at all. "You know she hasn't. I would have told you if she had."

Joeffrey nodded slightly, as if satisfied to find his own opinion confirmed. "And she's done nothing to . . . concern you?"

"Concern me? You mean, do I think she's going to kill me or Marott? You know I don't. She wouldn't." She'd tempted him, puzzled him, nearly driven him mad with wanting her, but that wasn't the same thing at all.

"Why not?"

Why not? A dozen easy answers rose to Tarl's lips, but he bit them back as a vision of Marna, stark naked and unwaveringly pointing a disruptor at his belly, formed in his mind. He'd had no doubt then that she was prepared to use the disruptor if she had to. He had no doubt she would use it in the future, if she considered it necessary. But somehow he didn't believe she would ever harm him, even if she had the chance.

''She could kill me if she had to,'' Tarl admitted at last. ''But just because someone's capable of killing doesn't mean they're killers. Marna isn't a killer. I'm sure of it. She doesn't have what it takes to be an assassin.''

''Some of the most effective assassins aren't cold-blooded killers, Tarl,'' Joeffrey countered. ''All it takes are loyalty and extreme dedication to a cause.''

''Like her loyalty to her people, you mean.''

''Exactly.''

''That's not good enough. Not for Marna, anyway. I'm sure of it.''

Joeffrey leaned across the table toward Tarl. His dark eyes, glittering under their heavy lids, were the only things that seemed alive in his ugly, wrinkled face. ''How can you be sure, Tarl? She has no cause to love a Grisaan. Any Grisaan. You've seen the reports. The Zeyn have suffered severely under your father's and your uncle's administrations. It doesn't matter that you can't be held responsible for their bad government. It doesn't mean anything that Marna refused to agree to her father's demand for the ceremony of bonding. Being pledged as Companion to you provides her more than enough opportunity to spy on you *and* your uncle—or kill you, if that's what she wants. So, *what makes you so sure she doesn't intend to kill you?*''

Tarl slammed his fist on the table hard enough to shake the pot of kava and the two cups. ''I will not listen to this. If you know of something against her, then tell me, but I won't sit here and let you slander her, do you understand?''

To Tarl's amazement, Joeffrey smiled, the innocent smile of a sweet, harmless old man. The breeze stirred by the fountain's crash and tumble of water lifted the sparse hair ringing his bald pate, reinforcing the false image.

''Well?'' Tarl demanded when Joeffrey remained silent. ''*Do* you know anything against her?''

Joeffrey shook his head. ''Not a thing.'' Before Tarl's anger could explode, he added mildly, ''Tell me why *you* are so sure you can trust her.''

Tarl dropped his gaze to the dark kava in the cup he held, struggling to get hold of his temper. How could he explain to Joeffrey what he couldn't easily explain to himself?

''Marna would give her life if it would save her people from harm,'' he said at last, picking his words carefully, ''but I don't believe she would ever stoop to assassination. She *couldn't.* She just isn't capable of it.''

He looked up to find Joeffrey watching him, listening to every word he spoke with the shuttered, unsettling intensity of a judge . . . or an executioner. Tarl's hands tightened around the cup he held, but he kept his voice level as he added, ''If you'd spent as much time with Marna as I have over the past three weeks, Joeffrey, you'd know what I'm talking about. She doesn't want to be here any more than I do. She's been abandoned by her father and pledged as companion to me, a man she thinks is an utter fool.''

Suddenly, the words came easily, hot and swift with the passion of his conviction. ''Everything here is entirely alien to her, yet she's made an incredible effort to adjust. She's curious, intelligent, and amazingly open-minded and fair. She's made *me* look at things in a different light, made me realize how much good there is in our society, as well as see more clearly what needs changing. She's showed me something of what it means to belong, really *belong* somewhere. She—''

Joeffrey held up his right hand. ''Enough! I believe you.''

Tarl stopped, then realized, to his amazement, that the old man was actually smiling again, but this time it was a real smile that lit Joeffrey's face with its glow. ''If you believe me, why—?''

''I wanted to know how you felt about her. You wouldn't

have told me half as much if I'd asked the question directly."

"What do you mean?" Tarl demanded hotly.

"I mean that I think Marna of Jiandu will make an excellent bound companion for you."

"Now just a minute—"

Joeffrey didn't give him a chance to finish. "We believe we've discovered Eileak of Zeyn's reasons for pledging his daughter to you, and why he wanted to force the ceremony of bonding."

"Why didn't you say so?" After all these years, Tarl thought angrily, he should have been used to Joeffrey's devious ways of approaching a subject, but this time his friend had gone too far.

"I didn't want to influence your judgment."

Tarl snorted. "Thanks for the compliment."

At least Joeffrey had the good grace to look abashed at that. "It wasn't a reflection on you. It's just . . ." He paused, obviously considering how to say what he wanted to say. "It's just that, for your safety, I had to be *sure*."

For an instant something glowed in the old man's eyes that Tarl had never seen before. If he'd seen it in anyone's eyes except Joeffrey's, he would have said it was fear. Whatever the emotion, it was gone as quickly as it had come.

"What's important," Joeffrey continued, "is that neither of us believes she will act against you. That supports the information we received that Eileak has formed a secret alliance with two of the Old Families, the Sherl and the Burnarii. They've been traditional enemies of the Zeyn, and their lands border the Diloran desert. So far as we can discover, they hope to use their combined influence to exact some favors from the central government."

"Meaning my uncle."

"Exactly."

Tarl frowned. "That doesn't explain Marna's being pledged to me."

Joeffrey frowned in return, clearly irritated at his pupil's slowness. "Of course it does. Once you, the legitimate heir to the controllorship, returned to Diloran, Eileak saw an opportunity to gain some additional advantages for the Zeyn. With you as controllor and Marna as your bound companion, Eileak would have some pretty strong leverage in the government. Instead of being the least influential partner in this little threesome they've formed, he'd be by far the strongest."

When Tarl didn't say anything, Joeffrey added, "The arrangement's to our advantage, as well. Once Marott is out of office, you'll have greater influence on the Zeyn than any other controllor ever has. It will be a perfect opportunity to end the quarreling that has plagued that region for years."

Tarl grimaced just as he had when he'd taken that first sip of Joeffrey's bitter kava. "What's Eileak going to do when I don't claim either the controllorship or his daughter?"

To Tarl's consternation, Joeffrey burst out laughing.

"Oh, I don't think we'll have to worry about that," the old man said at last with a grin. "I saw the look in your eyes when you talked about Marna. She's caught you, whether she intended to or not. And her influence might be just the thing to make you see that you can't leave Diloran."

"That's ridiculous!"

"Is it?" Joeffrey had stopped smiling, but there was no mistaking the look of satisfaction on his face. "Ever since you came back, you've talked about Diloran as if it were nothing more than a place you were visiting. 'Your government,' you said. 'Your problems, your decisions.' Well, Marna is obviously changing all that."

"What are you talking about?" Tarl demanded, fighting against an unpleasant sense of impending doom.

"When you were talking about Marna, you said '*our*' society, Tarl. For the first time you're talking as if you really belong here. And thanks to Marna of Jiandu, I'm beginning to believe you do."

Three weeks. A little longer than that, actually, Marna silently corrected herself. Three weeks and a few days. A long time to remain suspended between two worlds.

She bent to trail her fingers through the clear, cool water of the pond, watching the sunlight dance on the little ripples she stirred, and the delicate ribbons of light and shadow that quivered on the polished bottom in response. A small fish darted up to taste her fingers, then darted away again, disappointed, its iridescent scales as bright as precious jewels and far more beautiful.

Three weeks and a few days, and the ripples stirred by her refusal to obey her father's orders were still casting shadows across the surface of her life.

Her father had left that same evening, refusing to speak to her. In all the time since his departure, she'd had no word from him—or anyone else of the Zeyn. They had abandoned her here, perhaps as angry as he had been. Or perhaps afraid to contact her, unwilling to rouse Eileak's wrath against them, too.

Like every able-bodied adult Zeyn, she had the right to make her own decisions in life, but the demands of the communal life they lived encouraged acceptance of a leader's decisions. Marna had always accepted that. In insisting on her right of choice, she knew she had stepped outside the unspoken code that shaped her society.

What she hadn't expected was to find herself virtually exiled here in this strange, vast place that was both a luxurious fantasy and a prison from which she could not escape.

Everywhere she turned, Marna found a world that was radically different from anything she'd known before—her room with its rich furnishings; the crowded streets of the city and the empty, echoing hallways of the Palace; the food she ate. Even the language was subtly changed. Words had different meanings and the rhythm of speech here was quicker, sharper, as if no one had the time to spend in conversation, idle or otherwise.

She'd wanted to reject everything around her. Wanted to scorn and sneer and know that nothing was as good as what she was fighting to defend. To her surprise and growing unease, she found she couldn't. Oh, not that everything she saw was good, or admirable, or even desirable, but some things were. Enough that it was impossible for her to dismiss the entire society out of hand. Enough that she'd begun to question things about her own society that she'd always taken for granted.

What had taken longest to see and been hardest to accept was the fact that the concerns of the Zeyn did not loom so overwhelmingly large in Diloran affairs as she'd been taught and had always believed. Issues that were of paramount importance to her people were considered merely interesting or trivial to others, who were themselves immersed in what, to them, were far more pressing concerns about which she knew absolutely nothing.

It was a shock to see her people and society from the perspective of others, and to realize that the desert and the Zeyn were no more than a small part of a much bigger and far more complex world than she'd ever imagined. It made Marna wonder if her mission was an insane waste of time, like shoveling sand in a sandstorm, or if it was far more urgent than she'd imagined, because the Zeyn were too small and unimportant for anyone else to care about their fate.

All the while she'd studied this strange world around her, Marna knew the world studied her right back. To the palace residents, she'd become an object of curiosity and speculation. To Marott and Tarl Grisaan . . .

Marna violently swirled her hand in the water, frightening off the two jeweled fish who had ventured close.

She didn't care what Marott Grisaan thought about her or her decision. Her people had suffered for the limitations on trade he'd forced on them and the clandestine support he'd given to those who were encroaching on the desert that was their home.

But for some reason she couldn't explain, she cared what Tarl Grisaan thought. It was absurd, of course. Her people had sent her to destroy him, and her only interest ought to be what she could learn from him first. Yet the man intrigued her even as his silly mannerisms and his passion for tasteless clothing annoyed her.

After spending almost four weeks in the palace, Marna had come to realize that Tarl's choice of raiment wasn't quite as extreme as she'd first thought. There was a certain faction among the fashionably idle young men of Diloran Central that had opted for garish ostentation instead of good taste, and Tarl was one of them. Even his affected mannerisms were just an extreme version of the prevailing fashion.

It should have been easy to dismiss him as nothing more than another of those useless creatures who played at being men, yet Marna found she could not, and she was beginning to suspect it would be a serious mistake to try.

To begin with, she'd found he was a kind man. Simple acts of consideration, like finding Sesha a chair and something to eat that first night, came easily to him. He didn't even think about them. Not because such things weren't important, but because that sensitivity was so essential a part of him that it was as natural as breathing, or eating, or sleeping. And if he was kind in the small things, how much more generous might he be in the larger ones when he was Controllor?

He wasn't as foolish as he tried to make everyone believe, either. She'd lost count of the tours they'd taken of the city and surrounding countryside, or the official functions to which she'd been forced to accompany him in the past days.

At each of them Tarl had played his silly games and flashed his wild clothes, and at each of them, once she'd known how to look, Marna had seen another, more serious man hidden beneath the charade of silliness, silently watching and listening to all that went on around him.

She didn't think anyone else noticed. Had she not been of the Zeyn, and therefore accustomed to observing those around her, she would not have seen it either. Often, she wished she hadn't. It was . . . unsettling, and it made everything so much more complicated just when she longed for simple things and simpler answers.

A bird whistled in the tree above her, breaking her concentration. Marna stirred, suddenly restless, then found her eye caught by a bright flash of color in the water. The pair of jeweled fish had returned, searching, perhaps, for the odd, wiggling things they'd spotted earlier.

Marna smiled, diverted from her grim thoughts by their iridescent beauty. Taking care not to frighten them, she slid her fingers back into the water and gently waved them to and fro. One of the fish, either bolder or more hungry than its fellow, swam in close to inspect these strange additions to its watery world. Evidently satisfied, it darted forward and nipped the tip of her finger, then darted away just as quickly as it had come.

Marna gave a faint cry of surprise and pain and jerked her hand out of the water. Drops of water splattered the pool's edge and raised dark blots of wet on her gown, but she scarcely noticed, too startled by the unexpected attack to care.

She brought the injured hand up to inspect the wound. It had been a tiny nip, but deep enough to draw blood. A small red bead was already forming on her finger tip and threatening to spread. Irritated, Marna stuck the ill-treated finger in her mouth and sucked at the wound.

"Fierce little creatures, aren't they? They often catch people by surprise, even those who know what to expect."

Marna twisted around, startled. Tarl Grisaan stood on the grass a couple of meters away, watching her with his head cocked to one side, a slight but surprisingly friendly smile on his lips.

He was more conservatively dressed today than usual, which meant his robe was a subdued green rather than one of the blindingly bright colors he usually chose. He made up for the restraint in his choice of clothing by wearing an earring in garish shades of bright green and brighter pink, but even that was half hidden in the wild mane of black hair that had been his preferred headdress for the past five days. The black wig was absurd, but at least it was better than the red one that had preceded it, and infinitely preferable to the blond curls he'd worn when she first met him.

"Are you all right?" he asked, coming to her. He went down on one knee beside her and, before Marna realized what he'd intended, gently drew her hand away from her mouth, then turned it to inspect her finger.

His long, slender fingers wrapped around her hand, easily enclosing it. His touch was deft, extraordinarily gentle but firm. He delicately pressed against the pad of her finger near the bite, but no more blood appeared.

"Not too bad," he said, releasing her. "Sometimes they take out a good-sized chunk. But don't forget to clean it properly, first chance you get."

"I've had far worse injuries than this," Marna said sharply, burying her hand beneath the folds of her robe. The minute the words were out, she regretted their harshness, but it was too late to call them back. It grated to have this white-skinned male who had spent his life in comfort tell her, a daughter of the desert, how to care for a cut finger.

Beneath her robe, her hand tingled where he had touched her.

If her sharp reply bothered him, Tarl gave no sign of it.

Instead, he sank down to sit beside her at the pool's edge. His attention was fixed on the little jeweled fish who were now energetically darting back and forth, as though hunting the meal they'd found and lost.

"They're not from Diloran, you know," he said, pointing at the fish. "They were brought here by the people of Sharrai."

"Is that why they bite? They feel like strangers in this little pond?"

He looked up at that. A shadow passed across his face, darkening his eyes. "Perhaps," he said at last, slowly, as though weighing his words. "Is that the way you feel? A stranger in this great pond of ours?"

Marna frowned. She didn't care to discuss the way she felt. The loneliness and doubt that had become her constant companions were much too close to the surface. She couldn't risk them welling up, like the drop of blood on her finger, if he scratched her with his questions.

"I don't bite," she said sharply.

He smiled at that, a real smile that lit his face and made Marna, just for an instant, forget the silly wig and the earring and her own troubled thoughts.

"No," he agreed, "I'd say snapping's more your style."

"I don't snap!"

Tarl's smile widened. "You just did."

"I—" Marna bit down on her lip to keep from saying more. He was right, of course, and she didn't much appreciate the fact.

"You see what I mean?"

Marna stiffened, indignant. If she could have done so without appearing to be running away, she would have left him right then. "Is there some reason you came over?"

Was there some reason he'd come over? Tarl wondered, watching the subtle traces of anger and embarrassment flit across her face.

He'd come into this usually abandoned corner of the palace gardens in search of nothing more than a little quiet for himself. The moment he'd spotted her, he should have turned away and left her to her solitude, but he hadn't. There'd been something in the way her head bent as she watched the fish, something in the slight droop of her normally proud shoulders that drew him. Once he'd touched her he'd been completely incapable of leaving.

His skin still burned with the remembered feel of her hand in his.

"Was I supposed to have a reason for coming over?" he asked mildly.

If he were braver or more foolhardy, he'd admit he'd had a reason. But how could he tell her that the memory of her, clothed only in a curtain of midnight hair and shadow, haunted his thoughts, waking and sleeping? That when he was with her he was tormented by vivid mental images of taking down her braids and freeing her hair to float about her, just as it had that first night? That he dreamed of her, naked in that vast, curtained bed beside him, her body warm against his, her touch—

Tarl shifted uncomfortably on the hard, stone rim of the pool. Imagination and sexual hunger could be very dangerous when mixed indiscriminately, and of late they'd mixed not only indiscriminately but all too thoroughly in his brain.

"You just looked like you needed a little company," he said at last, in as casual a tone as he could manage, hoping she wouldn't hear the lie in his voice.

When she didn't respond to that, Tarl, groping for something to say, added, "I imagine you find all this greenery rather . . . overwhelming." A singularly inane statement, but he found he didn't want to be forced to leave simply because she couldn't be coaxed into carrying her side of the conversation.

She looked away, refusing to meet his gaze. "Yes."

Tarl hesitated, surprised by the sudden intensity in her voice.

"I've never visited the Diloran Desert," he said at last, gently. "As a child, my father made sure I traveled all over Diloran, but I never visited the desert."

He paused. Still no response. "They tell me it's very beautiful."

Her head came around at that, her eyes wide and eager. "Oh, yes! It's . . . it's . . ." She took a deep breath, then let it out slowly, on a long, low note of longing. "It's very . . . beautiful."

"Stark, they say," Tarl prompted, watching the light in her face. "Empty. Even dangerous."

She nodded, remembering. "That, too."

Tarl said nothing, letting the silence stretch, waiting.

"But that's part of the beauty," she said at last, picking each word with care. "To know that you are alive and that there is nothing living around you for . . . oh! for forever, because it seems the desert goes on that long, and longer, and . . ."

She faltered, and the light went out of her face.

"But it doesn't go on forever, after all," she said sadly.

Her gaze dropped to the green grass beside them. She bent forward abruptly to pluck some of the carefully cropped blades. They came away in her hands with a sharp tearing sound, but Marna seemed not to care. Frowning, she rolled them between her fingers, then opened her hand to study the crushed bits of grass and the smudges of green they'd left across her fingers.

"The desert dies where the grasslands begin," she said, "and the grasslands are everywhere."

Tarl watched her, wondering at the anger and the uncertainty he could read so clearly in her face. In a sudden surge of what might have been frustration, she shook off the bits of grass and swished her hand in the water. It was a wasted effort, for the stains were still there when she drew her hand back out.

"Perhaps I shall have to learn to like grass," she said, rubbing her fingers together. "There seems to be a great deal more of it than I ever imagined."

"It has its good points," Tarl said. He kept his voice noncommittal, but something within him twisted at the bleakness that hid behind her words.

"Such as?"

"Well," he said lightly, "animals can eat it. I haven't heard of any that survive on sand."

Did he detect the tiniest quiver of amusement at the corner of her mouth, Tarl wondered, or was that just his imagination? "And it doesn't blow in your face like sand. And it's . . . umm . . . it's much nicer to walk on than hot sand."

Silly words, but he was glad he'd said them because that was definitely the beginning of a smile on her lips.

"What difference does it make?" she asked. "If it's easier to walk on, I mean?"

"I wouldn't much care to walk barefoot in your desert," Tarl said, making no effort to disguise his own smile.

"Why would you want to walk barefoot anywhere?" To Tarl's surprise, she seemed honestly to want to know.

He scratched his chin and once more shifted his weight on the hard stone edge of the pool. This conversation was becoming more ridiculous by the minute—and strangely more enchanting. If he had any sense, he'd retreat now, before he got in any deeper.

Regrettably, he'd never had much sense.

"If you tried it once, you'd understand." Tarl struggled to make his words a calm statement of fact. He was having a serious problem keeping his unruly imagination in bounds, and right now it was delighting in tormenting him with images of Marna barefoot in the grass.

He bent forward and touched the folds of her robe, which hid her legs and feet. "You should try it. Take off your shoes and try it."

He'd only touched the fabric of her robe, Marna knew, but her body responded as if he'd caressed her bare skin.

The sudden heat angered her even as it sent her blood racing through her veins. She wanted nothing to do with Tarl Grisaan beyond what protocol and her own mission demanded, yet she found it impossible to ignore him. He was already pulling her to her feet.

"Try it," he said. Before Marna could object, he knelt again, lifted the hem of her robe, and gently wrapped his fingers around her ankle.

It was as though fire had engulfed her foot, then sent bright flares of heat shooting up her leg and into her body. Marna gasped, and swayed slightly.

"Just lean on me," Tarl insisted. "Put your hand on my shoulder, then lift your foot so I can slip your shoe off."

Too shaken to refuse, Marna placed her hand on his back, just above the shoulder blade, and lifted her foot. Even through the heavy fabric of his robe she could feel the warmth of his body and the way his muscles shifted as he worked. He seemed to take forever to tug her shoe off, but that was undoubtedly just her imagination, for his hands were as gentle and as deft as when he'd probed her finger. At each spot he touched her, the heat in her skin flared anew and the soles of her foot tingled and burned in a way that was totally unlike stepping on hot sand with too-thin shoes.

"All right," he said, interrupting the disturbing train of her thoughts. He released her now bare foot, then stretched to take her other foot in his hands.

His movements were precise and graceful, but Marna found herself suddenly awkward, off balance, and teetering slightly to one side. She shifted her hand from his back to his shoulder, then dug her fingers in to keep from toppling over. To her surprise, it was lean, hard muscle she found beneath his robes, not the sharp angle of bone she'd expected.

"There," Tarl said, setting her other foot down and carefully placing her shoe beside its mate. His voice sounded oddly choked, but that was surely as much the product of her imagination as the rest.

Marna let go her hold on his shoulder and straightened, suddenly conscious of just how absurd this whole game was. She was a grown woman. She shouldn't be playing childish games in the garden, no matter how appealing they seemed. The trouble was, she didn't feel like stopping now.

The stone was cool beneath her bare feet, but not unpleasantly so. The hem of her robe, which was cut to just brush the ground when she wore shoes, now bunched in small piles around her feet, hiding them entirely. Marna stared at the ground in front of her feet.

"Now what?" she demanded, suddenly embarrassed.

Tarl looked up at her from where he still knelt at her feet, an odd, twisted little smile on his lips. His eyebrow arched upward, raffish under the wild hair.

"You walk on the grass," he said patiently.

Marna shook her head, torn between embarrassment and excitement. He made it sound so easy, as if walking barefoot on the grass was something he did every day of his life. She'd never walked on grass in her life, barefoot or otherwise.

Tarl found he didn't dare stand. His limbs were too shaky after having made the mistake of touching her. Instead, he remained kneeling as Marna took a tentative step forward onto the grass, then quickly jumped back with an exclamation of disgust.

He couldn't help laughing at the look of distaste on her face. "What's the matter?"

"It tickles!"

"It's *supposed* to tickle."

"Why would anyone want to walk on something that tickles?"

"Just try it. You might as well," he added encouragingly when Marna grimaced. "You've already taken off your shoes."

"*You* took off my shoes!" she objected, but she stepped onto the grass once more, more firmly this time.

Tarl watched as she hesitated a moment, then took another step, then another. The trailing hem of her robe made things a little more awkward, but she appeared not to notice, too caught up in this strange new experience to worry about such trivial details.

She hadn't had to remind him that he'd been the one to remove her shoes. His fingers and the palms of his hands felt as if tiny electrical charges were racing back and forth across them, and the muscles of his shoulder and back burned beneath his robe as if her hand still pressed against him.

But even the torment he'd unwittingly—or perhaps not so unwittingly—caused himself was worth her delight in this new sensation.

With the exception of that one wild scene when she'd driven off the members of Internal Security who'd invaded her chamber, Marna had taken care not to let the freer, wilder side of her nature do any more than peep out now and then. She'd conducted herself with a dignity that was, at times, almost frightening in its cool detachment.

There was nothing either cool or detached about her now. And not much that was dignified, either.

As she adjusted to the unfamiliar sensation of cool, damp grass beneath her feet, she grew bolder and took longer, almost bouncing steps, as if testing the springy turf's resilience. When she took too long a step and found herself treading on her hem, Marna gathered up the skirts of her robe into two untidy wads of fabric, one at each side, and pulled them out of her way. The movement dragged her hem up so it straggled unevenly around her knees, but she didn't seem to notice or to care.

Tarl, however, noticed.

Her legs were slender and well shaped, her ankles trim, her feet narrow and gracefully arched. He'd seen women's ankles and legs before. He'd certainly seen far more of Marna that first night when he'd inadvertently crept into her room. But this was different.

This was far more . . . erotic, yet innocent and pleasing at the same time.

The unexpected, simple joy in her, the graceful way she lifted the skirts of her robe, the light, the sun, the very air about them . . . it was crazy, but Tarl felt as if all the forces of man and nature had combined to tempt him. And right now, he felt not the slightest urge to resist.

Chapter Eleven

She came back to him eventually.

"You're right!" she said, letting the skirts of her robe fall back into place. "It *is* better than sand! In the desert, grass and green things are too precious to treat so roughly but here . . ." She paused and looked around her, as if seeing the garden for the first time. "Here you have enough and to spare."

Tarl laughed, not at her but with her, glad to share the moment's pleasure.

"There's grass, but there's also water to wash it off," he said. "You'd better dabble your feet in the pond before you put your shoes back on."

"Put my feet in the pond!"

Judging by the horror in her face, he might as well have demanded she make human sacrifices to the water gods.

"Check the soles of your feet," Tarl suggested dryly. "They're going to be in a lot worse shape than your fingers were when you got grass stains on *them.*"

From her expression, Marna clearly suspected him of some devious trick, but she dutifully, if a tad doubtfully, lifted the hem of her robe, then balanced on one foot so she could inspect the sole of the other.

"It's completely green!" Marna stared, open-mouthed, first at her foot, then at him, then back at her foot. She changed to inspect the other foot. "They're both green!"

"That's what happens when you hop around on grass that's been mown recently."

"Mown?" She dropped the hem of her robe and glared at him. "You didn't tell me it had been mown."

"Would you have tried it if I'd told you what would happen?"

The glare softened to a frown. "No."

"And see what you would have missed?"

The frown disappeared entirely, to be replaced by a soft smile that made her look years younger. She didn't say anything and she didn't look at him; her eyes grew unfocused as she turned inward, remembering the joy of a few minutes earlier. The skirts of her robe began to rustle, very softly; then she seemed to grow a tiny bit taller, then to shrink again, then grow taller.

It took a second for Tarl to realize she must be curling up her feet underneath her robe, then rising, ever so slightly, onto the balls of her feet, then rolling back down. She was savoring the tiny taste of freedom she'd been granted, remembering the new sensations that, for one brief moment, had let her forget whatever burdens it was she bore.

At the thought, the smile on Tarl's lips faded. If only the troubles in life could be erased through the simple expedient of a barefoot walk in the grass! But they couldn't, and soon she'd remember, too, and the world would come pressing back in around them, and the pleasure they shared now would be gone forever.

Soon, but not just yet, Tarl vowed. Not just yet.

''You'd best wash off your feet,'' he said lightly. ''That is, if you don't want to trail back through the palace in your bare feet.''

She laughed at that, as pleased as if he'd said something witty, but when she glanced down at the pool, the tiniest trace of a frown reappeared on her face. ''But how can I wash off my feet? There's no basin or cloth.''

''I told you, you stick your feet in the pond and swish them around until the worst of the green comes off. It's just like the bath in your personal quarters.''

She stared at him blankly. It was his turn to frown. ''You take baths, right?''

''Of course not! And waste so much water? I have a basin, just as I would have in the desert.''

''Well, right now you don't have any basin except that pond, so you may as well put your feet in there and rinse them off.''

''I couldn't do that! Stick my feet in water that belongs to everyone? As if it doesn't matter?'' She was growing indignant even thinking about it.

''Here it's not considered ill-mannered to do that on occasion. Like now,'' Tarl said firmly. He patted a space beside him at the rim of the pool. ''Sit.''

Marna looked as if she was about to continue arguing, but then decided not to. Lifting the hem of her robe once more, she cautiously sat where Tarl indicated. Instead of dipping her feet into the water as he'd expected, however, she carefully scooped up half a handful of what, to her and her people, was the most precious commodity in all Diloran, then rinsed off all she could of the bits of grass clinging to her feet. It wasn't very much.

As Tarl watched her, the heat and high blood pressure he'd brought under control a few minutes ago returned, hotter and higher than before. He wanted to be the one to hold her feet in his hands, to rub his palms along her sole, to let his fingers curve into the arch and over her heel, then trace the delicate bones of her ankle before stroking up the swell of her calf and around her knee, up . . .

"You're doing it all wrong!" The words burst from him with explosive force, propelled by the frustration building within him. Without thinking, without heeding her gasp of astonishment, Tarl grabbed her by the ankles, swung her around, and thrust her feet into the pond with an impressive splash. "There! *That's* the way it's supposed to be done!"

For an instant she looked at him as if he'd gone mad—which Tarl did not doubt he had—then burst into a laugh loud enough to frighten three birds out of the bushes around them.

Tarl was panting from the combined effects of lust and his mad burst of activity, but somehow he found the breath to join in her laughter.

"Kick!" he said.

"Kick?"

"Your feet!"

She managed a quick flip upwards with one foot. "Like this?"

"Harder!"

She kicked with the other foot and managed to generate a little arc of water that splashed against the rim on the far side of the pond. "Like *this?*"

"Harder! Do you want the fish to eat your toes?"

Marna leaned back on her elbows, and with all the will in the world started to manufacture a boiling, frothing geyser of water. "How's this?" she demanded, halfway between a laugh and an exultant shout.

"*Harder!*" Even as he laughingly roared his order, Tarl realized that getting harder was exactly what was happening to him—or at least to a certain very personal part of his anatomy.

He gasped at the powerful surge of heat in his groin, then groaned as his body immediately responded to Marna's shout of "Is this hard enough?" by growing harder still.

By now Marna had created a major tempest in a very minor body of water. Water spouted in all directions, drenching them both, along with the surrounding grass and shrubbery. Tarl didn't care. All he could do was watch Marna and fight against the urge to take her right there at the side of the pond, to make love to her until they both collapsed from their frenzy.

The hem of her robe was halfway up her thighs and rapidly climbing higher with each energetic kick of her long legs. Her back was arched upwards, her breasts clearly outlined even under the heavy fabric of her robe, and her head thrown back to expose the long, graceful line of her throat under its high collar. She was panting and laughing and she was driving him wild.

His lustful thoughts were rudely shattered by the sound of a sharp "*Kiria!*" coming from behind them.

The shock, horror, and indignation contained in that one exclamation were more than enough to stop her laughter and bring both Tarl and Marna bolt upright. They turned to find Sesha standing a few meters away, eyes sparking and weather-worn face rigid with anger. She fixed her disapproving gaze first on Marna, then Tarl, then back on Marna, and with every second that passed her frown grew deeper.

As Tarl helped Marna scramble to her feet, Sesha stumped across the grass to them. Her crippled foot left a visible trail in the green, but it didn't slow her down much.

"What shame! Look at you!" she said, coming to a halt in front of them. "Look at your robes! Drenched! With water! How can *you,* of all people, be party to such a shameful waste, Kiria? What would your father say?"

Marna drew herself up straighter, her chagrin clear on her face. "I—"

"Her father would say it was right and proper that Marna do what she was doing," Tarl broke in, "because *I* told her to do it."

He couldn't have found a faster or more effective way to deflate Sesha's indignation. The maid puffed out her lips and gave a sigh that sounded like an air bladder going flat. "Oh!" she said. "Well."

"You ought to try it yourself." Tarl pressed his advantage. "I was just showing Marna how to wash off her feet after walking barefoot on the grass."

"Wash her feet? She was walking on the grass? Barefoot?" That was going too far. Sesha stiffened and drew in her chin. She clasped her hands together in front of her and straightened her shoulders as if she were a soldier on parade. "I don't believe it. Not Kiria Marna."

"It's true, Sesha. It's . . ." Marna groped for the words she wanted, unabashed by her maid's patent disapproval. "It's a rather wonderful experience, really."

"You should try it, Sesha. You'll like it!" The energy of that wild bout of water-splashing with Marna was still racing through his veins as Tarl grabbed Sesha's arm and tugged on it. "Come on. Just take off your shoes . . ."

The minute the words were out of his mouth he knew it was entirely the wrong thing to say.

Sesha stiffened, but this time her reaction wasn't from anger, it was from shame—shame and a pain that cut all the way to the woman's heart.

He'd forgotten she was crippled, but she hadn't and never would. Her people wouldn't let her, Tarl realized, remembering Marna's reaction to Joeffrey Baland. By the standards of the Zeyn, he should have ignored the woman and never, ever tried to treat her like a normal human being. For the Zeyn, she no longer was.

Silently, he cursed himself for an insensitive, unthinking fool. He'd stumbled into a mess, and he didn't know how to extricate himself without causing more damage. The trouble was, he couldn't just stand there and do nothing, either.

"Give it a try, Sesha," he urged, taking care to keep any hint of pity or condescension out of his voice. "Marna didn't think much of the idea at first, either, but she found she liked it."

"Tarl . . ." Marna said, clearly appalled by his blunder, but just as clearly without any better idea of how to retreat than he had.

Some small part of his brain took note of the fact that it was the first time since she'd appeared in the Hall of the Public almost a month before that she'd called him by his first name, but Tarl didn't have time to puzzle over the significance of that.

"Look, Sesha, I'll help you just like I helped Marna," he said, ignoring Marna's attempts to make him shut up.

Sesha shook her head and tugged her arm free of his grip on her. Her jaw was set as hard as the rock cliffs of her desert home, but there was a barely perceptible trembling in her lips that told him she was far more upset by this reminder of her infirmity than she would ever admit.

"Think of it as physical therapy," he persisted. "Only this way you can have some fun, too."

She froze, obviously puzzled and not a little suspicious. "What do you mean, physical therapy?"

Tarl blinked, disconcerted. He wouldn't have been surprised if she'd hit him, or run away, but he hadn't expected that particular response. "Physical therapy," he said. "You know, the exercises and treatments you go through for your leg. To make it strong again."

Shesha stared up at him from under furrowed brows, as if she suspected him of trying to play some very unpleasant joke on her. Marna wasn't much better. She was looking at him as if he'd gone slightly mad.

Tarl started to speak, then stopped. The thought that had

just popped into his head was too absurd to be worth considering, yet something about the expressions of the two women in front of him made him wonder.

"Sesha," he said at last. "How did you become crippled? What happened to your leg?"

The older woman scowled. "It was a long time ago. It does not matter now."

She started to back away, but Tarl reached out to stop her. "What happened? I want to know."

If he hadn't been the heir to the Controllorship and pledged to her mistress, Tarl knew he never would have gotten an answer. As it was, the words came slowly and with great reluctance.

"I was hunting," Sesha began, then stopped. Her head came up proudly. "I *was* a hunter," she said, as if she expected him to doubt her. "One of the best."

"It's true," Marna added, obviously uncertain where the conversation was headed but anxious to support her maid in whatever way she could. "Sesha was famous for her skill and daring. Hunters are very important people in our society," she added. "They destroy the desert stalkers that prey on our herds, but it's very dangerous work."

"Yes. That is so. And I was one of the very best." Sesha was nodding eagerly now, her face alight with the pleasure of knowing her achievements had not been totally forgotten. The pleasure didn't last long.

Her eyes darkened again and the light faded from her face as quickly as it had come. "I *was* a hunter. I'm not anymore."

Tarl could hear the pain in her voice and an even deeper regret, but he detected no trace of bitterness. Sesha had faced the consequences of her injury with the same courage and quiet strength she must have shown as a hunter.

"I was caught in a rock slide when trying to rescue another hunter,'' she said at last. ''He died. I lived. That is all.''

''But the doctors,'' Tarl protested. ''Couldn't they do anything? There's physical therapy, and artificial bones and joints, and—oh! I don't know what else. Didn't any of that help?''

Sesha frowned again, more puzzled than distrustful now. ''The doctors kept me alive. I do not know about the rest.''

''But surely they tried to rebuild your leg! They couldn't just leave you—'' Tarl stopped short as understanding dawned. Sesha had survived her accident, but among the Zeyn, the communal resources went first to the young and strong. A hunter who would never hunt again might as well be dead so far as her standing in Zeyn society went.

Marna looked as if she was on the verge of crying, but Sesha had had years to learn to live with the truth. ''The Zeyn doctors do not rebuild crippled legs, Kiri Grisaan,'' she said with dignity. ''It is not possible . . . and it is not our way.''

With that, Sesha turned from him to take Marna by the arm. ''Come with me, Kiria,'' she said sternly. ''You must change for the Controllor-Regent's dinner tonight. You represent our people, you know. You have a responsibility to be at your best.''

She shook her head in disgust. ''Look at you. Dripping with water. There must be a full day's ration soaked into your robe. What shame!''

With only a pause to let Marna collect her shoes, Sesha led her charge away, lecturing and scolding with every dragging step she took.

Tarl stood watching without moving until they disappeared from sight, two strong, intelligent women—one bound by duty, another by physical limitations—who faced life's challenges with courage and dignity in spite of the demands their society imposed on them.

What would the Zeyn do if people like Marna and Sesha

ever rebelled against their society's dictates?

What would the people around him do if he—no, *when* he refused to meet their expectations for him?

A tiny splash beside him drew Tarl's attention back to the pond. One of the jewel fish had grabbed an insect from the surface and was now devouring it in great gulps. If the little creature had suffered any harm from the wild storm Marna had kicked up, Tarl couldn't see any sign of it. It had weathered the tempest in its little world and was getting on with its life, as unconcerned about any storms the future might bring as it was about any disturbances in the past.

He hated to admit it, but Tarl couldn't think of any human who would be that practical.

Sesha didn't say a word all the way back to the guest quarters. Marna found herself at a loss to know if she ought to open the conversation herself, or simply ignore the specters raised by Tarl's clumsy, but well-intentioned questions. Guilt for her own childish behavior, and especially for her inexcusably wasteful play in the water, made her even more uncertain of the best course to take. She almost would have preferred a harsh scolding to the strained silence between them.

Worse, she'd never been more aware of Sesha's halting gait than now, and Marna suspected that Sesha knew it. Sesha had cared for her since she was a child, but this was the first time Marna had ever really noticed the odd rhythm of her maid's walk, the slight scrape as Sesha dragged her foot up behind her, the sway of her torso as she swung her foot to the front, followed by the soft thump as her foot landed and a half-hop as she transferred her weight to her bad leg and stepped forward. It was an awkward, complex movement compared to the simple one-two beat of a normal person's stride, and must have been an inescapable reminder to Sesha of just how much a rock slide had changed her life all those years ago.

Yet even as Marna felt the sympathetic pain of Sesha's loss, she was conscious of her own resentment at being reminded of the differences between her and her maid. There was nothing she could do about the older woman's crippled leg—nothing anyone could do about it—so it was ridiculous to suddenly feel guilty, as if she had somehow let down Sesha and all the others like her by not being crippled herself.

And what could she say, anyway? Among the Zeyn, it was horribly impolite to discuss such matters. Wouldn't bringing the subject up now merely make an already uncomfortable situation more uncomfortable?

Marna was ashamed of her sense of relief when Sesha, after making sure her braids were still in their usual neat arrangement, left her alone to tend to such mundane tasks as washing off her dirty feet and changing her damp robe for a dry one that would be more appropriate for the formal dinner scheduled for that evening.

As she scrubbed at the recalcitrant green stains on the bottoms of her feet, however, Marna discovered she'd merely exchanged one set of uncomfortable thoughts for another. Instead of thinking about Sesha's awkward walk, she found herself remembering the feel of Tarl's hands on her ankles and feet, the comforting solidity of the man when she'd leaned on him for support. Instead of wondering what to say to Sesha, she wondered what Tarl had been thinking as he'd watched her, there in the garden. For a short time, he'd let down his guard, stopped playing the fool, and simply relaxed and let himself enjoy the moment.

As she unfastened her robe, then slipped out of it and let it slide to the floor, Marna found herself remembering the avid way he'd watched her. She could feel his eyes on her even now, and the memory stirred an uncomfortable heat within her.

Sands help her, she'd *enjoyed* him watching her, even as

she'd reveled in the new sensations he'd introduced her to.

She'd delighted in the feel of the sweet, cool grass beneath her feet and the warm sun on her legs. She'd relished the blissful moment of childish, irresponsible pleasure.

But she'd enjoyed having his eager, hungry gaze on her even more.

There'd been no need to lift the skirts of her robe above her knees, but she had, just so she could savor the almost physical caress of his watching her. There'd been even less cause to let herself indulge in that mad shower of water and laughter, but she'd done that, too. She'd lain back on her elbows and let her robes slide up her thighs, and she had laughed as he had, wildly, in utter, uncaring abandon.

The memory brought a painfully hot blush to her cheeks. Tarl had been as aroused as she was, and she had burned with a heat that even the cold water of the pond could not assuage.

What would have happened if Sesha hadn't interrupted them? Was she glad or sorry that Sesha appeared when she did? Did she even want to know?

With a short exclamation of disgust, Marna kicked aside the damp robe that lay on the floor at her feet; then, ashamed, she immediately bent to pick it up and shake it out. What had she come to that she could be so careless of her clothes, or so heedless of her responsibilities that she would let down her guard as she had in the garden?

She hung the robe on a hook where it could drip dry, then picked up the basin of water she'd used to wash her feet and carried it over to the vast, tiled bath to dump its contents.

As the water splashed against the bright blue tiles, Marna was shaken by a sudden, vivid image of water splashing over the edge of the pond and onto Tarl's dark green robe. She could hear his laughter as he urged her to kick harder, then harder still.

And with that memory came another, of a different man's laughter—laughter that was lower, softer, more restrained but no less sense-stirring.

Marna's fingers tightened around the edge of the basin. For the past three weeks she'd refused to let herself remember the dark stranger and his tormenting kisses. Each time her brain conjured up thoughts of shadows and heat and his dark presence in her room, she'd firmly squelched them. Whoever he was, whatever his purpose, she had to remember he had no place in her life, especially not now.

Yet though she had forced away any thought of the man, Marna continued to cling to his words when her doubts and her lonely longing for home were the strongest. She'd found she needed a reminder, every now and then, of why she'd chosen to go against her father's will.

But not now. Now she would do well to forget the stranger and his words, to forget Tarl and Sesha and everything except the task of dressing for a dinner she didn't want with people she didn't care to know.

Strangers in the dark and bewigged men in the garden, laughter and light and the sweet, soft touch of a man's hand on her skin—they were all transient, unimportant things that had nothing to do with her or her reasons for being here. She had to remember that, always.

Marna tried to ignore the glistening drops of water on the tiles as she set the basin down on the edge of the bath, but she couldn't. With angry haste, she bent and swiped a hand across the cool tiles, sluicing the remaining water into the drain. Even drops of water carried memories.

If only the memories themselves were so easily thrown away.

Marna had donned the simple white robe and embroidered over-robe that Sesha had laid out for her, and was debating how to spend the remaining time until her presence would be required, when a low knock at the door startled her from her thoughts.

A male servant Marna didn't recognize stood in the hall. He bowed and extended a small, cloth-wrapped packet to her. "For you, Kiria," he said. The minute she had it in her hands, he turned and walked away, not so quickly that he appeared to be rushing, but not dawdling, either.

Marna opened her mouth to call after him to ask what the packet was and who it was from, but he was already gone. Two attendants lounged at their posts at the far end of the building, but they didn't seem to be concerned about the man's abrupt appearance and disappearance. There was no one else around.

Frowning, Marna shut the door and crossed to the windows, where there was better light. The cloth wrapping proved to be a small pouch, tied at one end with a drawstring. She pulled the string to open the pouch, then drew out a small leather box which opened at a touch on its metal clasp.

The box was unimpressive, but its contents made Marna gasp and started her heart thudding painfully in her chest. Her fingers trembled as she tipped the box and poured a couple of grams of red-gold sand into the palm of her hand. Desert sand.

With a low moan that was half plea, half protest, Marna flung the sand and box and its pouch out the window, then slammed the windows shut and locked them.

It was the message her father had said he would send, the message she'd hoped she would never, ever receive.

She had exactly one week to kill Marott and Tarl Grisaan.

To Tarl, the dinner dragged interminably, even though it lasted barely two hours. Protocol had placed him directly across from Marna, and throughout the meal he was uncomfortably aware of her, even though she was clearly trying to avoid looking at him. He was aware of her voice, the way she lifted her goblet to drink, the way she bent her head to listen to the comments from the people on either side of her. Yet no matter how entrancing Marna's appearance was now, he found he couldn't suppress the vivid memory of her barefoot in the grass with her robe hiked halfway up her thighs and her eyes aglow with mingled wonder and delight.

Just the thought was enough to make his temperature rise and his body ache with a wanting that was all the fiercer for being so impossible to fulfill.

Tarl couldn't help but be grateful when a servant brought a message bidding him to report to Joeffrey's private quarters when the dinner was over. Even if the old man launched into another of his lectures about duty and destiny, it would at least provide a diversion from the all-too-distracting mental images that Marna's presence roused in him so easily.

Fine words, but Tarl had to admit to a twinge of disappointment when Marna managed to slip out of the dining hall in the confusion at the end of the meal without his having a chance to bid her good night.

Or maybe she just had the good sense he lacked. There was no advantage to either of them if the attraction that had flared between them in the garden was allowed to go any further. He would soon be gone from Diloran and she had her own concerns, concerns that he would be wiser not to meddle with.

Telling himself to be sensible didn't make him that way, however. All the way to Joeffrey's personal quarters, Tarl found his thoughts dwelling on things he would be much better off forgetting. Things like Marna, naked in the moonlight, or laughing in the garden, or—

Tarl cut his thoughts off sharply when he reached the entrance to Joeffrey's quarters—quarters that, for the old man's convenience, were unusually close to the public rooms and offices of the palace. He rapped sharply on the outer door with his knuckles and was admitted by one of Joeffrey's servants. After a quick glance to assure himself that everything was in order, the servant left, leaving Tarl alone with his former mentor.

Joeffrey Baland might have been one of the most powerful men on Diloran, but that power wasn't evident in the two small, spare rooms that comprised his personal quarters. Nothing had changed since Tarl had last been summoned to these rooms over thirteen years earlier. The sitting room walls were lined from floor to ceiling with old-fashioned books and papers and a bank of monitors connected to the central government computers. A simple table and four chairs, one of which was specially designed to accommodate Joeffrey's twisted body, were the only items of furniture. The bedroom contained a narrow bed and a cabinet for Joeffrey's personal possessions, nothing more.

"Nothing's changed," Tarl said, sitting down in the chair Joeffrey indicated. "It seems a little . . . strange to find this place so familiar, when so much else is different."

"Keeping things from changing is a prerogative of the old," Joeffrey replied dryly. He set an exquisitely formed blue glass decanter on the table, then made another trip for two glasses of the same delicate blown glass. Carefully balancing himself by leaning on the table with one hand, he lifted the heavy decanter and poured a generous measure of brandy for Tarl and an equally generous measure for himself. Then he restoppered the decanter and cautiously lowered himself into his chair directly across from Tarl.

Tarl lifted his glass and sniffed appreciatively at its golden contents. "Verelian?"

"The best to be had." Joeffrey raised his glass in a silent salute, took a delicate sip, then set the glass back down with great care. "That's one thing that's changed, at least. I don't recall ever offering you brandy when you came to me for your classes.''

''No. But I seem to remember a rather stringent lecture on the evils of drink.''

''That was only after you and Jarfall of Nalmor raided his father's private stores. Though I imagine the hangovers you two suffered were far more effective than my lecture.''

Tarl smiled, remembering. ''It's the only time I've ever gotten drunk.''

''You see the value of experience? What were you? Thirteen?''

''Twelve and a half.''

Joeffrey nodded a thoughtful agreement. ''Twelve and a half. One lesson, all those years ago, yet you remember it well enough to avoid the consequences of over-indulgence ever since.''

He picked up his glass again, but this time he didn't drink, just rolled it thoughtfully between gnarled hands. ''How many other lessons has life brought in the years since then, Tarl? Have you learned them as well as you did that one?''

Tarl frowned, but said nothing. Joeffrey had a purpose in inviting him here beyond indulging in nostalgia; he just wasn't certain what it was.

When the silence had stretched sufficiently to make Tarl uncomfortable, Joeffrey said, ''One of the things that most impressed me about you as a boy was that you learned so quickly and adapted so easily to the challenges we set you. That is a very useful trait for the Controllor of Diloran, you know.''

''Undoubtedly. But since I'm not going to be the Controllor, it doesn't matter much, does it?'' His response verged on the childishly belligerent, but Tarl didn't care. ''As soon as my uncle is safely removed from office, I'm leaving.''

''You're wrong, Tarl. You're not leaving here, no matter what you say.''

Chapter Twelve

"You *can't* leave." Joeffrey forged ahead, too canny to let Tarl have a chance to protest before he'd managed to say all he was going to. "Some of the leaders of the Tevah have just informed me that they're calling a special meeting for midnight. They've decided to formally recognize you as their official leader, and to give allegiance to you as the legal Controllor of Diloran."

"What?"

"Under your guidance, our plans have moved faster than anyone expected. They're anxious to make sure that there will be no problems with the transition of government once Marott is gone. I didn't want to press the issue this soon, but I understand why they want to."

Joeffrey hesitated, studying Tarl for a moment before adding, "They *need* you—as much as Diloran does, Tarl. I worked for years to bring them together. You've seen the quarrels, how each leader only sees *his* group's side of any issue. Without your leadership, I don't think we would ever have come as close as we are now to getting rid of your uncle."

"They'll have to start learning, then. Just like everyone else on Diloran will."

"It's not that easy and you know it. You have no choice, Tarl. You are a Grisaan. You were *born* to lead Diloran."

The old man, head sunk beneath the weight of the hump he bore, studied Tarl as coldly and dispassionately as if he were a collector of rare objects and Tarl a specimen for his collection.

"I taught you, shaped you, shared my knowledge with you. I have watched you since your return to Diloran, just as I watched you when you were a child, and then a young man testing himself against the worst this galaxy has to offer. Testing yourself and winning, Tarl. Every time. No matter what the odds against you."

Joeffrey leaned forward to study Tarl, his eyes like glittering black ice beneath his heavy lids, his massive, misshapen jaw set at a belligerent angle.

"You are all the man I'd hoped you would be, Tarl Grisaan, and you are *ready* for this." He thumped the table with the tip of one gnarled finger for emphasis. "Everything in your life has prepared you for this moment when you can claim the position that is rightfully yours, not by inheritance, but because you are the only man to fill it! You are the man who can lead Diloran, the man who can keep us from tearing ourselves into pieces and give us peace again. No matter what you think, you *can't* refuse."

Tarl angrily shoved back in his chair. He wanted to throw the contents of his glass in that familiar, ugly, determined face. He wanted to pick up the table and toss it in Joeffrey's lap. He wanted to walk away. Now. From everything.

He couldn't. Something kept him chained to his chair, listening to an old man's fantasies even as he raged against them, deep inside.

He shook his head, so hard he could feel the muscles at the back of his neck strain at the force of the motion. "You're wrong, old man," he said, not caring if his words sounded like a threat. "You don't know me. If you did, you would know that I not only *don't* want this grand position you offer, I won't take it. I don't want to rule anyone, let alone an entire world."

Joeffrey smiled, just a confident little lift at the edges of his thin lips, but it was enough to strike fear in Tarl's heart. The old man had lived with secrets all his life. What secret did he possess that made him so sure Tarl would give in to his demands now?

"I know you don't want the power, Tarl, and that's one of the reasons you're the best man to have it. Your father lived for his power. Your uncle craves it even more. Between them, they've come close to destroying the political structure of this planet. Your uncle knows that if he succeeds in inciting the various factions of Diloran to quarrel with each other, they'll weaken themselves and strengthen him. If Marott is allowed to continue, he may well bring on civil war. Is that what you want, Tarl? To see your uncle gain even greater power than he now possesses—at the expense of the suffering and misery of others? Will you really stand by and let that happen, knowing you can prevent it? If you were Controllor—"

Goaded, Tarl kicked back his chair, relishing the angry grating sound it made against the floor. He banged both fists on the table and leaned forward to glare at his old tutor.

"Stop playing with me, Joeffrey. I said I would do everything I could to help you and your people get rid of Marott. I haven't backed down from that promise and I won't. But I never, ever, said I would stay as Controllor. You go too far when you try to manipulate me with guilt or these absurd claims that I'm the only man who can keep this world together."

Joeffrey hadn't even flinched when Tarl kicked back his chair. Not by so much as the flicker of an eyelash did he indicate that he was affected now. Tarl found the old man's steady, probing gaze far more disconcerting than if he'd threatened him with a disruptor, but he wasn't prepared to acknowledge defeat.

"You've deluded yourself, Joeffrey. You're letting your loyalty to tradition and the Grisaan name lead you astray, and all because my grandfather gave you a chance when no one else would. I *know* you. You haven't changed since that day you dragged me down the palace halls by the scruff of my neck because I'd said something disrespectful to an Elder of one of the Old Families. Remember?"

The sudden quirk at the corner of Joeffrey's mouth made it clear he remembered the incident, but Tarl didn't give him a chance to interrupt. "You haven't changed, Joeffrey, but *I* have. I was a boy when I left here thirteen years ago. I'm a man now, a man you know nothing about. You'd be a fool to put someone you don't know in the Controllorship."

"I know you far better than you think, Tarl. Better than you know yourself. And everything I know tells me that you are the man the people of Diloran need as Controllor. The man who can lead us back to the peace we once knew."

Joeffrey hesitated a moment, his gaze unblinkingly fixed on Tarl. "When your troop was captured and presumed dead on Saltos III, did you follow orders, give up, and go back to the comfort of your ship? No. You spent seven weeks alone in that hell and risked your life to rescue your people and get them to safety."

At Joeffrey's casual mention of the incident, Tarl slumped into his chair, stunned. He'd thought that particular exploit long since forgotten. How had Joeffrey learned of it?

"When you delivered those emergency supplies to the outpost on Beurig's third moon, you were supposed to do nothing except wait for a battalion of Marines to arrive. Instead, you organized a decidedly unorthodox defense that drove off the larger and better armed force of Fashil which attacked earlier than expected. If you'd followed orders, the outpost would have been destroyed long before the main force could have reached you."

Tarl listened to Joeffrey's recitation, too dazed to react. Against the advice of his superiors and, occasionally, their direct orders, he'd refused every medal the Galactic Marines had ever awarded him, and had officially requested that any record of his activities be buried in the Marines' classified files. Joeffrey should never have heard of Saltos III or the invasion of the outpost on the third moon of Beurig.

Joeffrey paused, obviously enjoying his former student's confusion. "There's a great deal more, of course," he said at last, when Tarl didn't speak. "Would you like me to go on?"

"How did you learn about all this?" Tarl demanded hotly. "Those records are sealed. No one is allowed access to them."

That remark generated an amused snort that, for Joeffrey, almost qualified as a laugh. "If you'd spent more time dabbling in politics, you'd know there is no such thing as a sealed record. You might be surprised at how many people of influence in galactic affairs know of your achievements. For instance, you probably didn't realize that five individuals submitted notarized statements regarding what really happened on Orgon station. Your attempt to protect those settlers was noble, but misguided, Tarl. One of the statements was submitted by Amon Shay himself. He was the one who recommended you for the Medal of—"

"Enough! I don't know how you got all this information, but it won't do you any good. I—"

"Actually, it's already done its good work, Tarl. Did you really think all the hard-nosed leaders who form the Tevah would have accepted you for Controllor unless they were convinced you were the man they needed? And what better way to convince them than to share all those fascinating items in your personal file with them?"

"You showed them my file?"

"Of course. They saw everything almost as soon as it was entered. As a matter of fact, one of them was just commenting on how impressed, as well as amused, she's been with this absurd role you've adopted since your return. It was totally unexpected, and it's managed to keep your uncle and his supporters off balance far more effectively than anything we might have proposed would. Flexibility and a willingness to try something new are hallmarks of a good leader, Tarl." He frowned and added, "Even though I still don't like those damned earrings you wear."

Rage and an overwhelming sense of betrayal coursed through Tarl. He'd thought he'd escaped thirteen years ago, but instead he'd been watched and studied and judged just as if he'd remained on Diloran. He was as much a prisoner of his history as he'd ever been.

He turned away from the table and the man who was at the heart of his betrayal, but there was nowhere to go.

"The meeting of the Tevah tonight . . ." Joeffrey let the words hang on the air until Tarl reluctantly turned back to face him. "We have worked for years to bring Marott Grisaan down, but it will all be wasted if there is no one to take his place."

Joeffrey frowned and his eyes grew unfocused, as if he looked beyond Tarl to a future that frightened him.

"Without someone strong enough to hold the central government together, Tarl, this world will descend into civil war. The Old Families and the independent states will start fighting among themselves for more power, more wealth, more land, more of whatever they think the others have that they don't. They'll—"

Joeffrey stopped, and this time his black eyes fixed on Tarl's with the same fierce determination that had driven him to overcome the limitations of his physical body. "They'll destroy Diloran, and there will be no one to stop them. That's why you can't refuse the controllorship. It *is* for the best, Tarl. For Diloran—*and* for you."

He swam without stopping, back and forth and back again in an endless circle of exertion that swallowed his inner turmoil in the surging waters of the pool—but only for so long as he kept moving. The minute he stopped to hang, gasping, on the water-slicked edge, the turmoil came rushing back.

What was he to do? What was he to say to those grim men and women who would face him in their shadowed meeting chamber, demanding an answer he did not have and could not give? Not yet, anyway.

Not yet. Tarl grimaced and shut his eyes against the rivulets of water streaming down his face. He leaned his head back against the cold stone, his mouth open, his chest heaving as he fought for air.

Not yet. Two simple words that contained a lie within them, for they promised that there would be an answer, sometime. He wasn't sure he *had* an answer, or ever would.

The waves he'd churned up slapped against the stone, lifting his body and lightly twisting it, first to one side, then to the other, then back again, pushing him against the pool's edge, then pulling him away in their dying wake.

Tarl tensed, too tired to fight against the tug of the water, yet suddenly resentful of its power. It was too much like the conflicting forces in his life now, pulling him back and forth, dragging at him, making him fight against them just to keep his balance.

With a sudden, angry surge, he pulled himself from the water, letting it sluice off him in cascading runnels that traced the muscles of his back and belly and thighs before slipping into an untidy puddle beneath his feet.

If only life were like that. If only he could let all the clamoring demands of duty and responsibility and the expectations of others slide away from him so easily.

He couldn't, and he knew it. Yet if he gave in to them, they would pull him under and he would drown, just as he'd drown in the waters of the pool if he ever surrendered to their insistent pull.

Tarl raised his head to find his image reflected in the flat, black glass of the surrounding windows. It was as if he were looking at himself from a great distance, a naked, defenseless man almost lost in the dark, while behind him shimmered the waters of a life that could pull him under if he let it.

There was nothing else, for the world beyond the windows had been swallowed up in the dark. No light pierced the barrier of glass and shadow, not even a hint that there was life behind the dim reflection staring back at him, unspeaking.

Tarl walked toward the windows. His reflection walked toward him, becoming darker and more indistinct with every step he took. The lights of the pool were too bright. He disappeared in their radiance until he was nothing more than a dim, dark shadow pressed against the unyielding glass.

Marna was out there someplace. As alone as he was. As lost in the dark as he was. As driven by the needs and wants of others as he was, and just as uncertain about her right to fight against them.

Tarl cupped his hand over the glass and leaned closer, trying to shield his eyes against the light so he could peer out. Nothing. Just a blacker shadow where nothing showed, not even his own face. The protective film imbedded in the glass which made it impossible for anyone outside to see in, now made it impossible for him to see out, leaving him a blurred shadow floating between light and dark.

Angry, now—at himself and his world and the world that lay hidden beyond the black curtain of glass in front of him—Tarl dropped his hand and turned away.

The water in the pool was calmer, the waves he'd generated fading into a slowly shifting quilt of light, tranquil and inviting. Tarl watched the ever-changing, faceted surface, waiting for it to grow calmer still.

It wasn't a matter of finding a place for himself in this life they offered. It was a matter of choosing. Just as he could choose not to dive into the pool, so he could choose not to accept the life they now dangled before him.

He wasn't the leader they wanted and never would be. Three hundred years ago, Yerlaf Grisaan had brought peace to a warring world by assuming control over the entire planet. And for three hundred years, the peace he'd imposed had held, shaky but intact.

What Joeffrey and the Tevah refused to see, however, was that Diloran and its people had changed in those three hundred years. No one man could enforce the kind of government his ancestor had. If Diloran was to survive, the various quarreling factions would have to lay down their arms and set aside their claims in order to work together. Peace—real, lasting peace—had to come from within. It could not be imposed by one man standing outside the social and political structure of Families and states, no matter how much some people wanted to believe it could.

He would tell them no, Tarl decided. Tell Joeffrey and those grim-faced men and women who awaited him that they would have to build their own future in their own way, just as he would have to build his.

But first . . .

First he would go to Marna.

The sound of pebbles clinking against the open window drew Marna from her bed. More than three weeks had past since the dark stranger had promised never to return, but she had no doubt who it was. No one else arrived at her window seeking entrance in the middle of the night.

For a moment, she debated ignoring him. She'd asked him not to return and he'd given his promise he would not, a promise he'd clearly broken. She ought to be angry, but tonight she welcomed the intrusion. All the anguished doubts that her father's message had stirred this afternoon now threatened to suffocate her, alone here in the dark.

Another flurry of insistent little clicks echoed in the room as he tossed a second handful of pebbles at the window.

Marna slipped on her robe but didn't bother to fasten it, just clutching it against her as she crossed the room in the dark. She leaned out the open window to find him standing in the garden below her, his lean, black-garbed figure outlined against the shadowed night. She gestured for him to come in, then stepped back as he easily pulled himself over the sill and into her room.

This time he didn't speak, just stood there, his back to the window, his eyes fixed on her with an intensity that was wholly unexpected . . . and deeply disturbing. The tension vibrating within him was an almost living thing, radiating from him in waves so powerful that Marna found her own body aching in response.

''What is it?'' she demanded in a hoarse whisper, as shaken by his silence as by his presence.

He sighed, then, a long exhalation of pent-up emotion, and moved to stand in front of her, so close she could feel the heat of his body, even through the delicate fabric of her robe.

''If you could, would you go with me?'' he asked, his voice low and carefully restrained.

''Go with you?'' Her fingers tightened around the edges of her robe. His question made no sense.

''Away from here, from Diloran. To another world. To start a new life.''

''But . . . why?''

He breathed deeply at that, as though searching for the words to explain. Even in the dim light, Marna could see the tightness in his jaw and the corded tendons in his neck.

Instead of answering her question, he asked another. ''Of your own choosing, would you have come here? Here to Diloran Central? Pledged yourself to Tarl Grisaan?'' When she didn't immediately answer, he grabbed her by the upper arms and dragged her even closer. ''*Would* you?''

She should have jerked away, should have grown angry at his presumption and his violence. Instead, she said, very slowly, ''No.''

''No.'' He said it low, as a sigh more than a word.

He released her, then, but didn't step away. His hands slid up her arms, under her tumbled hair to the top of her shoulders, dragging the sleeves of her robe upward in an erotic brush of silk and heat.

Then his fingers clamped over her once more, holding her bound to him with the same urgency that vibrated in his voice. He stooped, until his head was on a level with hers, his eyes glittering black diamonds in the shadowed angles of his face.

''Would you come with me *now?* Away from here? I don't care where, just somewhere far away where we can both be free?''

Bewilderment changed to anger as the full import of his words struck her. ''I can't do that!''

''Why not?''

''Because . . . Because I *can't.*''

''Or won't?''

''What difference does it make?''

His grip on her shoulders tightened. ''It makes a great deal of difference. It makes the difference between your choosing your course in life and letting someone else choose it for you. It makes the difference between living—really *living,* Marna!—and merely enduring while someone else tells you what to do, what to think, what to say."

"It's not like that!" His words bit deeply, as sharp as a finely honed dagger driving straight to the heart.

He wasn't asking any question she hadn't already asked, saying anything she hadn't already told herself a hundred times over. But he could speak of going away, of making a new life, and she already knew that escape wasn't possible. The needs of her people and the dictates of her Elders decreed that she accept the path they'd chosen for her, regardless of where her heart led her. The Family of the Zeyn must come first.

"You said you wouldn't have come if it weren't for others," he insisted, ignoring her protest. He pulled her closer still, his eyes glittering, his passion like a live thing writhing between them. "I don't care why you were pledged to Tarl Grisaan. Political alliances, economic privileges, a blood tie to the next Controllor of Diloran—whatever the reason, it doesn't matter. What matters is that you not give in to them. Do you understand?"

Political alliances! Marna was caught between mad laughter and a choked cry of denial. She'd been sent to kill a man she scarcely knew, sent to destroy a political dynasty that had hundreds of years of history behind it, and all because her people, her Elders—her *father*—said she must. If only it were political alliances!

"No! I don't! Not in the way you mean. My people have asked this of me, and that's all that matters. Not what *I* want, but what *they* need. Can't you understand that?"

Marna stopped, then breathed deeply, struggling for control. He had drawn her so close that her hands, still clutched around the edges of her robe, were crushed between them.

It was the only barrier that divided them—and she would have removed that, if she could have moved at all.

It was insane to argue. He understood the conflicting claims of duty and desire. Whoever he was, whatever it was that drove him, he understood. Of that she was absolutely certain. He would not have come to her with his mad plan to leave Diloran otherwise.

She wished she could ask him about it. She would have given almost anything to share her own burden of doubts, but that was impossible. They had walked the same path only to arrive at very different destinations, and there would be no turning back now.

Without thinking, Marna pulled a hand free from between them, then reached up to gently trace the hollow of his cheek.

At her touch, his grip on her shoulders eased. "I understand," he said, and suddenly the tension and the anger drained out of him, like bitter wine spilling from a cup. Marna could feel it go, feel the emptiness it left behind.

He sighed and slid his hands down to knot them together behind her back, then closed his eyes and dropped his head, bringing his forehead down until he could touch hers.

Heedless of her gaping robe, Marna brought her other hand up to cup his face, letting her fingers slide over his ears to touch his neck and hair. His hair was short, slightly coarse, but his skin was soft and warm under her fingertips. She could feel the muscles in his jaw and the side of his neck tense slightly at her touch, but he made no move to stop her, or to begin an exploration of his own.

Marna tightened her hold and pushed his head back, forcing him to look at her. This close, his eyes no longer glittered. They were wide and black, and even in the dark Marna could read the doubt inside him.

He hadn't found the answers to his questions after all. His brave speech about choosing his course in life was just that. A speech. Something he said out loud to convince himself that he'd found the answer when he was simply running away from the question.

If she could, she would run with him, but she had nowhere to run to, no place she belonged except with her Family. She was Zeyn and he . . . he was whoever he was.

"Stay with me," she said, pressing her hands hard against his face so he couldn't pull free. She could feel the shock of her request jolt through him, and the desire that immediately followed.

He unknotted his hands from behind her and tried to shove her away. "I can't."

"Then stay an hour. A half hour, if that's all you have." Still she refused to release him, refused to yield to the pressure of his hands at her hips and waist.

If a half hour was all they had, she would make it enough. It wasn't love between them, nor even lust. It was need and the shared search for answers in a world that offered far more questions. Thirty minutes were not too much to ask.

When he didn't respond, she said, "You want to stay."

He groaned then, and his fingers dug into her side. "I've wanted to stay since the moment I first saw you."

Something eased inside her then, some fear she hadn't realized held her. The corner of her mouth twitched. "I threatened to shoot you."

"More than once." She could see the corner of his mouth turn upward, too. "And threatened to have my head."

This time her mouth curved upward in a full-blown smile. "Which I've achieved." Marna dragged his head downward.

He didn't resist. His mouth closed over hers as his hands slid up her back to hold her tightly against him.

He tasted of night and longing and dreams. Marna opened to him, taking as much as she gave, demanding more. She pressed her body against his, thigh and hip, belly and breast, straining to bring them closer still. Her robe slipped back and off her shoulders, leaving her bare to the tormentingly rough brush of his clothes, the heat and solid strength of him, against her skin.

She shifted her weight, letting her body lean into his, only to have him groan and push her away.

"I can't give you promises."

"I didn't ask for any. I wouldn't claim them if I could."

"I'm leaving. Do you understand?" he said, so low and fierce that Marna couldn't help wondering who he was trying to convince, her . . . or himself.

"Not yet," she said, and smiled in the dark, knowing that, at least, was true and honest. No lies between them now. No promises. Just the moment and the night and their own, aching need.

"No, not yet."

He nodded, breathed deeply, and in one deft sweep pulled her robe off and tossed it aside. Then he bent and gathered her in his arms and carried her across the room to the vast, curtained bed.

He laid her down, but remained leaning over her, his hands at each side of her shoulders, half-hidden in the spreading glory of her hair. Despite the deeper shadows within the curtained recess of the bed, Marna thought she detected a smile softening his face.

"No boots this time," he said. If they had only this brief time together, then clearly he would sweeten it with laughter, not tarnish it with tears.

She laughed. "No boots. And nothing else, either."

Still laughing, she grabbed the front of his shirt and pulled him down on top of her. He immediately shoved back, but only just enough to carry his weight on his forearms. The arc of his body pushed his hips into hers, hard against her softness, the fabric of his clothes rough against her skin.

Liquid fire coursed through her, making Marna arch against him with a low, soft cry of pleasure.

"How am I going to manage the boots if you don't let me

go?'' He asked the question wickedly, teasing her with the knowledge of her response.

''As I recall, you're not that good at managing such things by yourself.'' The words weren't quite steady, punctuated with tiny gasps of pleasure as he gently shoved against her once, twice.

Wrapping her legs around his hips so he couldn't squirm free of her, Marna reached down to tug his shirt free, then shove it slowly up his ribs. The shirt bunched in front of her hands, sliding easily over smooth skin and hard muscles until she reached his arms. He didn't move, even when she shoved hard against the backs of his arms.

He hung above her, grinning and not budging an inch. ''So what comes next?''

It might have been easier to think what came next if he had not tangled his fingers in her hair, if he were not tugging on it, playing with it as if he'd found a delightful new game to while away the time. Marna abandoned his shirt and reached to seize his wrists, but he was ahead of her.

He captured her hands without abandoning the locks of hair he'd claimed. His fingers laced with hers, sliding over and through the long strands of curls until they were bound, one to the other, in a web of silken threads.

And then he bent and claimed her mouth, and when the taste of her was mingled with the taste of him, he kissed her cheek and eyes and brow, and then her mouth again, hungrily. Marna moaned and twisted beneath him, her legs still locked around his hips, seeking freedom, reveling in her captivity.

He moved then, slowly brushing his bare chest across her breasts, from side to side, then back again. Soft curls skimmed across her nipples, teasing them to hard peaks. He deepened his kiss, demanding more and taking it even as he moved closer, so close that she could feel the small, round tips of his nipples brush against hers.

Then somehow she was past all rational thought, all care for anything but his heat and his touch and their joining.

Somehow his clothes came off, including the boots. Somehow she was freed to touch, to explore, to make her demands and to claim her reward. Marna was past knowing how it happened or why, only knowing that it *was.*

There in the dark he was all fire and hunger. His touch, his scent, the sheer male power of him, consumed her, rousing a hungry fire deep inside her that answered to the fire in him, and cried for more. More of his touch, more of the hard, hot feel of him against her, more of the need within him that fed the need in her. It was all fuel for the flames that licked across her body, consuming her every nerve and muscle and bone in the spreading heat.

She needed this. Needed *him.* Now.

And he needed her.

She could feel it, feel the aching emptiness inside him that her touch had filled, feel the need that flared within him as hot as the hunger that drove him.

He was a man of shadows. He came to her out of the dark and he left her, always, in the black, velvet silence of her room. Alone. Wondering.

But he would not leave her now. Not just yet. Not because he had not yet taken what he wanted, but because he *could* not leave her and did not want to.

And that would have to be enough.

He left her in the great bed, alone with the shadows and the storm-tossed sheets and the silence. His body felt heavy, sated, yet still he ached for more of her. His face still burned where, afterward, she had delicately traced each line and curve and hollow, letting her fingers see in the dark what her eyes could not.

That subtle exploration had shaken him more than he cared to admit. He'd instantly known it for what it was, an offering to memory . . . and a farewell. Marna already knew what he lacked the courage to tell her.

He would not visit her again. Not like this. He wasn't strong enough or brave enough to touch that kind of passion and not want to claim it for forever.

She hadn't said a word, not even when he'd drawn away from her, gathered his clothes, and fled.

There was still the meeting of the Tevah ahead of him, and he was already late.

As Tarl slipped through the gardens and out into the night-shrouded streets of Diloran Central, he forced away the memory of Marna and tried to keep alert for any sign of an Internal Security patrol among the dwindling flow of traffic.

Yet even as he maintained a wary eye for possible pursuit, Tarl found himself studying the city around him, noting the trick of lighting on a building, or the cool drift of the night air, or the way a solitary resident, shoulders hunched against the darkness, hurried down the other side of the street, intent on reaching home and his bed.

Simple, ordinary things. Things he would soon be leaving behind forever, because once he left Diloran, there would be no coming back.

The thought made Tarl falter, just for an instant. Then anger rose to his defense. If he could leave Joeffrey and the life of power and wealth that was his for the taking, if he could leave Marna—

Marna!

Tarl stopped dead in his tracks, heedless of possible observers.

He would never see Marna again.

The thought hit him with all the force of a laser blast.

He'd known it. Known it when he'd entered her room tonight. Known it when he'd taken her in his arms and let the fire within her burn away the anger and pain in him. Known it when he'd left her without a word of farewell, there in the shadowed, secret bed amid the tumbled sheets.

Yet knowing was, somehow, not the same as understanding. He felt like a child who knew he might be hurt if he jumped out of a tree, but hadn't understood just how long the drop and how painful the landing could be until he actually jumped.

For the first time, there in the silent streets, Tarl understood what it was to jump. Worse, he had the awful feeling that he was still a long way from landing, and that the landing, when it finally came, was going to be far more painful than he'd ever imagined.

Dazed, he shrank back into the shadows of a building's entryway. He felt as if the wind were rushing past his ears with the speed of his fall, as if he were twisting in mid-air, madly trying to stop, yet all the while knowing it was far too late to try. He slumped against the cold, hard wall at the back of the entrance, grateful for its solidity.

How many nights, now, had he dreamed of slipping into Marna's room to whisper foolish stories and talk of silly things? Just for the pleasure of listening to her, there in the dark? So he could be with her, even if only for a few moments?

How many days had he spent watching her, talking with her, longing to put aside a charade that had long ago ceased to be an amusing game and had become a galling burden?

All that time he'd known he would be leaving, but he'd always thought in terms of escaping, never in terms of what he might be leaving behind.

Now that he'd thought of it, nothing seemed quite as simple as it had been. Absolutely nothing.

Tarl had no idea how long he remained in the shadowed sanctuary of the building entrance, desperately trying to regain his balance. A minute or an hour, it didn't matter. By the time his heart had stopped its mad pounding, he knew he couldn't face the meeting of the Tevah. Not just yet, anyway.

In the space of a few hours he'd gone from doubt to certainty to even more unsettling doubt, and he didn't know how to sort it out. He only knew he couldn't do it here.

With an effort of will, Tarl forced himself to stop thinking and feeling and to concentrate on listening and seeing. He had to get back to the palace and his personal quarters. Now.

He crept to the edge of the shadowed entryway and peered out. Nothing. The streets seemed inordinately still. In the dark, the graceful buildings around him were transformed into silent, watching creatures, spying on his every move.

Tarl shook his head, trying to shake off the fanciful notion. He wished, suddenly, that he'd accepted the escort Joeffrey had often suggested he take with him. He would have liked some company right now.

Too late for that. He would have to get back to the palace grounds and to his quarters on his own. How hard could that be, after all? He'd done it numberless times already, and always without incident. Despite his present emotional confusion, he could do it again now.

He was almost over the wall and back into the garden when the Internal Security patrol shot him.

Chapter Thirteen

Even on the best of days, Marna found it difficult to endure the official functions that so often fell to her lot as Tarl's pledged companion. Today, the hours spent in morning meetings and a formal luncheon for visiting dignitaries dragged unbearably.

She desperately needed time to be alone, time to think and to untangle the increasingly knotted threads of her life, but she didn't know how to ask for it. In the caverns, there would have been no need to explain. Here, all she could do was wait until the demands of protocol freed her for a little while. Until then, her thoughts spun endlessly in a dizzying circle that made her head ache.

Yesterday, in the garden with Tarl, she'd found the emotional barriers she'd erected with such care crumbling away, leaving her unprotected. She'd felt so lost and he had been so very, very kind.

Marna remembered with stunning clarity the warmth of

his hands against her skin, the heat and solidity of his back when she'd leaned on him, the power of his shoulders when she'd clung to him to keep from falling. He'd been so close, and she'd wanted him to come closer still.

Yet even as she explored these decadent new pleasures he offered her, Marna had been achingly aware of Tarl watching her, of his *wanting* her. The knowledge that he desired her had been as unsettling as it was stirring.

What kind of man was he, that he could so easily give her the gift of laughter and, for those few brief, precious moments, the gift of forgetting everything except the present?

What kind of woman was she, to want to destroy him?

She'd thrown the sand that bore her father's message out the window of her room, but Marna hadn't been able to toss out her own responsibility, or the remembrance of her sworn promise, with such ease.

One week. That was all she had. One week to eliminate Tarl Grisaan and his uncle—or to find some other solution that destroyed the Grisaans' power over the Zeyn. But what? And how? And even if she could discover that unknown solution, was she justified in following it, knowing that she had already sworn herself to the task the Elders had given her?

The anguished, unanswerable questions had chased each other through her thoughts all during the dinner last night and might have continued tormenting her long afterward if it hadn't been for the return of her dark stranger.

She couldn't call him Toff. The name was too absurd, too childish for a man who could so easily set her blood afire. The tips of her fingers tingled still with the remembered curves of his cheek and brow and chin, the soft heat at his temple and the roughness of the faint beard beneath his skin. She had never seen him clearly, scarcely ever heard him speak above a rough, intense whisper, yet her body could recall his in exquisite, aching detail, the hard heat of him and the hungry, tormented need that had driven him to her bed in the first place.

Deeper than the ache and far more troublesome was the unfamiliar longing he'd stirred within her. Not for sex, though Sands knew she ached to feel his body on hers once more, but for closeness with another human being with whom she could share some, at least, of her doubts and fears and overwhelming uncertainties.

Sesha couldn't take that place, no matter how long they'd been together. Between them lay a gulf created by their society and the long years of the older woman's service. There was no such gulf dividing her and the stranger. He understood her dilemma—had understood it from the first, regardless of whether he knew the details or not.

Yet even though he understood her, his presence, his words, and his tantalizing kisses had made what was already confusing even more complex, until there seemed no way of knowing what she ought to do, or why.

When the interminable luncheon eventually ground to a halt, Marna was finally free to seek the privacy and the silence of her own quarters. Using the less-traveled corridors as much as possible, she worked her way through the labyrinth of the Government Palace, keeping her head down so she wouldn't be forced to greet anyone who might delay her, taking care to lift the long skirts of her robe out of the way of her hurrying feet so she wouldn't trip. Her steps echoed with a hard, hollow sound that seemed to chase her through the twisting passageways, mocking her with their emptiness.

She turned and headed down a long flight of steps, her fingers skimming the shaped plascrete rail at the side. Beyond lay the guarded passage that connected the palace with the guest quarters. The guards knew her so well, they smiled at her when she passed, but Marna only nodded in return, too intent on reaching the sanctuary of her rooms to stop.

To Marna's dismay, Sesha was waiting for her, seated in one of two uncomfortable chairs set at the side of the room farthest from the windows. She sat rigidly erect, her feet together, her hands in her lap. Her dark, weather-beaten face appeared carved from the rocks that had crippled her, while her eyes, deep sunk in their sockets, seemed to be focused on something far beyond the confines of the room.

"Sesha?" Marna asked, crossing the room quickly, suddenly anxious. In all the years they'd been together, she'd never seen the kind of strain in her serving woman's face that she saw now. "Is anything wrong? Can I help?"

Sesha blinked, then stirred slightly on her chair and looked up at Marna. "Kiria Marna."

"Yes. Are you all right?"

"I wanted . . ." The words seemed to catch in the older woman's throat, as though they were too big to get out. Sesha swallowed hard and tried again. "I wanted to talk to you, Kiria. If I may."

"Of course you may. You know that." Marna stifled a small surge of resentment, ashamed that she should begrudge Sesha her time when the older woman had asked so little of her over the years. "Tell me what you need."

Sesha started to speak, but bit her lip instead and slid her hand into a pocket of her robe to pull out a small, folded piece of heavy paper.

"I received this a little while ago, Kiria." She made no effort to hand Marna the piece of paper, just sat staring down at it as she turned it over and over between her fingers.

Worried now, Marna sank into the chair opposite without ever taking her eyes off the older woman. "What does it say? Who is it from?"

"It's from a doctor. A doctor named Borsen Prale." The words came slowly, hesitantly, as if Sesha still wasn't sure of their meaning, or doubted their truth. ''He says Kiri Tarl spoke with him last night. About me. About my leg. He says—'' Sesha stopped and looked up at Marna. ''He says there may be a small chance they can heal my leg. He says there are new treatments, new techniques . . .'' Sesha let her words trail away, too overwhelmed by their implications to go on.

''They can help you? Make you walk normally again?'' Marna could feel her eyes going wide at the thought. ''But Sesha, that's *wonderful!* When can he see you? What do you have to do? What else does he say?''

With great care, Sesha refolded the paper and returned it to her pocket. ''He says he will give me a date to meet with him and take some of the necessary tests.'' Without looking at Marna, she licked her lips nervously, took a deep breath, and added, ''I don't know if I will go.''

Marna jerked upright at that. ''Don't know—But why? Why wouldn't you want to see him?''

Sudden anger broke through the emotions that had held Sesha frozen and brought fire into her eyes. ''Why? Because I don't need anyone's help. Do I not fulfill my duties? Do I not work as hard as anyone else in the caverns? Just because I am crippled doesn't mean I need anyone's pity! I never have, any more than I needed anyone's help when I hunted the desert cats alone in the sands and among the rocks. I—''

The torrent of words stopped as quickly as it had begun. The fire in Sesha's eyes sputtered, then died, and she drooped in her chair, as uncertain and afraid as she had been earlier.

''I am afraid, Kiria,'' she said at last with painful honesty, her voice cracking with emotion. ''All these years . . . trying to accept that I'm not the woman I once was, that I'm a servant and nothing more. That I have no rights and am of little value to my people. It has been hard—so hard!—but I have learned because there was nothing else

I could do and nowhere else I could go."

The courage that had sustained Sesha for so long came to her aid once more. She straightened and turned to face Marna squarely, eyes bright with the tears she would not permit herself to shed. "I am afraid to hope, Kiria, because I am afraid they will tell me there is nothing they can do. It will be so much worse to have had a moment of hope and then . . . to lose it . . . forever."

Marna sat still and silent, not knowing what to say or do. The anguish and the uncertainty that vibrated in every one of Sesha's words were almost more than she could bear. All these years and she'd never known, never even guessed that Sesha felt like this. Until she'd come here, she'd never thought about the matter at all. Sesha was her maid, her friend, almost her mother, but she was also a cripple and that, among the Zeyn, overruled every other consideration.

When the silence finally became unbearable, Marna said with difficulty, "You must do whatever you think best. It's your choice, Sesha, not mine, but . . ." She hesitated, wondering if she was making things better, or worse, then continued, "But what if they *could* help you? What if they *could* heal your leg?"

Sesha looked at her, and the look was like a physical blow, for in it Marna read an angry scorn she'd never seen before. Just as she'd never seen the pain, she thought with shame, reeling under the impact.

"What if they could, Kiria?" Sesha demanded. "I can't be a hunter again. I'm too old. The Elders would not even let me be a teacher to the young because it's been too long since I last hunted." She stopped abruptly and her lips twisted in a bitter grimace. When she spoke again, her voice was lower, tight with an anger that had spent half a lifetime festering. "Once, I might have been a teacher, but that was over twenty years ago, when I was first injured. They wouldn't permit it, though. I was a cripple, after all."

Each word stung, like stones thrown with the intent to hurt, but Marna didn't try to dodge them. It wasn't really she Sesha was aiming at, anyway.

"I have seen Kiri Baland," Sesha added, a little less vehemently, but no less directly. "They tell me he is a very wise and powerful man, yet he cannot stand straight nor walk very far without the aid of a cane."

She didn't look at Marna, but sat staring at something only she could see on the far side of the room. Her heavy bosom rose as she took a deep breath, then fell slowly as she let the air out through her nose in a soft, sighing sound of release. For a moment, silence held them in its grip; then Sesha added, very low, "Every time I see him, I wonder what I might have been allowed to become if I had not been born a Zeyn."

Marna didn't say anything when Sesha rose to her feet. She just sat, stunned, and watched while the older woman made her way to the door, dragging her crippled leg behind her.

Even long after Sesha was gone, Marna could have sworn her last words were still echoing in the room.

She had to talk to Tarl.

After what seemed like hours sitting alone in her room, too stunned by Sesha's revelations to deal with either her own problems or her maid's, Marna knew she needed someone else's perspective. Who better to ask than Tarl, the man who had precipitated the situation in the first place?

To Marna's surprise, the attendant outside Tarl's quarters refused to announce her, even though he conceded that Tarl was in.

"He said he was busy, Kiria, and didn't want to be disturbed."

"But this is important!"

"He said I wasn't to let even the Controllor-Regent in, Kiria. Something about some reports he had to review."

For an instant, Marna had a vivid mental image of the heaped piles of official documents that had buried the table in Tarl's quarters the first—and only—time she'd visited him. She'd long ago decided that Tarl had deliberately started the avalanche of paper, though she still wasn't sure why. Not that it mattered. Right now she didn't care whether he truly had work to do or was using his untidy collection of "documents" as an excuse to hide from her and anyone else who wanted to disturb him. She wanted to see him and see him she would.

"Open the door," she said.

"But, Kiria—"

"Kiri Grisaan will want to see me," Marna said firmly. "After all, I am not the Controllor-Regent. I am his pledged companion. That is a very different thing." She wasn't sure if it was her words or the threatening look she gave the attendant, but something worked.

With a nervous grimace, he opened the door for her. That was as far as he was willing to go. He made no effort to announce her and swung the door firmly shut behind her the minute she was through.

The outer, public chamber, which was as far as Marna had been the first time, was empty. The documents she'd last seen heaped in untidy profusion on the floor were once again stacked on the table, albeit in not much better order. Tarl's heavy chair stood near the table, a bound document open but upside down on its seat. The remaining chairs in the room were pushed back against the walls and looked as if they were never used.

Perhaps they weren't, Marna thought in surprise. She'd never considered it before, but she couldn't remember ever seeing Tarl with anyone except, perhaps, Joeffrey Baland, whom she would have thought a friend. He was often surrounded by people—his position as heir to the controllorship guaranteed that—but he never seemed to be *with* anyone. As though he were just as much a stranger here as she was.

The thought was as unsettling as his touch had been yesterday.

Marna hesitated, uncertain. Perhaps she shouldn't have insisted on entering. What could he tell her, after all, that wouldn't be better coming from the physician himself? And considering her purpose in being pledged to him, there was no honor in accepting his favors, even on Sesha's behalf.

She turned to leave, but stopped just as suddenly, stung by the memory of Sesha's revelations. All these years together, yet never once had she realized just how much her servant—her *friend*—had suffered for her injury. Didn't she owe it to Sesha to do whatever she could to help? Or was there some other way to obtain medical help for Sesha without relying on Tarl, or anyone else?

Should she go? Or stay?

Marna nervously shifted her weight from one foot to the other, but made no move toward the two doors that stood half open on one side of the room.

Perhaps Tarl wasn't really here, after all. He could have slipped out through some other entrance without informing the attendant at the door. Or he might be sleeping. Late afternoon seemed an odd time of day for that, but it was always a possibility. Then again, he might actually be working and would resent her intruding against his specific orders. She could return some other time and—

Coward! she scolded herself. You're afraid to ask for fear you'll find his generosity as large as it seems. And then what will you do? Accept, and face the dishonor of killing him later? Refuse, and deny Sesha the chance to be whole again?

No answer came to her out of the silence. She hadn't expected any. Willing herself into motion, Marna crossed to the half-open door closest to the wall of windows that looked out on a section of the palace gardens and the public buildings beyond. After only a heartbeat's hesitation, she pushed the door farther open and stepped through.

No one. The room was empty.

Most of the space was taken up by a pool, whose blue-green waters were as still and flat as glass. It seemed an odd place to have a pool, for there were only a few potted plants in the corners, certainly not enough to call it a garden. The floor around the pool itself was of rough stone, but that of the open area on the far side of the room was covered with thick exercise mats that glowed a soft green in the sunlight pouring in from the floor-to-ceiling windows lining the room on two sides. Except for the pool, the mats, and the few plants, the room was empty. Tarl wasn't here, at least.

A wide archway set in the wall to her right showed a glimpse of another room beyond with its own wall of windows, but nothing more. As the heir, Tarl had been given a corner suite that could have housed several dozen of her own people with comfort and room to spare.

Skirting the pool, Marna crossed to the archway. The room beyond was larger than the public chamber, but a good part of its space was taken up by a vast platform bed whose covers, even at this late hour of the day, were as disordered as if the bed's occupant had only recently risen from it. A bright blue robe Marna recognized as the one he'd worn to dinner the night before had been flung haphazardly across a corner of the bed with half of it left to trail on the floor.

A massive chair in a far corner was turned, back to her, facing the gardens visible through the windows. A dressing table stood against one wall, its surface covered with an untidy jumble of vials and bottles and boxes. Another two robes were draped over a nearby chair with no more care than if they'd been rags. Clearly, Tarl Grisaan didn't set much store on keeping his possessions in any sensible order.

An open door near the table undoubtedly led to a dressing room, while the larger, half-open door nearest her led back to the public chamber. A quick glance showed that the dressing room and bath were as empty as the rest of the suite.

Marna couldn't help a small sigh of relief that she wouldn't have to confront Tarl just yet, even though she knew the delay wouldn't make things any easier. She turned to leave, then stopped at the sight of the heavy chair in the corner.

Its solid base and broad wings could easily conceal a man behind them, but surely Tarl would have spoken by now if he were there. Even if he'd fallen asleep sitting up, he would have roused at the swish and sweep of the hem of her robe across the thick carpet. She hadn't made any attempt to keep quiet.

Marna was halfway to the door to the public chamber when she stopped. She had to check the chair. She suddenly knew she couldn't leave until she had, though she wasn't sure why. Her stomach tightened uncomfortably with a return of nervousness, but she ignored the physical sensation, just as she ignored the doubts behind it.

Not until she stood at the side of the big chair could she see Tarl slumped in its depths. He was tilted to one side, his chin on his breast, his head propped at an awkward angle by the wing of the chair. His eyes were shut and his lips parted slightly, as if the muscular effort required to keep them closed was too much for his unconscious body to manage. His skin, normally pale, had taken on a faint but unmistakable gray cast that spoke of pain and exhaustion. The dark shadow of a day's growth of beard made the already disturbing color of his skin even more worrisome.

His hands lay in his lap, palms up, his long fingers slightly curled, like a child's in sleep. He wore a deep green robe, loosely sashed at his waist, that gaped open at the top to expose his throat and some of the curly, light brown hair covering his chest, then fell open again where his knee bent, exposing a slim, yet strongly muscled lower leg, a trim ankle, and a slender, well-shaped foot bare of covering.

Despite the disconcerting color of his skin, Tarl seemed oddly changed, the lines of his face and body somehow harder and far more masculine—strangely familiar, yet undeniably different from what she remembered. It took a moment for Marna to realize that she'd never before seen him without a wig. The wild black curls he'd been wearing for the past week lay on the floor near his feet looking like some sort of dead, furry animal, limp and abandoned.

His own hair was dark brown, cut just above the ears, matted with damp and the pressure of the wig. Without thinking, Marna reached to brush away some of the strands plastered along his temple, but instantly drew back at the clammy cold of his skin.

Was he dead?

The thought made her breath catch in her chest and her legs grow suddenly weak. A cry of protest rose in her throat, but she choked it down by ramming her fist against her mouth and biting down hard on a knuckle. She didn't want the attendant in the corridor to come bursting in right now.

Or did she?

The thought stopped her. Did she? If Tarl really was dead, then part of the task the Elders had given her was completed. It wouldn't matter if it had been her hand or another's that had accomplished the deed. Tarl would be eliminated and only Marott Grisaan would be left for her to deal with.

Relief surged through her, immediately followed by black disgust. Had she come to this, then? That she could be glad of a man's death so long as she didn't have to face her own guilty intentions?

Eyes wide, she studied Tarl, searching for some sign that he was alive. She could see no rise and fall of his chest, but the heavy dressing robe he wore might disguise that. He hadn't moved. His face seemed even paler, the flesh more hollowed out beneath his eyes and the strong, fine curve of his cheek bones, but that might be her imagination and nothing more. She could see no hint of what it was that made him so still and gray and cold.

He didn't look alive, but what if he wasn't dead?

She'd been taught a hundred ways to kill a man, all of them as acts of self-defense. Any one of those ways would be more than adequate for murder. What someone else had begun, she could easily finish here, and who would say that Tarl Grisaan wasn't dead before she'd forced her way in against the attendant's protests?

Marna bit down on her knuckle, hard enough to draw blood. She wanted to shut her eyes, but she forced herself to stare into Tarl's pale face instead. If she was to be his murderer, she would somehow have to find the courage to confront the act *and* her victim.

When she'd sworn to destroy Tarl, Marna had thought him the enemy, the inheritor of an oppressive rule that had forced years of suffering on her people. Now, Marna knew better. Marott Grisaan had earned her people's enmity, but this man had not.

Marna blinked, suddenly fighting back hot tears of shame.

Today Tarl had offered Sesha a chance at a life her own people had denied her for over twenty years. He'd asked no thanks and demanded no return for his efforts. She had forced her way into his quarters because of it, and now she found herself contemplating a despicable, cowardly act of murder instead.

With a sharp exclamation compounded of self-loathing and regret, Marna dropped to her knees beside the chair and wrapped her fingers around Tarl's wrist, desperately groping for a pulse. At first, she could feel nothing but the coldness of his skin and the hard framework of the bones beneath. When her probing fingers eventually found the faint but steady beat she sought, the breath she didn't realize she'd been holding burst from her in an explosive gasp.

Alive, then.

Relief washed through her, scalding in its intensity. Her hold on his wrist tightened, and Marna had to grip the arm of the chair to steady herself.

Tarl was alive, and he would remain so if she had any say in the matter. With relief had come the unnerving certainty that she would never carry out the task the Elders had given her, despite her sworn promises. She would give her life to help her people, but she could not commit murder. Not now, and not in the future.

Tarl groaned suddenly and shifted in the chair. Guiltily aware that she had wasted precious minutes in indecision, Marna released his wrist and rose to her feet. She had to get help. She hadn't the slightest idea who or how, but the attendant outside would know.

Before she could take a step, Tarl's right hand wrapped around her arm. A sound that was almost a snarl burst from his lips as he pulled her down across the arm of the chair until she was half kneeling beside him, half lying across his lap. "What do you think you're—Marna!"

He was panting with effort, awkwardly twisted in the chair so his left side and arm were protected while his right had full freedom of movement. His eyes were wild and flashing fire, but as it dawned on him who he held, his eyes widened further and the fire in them flickered, then died altogether.

When Marna pulled her arm away, he released her without protest and sank back into the chair. "How did you get in here?" he demanded weakly. "I told—"

"I made him let me in," Marna replied. She pressed the back of her hand to his brow. His skin was still far too cold and clammy. With a worried frown, she once more knelt beside the chair.

"What happened to you?" she demanded. "I thought . . ." She bit her lip abruptly, remembering exactly what she'd thought.

When he simply sat there, looking at her with a dazed expression on his face without saying anything, she added, "I thought you were dead." That much, at least, was true.

Tarl tried to laugh, but the laugh immediately turned into a sharp gasp, then a low groan. With an effort, he shifted his position in the chair. Even that slight movement left him panting and paler than ever.

"Fever," he said, clearly unwilling to waste his remaining strength on too many words.

"Fever! You're suffering from shock, not fever."

"Daiphan fever. Comes in bouts every now and then. Always leaves me shaky."

"Well, you should have asked for help," Marna said firmly. "I was just going to call the attendant. He'll know whom to summon if you won't tell me." She rose to her feet, but Tarl once more grabbed her arm to stop her.

"No! I'm fine. Really."

The fact that he had to stop for a moment to regain his breath before adding, "I just need to rest," indicated clearly that Tarl was very far from being as fine as he claimed.

Marna hesitated, uncertain. She didn't for a minute believe he was "fine," but Tarl Grisaan was no fool, no matter how hard he'd worked to convince everyone otherwise. He had to have a very good reason not to call for help, even if she didn't know what it was.

"Tell me whom to call, then," she said firmly. "I don't know anything about Daiphan fever, or whatever it is that's bothering you, but I do know you need help. If you won't tell me who to get, I'll . . . I'll call that Borsen Pale."

"Prale."

"Whatever. I'll call him."

To Marna's surprise, he smiled at that, an odd, slightly lopsided little smile that was strangely appealing.

"You'd do that, wouldn't you?" he said, clearly amused by her determination.

Her hand clamped over his where it wrapped around her arm. His skin was still cold and she could feel a slight tremor in his fingers, as if he found the effort of holding her too much for his limited strength. "Do you really think you can stop me?" she asked, carefully freeing herself from his grip.

He let his hand fall back in his lap with a soft sigh of resignation. "Not right now, no."

"Then whom do you want me to call," Marna insisted. Tarl might be sitting up and talking, but she didn't like the deepening gray cast of his skin or the trembling in his hand. He was clearly suffering from shock, but she could only guess at what had caused it.

Guilt stabbed at her. If she'd gone for help when she'd first found him, rather than debating the merits of murder or leaving him to die unattended, help would have been here long ago.

"I'll call whomever you want," she said then, more gently. "But I *will* call someone. I'm no healer, but we both know you need help."

Tarl closed his eyes and leaned his head against the seat back, as if he were suddenly too tired to argue. "Call Joeffrey," he said. "He'll know what to do."

Marna didn't bother answering. She was already on her way out the door. The attendant outside would be able to track Joeffrey down through the palace's complex communications system far better than she could.

She couldn't have been gone more than a couple of minutes, but by the time Marna got back to Tarl, his shallow breathing and the fragile, bruised look about his eyes and mouth told her he was weaker. She leaned down to gently take his hand in hers. His eyes opened at her touch, but he had trouble focusing at first and he squinted slightly, as though he wasn't really sure she was there. The usual brown of the irises seemed to have paled into a muddy color tinged with the same gray that discolored his skin.

Pushing down the fear that suddenly assailed, her, Marna bent over him and said as encouragingly as she could, "Come on, Tarl. Help me get you in bed. You need to get warm. Lie down and rest."

He frowned at that, as if searching his memory for some forgotten bit of information. "Where's Joeffrey?"

"He's coming. But in the meantime . . ."

With a great deal of urging and support from her, Tarl got to his feet, then stood swaying and peering about him like a drunken man staggering from a tavern, uncertain what came next. The heavy dressing robe seemed to hang on his frame, burying him in its folds.

"All right now," Marna said, slipping his right arm over her shoulders and wrapping her arm around his waist. "It's just a little way. Just over to the bed."

Tarl frowned, but he was too dazed to object. At her command, he obediently took a shambling step forward.

Either he was far weaker than she thought, or he was dizzy from the effort of standing. At the very first step, his leg crumpled beneath him and he pitched forward.

Marna swung around, trying to prop his body with hers, but he weighed more than she did. As she flung out her free hand in an effort to prop him up, she hit his left shoulder, far harder than she'd intended. The instant she touched him, Tarl cried out in sudden pain and collapsed on top of her, completely unconscious.

It took an effort to shove Tarl's limp body off her, and though Marna tried not to be rough, he groaned as she rolled him over onto his back. As he rolled, the heavy fabric of his robe caught under him, so that the front pulled open to expose what he had been at such pains to hide from her.

Marna gasped and swallowed hard, staring at the crude, blood-soaked bandage Tarl had bound over his left shoulder and around his ribs. She'd seen blood before, but she couldn't remember ever seeing quite this much of it. Tarl's shoulder, chest, and upper arm were stained red, and rivulets of blood had traced ugly scarlet tracks down across his ribs and side until they disappeared beneath his robe. She couldn't tell how bad his wounds were or what had made them, but Marna had enough emergency training to know that the blood loss alone was enough put Tarl's life at risk.

Someone, it seemed, had tried to kill the heir to the Controllorship of Diloran.

Chapter Fourteen

Tarl moaned at her gentle probing of his bandages, but didn't regain consciousness. Before he could come around, Marna grabbed his robe by the back of the collar, dragged him across the room, and heaved him onto the bed. Grimacing at the incredibly bad joke that had thrust her into this position of trying to save a man she'd sworn to kill, she checked to make sure her rough handling had caused no more damage to his shoulder, then quickly tucked the bedcovers around him for warmth.

A quick search of Tarl's quarters yielded a basin, some soft cloths, and the remains of the robe Tarl had ripped up to make the first inadequate bandage. Marna could feel her heart thudding painfully in her chest as she filled the basin with warm water, then deposited basin, cloths, and more strips of the mutilated robe on the small table she'd pulled up beside the bed.

She'd had no more than the basic emergency training that

all Zeyn received before they were allowed to venture into the desert, but she couldn't afford to wait for Joeffrey. She seriously doubted that he had any more skill as a healer than she did, anyway, and Tarl might well bleed to death before Joeffrey could find a proper healer who could be trusted.

Marna pulled out the knife she always carried under her robes; then, with a deep breath to still her trembling, she sliced through the wad of blood-matted bandages. The wound itself, an ugly tear across Tarl's chest and over his shoulder, didn't look life-threatening, so far as she could tell. The bleeding from the ragged edges of flesh was another matter entirely.

At least he hadn't been hit by a charge from an energy rifle. The burns left by that weapon might well have been fatal.

Marna made no effort to clean the wound, but simply packed folded strips of cloth over it as tightly as she could, then bound them firmly in place with the longest strips, which she wound over his shoulder and around his chest. She made sure to pin his left arm against his side in the process so he couldn't tear the wound open again by any sudden movement.

As she tied the last knot, Marna glanced at Tarl's face. He hadn't stirred and had moaned only twice throughout the whole process. His head was slumped to the side, and his skin looked waxen against the fine white pillow covering.

His stillness frightened her, but there was nothing more she could do for now except keep him warm and wait for help. Marna doubled over the heavy bed covering for added warmth—given the size of the bed it covered, that wasn't difficult—and carefully tucked it in around him. Then she went in search of more blankets.

By the time she found something that would serve her purpose, Joeffrey Baland had arrived. At least, she hoped he was the one stumping slowly across the outer chamber. She hastily spread the long, heavy cape she'd found over Tarl, then crossed to the door leading to the room beyond.

Joeffrey Baland reached the door first, but stopped dead at the sight of her. "Kiria Marna!"

He appeared incapable of saying anything more. His bright, hooded eyes were glued to the even brighter red splotches on her sleeves and across the front of her gown. His mouth dropped open, but before Marna could say anything, his gaze shot to the bed behind her. "Tarl!"

There had been shocked surprise in his voice when he spoke her name; there was unmistakable fear when he spoke Tarl's.

A sound like that made by a wounded animal emerged from deep in his throat. Before Marna could stop him, Joeffrey pushed past her and hobbled across the room as fast as his crippled body would let him. When he reached the bed, he halted abruptly and leaned forward, both hands wrapped around the head of his cane as if he were afraid of falling without its support. His eyes fixed on Tarl's pale, still face, but he said not one word.

If love and sheer force of will could have cured his wound, Marna thought, Tarl would have thrown back the covers and bounced out of bed right then.

Though Joeffrey Baland had never given her any reason to like him during the past three weeks, Marna felt her heart twist at the old man's obvious anguish.

She touched his shoulder, heedless of the ugly hump on his back, and said gently, "He's been shot, but he's alive, Kiri Baland."

"Who—" The old man choked on the words and his hands clenched tighter on the cane. She could see the movement of the muscles in his throat as he swallowed with difficulty, then tried again. "What happened?"

"I don't know. He didn't tell me. He just said I should

call you.'' She hesitated before adding, ''He wouldn't let me call anyone else.''

Joeffrey turned his misshapen head at that, but he seemed to look through her, rather than at her.

''I've changed the bandages and covered him to keep him warm,'' she said. ''The wound isn't too bad, but he's lost a lot of blood. I suggested calling a doctor he'd dealt with, a Borsen Prale, but he refused.''

At the name of the doctor Tarl had recommended for Sesha, Joeffrey shook his head. ''Good doctor. Wrong man.'' He turned back to stare at Tarl, then added in a low, tense voice, as if he were speaking to himself, ''No one here right now. No one we can trust, at any rate. If only . . .'' He thumped his cane on the floor suddenly, clearly frustrated and afraid.

His fear only made Marna's worse. ''Surely there's some doctor here—''

He turned on her angrily. ''No one! No one who can know of this. It's too risky. For Tarl *and* for—'' Joeffrey stopped abruptly, then added more calmly, ''Some of them would let him die because his uncle would tell them to. The rest . . .'' He shrugged.

Marna almost burst into hysterical laughter. She stopped herself only just in time by hugging her arms across her chest and biting down on her already abused knuckle. What horrible irony if Tarl should die now, and all because the only person he'd let her call was afraid to act on his behalf!

''I thought you were his friend,'' she said sharply.

''I am. Too much a friend to give Marott Grisaan the chance to kill him.''

Something of Marna's shock must have shown on her face, for he added, ''Tarl's uncle has been looking for the opportunity to get rid of him ever since I brought him back to Diloran. Nothing would suit Marott's purposes better than to make a show of providing the best medical care possible while letting Tarl die.'' He snorted in disgust. ''He'd probably even take advantage of the situation to blame Tarl's murder on a few of his enemies, which would give him the perfect excuse to get rid of them, too.''

There was nothing Marna could say in response to that. The old man was right and she knew it, even if she understood none of the political complexities behind it all. She'd seen enough of Marott Grisaan during the past three weeks to know he wouldn't readily relinquish the controllorship of Diloran. If the legal heir was dead, he wouldn't have to.

How much easier her life might have been if her father and the Elders had realized just how much plotting went on behind the carefully maintained facade of Diloran government! If they'd known more, they might have left their assassination plots to others.

Without a word of apology, Marna shoved past Joeffrey as abruptly as he'd shoved past her earlier, then bent over Tarl. He didn't stir when she gently laid the back of her hand against his forehead and along the side of his face. Again she had that odd, fleeting sense of familiarity, but she squelched it ruthlessly. Now was not the time to rummage through her memories trying to track down the vague feeling that she'd known him somewhere before.

Tarl's skin seemed marginally warmer and a fraction less pallid than it had been earlier, but that could easily be her imagination. She pulled back the covers and checked his bandages. There was no hint of blood yet, but that didn't mean the bleeding had stopped, and removing the bandages now to check could only make things worse.

With a tenderness that was, she realized, the best she could offer as an apology for ever having contemplated doing him harm, Marna tucked the covers back up around Tarl's chin and turned to confront Joeffrey, who had remained where he was, quiet, but tense, awaiting her judgment.

''Well?'' she demanded coldly, meeting his questioning

gaze. "What are we to do? Don't you know of *anyone* who might help?"

His eyes dropped first. "My personal servant is waiting outside. He can get the medicines and bandages you need, then track down someone we can trust who knows about"—Joeffrey's gaze flicked toward Tarl, then back to the carpet he was studying so diligently—"about such things."

The decisive, demanding Joeffrey Baland Marna had so far encountered was gone, leaving in his place a badly frightened old man whose decisions would clearly be dictated by political necessity as much as by his concern for Tarl. That left her with all the responsibility.

Marna inwardly winced at the thought. It wasn't a charge she could refuse, no matter how little she liked it. She owed at least that much to the man she had intended to murder.

"I'll write him a list of things, then," she said. "You'll tell him what to do? Send him after help?"

Joeffrey nodded, suddenly wary, but Marna decided to ignore that. They had no time for mutual mistrust. She tore a page off one of the documents piled on the table in the outer room and on the back wrote a list of items she needed, including a request for whatever medicines were appropriate to deal with infection, blood loss, fever, and anything else she was afraid she might encounter.

While Joeffrey gave his instructions to his servant in the public chamber, Marna paced at the foot of Tarl's vast bed, trying hard not to glance at the still unconscious man half-buried under the pile of covers and the heavy cape she'd heaped over him.

When Joeffrey returned, he briefly bent to touch his hand to Tarl's forehead, as though anxious to reassure himself that his former pupil was still alive; then he sank without a word into the chair Marna drew up beside the bed for him. A few minutes later he was slumped forward, his forehead propped on his hands where they clutched his cane, as though his worries for Tarl pressed down on him as unbearably as the heavy hump on his back.

Joeffrey's servant returned in a little over a half an hour, though it seemed far longer to Marna. As instructed, he'd bundled everything into a nondescript bag and, on his own initiative, had brought a basket of food and wine, as well. Unfortunately, he also brought word that Marott Grisaan had demanded Joeffrey's presence at a meeting that would begin in little over an hour. As soon as he'd delivered bag, basket, and bad news, he disappeared again to carry out the far more difficult task of finding one of the two or three doctors Joeffrey trusted, all of whom were at present out of the city.

Marna quickly sorted through the bag's contents, pulling out the fresh bandages, antiseptic sprays, and other miscellaneous items she needed immediately, and setting aside the rest for later perusal. To her relief, the wound had stopped bleeding and even removing the pads of fabric she'd used earlier didn't cause much new blood to flow. Joeffrey helped where he could, reading instructions to her from the manual his servant had wisely included and handing her the various items she needed as she asked for them.

Through it all, Tarl lay silent and unmoving, even when she must have hurt him. Marna found herself pausing more than once to watch the slow, almost invisible pulse in his throat just so she could assure herself that he was still alive.

Joeffrey reluctantly left at last with a promise to make sure the attendant assigned to guard Tarl's door through the night would be someone he trusted. At Marna's request, he agreed to convey a discreet note to Sesha to allay the older woman's worries and cover Marna's absence. For once, there was no official dinner planned that required either Tarl's presence or hers, which eliminated one problem, at least.

Marna remained seated by Tarl's bed, but she couldn't help flinching at the sound of the outer door closing behind

Joeffrey. How long would she have to wait before his servant found someone who could help? What if Tarl became worse in the hours ahead, when she was the only one here to care for him?

Although she'd done so reluctantly, Marna had agreed with the old man's arguments that it would be safer for Tarl if she remained through the night. Little though she liked the thought, no one would question her presence, since pledged companions seldom waited for the formal ceremony of bonding before they began sleeping with each other. Palace gossips would simply assume—or so Joeffrey hoped—that she and Tarl had decided to make the most of their situation.

Like a quick desert wind stirring the sleeping sands, the thought of making love to Tarl instantly roused hot, sensual memories of another night and another anguished man who had lighted the dark with his touch.

They'd had so little time together—two, perhaps three brief, sweet, aching hours that now seemed mere fragments torn from real life—but that didn't stop her body from responding to the heated images. Marna gasped at the sudden flare of fire in her veins and the hunger that grabbed hold of her insides. Desperate for an anchor against the sensations rocking her, she clutched at the heavy bedcovers, only to brush against the solid outline of Tarl's hand beneath.

It was a glancing contact, blurred by the layers of cloth that covered him, but it was enough to jerk Marna back to a sharp awareness of the present.

Ashamed, she forced away the unsettling memories and went to find the room's heating and light controls. The light coming in through the wall of windows was fading with the setting sun, and the coming hours of night suddenly loomed long and lonely before her.

The fever started a little past midnight.

Earlier, Tarl had briefly roused to semi-consciousness, and

Marna had taken advantage of the opportunity to get several draughts of restorative medicines down his throat. They'd evidently done little good, for now he tossed in feverish, incoherent dreams, unconsciously fighting against the pain in his shoulder and the heat consuming him.

At the first hint of an increase in his temperature, Marna injected the contents of a hypospray whose label declared it to be an effective febrifuge. Either the label lied, or Tarl's body was battling a spreading infection. His temperature continued to climb, and Marna was eventually reduced to applying cool, damp cloths to his forehead in an effort to bring down the fever.

Because the room's strong, artificial lights seemed to bother Tarl, Marna had turned most of them off until the only illumination came from a fixture set far back in the dressing room and another, dimly lit, mounted on the wall at the far side of the room.

In some ways, the darkness was less frightening. There was enough light so she could just manage to see what she was doing, but not enough to see the ravages of pain and fever on Tarl's features. Listening to his mutterings and his painful, restless tossing was bad enough.

She felt helpless and, somehow, even more guilty, as though she'd had some part in Tarl's wounding. In the long hours since Joeffrey had left her, Marna hadn't had time to think about what her decision to help Tarl would mean—to her, to her father, or to her people—but she'd found she didn't regret what she'd done.

Whatever the future brought, murder wasn't the solution to the problems of the present.

Perhaps tomorrow she would be able to think clearly about what she would tell Tarl and how they could end their pledge. Tonight, she would do what she could to keep him alive.

Marna bent to remove the cloth from Tarl's forehead. It

was almost dry and warm from the heat of his skin. She picked it up and dipped it into the basin of cool water set on the chair beside the bed, then wrung it out, refolded it, and turned to replace it. Just as she removed her hand, he twisted away from her with a sharp cry, then jerked back again, throwing the cloth off.

Tarl's head was little more than a dark shape against the marginally paler pillow cover. The lost cloth was invisible in the shadows. Marna groped at one side of his face, then the other, searching for the rag.

Tarl turned again and the tip of his nose brushed her finger. Instinctively, Marna pressed her palm against his cheek, testing the fever, hoping her touch might calm him.

The simple gesture served as the final bridge between memory and the vague, troubling impression that she'd somehow known Tarl in some other way, some other time.

With a soft cry of shock and recognition, Marna sank to her knees beside the bed and stretched both hands to explore the familiar lines of brow and cheek and jaw that she'd learned so intimately in the dark of the night before.

His skin burned beneath her fingertips. The short, soft hair at his temples was damp with water as well as sweat. His eyes and the hollows of his cheeks were more sunken, the bones more prominent than they'd been last night, but there was no mistake.

Tarl Grisaan, heir to the Controllorship of Diloran and Marna's pledged companion, was her dark stranger.

Either the medicine in the hypospray had been more effective than she'd thought, or Tarl's constitution was a great deal stronger than she'd given him credit for, because his fever broke just after dawn, leaving him limp, drenched in sweat, and still unconscious.

Marna changed the dressing on his shoulder and was relieved to see that the ugly wound was already beginning to heal. As best she could, she quickly bathed off the sweat and the crusted tracks of blood that trailed down his side, then covered him back up to his chin.

For some reason, she felt as if she had to protect his privacy. Not that it mattered. She would never sleep with Tarl again.

He had come to her a stranger, seemingly as much a prisoner of his circumstances as she was of hers. Their coupling had been born of their isolation and their need. It had been passionate and deeply satisfying, but it had not been love. Neither of them had tried to pretend it was.

Now that she knew the secret of Tarl's double life and had admitted, by her own actions, that she could not carry out the mission to which she was sworn, there would be nothing left between them.

Just as well. He had his own life to lead, whatever it was he sought, and she could not remain here. She'd failed in her task and ahead lay . . .

Marna's grip on the damp, blood- and sweat-stained cloth she held tightened. Ahead lay difficulties she'd so far refused to consider. Before she'd left the desert, she'd worried about the possible dishonor of the task she'd undertaken. She had no doubts about the dishonor of her present refusal to complete the mission to which she was sworn, regardless of the right or wrong of it. The Elders—even her own father—might well refuse her permission to return to the caverns. What would she do then?

With an angry shake of her head, Marna tossed the cloth back into the basin, heedless of the dirty water that slopped over the edge. She'd deal with the future when she had to. Right now, there were more important matters to attend to, not the least of which was caring for Tarl until someone with more knowledge and greater skill took over the task.

Taking care not to jar the new dressing she'd tied about Tarl's shoulder, Marna shifted him to the far side of the bed where the sheets were cool and clean, and once more buried him under the doubled-over cover. The cape she'd thrown aside when he was twisting with fever.

She picked up the cape, along with the basin, used cloths, and discarded bandages, and hauled everything into the dressing area. The bandages she disposed of in the trash chutes, where all the palace waste was burned and converted to electrical energy. The cape went back where she'd found it, and the cloths she rinsed out for future use.

Each action seemed more difficult than the last. Her mind and her body were giving out after a long, difficult night, but she couldn't sleep yet. Not until she received some word from Joeffrey, anyway.

Marna frowned at her disreputable image reflected in the dressing room's wall of mirrors. Her heavy braids had slipped out of their ornate arrangement and now fell over her left ear. A number of loose curls straggled at neck and cheek. One dangled in the middle of her forehead, tickling the tip of her nose. She hadn't even noticed. The skin beneath her eyes looked bruised, and there was a smudged streak of dried blood across one cheek. Her robe—

Marna closed her eyes rather than get too clear a look at her rumpled, water-spotted, blood-stained robe.

With a sudden surge of determination, she turned from the mirrors and stripped off her robe and undergarments and kicked them into an untidy heap in the corner. A quick bath and a clean robe ought to improve matters considerably, then some food from the basket Joeffrey's servant had left the night before. She'd had a glass of wine during the night, but had been too tense to eat. Now, to her surprise, she realized that she was hungry as well as tired and dirty.

Marna emerged perhaps twenty minutes later, considerably refreshed and loosely wrapped in a pale green robe from Tarl's collection, with her hair unbound and floating free about her shoulders.

A quick check revealed that Tarl seemed to be sleeping restfully. His pale skin had lost the last of its gray tinge and his mouth had softened, the tension at the corners disappearing as his pain eased.

Relieved, Marna circled the bed to the small table and the two chairs where she and Joeffrey had sat during their shared watch. Hastily stuffing the unused medicines and bandages into their bag, she set the bag on the floor, out of the way. She'd had more than enough of such things through the night; she didn't care to see them as she ate breakfast, too.

She retrieved the bottle of wine she'd opened previously—it was far too early in the day for alcohol, but she needed a boost right now—and righted the wine glass she'd tipped over some time in the night without realizing it. There was nothing she could do about the red stain on the carpet. Burrowing in the basket, Marna came up with a clean glass, a napkin, and a surprising variety of meats, fruits, cheeses, and the like. Even if she were left on her own for another day, she wouldn't starve.

Bread, cheese, and a glass of wine. A strange meal to start the day, but satisfying, Marna decided a little while later. She hadn't managed more than half a glass of the wine, but she devoured everything else as she sat and stared out at the bright day beyond the windows.

She'd made it through the night, and so had Tarl. Joeffrey ought to come soon, and perhaps the doctor his servant had summoned would be with him.

Marna glanced over at Tarl. He was beginning to move a bit and would probably wake soon. She sincerely hoped *someone* was here when he did, because she wasn't at all sure what she'd say to him.

The sound of the outer door opening brought Marna upright in her chair with a smile. The sound of angry debate wiped out the smile and brought her out of her chair an instant later.

Clutching Tarl's robe closed in front of her, Marna darted

across the room to the door that opened on the public chamber. She was just in time to see Marott Grisaan slam the door to the outer corridor in the face of the anxious, protesting attendant and angrily turn back into the room.

Chapter Fifteen

Marna wasn't sure who was more startled, Marott Grisaan or her. She automatically clutched the loose robe more tightly about her, wishing she'd chosen one that closed all the way up to the collar.

"Kiria!" Marott stopped short as if his boots had suddenly taken root. "What—?"

"Kiri Grisaan, good morning." Still clutching the robe, Marna abandoned the doorway and languidly crossed toward Tarl's uncle, desperately trying to ignore her racing heart and the sick heaviness that had suddenly claimed the pit of her stomach.

"I'm afraid we—that is, I—er, didn't expect to see you here," she said politely. "Certainly not this early."

She'd rather have faced a hungry desert cat than Marott Grisaan. No matter that she'd driven off the Internal Security guards with a pillow when the dark stra—no, *Tarl*—had broken into her room that first night. Then, at least, she'd had the satisfaction of physical violence to help her carry the bluff. Now the stakes were far higher and she was armed with nothing more than her wits. She'd never felt more defenseless.

"I apologize, Kiria." Marott bowed slightly, clearly still shocked at discovering her in Tarl's room in such a state of undress. "I had not . . . expected to find you here at such an hour."

Marna laughed. It was rather a good laugh, too. Light, amused, with just a touch of embarrassment. Just a touch. No Zeyn would apologize to a soft city-dweller.

"But you expected to find Tarl," she said.

"He *is* usually here at this time of the day," Marott snapped.

He'd heard the mockery in her voice. Marna didn't miss the contempt in his.

"Well, he's here, of course, but . . . I'm afraid he's not awake, yet. Perhaps I could take a message? For . . . later?"

Marott's dark eyes—so disturbingly like his nephew's, Marna realized suddenly—flicked down to her bare feet, then to the open door behind her. He frowned in sudden disapproval, or possibly in distaste, then abruptly strode past her, headed directly for the door to Tarl's bedchamber.

He didn't get far. Marna caught up with him in three long steps, grabbed him by the arm, and jerked him to a halt.

Marott swung around, too startled by her temerity to protest. By the time anger and indignation rose to his defense, Marna was in full cry.

"Your pardon, Kiri!" she said indignantly. "I told you that Kiri Tarl still sleeps." She drew herself up to her full height, only a few centimeters less than his. "As a Zeyn, I am not accustomed to having my privacy invaded in such a manner. Perhaps such lack of manners is more common among your people?"

Marott opened his mouth to respond, but Marna swept onward. "Certainly I have been shocked by a great many things I have seen in your city. The rudeness in the streets, the lack of courtesy in the passageways of your palace, the wasted space and your positively *shameful* waste of resources. But I don't speak of that now!"

"I—"

"I resent your appearance here without the courtesy of being announced first, Kiri! I most especially resent your insistence on ignoring me when I tell you that Kiri Tarl is still asleep and that I do not wish him to be disturbed. How is it that you—"

This time Marott, harassed, didn't try to argue. He simply pulled free of Marna's grip on his arm, then swung about and strode toward the open door, anger visible in every line of his lean body.

She grabbed up the dragging hem of her robe and raced across the intervening space, intent on stopping him before he entered the bedchamber.

Too late. Back and shoulders rigid with scarcely repressed anger, Marott Grisaan disappeared through the open door.

The best she could hope for now was to somehow stop him from trying to shake Tarl awake. There was a slim chance her bluff would still work, but everything would shatter if Marott saw the bandages on Tarl's shoulder.

Marna was almost on top of Marott before she realized he'd stopped just inside the doorway and was staring indignantly at the scene before him. There was the small table with its untidy remnants of a meal and the two used wine glasses, one still half full. There was the wine stain on the carpet that was glaringly apparent, even halfway across the room. And there was the vast bed with its wildly rumpled covers, the two pillows that still showed the indentations where heads had lain, and the crushed and sweat-stained sheets.

It was all there for Marott Grisaan's inspection. All, that was, except Tarl. The bed was empty.

Before Marna had a chance to gather her spinning thoughts, a pale, disheveled Tarl, clad in a bright purple and pink robe, appeared in the dressing room doorway, yawning and rubbing his hand over his already wild brown hair. He staggered a bit, as if still trying to get his feet to working after a long night filled with strenuous physical activity, then casually propped his right shoulder against the door frame and blinked stupidly at his uncle.

"I thought I heard voices," he complained. The words were slightly muffled because he tried to say them through another wide-mouthed yawn. "Can't say I think much of your timing, Uncle. Did you bring any kava with you?"

For a minute, Marna thought Marott Grisaan was going to explode. His pale face grew red and his chest swelled as he kept breathing in, but forgot to breath out.

"No, I did *not* bring any kava with me!" he managed to get out eventually, almost strangling on his fury.

"Pity." Tarl yawned again, then staggered over to the bed and plopped down on the edge. "I could have used some." He grinned stupidly and tried unsuccessfully to leer in Marna's direction. "It was a long night, you know."

And with that profound statement, he groaned, flopped back on the pillow, covered his eyes with his right forearm, and muttered to no one in particular, "I *really* shouldn't have had that last glass of wine."

Outraged by his nephew's behavior, Marott crossed the room to stand by the bed, and said testily, "I have an assignment for you, Tarl."

Tarl groaned softly, but didn't bother to open his eyes.

"This is important. Sit up, man!" He eyed his nephew with disfavor as Tarl reluctantly pushed himself to a sitting position with a pillow propped behind him for support. "Perhaps next time you'll remember to restrain yourself when you're tempted to overindulge."

"It wasn't a matter of temptation, Uncle," Tarl assured him fervently. "I—"

"I'm not interested in your personal concerns!"

Marott didn't bother to glance at Marna as she came to stand at the foot of the bed, where she could see both combatants clearly.

"I came," Marott continued, "because I have a mission for you. Since it affects the Zeyn, I suppose it's just as well you and Kiria Marna have become such . . . intimate companions. You'll accomplish more with her help than you could otherwise."

Marna had to bite her lip to keep from blurting out questions. Tarl made no such effort.

"The Zeyn, Uncle? What's going on? What can possibly—"

"The Sherl and the Burnarii have signed a secret agreement to combine their forces against the Zeyn."

At that, Marna quit biting her lip and opened her mouth.

"I have tried to send word to Eileak of these plans, but the local representatives of the Zeyn are refusing to believe my sources. For that reason, I want you to go as my personal emissary to alert Eileak of the dangers."

"But why are you concerned about such things now? You never worried about them before," Marna demanded, unable to keep silent any longer. Over the years, her people had indulged in feuds with a number of the Old Families, including the two Marott had mentioned, but no one had ever bothered to alert the Zeyn leaders before.

Marott cast an irritated frown her way, but must have decided it made better sense to humor her. "The heir to the controllorship was never before pledged as companion to the daughter of the Zeyn leader. That makes it a little more difficult for me to ignore your people's quarrels, don't you agree?"

Marna wasn't sure she did, but there was nothing to be gained by arguing. "What makes you think my father will listen to Tarl when his representatives won't listen to you?"

"I don't think he will, but I feel obligated to try." Marott's eyes, so very like his nephew's, narrowed thoughtfully. "Unless you'd care to go along, Kiria. Your father would listen to you, wouldn't he?"

What would Marott think, Marna wondered, if she told him of all those long, fruitless arguments when she'd pleaded against Eileak's plans? Her father hadn't listened to her then. She couldn't imagine why he would be interested in second-hand rumors provided by Marott Grisaan now.

On the other hand, this was her chance to return to the caverns. She certainly couldn't let Tarl venture there alone. Her father wasn't fool enough to try to harm Tarl while the heir was in Zeyn territory, but that didn't mean he wouldn't try to take advantage of the situation. Diloran history had plenty of tales of hostages taken to further one side or another's political ambitions. There were other tactics, as well, possibilities she'd just as soon not consider.

Under the circumstances, lying seemed the best course of action. "Of course my father would listen. How soon—" Marna stopped, remembering Tarl's shoulder. Without glancing at him, she continued smoothly, "I can't go for another day or two, however. At least. My . . . my maid won't be able to travel until then."

"Your maid!" There was no mistaking the disbelief mingled with distaste in Marott's exclamation.

"Tarl has arranged medical care for her," Marna said, nodding in Tarl's direction. It was long past time he took a part in this conversation.

"That's right." Tarl shrugged. Both shoulders, Marna noted with surprise. And he hadn't even flinched. "For her leg. Borsen Prale thought he might be able to help her."

Marott's eyebrows came together in an irritated frown.

''What's wrong with her leg? And why does it matter anyway?''

Sudden, sharp anger at Marott's callous indifference flared in Marna, but Tarl answered the questions before she could respond.

''She was crippled years ago and the injuries never healed properly. And Marna doesn't go anyplace without her. They've been together for years, you know.''

''That's right,'' Marna said crisply when Marott glanced at her for confirmation. She didn't dare say more. Marott Grisaan might look like his nephew, but there the similarity clearly ended. Tarl had immediately responded to Sesha's condition with unpresuming consideration. Marott had never noticed Sesha at all; a maid was too unimportant to be worth the effort.

''What would your father say if he knew you'd delayed bringing him such information, and all for the sake of a maid?'' Marott demanded, breaking into her brief reverie.

He'd be furious, Marna thought—but only if the information really was urgent, which she doubted. In any case, delaying a message would be a minor infraction when weighed against her own, all too evident, failure to kill the Grisaans. She couldn't say that, however. ''Loyalty is important to a Zeyn, Kiri Grisaan,'' she said coldly.

And with that, Marott had to be content. He stalked away a few minutes later, clearly undecided whether to be angrier about Marna's hauteur and lack of enthusiasm for carrying messages, or his nephew's determination not to take anything seriously, including the threat against the Zeyns.

As soon as the outer door closed behind Marott, Marna sank down on the edge of the bed at Tarl's feet. Her legs were trembling too much to hold her.

For his part, Tarl sank back into his pillow with a sigh and once more covered his eyes. ''That man has an uncanny sense for knowing exactly when he's not wanted.''

''At least he was kind enough to assume . . . what he assumed,'' Marna said, grateful Tarl's eyes were closed so he couldn't see the slight flush she could feel stealing up her throat.

''Putting those two wine glasses out there was inspired.''

''I didn't put them out. I drank from one last night, and the other this morning.''

Tarl peered out at her from under his arm, one eyebrow raised in disbelief. ''Wine? For breakfast?

''As you so neatly put it, it was a long night,'' Marna said tartly.

He had the grace to look vaguely ashamed. ''As bad as that, was it?'' he said.

''I don't know about bad, but it *was* long. I . . . I've never cared for anyone who was injured before. When your fever set in . . .''

She compressed her lips and folded her hands in her lap, unwilling to discuss it further for fear that all the anguish of the long night would suddenly come rushing back to claim her.

''I'm sorry you had to get involved in this,'' Tarl said at last. He dropped his hand, but not his gaze. ''I didn't realize I was bleeding that badly. Bandaging my own shoulder one-handed wasn't the easiest thing I've ever tried. I guess I lost too much blood and passed out.''

His lips twisted in a wry grin, but there was no laughter in his voice. ''Lucky for me you showed up when you did. I'd hate to think what would have happened if my beloved uncle had been able to drag his doctors in. You'd probably be making plans to bury me right about now.''

''That's what Joeffrey said.''

''Joeffrey? He's in on this, too?'' Tarl sat up at that, grimacing at the effort it cost him even though he waved away Marna's offer of help.

"You said to call him. In fact, you wouldn't let me call anyone else."

"I wouldn't?" He frowned. "I don't remember that. I don't remember much of anything, in fact. Not you, not Joeffrey . . ." He shrugged again, but this time he winced at the stab of pain the motion must have caused him.

"Joeffrey ought to be here soon," Marna said, suppressing a quick stab of irritation that she'd automatically winced at the same time he did. "He couldn't stay, but he promised to find a healer, a doctor for you. Someone he could trust. He said . . ."

"What did he say?" Tarl prompted when she didn't continue.

"He said we'd be all right, because everyone would assume we'd . . ."

"We'd?"

"Become lovers," Marna snapped.

"Joeffrey's always right."

The angry heat in Marna's cheeks flared until Tarl would have had to be blind not to notice.

He slid along the edge of the bed until he was close enough to caress her cheek with the tip of one finger. Not blind, then. As if she'd had any doubts.

"Well, isn't he?" Tarl prodded gently. "I'm not such a fool as to think you haven't realized who I am."

Marna shoved her clasped hands deeper into her lap, squeezing them tightly between her thighs. He'd lain between her legs, and the memory was enough to stir a moist, dull ache at their juncture. It didn't help that he was watching her, silently waiting for some sort of response, some acknowledgement of what had passed between them.

All she could think of to say was, "Why?"

"What?"

"Why the masquerade? The earrings and the wigs and . . . and . . ." Her fingers tightened their grip around one another, but she didn't dare free them because she was afraid she might, against her will, reach to touch his cheek, just as he had caressed hers. Tending him while he was unconscious had been sufficiently disconcerting last night. Having him sit beside her at the edge of this vast bed was even more unsettling. "Why the skulking around in the dark? Why the Internal Security guards that first night? And why . . . who shot you?"

Tarl sighed and awkwardly rose to his feet, his right hand clutched around his left arm to keep from jarring his shoulder. "That's a lot of questions. Will you object if, first, I try your breakfast recipe of wine and whatever else might be available?"

His shoulder ached abominably and his limbs weren't at all enthusiastic about doing what he wanted, but the wine served as a welcome restorative and the bread, cheese, and smoked meats filled a rather large hole in the middle of his belly.

The explanations were a great deal more difficult to manage. Nothing was simple. He'd had no difficulty understanding Marna's situation, but she seemed completely incapable of believing him when he insisted he didn't belong on Diloran and didn't want anything to do with the inheritance so many people were anxious to foist on him.

"But you were born to be the Controllor of Diloran," she protested, brows furrowed in puzzlement. "It's your duty to take up your responsibilities. Especially," she stressed the word, "when your uncle has abused his power for so long. You *can't* just walk away from that."

"I'm not going to walk away from it." Tarl slumped back in his chair, suddenly too tired to tolerate one more person trying to tell him what to do with his life. "I told you. Another week or so and my beloved uncle will be looking for a new job, preferably on another planet altogether. Though why I'm telling you all this, I can't imagine. I still don't know why you're here or what your father intended when he pledged you to me."

Marna flinched at that, as if he'd struck her, and her face went white.

"I'm sorry," Tarl muttered, looking away. He squeezed his eyes shut and pressed his thumb and forefinger on either side of the bridge of his nose, trying to block out the headache that was beginning to pound behind his skull.

"No, *I'm* sorry." Marna was at his side in an instant. "You should be in bed instead of listening to me lecture."

She leaned over him and gently pressed the back of her hand to his forehead. Her cool touch was like magic, her nearness a stimulant to Tarl's flagging senses. He breathed deeply, drinking in the faint, sweet scent of her skin. Her hair, the same wild, silky mass of curls that had filled his dreams ever since that first night, brushed against his shoulder, tickling his ear and the side of his neck.

Without conscious thought, Tarl freed his right arm from where the firm planes of her stomach held it pinned against him, slid it around the back of her legs, then dragged it upward until it was firmly anchored just were her thighs flared to the soft curves of her buttocks. His fingers dug into the folds of her robe and pulled her closer yet.

She grabbed at his hair with one hand, his good shoulder with the other, fighting for balance. Tarl tilted his head to look up at her, only to find her staring down at him, wide-eyed, over the swelling arch of her silk-covered breast. He blinked, swallowed hard, then let instinct, which had been doing just fine to that point, take over entirely.

Two seconds later, Marna was in his lap and he had his arms around her, heedless of the dull throb of pain in his left shoulder. His right hand slid up her back, under the cascade of her hair, pressing her close so she had no choice but to lean into his chest.

It wasn't self-defense that made her wrap her arms behind his neck, however, or slide her fingers through the short hair at the nape. With a soft moan, she pulled his head down to meet hers.

It would have been impossible to tell who claimed the first kiss, and totally unimportant. Her mouth was as warm and welcoming as he remembered, and the soft, quick exhalations of her breath across his lips were just as enticing. Tarl groaned and knotted his fist in the curly mass of her hair so she couldn't escape him, even if she'd tried. She didn't try.

The kiss seemed to go on forever. They were interrupted by the unmistakable sound of a human throat being cleared behind them.

"I trust we're not intruding?"

Marna gasped and jerked back, jarring Tarl's shoulder in the process. Tarl gasped at the sharp pain that shot through him, but had the presence of mind to tighten his grip on Marna so she didn't fall off his lap.

"Kiri Baland!" Marna scrambled to her feet with more haste than dignity, desperately trying to push back her hair, straighten her robe, and wipe from her mouth the clear signs that she'd been well and thoroughly kissed, all at the same time.

Shaken by the combination of pain and newly roused but unsatisfied lust, Tarl settled for scowling and awkwardly twisting around in his chair. "Well, Joeffrey?"

Joeffrey Baland, accompanied by a stout, gray-haired man, stood just about where Marott Grisaan had stood earlier, but Joeffrey's expression was one of inexpressible satisfaction rather than angry mistrust.

"So," he said. "You've decided to get out of bed before midday, have you? Then you might want to meet an old friend. You'll remember Doctor Alarrin. He tended you when you were a boy, you know."

Tarl blanched. He remembered Alarrin quite well, but he would just as soon not have. There was one particularly embarrassing episode—

Joeffrey's smile widened as he added jovially, "The good doctor assures me he's quite forgiven you for throwing up on him when you had the pox at the age of six."

It didn't help that Marna giggled.

Marna delivered herself at Tarl's door shortly after dark, considerably refreshed by the combination of several hours' sleep and clean clothes that were her own, not someone else's. Neither sleep nor clothes nor the substantial meal Sesha had left her were capable of making her glad to be there, however. If it hadn't been necessary to continue this charade—for her sake, as well as for Tarl's—she would happily have locked herself in her own quarters until they could leave on Marott's "mission of mercy."

Or whatever plot it was that he'd concocted. Marna didn't believe he cared about her pledge to Tarl any more than he cared about the welfare of her people.

She hadn't had a chance to talk to Tarl about this proposed trip earlier. Of necessity, she'd stayed while the doctor Joeffrey had brought tended Tarl's shoulder. She'd answered his questions and withstood Tarl's teasing glances as best she could, then gratefully slunk away when Tarl, tricked by Alarrin into taking a soporific, finally fell asleep and was tucked back into bed.

Joeffrey and Alarrin had remained, under the pretense of the elderly doctor wanting to spend the afternoon reminiscing with his former patient, but she'd reluctantly agreed to return after dark. Palace gossips would already have heard of her spending the previous night in Tarl's chambers. They would expect her to do the same tonight.

And so she would, Marna told herself grimly. But not in Tarl's bed. A pillow and the cape she'd used the night before would make a more than adequate bed in another corner of the room. The heavily carpeted floor couldn't possibly be more uncomfortable than some of the caves where she'd been forced to make her bed in the desert.

Filled with stern determination to keep her distance from Tarl, Marna scarcely noticed the attendant outside his quarters. She sailed through the door the man held for her, then stopped abruptly, startled to find the public room in darkness.

At the sound of the door being pulled shut behind her, Marna jerked back around, suddenly rattled at the prospect of continuing what she'd begun. Too late. The electric *snick* of the locks being set was unmistakable.

She frowned at the solid doors. A pity the locks weren't inside, rather than out. A few, properly placed, might have kept Marott out this morning and prevented Joeffrey's intrusion this afternoon.

It also would have kept her out.

Marna couldn't decide whether she would have preferred that outcome, or not. It didn't matter anyway. The past was nothing more than sand blown before the wind, gone past any hope of retrieving.

Screwing up her determination—why did one injured man seem so intimidating?—Marna cautiously picked her way across the dark room toward the odd blue-green light coming through the doorway that led to the pool area.

To her surprise, the water in the pool was no longer the silent sheet of glass it had seemed that first time she'd ventured into the room. Now it rocked and shifted and every once in a while hit the constraining walls with a soft slap. The only illumination in the room came from the underwater lights set in the pool walls. It took a moment for Marna's eyes to adjust enough for her to see the brown-topped form propped in one corner.

"What are you doing?" she demanded, aghast. "What about your shoulder?"

Tarl gave the surface of the water a dismissive flick with his left hand. "My shoulder is fine. Alarrin sealed it up, then covered it in a waterproof bandage I can take off in a day or two. After that, he poured some sort of appalling restorative down my throat, told me to run off and play like a good little boy, and left. As to what I'm doing, I'm swimming."

He chuckled, as if amused by some thought that had suddenly occurred to him. The water magnified the sound, bouncing it from one side of the room to the other, making it come out hollow and echoing. "Actually, I'm floating around trying to recover from the abuse I've suffered in the past couple of days."

"Abuse!" Marna sniffed indignantly and came around the end of the pool. "And why would you be swimming? Only the folk who live near the sea swim."

"You know all about that, do you?"

Marna's lips thinned in irritation. "Just because my people live in the desert doesn't mean we're uneducated. We're taught about the rest of Diloran when we're young."

"Is that right?" Tarl stood with a sudden swoosh and splash, setting off waves that pounded the sides of the pool as he plowed through the chest-high water toward her. He came to a halt only a few meters away and looked up at her, head cocked to one side in curiosity. "And how much do the things you've seen so far resemble what you were taught?"

She would have had a hard time answering his question honestly—it grated to admit her education had erred on more than a few points—but Marna found herself confronting more distracting matters. The choppy waters of the pool distorted everything beneath them, but not so completely that she couldn't see a few essential details.

"It might have been mistaken on a point or two," Marna said, resolutely fixing her gaze on a point just above his left eyebrow. "Like the matter of swimming clothes. You don't appear to be wearing any."

Tarl grinned, a lopsided grin that made her breath catch

somewhere in her chest, hot and uncomfortably tight. ''You noticed.''

''I still don't understand why you're . . . well . . .'' Marna flapped her hands helplessly. It irritated her to be at a loss for words, and this man seemed to deprive her of them rather more often than was comfortable. ''If you have to sit in water, you have a perfectly good bath. Why waste so much water by . . . this?''

''Why not join me and find out?''

''I don't swim.''

''You're never too old to learn.''

''Perhaps, but I doubt it's a skill I'll have much need of in the desert.''

''Mmmm.'' Tarl slowly swirled his hands back and forth through the water as he studied her, his grin subsiding into an even more unsettling, and far more sensual, smile. The waterproof dressing Alarrin had strapped over his shoulder appeared not to bother him at all.

Marna wished *he* didn't bother *her,* but that was a wasted wish. Tarl Grisaan had bothered her from the first moment he'd climbed in her window, and he hadn't stopped since.

''You know what I think?'' Tarl said, breaking into her uncomfortable reverie. ''I think you're afraid.''

Marna stiffened at that. ''Absolutely not!''

''Then take off your robe and join me.'' When she didn't say anything, his voice dropped and he added, half wheedling, half coaxing, ''Just once. It's like paddling your feet in a pond, only better.'' When she didn't respond, he added, ''Think of it as one of your sweet caves, where men and women mix and clothes aren't required. Nothing to it. Trust me.''

Trust him! She didn't trust him at all, but then, she didn't trust herself, either.

And it definitely wasn't the water she was afraid of.

Chapter Sixteen

Despite the unmistakable challenge in Tarl's expression, Marna held her ground. The temptation to run was ferocious, but where would she run? And why? He was safely in the pool and . . .

Tarl turned and slowly made his way to the steps at her side of the pool.

The weight of the water turned his progress into a slow-motion dance, each movement flowing into the next, his body a fluid sculpture of grace and power. He moved onto the first step and the water lapped around his ribs. At the second step, it fell to his navel; at the third, to the jutting edge of his hip bone.

He stopped at the third step, smiled, and held out his hand to her, like a god offering inhuman pleasures to the mortal who stood before him. "Join me, Marna," he urged. "Try it."

Marna blinked and grabbed hold of the skirts of her robe,

as if they were capable of protecting her, stopping her from yielding to the urge to place her hand in his and join him in the softly lapping blue light that surrounded him.

She'd be a fool to risk such temptation.

She'd be a greater fool to risk his leaving the pool, to invite his touch by refusing his challenge.

And yet . . .

Quickly, before she could think of all the reasons why she should not, Marna shed her clothes and crossed to where Tarl stood waiting for her, all too aware of the way her breasts had firmed and her nipples peaked, of the tightness in her muscles and the unsteady pounding of her pulse. She ignored his proffered hand, afraid that even so slight a touch might be her undoing, and stepped into the water, head high and back straight.

At the first touch of the cool wetness against her feet and ankles, she gasped and pulled back.

"It's no crime, you know," Tarl said gently as she hovered at the edge of the pool, staring doubtfully at the blue-green water licking at her toes. "Not here."

Before she could object, he grabbed her hand and tugged. She had no choice but to step into the water of her own volition, or be pulled in bodily.

Marna sucked in her breath as the cool water swirled around her waist, then up her ribs to her breasts.

Tarl laughed, then drew her deeper until only her shoulders and head were above water. "It will feel warmer in a couple of minutes. I promise."

"I can't . . . stand," Marna gasped as the water threatened to lift her off her feet. She tightened her grip on Tarl's hand, suddenly grateful for his steadying strength.

"Relax and let the water lift you. That's the pleasure of it." He was beside her now, his lips close to her ear so his soft murmur wasn't lost in the loud beating of her heart.

"Like this," he said, and gently pulled her off her feet

and back against him, until her head was lying on his shoulder and his hand was between her shoulder blades, holding her up.

"Don't fight it," he added a moment later when she twisted in sudden panic, struggling against the loss of control. "Gently. Gently."

His voice eased some of the unreasoning fear within her. Enough, at least, that she stopped fighting him and the water.

"Just be calm," he murmured, pressing his free hand upward against the small of her back until she relaxed enough to let the water bear her. "Let your body float. All you have to do is enjoy it," he added as he towed her to the end of the pool, then slowly swung her in a half circle and started back the way he'd come.

With each step he took, Tarl murmured soft words of encouragement, but Marna, teeth gritted, kept her gaze firmly fixed on the shadowed ceiling overhead, too intent on fending off panic and forcing her unwilling body to relax to heed much of anything else.

What she couldn't ignore was the feel of his hands against her back, pulling her forward, holding her at the surface. His touch was sure, gentle, and infinitely reassuring. Strangely, it wasn't nearly as erotic as she'd feared, as though the water absorbed the sexual heat and left her with the comforting strength.

By the time he'd completed a fourth circuit of the pool, Tarl had removed the hand at the small of her back and placed it where her head rested on his shoulder; his other hand pressed between her shoulder blades. To her surprise, Marna found herself reveling in the soft, uneven tugging of the current created by their motion, in the seductive flow of water over her breasts and belly and thighs. The tension that had held her was gone, leaving in its place a sensuous languor that threatened to turn her limbs to limp rags.

For the first time since Tarl had pulled her onto her back, Marna worked up the courage to take her gaze off the ceiling. She tilted her head forward, and for a brief, gratifying moment, felt rather proud that she hadn't flinched when the water surged up over her chin. Then her mind focused clearly on what her eyes were seeing. She choked and struggled to regain her feet.

All she succeeded in doing was to wrench free of Tarl's supporting hand, which sent her plummeting beneath the surface, arms and legs flailing as she desperately tried to right herself. Her eyes were wide open, yet blind to everything but the blue-gold light that threatened to swallow her whole. Marna opened her mouth to scream and water rushed in, choking her.

In that moment she knew, with horrifying certainty, that she was going to die.

Marna's violent transformation caught Tarl by surprise. He staggered, then grabbed for her as she sank.

By way of gratitude, she gave him a hard blow to the mouth from one thrashing hand, then a harder kick to his ribs as she spun down through the water, struggling madly.

In the end, Tarl settled for seizing Marna by her hair and dragging her to the surface. She emerged, choking and spluttering and retching, and instantly wrapped herself around him with a coughing sob.

"It's all right." Tarl thumped her back, trying not to laugh, yet all too uncomfortably aware that his own heart was pounding madly in reaction to her panic. "It's all right."

She didn't cry, but it took a while for her coughing to stop and the tremors that racked her body to ease. Her hair, which had been only loosely bound on top of her head, fell about them in sodden hanks, the ends trailing across the surface of the choppy water like dark sea grass. Her skin was rough with the cold. Her nipples poked his side and chest where he held her against him, their firmness muted by the softness of her breasts, and her legs . . .

Too late, Tarl realized that taking a deep breath under such circumstances was *not* a good way to get his mind off the sensations afflicting him.

Gently, he loosened the hold of her legs around his waist and shifted her so she had no choice except to let go. Marna stiffened in protest and tightened her grip around his neck, but he made no effort to slip free, just settled her against him while the water slapped at their sides. She pressed her forehead to his shoulder and refused to look at him.

"What made you panic like that?" he asked at last, when she was calmer. "You were doing so well. Did I do something to frighten you?"

Marna jerked in her arms and would have pulled free if he hadn't tightened his hold. When she didn't reply, he said, very softly, "Marna?"

She looked up at that, her eyes wide. He could see a muscle at the side of her jaw jump, and the cords of her neck stood out, tight with tension. He suspected it was pride, not a compulsion for honesty, that made her say, "You didn't frighten me. I just . . ." She clamped her mouth shut suddenly, as if biting back the words that threatened to escape.

"You just . . . what?"

"I saw . . . me."

If there was an intelligent response to that, Tarl couldn't think of it. He gave her a blank look instead.

Goaded, Marna added, "My . . . breasts." She grimaced, as if she'd just drunk bad wine, and added reluctantly, "Breasts and . . . curls. You know. Floating."

The blank look served Tarl a good five seconds longer before understanding dawned. He choked, then burst into a roar of laughter.

Between fighting to keep his hold on Marna and regain control of his powers of speech, it was a good while before he managed to gasp out, "You think *you* float, you should see me! It's a sad sight. Limp and bobbing around and—er, that is . . ."

Tarl swallowed the words he'd intended to add. The item in question was no longer just "bobbing around." It had, in fact, become quite capable of standing on its own.

Marna didn't need any clearer explanation. She could feel Tarl's erection rubbing and bumping against her thigh, moved by the water and its own inner energy until it seemed a live creature with a mind of its own.

Unfortunately, its presence was generating some distinctly unsettling thoughts in her, as well.

She had no intention of giving in, of course. Thoughts were one thing, acting on them quite another.

She'd slip out of his arms and walk to the steps, just as he had earlier. She'd climb out of the pool and retrieve her robes and leave him to his forbidden splendor and . . .

She couldn't.

Blame it on the water.

It robbed her of both balance and leverage, lifting her out of the solid world she knew and setting her afloat in a sensual wonder of wetness and warmth.

Blame it on Tarl.

When her feet swept out from under her as she tried to break free, he simply laughed and dragged her back so that she had no choice except to wrap her legs around his hips once more.

No, blame it on her own heated longings.

She didn't resist his kisses.

She didn't fight him as his arms tightened around her, drawing her fast against him, breast to breast, belly to belly.

Instead, she clung to him as he pressed her back against the side of the pool, then grasped hold of the edge to anchor them against the water's pull. And when he entered her with a swift, sure thrust, she cried out in pleasure and surrendered to the aching, irresistible wanting.

Their ability to move was limited by the necessity of remaining anchored to the solid wall of the pool, but still they set the water churning. It splashed Tarl's back and sent spray flying across Marna's cheeks and into her mouth. It swallowed them in its fluid mass, yet left them floating free in their heat and their need, incapable of quenching the fire within them.

Tarl drove deeply. With each thrust the muscles of his arms and shoulders and back strained with the effort of holding them fast. He grunted, breathed deeply, then let his breath out with a ragged gasp, hot against her skin. His mouth slid over her wet flesh, sucking, nipping, licking away the glistening drops of spray; his tongue caressed what he could not touch with his hands, driven by his hunger and her own responsive demands.

For Marna, pinned between Tarl's straining body and the wall behind her, the world had washed away from her until there was only the two of them—her hands, clasped tightly about his head, holding him to her breast; his mouth, so exquisitely alive on her flesh; the straining, aching center of them where the fires within each met and roared hotter, faster, hungrier.

He climaxed first, arching against her, his face tight with the strain of his passion, the muscles of his arms and back knotted with his struggle . . . and his surrender.

At the moment Tarl gave himself fully to her, the last vestiges of Marna's own control shattered, abandoning her to the consuming flames. She groaned and arched to meet him, then shuddered, whimpered, and collapsed against him, utterly spent.

They drew apart at last, too shaken to resist the tug of the water around them. Instead of abandoning the pool, however, Tarl led Marna to a shelf set into the corner of the pool where she'd first found him. The shelf made it easy to sit side by side, their heads propped on the rim of the pool, while the water sloshed up to their chins and their arms and legs floated beneath the surface.

The underwater lights surrounded them in liquid gold and blue, sparkling through the floating strands of her hair like sudden bursts of stars in a watery heaven. Beneath the restless surface, their bodies appeared oddly distorted, as if the heat that had raced through them really *had* transformed them into molten, malleable flesh.

Marna lazily watched the shifting images as her thoughts floated on the surface of her mind, trivial and undemanding. It would have required a deliberate effort on her part to force them deeper, and she didn't care to make the effort. There were too many pressing questions that had to be answered, too many serious issues to be faced, and right now, she didn't care to deal with any of them.

Tomorrow, maybe. She might think about them tomorrow. But not now.

"I told you, didn't I?" Tarl said dreamily.

"Told me what?" Marna glanced over at him, startled. His gaze was fixed on something in the water, not on her.

"That I'm a sad sight in the water."

Marna snorted. She couldn't help it. "Maybe sometimes, but . . ." She wrenched her gaze back to Tarl's face and found him watching her, his brown eyes twinkling in the golden light.

The corner of his mouth twitched. "But what?"

The corner of Marna's mouth did more than just twitch—it turned right up into a smile. "It seems to do all right if you don't keep an eye on it."

"Maybe that's what it is. You were staring so hard, I was beginning to wonder if you had doubts about it—or about me."

At the word "doubts," Marna's smile disappeared and she shifted uncomfortably on the shelf. The slight motion destroyed her precarious equilibrium and she tilted to one side. Her hips slid off the shelf, her legs went up and her head went down, and she would have gone under, despite her desperate grab for the rim of the pool, if Tarl hadn't taken hold of her arm and pulled her back upright.

"For someone who doesn't approve of pools, you're spending a lot of time getting dunked in one," he teased.

Marna didn't answer. She couldn't. She was off balance, out of her normal element in more ways than one, and suddenly she was very, very tired of it all. She was tired of feeling cast adrift, tired of lying, tired of spying, tired of trying to balance honor and right and the demands of others against her own longing for the safe, sane world she'd always known. She was tired of fighting against her doubts, tired of trying to find answers she wasn't sure existed to questions she didn't want to deal with.

She closed her eyes, blocking out the sight of Tarl staring down at her, brown eyes dark with worry. Suddenly, she longed for the hot sun and the unforgiving sands of home with an intensity matched only by the lovemaking she had shared with Tarl. She wanted something—anything—that was sure and real and true.

With a faint moan, Marna opened her eyes and stretched out her arms to Tarl. "Hold me," she said. "Just hold me."

Tarl gathered her into the sheltering circle of his arms and led her from the pool, then wrapped her in a vast, soft towel, and took her to bed and held her close.

Marna told him everything—everything except the real reason for her being pledged to him as companion. No purpose could be served by revealing that, she thought.

If Tarl suspected that she hadn't been completely truthful with him, he gave no sign of it. When she had talked herself out, he pulled her closer against him, pillowing her head on his chest where the soft curls tickled her nose and the corner of her mouth, then quietly told her about his own doubts, the doubts he hadn't admitted before.

Marna listened to his tale with one ear and to the steady beating of his heart with the other, and was comforted.

Tarl fell silent at last, his chin propped on her head, his hand slowly rubbing up and down her arm in a soothing, intimate rhythm that gradually slowed, then stopped altogether as he slipped into slumber.

Caught on the borderland of sleep herself, Marna lay quiet, listening to his breathing, wondering if it would ever be possible for them to go back to the lives they had known before. She had changed in these past few weeks, and so, she suspected, had Tarl. It might not be so easy to pick up where they'd left off, no matter how badly they wanted to.

Although Tarl had claimed he owed no allegiance to Diloran, Marna had sensed a deep and abiding love for his troubled world inside him. She'd heard it in his voice, felt it in the subtle tensing of his body when he'd talked about the people of Diloran and their problems. No matter how much he denied it, she thought muzzily, Tarl Grisaan belonged here on Diloran, just as much as she did.

As the tendrils of sleep reached to claim her, she ran her fingers across the silken curls on his chest, watching the way they bent, then sprang back up. Her eyes were growing unfocused, her limbs unwilling to respond to her commands, but she could still smell the clean, male scent of his skin and feel the warmth of him beneath her cheek.

Tarl belonged here. With her, Marna thought, and she gently drifted off to sleep.

A servant brought breakfast for two and a message for Marna the next morning. Tarl poured kava for them both and watched as Marna read the short note, then thoughtfully folded it up and tucked it under her plate.

"Is there anything wrong?" he asked, setting the steaming cup of kava in front of her.

Marna looked up at that, startled. "Wrong?" She frowned. "No, nothing's wrong. It's Sesha. Her appointment with that doctor has been set for this morning. She's . . . decided to go."

"You sound as if you don't approve."

"Of course I approve! I'm very grateful that you arranged it for her."

Even given Marna's dusky skin, Tarl could see the quick flush of anger on her cheeks. "Then why the frown?"

"I . . . It's just . . ." Marna's gaze dropped to the edge of the note showing beneath her plate. "She's afraid, you know. Afraid to hope and then find out . . ."

She bit her lower lip and slid the note farther under the plate, then raised her eyes to meet his. "I never knew it bothered her so much . . . not being able to hunt, being a servant. I don't think I even thought about it, about what it meant to her . . . until I came here."

The admission came hard for her. Tarl started to say something soothing, then realized she wouldn't thank him for it. "And now?"

"Now?" Her eyes fell again. She nervously shoved a spoon away from her with the tip of her finger, then dragged it back again. "Now, I am . . . ashamed. A little. And sorry. And . . ."

She straightened in her chair, forced her shoulders back, and looked straight at him, like a prisoner facing the executioner.

Suddenly, all the light went out of the morning for Tarl. He knew what she was going to say next, even though he had no idea *how* he knew. She was going to tell him she was returning to her people. There'd be more, of course, but none of it would be as important, or as painful, as the words that would tell him she was leaving.

He'd known it would happen. Known it *had* to happen.

Knowing wasn't going to make it any easier, because Tarl suddenly realized he *couldn't* let her go.

Marna kept on speaking, too focused on her own painful confession to notice any change in him. "I just wanted you to know that when I go back . . . to my people . . . I will do everything in my power to change our customs. Our ways. It will take time, of course. I—we can't change overnight, but we *can* change. We *must.* And—"

The outer door opened abruptly and without warning. The wide-eyed attendant, who had been firmly instructed not to admit anyone, stood at attention as Marott Grisaan stalked through. Joeffrey Baland followed a few seconds later.

Tarl jumped, startled by the unexpected intrusion, then quickly forced his features into their usual fatuous expression. He could sense Marna's start of surprise, but he didn't glance at her. He kept his own gaze firmly fixed on his uncle as he raised his cup of kava in salute. "Good morning, Uncle. Another personal visit! Two days in a row, too! If you'd warned me, I would have ordered extra cups and kava."

Marott snorted dismissively. "I ate hours ago. As you should have." He caught Marna's eye, and had the grace to look embarrassed. "That is, were it not for Kiria Marna, of course."

Marna simply stared back at him, her head high and her face carefully expressionless. The effect would have been daunting, Tarl thought, if her hair weren't loose in an unruly tangle. The wild black tresses gave her an appearance of wanton sexuality far different from the usual prim image her braids created.

Even Marott appeared affected, but only for a moment. He straightened and returned his attention to Tarl. "The arrangements are made," he said curtly. "You and Kiria Marna will leave this afternoon. I have put one of my fastest ships and best pilots at your disposal. You should reach the central Zeyn caverns by sunset."

"So soon?" Marna's protest echoed Tarl's thoughts. "But my maid—"

"Your maid will be taken care of," Marott snapped. "If she cannot accompany you, we will find someone who can."

"I can't leave without Sesha." Marna might look wanton, but there was no hint of softness in her voice. She hadn't let Marott bully her before, and she clearly wasn't going to let him start bullying her now. "It's impossible! And I can't ask her to go with me until the doctors have decided if they can help her."

Her arguments weren't enough to sway Marott. "I do this for all your people, Kiria," he said. "It is impossible to delay just for one serving woman."

"I'm sure something can be arranged," Tarl murmured, trying to defuse the tension. "In the meantime . . ." He rose and brought a chair to the table.

"Take my cup of kava, if you like, Joeffrey. It's not as strong as you usually drink it, but it's the best I can do, I'm afraid." He shrugged helplessly and gave a little titter. "You can't complain if you don't let me know when you're coming, after all."

The old advisor grunted and glared at the half empty cup at Tarl's place, but said nothing as he carefully eased himself down into the chair Tarl had brought.

"Joeffrey will explain all the details," Marott said, trying, and failing, to conceal his distaste for Tarl's manners. His sharp, dark eyes flicked from Tarl to Marna, then back again. "I will have documents, computer-coded message disks, and a personal letter to Eileak of Zeyn for you when you are ready to depart. Until then, do as you like."

Marott's eyebrows twitched, as if he couldn't quite bring himself to believe that either Tarl or Marna would have anything important to do in the intervening hours. He was gone a moment later, leaving Tarl to stare blankly at Joeffrey.

"Well?" Tarl said gently, a full thirty seconds after the door had closed behind Marott. "What is it you're supposed to tell us?"

To his surprise, Joeffrey swung his heavy head to look directly at Marna.

"If you would excuse us, Kiria?" the old man said politely, but without any hint of warmth. "Tarl will share his instructions with you, but for the moment, I would like to speak with him alone."

For an instant, Marna hesitated, then pushed back her chair and rose to her feet. "I'll go check on Sesha," she said.

She was halfway across the room by the time Tarl caught up with her. When she looked up to meet his gaze, the somber shadows in her eyes startled him.

He lightly touched her arm. "Don't worry about Sesha. Joeffrey will make sure she gets whatever help she needs."

She nodded—one quick, downward dip of her head—as if she didn't want to discuss it.

Tarl let his hand drop. Marna half turned away from him, then stopped and abruptly turned back.

"I don't trust your uncle," she said, low and intense. "There's no reason for him to warn my father. The Sherl and the Burnarii have always been against us. Always."

Marna hesitated, her eyes fixed on his, as if weighing whether she should say more. When he didn't respond, some of the fire went out of her, to be replaced by an expression of sadness.

"I don't want to leave yet," she added, finally. "Last night . . ." She bit her lip, then let her breath out with a small sigh and shook her head. "Never mind."

She didn't have a chance to say more, for Tarl bent and lightly brushed a kiss across her mouth. "We'll talk. But not now."

Marna glanced at Joeffrey, then back at him. "All right."

Tarl carefully closed the door behind her and crossed back to take his seat across from Joeffrey. "So tell me," he said. "What's going on?"

"A great deal, and none of it good." Joeffrey took a sip from Tarl's cup, grimaced in distaste, and set the cup aside. "For starters, Marott made arrangements to have your shuttle rigged to explode over the Diloran desert."

Tarl jerked upright in his chair. "That's absurd. Not with Marna on board. Even if he blamed it on one of the other Families, he wouldn't want to deal with the war that would follow."

"That's what I thought, too. Until about two hours ago, when information reached me that the Zeyn are in league with both the Sherl and the Burnarii. The three Families plan to take over the central government by force, if necessary, and it appears they might just succeed if they aren't stopped in time."

"What? I don't believe it!"

"Believe it. It's true." Joeffrey took another sip from Tarl's cup, then scowled at the hapless pot of kava in the center of the table. "How you can drink this pap is beyond my comprehension." He refilled his cup, then added gruffly, "It seems we in the Tevah spent so much time watching Marott that we forgot to keep an eye on what else was going on."

He paused, staring at the cup he held, then reluctantly added, "I remember you warned us about that shortly after you came back. More than once, actually."

Tarl waved his hand in dismissal. "Too late to worry about that now. At least you've found out about their plans in time. I assume the trip will be canceled, then?"

A muscle at the corner of Joeffrey's right eye twitched. "No. Your trip will go ahead, but with a few changes. We want you to talk to the Elders of the Sherl and Burnarii, and the easiest way to get you there is to pretend that you're following through on your uncle's plans. You needn't worry about the transport, of course,'' Joeffrey added hastily. ''We already have people working on it. They found the explosive device Marott's men planted without any difficulty. It's been disarmed and its tracking signal has been modified to provide false data to anyone trying to follow you.''

''We can discuss that later,'' Tarl said curtly. ''Right now I want to know what you think I can accomplish by meeting with a lot of Elders who obviously aren't too fond of the name Grisaan.''

''It's your uncle they hate, Tarl, not you. This is the perfect opportunity to get them on your side, before he learns of their intentions.'' Joeffrey leaned across the table toward Tarl. The wrinkled skin on his face and neck had a worn, papery look, and his hands, pressed flat against the table top to support the weight of his twisted back, trembled as if with palsy.

He looks *old,* Tarl thought in shock. Old and tired and desperate.

''We haven't much time,'' Joeffrey insisted. ''There won't be a second chance. If these three Old Families move against the central government of Diloran, the other Families and the independent states will fight. Once the fighting starts, every one of them will be trying to get control of the entire planet. Not just from greed, but because they're afraid of every one else and because they'll see no alternative. They've worked together for three hundred years because none of them had the advantage. Now—''

Joeffrey's voice broke at that. He slumped back in his chair and shut his eyes, unable to continue.

Tarl gripped the edge of the table, fighting to control the anger that was threatening to explode within him.

What he'd feared and railed against for years was now coming true and no one, not even Joeffrey, had ever really believed it could happen. They'd all chosen to cling to tradition and the hope that a Grisaan would somehow be able to keep everything functioning, just as all the previous generations of Grisaans had.

Tarl had to force himself to release his grip on the table. There was too much that had to be done, too many plans that had to be made, for him to indulge in anger now. And there was another, even more urgent question for which he needed an answer.

''What about Marna?''

Joeffrey stirred, opened his eyes, and blinked. ''Marna?''

''Will she be at greater risk if she comes with me, or if she stays here?''

Joeffrey laughed—a short, bitter laugh that startled Tarl with its harshness. ''Don't worry about her. She's not the one at risk, Tarl. You are.''

''What do you mean?'' Tarl demanded sharply.

''Did you never guess? I didn't. She has sworn to kill you, Tarl. Marna of Jiandu is an assassin for the Zeyn.''

Chapter Seventeen

Marna sat at the open window in her room, blindly staring at the garden outside as she combed her hair. After all that time the pool last night, the long strands had matted and tangled, and tugging at the snarls brought tears to her eyes. The tears stung and blurred her vision until all she could see were amorphous smudges of color and shadow.

Life seemed like that at the moment, out of focus and full of shadows. Marna wasn't sure if she would ever see things clearly again, without confusion and uncertainty.

She longed to be home, to be back in the desert with her people, and yet she didn't want to leave Diloran Central.

Her lips still burned with Tarl's kiss. Her body ached with the memory of their lovemaking. Last night, falling asleep in his arms, it had all seemed so simple.

It wasn't simple at all. Nothing was.

Her doubts angered her, yet she no longer had any confidence in the truths she'd always believed in. There were so many things she'd always taken for granted that now seemed wrong—or at least imperfect—after she'd looked at them with different eyes and from a different perspective.

Marna set aside her comb and pulled her hair to one side, then slowly worked her fingers through its length, dividing it into sections for braiding.

If only she didn't have to return to the desert so soon. Given time, she might manage to sort out the tangles in her life and in her thoughts, just as she'd sorted out the tangles in her hair.

Unfortunately, she didn't have any time. The only way she could stop Tarl from venturing into the desert was to reveal the true reason for her presence in Diloran Central, and she didn't dare do that—for her people's sake, as well as for her own. She couldn't let Tarl approach the Zeyn alone, either. She had to protect him, and at the same time she had to explain to her father and the Elders why she refused the task to which she was sworn.

And what then? Would she stay in the caverns? Or come back with Tarl? What would she come back to, and for how long? And what about Sesha?

Better to leave those questions for the future, Marna decided with a sigh, tying off the one long braid she'd made and flipping it back over her shoulder. There were more than enough questions for the moment, and not one of them had an answer.

The skimmer and driver she'd requested were waiting for her at the entrance to the guest quarters; the trip to the building where Sesha had asked to meet her took little more than ten minutes. Working her way through the bureaucracy of the place proved to be more of a challenge than Marna had expected, however. With people coming from all over Diloran for treatment, the medical center was bustling and no one had the time to help one more stranger through the maze.

The rush and the impersonal, distant attitude of the place reminded Marna all over again that there were a number of things the Zeyn could teach others—things like courtesy, and taking time to help, and not ignoring others. By the time she reached the waiting area that Sesha had designated as their meeting place, Marna was tense and angry. She nursed her anger while she waited, grateful for anything that distracted her from her worries and her doubts.

She wasn't sure what made her look up to find Sesha standing at the far side of the waiting area, where a hall disappeared into the depths of the building. The older woman didn't speak and didn't move. She just stood there watching Marna, wrapped in a cold, gray calm that was far more unsettling than anger or tears would have been.

Marna rose to her feet, suddenly hesitant to face this woman she had known most of her life. "Sesha?"

Sesha stirred then, as if shaking off the remnants of a bad dream, and slowly crossed to where Marna stood. Her lame leg made almost no noise as she dragged it across the polished floor.

She stopped an arm's length from Marna and primly folded her hands in front of her. "Thank you for coming, Kiria."

"I would have come with you, if you'd told me. You know that, Sesha."

When the older woman didn't say anything, Marna burst out, "Well? What did they say? What can they do?"

Sesha blinked and took a deep breath. "Nothing."

"They didn't say *anything?*"

Sesha shook her head, clearly angry now. "They can't *do* anything. Nothing. Absolutely nothing."

"Then why did—"

"They could have healed me completely, twenty years ago," Sesha burst out. "They said if I'd had proper treatment when I was first injured, I would have been able to continue hunting. I could have been whole and strong. But I didn't have proper care, and now it's too late.''

Marna had been caught in desert storms that were less fierce and dangerous than Sesha's anger—and the storms hadn't frightened her half as much, even if she'd been just as helpless before their fury. She felt sick. Sick and ashamed and angry.

''I don't know what to say. I—''

''There isn't anything *to* say, Kiria.''

Marna took a deep breath and stood up straighter. ''No. No, I suppose not.'' After a moment, when Sesha showed no sign of wanting to speak, she added diffidently, ''We'll be going back to the desert this afternoon. Kiri Marott is insisting—''

''I will not be going with you.''

''Not going—But why? If the doctors here can't help you, there's no reason to stay.''

Sesha's mouth hardened. ''There's no reason to return, either. Kiri Prale said there are people here who can help me find work, a place to live. I will ask them.''

''But what can you do that—?''

''*That* is why I am staying!'' Sesha broke in hotly. ''Even you, for all the years I've served you, think I am good for nothing but serving others. Even you! If I go back to the caverns, I will never have a chance to see if there are things I can do besides hunt and wait on someone else.''

Marna flushed hot with shame. ''I didn't mean . . .'' Her words trailed off.

She *had* meant it. Without realizing it, she, too, had absorbed her people's attitudes and narrow-minded prejudices. There was little to distinguish her assumptions from her father's; the only real difference between them was that hers didn't show on the surface quite so clearly.

''I'm sorry. I know that isn't worth much, but I am. About . . . everything.'' Marna hesitated, then added carefully, ''If there is anything I can do to help, you will tell me?''

Sesha nodded and some of the anger seeped out of her. Not all of it, but enough that she could say calmly, ''I will tell you. But I think you will have enough to worry about.'' This time it was her turn to hesitate. ''You and Kiri Tarl. Are you . . . going to accept the ceremony of bonding?''

Marna shook her head. ''No.''

''Then what will you do? Can you go back to the desert as if nothing has happened?''

''I . . . don't know.''

She didn't know what else to say, and was saved from trying by the appearance of a young man who stopped in the entrance to the waiting area and nodded respectfully to Sesha.

''Kiria? If you are ready?''

Sesha gestured to the young man to wait and turned back to Marna. ''You see, Kiria?'' she said softly. ''Already the world has changed. In the caverns I am only Sesha. Here I am Kiria, just like you.''

Marna nodded and tried to smile, but her mouth twisted as she fought back the tears that suddenly threatened. Just one more thing she'd never noticed, never even thought of. ''I see . . . Kiria,'' she said.

Impulsively, she took a step forward and caught Sesha in a hug that was more than willingly returned.

''May the rains fall sweet,'' Marna said softly at last, pulling free of the older woman's embrace.

''And the sands never blow.'' Sesha choked on the traditional Zeyn words of parting.

For a moment, Marna thought she was going to say more, but she turned abruptly and limped toward the young man who was waiting for her.

Marna remained standing until Sesha and her escort were out of sight; then she, too, turned and walked away. Her old wooden chest needed to be packed if it was to be ready in time for their departure, and there was no one now to help her.

Sesha's absence would be one more item to add to the list of things she would have to explain to her father, but Marna knew the matter would be dismissed as unimportant—if it was noticed at all—and that fact shamed her even more.

The transport was fueled and waiting for them. The pilot had already completed his pre-flight inspection and was at the controls running through one last check of the transport's systems. Joeffrey had not come. Tarl had not expected him to. By now, his old mentor should be in the safe haven of the Tevah's hidden control center, securely out of Marott Grisaan's reach.

Joeffrey might not be at the transport dock, but Marott was, his expression distant and vaguely forbidding. His equerry followed a respectful two paces behind, a small, sealed portfolio under his arm.

A number of security guards were posted at various points around the dock. There was no way to tell which were members of the Tevah, and thus to be trusted, and which were not. It didn't matter, anyway. Just before Tarl left the palace, Joeffrey had assured him that the transport had been inspected and cleared.

Tarl preferred to reserve judgment, but he hadn't told his old mentor that. Joeffrey was already sufficiently upset at the discovery that all his years of planning and scheming might have been for naught, and all because he, like the majority of Dilorans, had put his faith in the power of one man to hold an entire world together.

In honor of the occasion, Tarl had chosen to wear a severely styled wig in a dull coppery color that blended well with his rust-colored robe. The only garish note was the ornate earring he wore. When he'd pulled it out of the jumble on his dressing table, he'd wondered if Marna would notice that it was one of the hideous pair he'd bought on that first tour of the city.

So far, he hadn't had a chance to find out. She hadn't arrived yet. She'd refused both his and Marott's offer to take her with them in their respective skimmers and had made her own arrangements instead.

Tarl resolutely pushed aside his worries. Marna had absorbed far more than her fair share of his thoughts in the past few weeks—in the past two days she'd been all he could think about. He couldn't afford to let his heart lead him into entanglements he didn't want, any more than he could risk letting his guard down now.

Especially not now.

Marott evidently had his mind on her as well, and it appeared his thoughts weren't kind. "You're sure the driver of her skimmer knew where to go?" he demanded of his nervous equerry.

"Yes, Excellency. When she refused your invitation as well as Kiri Tarl's, I handled the arrangements myself. She should have been here ten minutes ago."

If Marott Grisaan intended a reply, Marna's arrival cut it short. She refused a guard's offered hand as she climbed from the skimmer, then turned to direct the driver in the removal of a battered wooden chest from the skimmer's carrying compartment. Not until she had assured herself that the chest was loaded on the waiting transport did she deign to turn her attention to the two men who had been awaiting her.

"I was beginning to wonder if you were coming, Kiria," Marott snapped. "I trust the driver was not the cause of your delay."

"He wasn't." Marna serenely crossed the dock to them, as icily composed as she'd been that first day when she'd followed her father into the Hall of the Public. The only difference Tarl could see was that she was dressed in the traditional dull-gold robe of the Zeyn, and her braided coif was far less intricate and slightly lopsided. "I wished to assure myself that my chest was properly packed. That is all."

Marott's right eyebrow slid downward suspiciously. "I don't see your maid."

Tarl could have sworn Marna flinched. "She is not coming with me this time. After all, our trip will be a short one, will it not?"

"Indeed." Marott bowed courteously, but made no effort to disguise the note of sarcasm in his voice. He snapped his fingers at the equerry as he turned to face Tarl. "I have here the documents and other material you are to provide His Excellency, Eileak of Zeyn, in support of the message you bring. Do not fail. It is urgent he be informed of these affairs that affect his people."

Tarl tugged on his earring in a restrained display of nervousness. Now was not the time to overplay his act. "Of course, Uncle. I'm to tell him—"

"Not here, you idiot!" Marott hissed, too low for any of the nearby guards to hear him.

Tarl slapped his hand over his mouth. "Oh! Of course. I'm really very sorry, Uncle."

"Just remember what I told you. The details are all in here," he added, passing Tarl the portfolio his equerry had handed him. "No, don't try to open it now. There's no need to waste more time. Just go."

They went. Marna carefully avoided looking at him as they took their seats in the transport and strapped in. Their pilot ignored them as he conducted the last pre-flight check, then eased the transport out of the dock and into the air.

As promised, the transport was fast. They were away from Diloran Central in a matter of minutes. Marna kept her attention on the viewport and the countryside passing beneath them, unwilling to face the man across the aisle from her. Yet even though she refused to look at him, she couldn't help but be intensely aware of him, of the soft rustling of his robes when he shifted his position, of the almost imperceptible beat as he drummed his fingers on the arm of his seat.

Whatever had flared between them was over—by force of circumstance, not choice—but over nevertheless. She ought to be grateful for this enforced break. They had no future together and never had. It was better that she return to the desert and her people now, before she had to deal with the consequences of a broken heart as well as a broken promise.

Easy to say; not so easy to believe.

It might have been easier if Sesha were with her—comfortable, no-nonsense Sesha, who would have scolded her and reminded her that there was no use crying over what might have been.

But Sesha wouldn't be coming back, and her absence was going to be a constant reminder that the world Marna had always known was no longer the perfect place she'd thought it was, not because it had changed, but because she had.

Marna blinked, fighting against the tears of loss and regret that threatened to spill down her cheeks. She had no time for such self-indulgence. Ahead of her lay the question of what she was going to do about the imperfections she now knew existed in her world. Right now, there were more urgent problems to be faced. Problems like keeping Tarl alive; problems like whether her father would exile her from the caverns or welcome her back and listen to what she had to say. So many problems. So many questions. And not one answer.

Tarl watched Marna from the safety of his seat at the opposite side of the transport. He longed to go to her, to hold her in his arms and kiss away the tension he could sense within her. Instead, he left his safety belt fastened and drummed his fingers on the arm of his seat for distraction.

So many things to balance and weigh, so many plots to

second-guess—Joeffrey and his warning, Marott's murderous machinations, political intrigues among the Old Families and the independent states, the Tevah and its plans. Before, he'd reveled in such dangerous complexities. He wasn't reveling in any of it now, and there was still too much to do, too many things that could go wrong.

The transport banked slightly as it turned onto a new course, and for a moment the sun poured in the viewports on Marna's side, showering her in bright gold light. Tarl forced his gaze away from her and glanced out the viewport on his side, where the downward angle allowed him to see the network of roads below them clearly. The transport almost immediately leveled out on the new heading, cutting off the view below, but Tarl had seen all he needed to see.

The course correction was the standard one for flights into Zeyn territory. The pilot was still operating under Marott's original orders, not Joeffrey's revised instructions, which meant he was probably a spy who had infiltrated the Tevah's ranks. Chances were even better he had no knowledge of the fiery ending that Marott had planned for this particular flight.

Anger surged through Tarl. The muscles in his jaw clenched in reaction. There were times he didn't like being right, and this was one of those times.

With an angry jerk, he opened his safety belt, then pulled off his gaudy earring and tossed it into the seat behind him. His wig followed immediately after. He sighed, glad to be free of such annoying fripperies. Whatever happened in the next couple of days, at least he wouldn't have to worry about color-coordinating whatever he was wearing.

As he bent to retrieve the bag he'd stuffed under his seat earlier, Tarl caught Marna twisted around in her seat, watching him wide-eyed and open-mouthed. He placed his finger over his mouth in a gesture for silence, and when she nodded in puzzled acquiescence, he opened the bag and fished out the palm-sized device he'd hidden there.

As he started up the narrow aisle toward the cockpit, Marna released her safety belt as if to follow him. Tarl motioned her back in her seat. The door between the cockpit and the passenger area slid open soundlessly, but the slight change in air pressure was enough to attract the pilot's attention. The man turned to look back over his shoulder, frowned slightly, then nodded in polite recognition, obviously not quite certain why his passenger looked so different all of a sudden.

Tarl didn't give him a chance to figure it out. He was across the cockpit in three steps and had his palm pressed tight against the man's neck. The pilot stiffened, prepared to struggle against this unexpected attack, but the tranquilizer injected by the needler Tarl carried was faster. With a soft exhalation of air, the pilot slumped over the arm of his seat, unconscious.

"Did you kill him?" Tarl could hear the doubt in Marna's voice, but he didn't bother to look around. He was too busy making sure the autopilot was safely engaged.

"Did you?" Marna insisted, abandoning her position at the door to move into the cockpit.

"No, but he'll be unconscious for at least six hours. Grab his feet, will you? I need his seat. We can put him in one of the passenger seats for now."

To Tarl's relief, Marna didn't question his commands. Together, they carried the limp pilot back to the passenger area and dumped him in a convenient seat. Without asking, Marna pulled out the seat's safety belt and fastened the man in while Tarl returned to the cockpit. By the time Marna was back at his side, he'd already disengaged the auto pilot and was bringing the transport down to an altitude where he could see the ground clearly.

"What are you looking for?"

"An open field that's far enough away from any habitation

that we're not likely to be spotted. Someplace where I can set down for an hour or so, and where I can dump our passenger when we leave. I want him so far from anywhere that he'll have to spend several hours walking before he can find help—once he comes around, that is."

A few minutes later, Tarl spotted what he was looking for, a high plateau meadow surrounded by trees far from any settlement. He took the transport down, then cautiously landed on the uneven grass. As the engines shut down, the silence in the narrow cabin seemed magnified. Tarl forced his hands to unclench from the steering sticks, then leaned back in the seat and let out the breath he'd been holding.

"You look as if you weren't sure we were going to get down safely," Marna commented from the jump seat behind him, where she'd been watching his performance, waiting for a chance to speak.

"I wasn't."

She moved up beside him, her expression guarded. "Why not? From what I could see, you must be an experienced pilot."

"I am, but there may be an explosive or an incendiary device on board, and I couldn't be sure it wouldn't explode before I got down." He shoved out of the seat to stand beside her. "Give me a few minutes, then I'll explain. All right?"

Marna nodded, still wary, and stepped back so he could slide past her. She watched from the doorway to the cockpit as he shrugged out of his robe to reveal the sturdy desert-tan uniform of the Galactic Marines underneath. Tarl once more rummaged in his bag and pulled out some sort of hand-held device covered with an array of readouts. He pressed a button that lit the readouts, then started scanning the transport's interior.

* * *

A little over an hour later, Marna watched as Tarl cut the last lead to the simple, but highly effective bomb the detector had located high up inside a seldom-used hold on the outside of the transport. He rocked back on his heels, staring at the tangle of wires and equipment above his head. "That should do it. I hope."

Marna sighed and sank down to sit on the ground a couple of meters away. Under Tarl's guidance, she'd helped where she could during the past hour, opening panels, carrying tools, and keeping an eye out for any unexpected visitors. She still didn't know what it was all about.

Tarl tossed the cutters back into the bag of tools beside him and wiped away the sweat on his brow with the back of his arm, then he, too, slumped on the grass. "I'm sorry. I didn't think it would take this long."

"Who put it there?" Marna demanded, studying him. During the past hour she'd seen a man she hadn't known existed, an intense man totally focused on the task before him and seemingly oblivious to everything else. There'd been no joking, no teasing, and absolutely no lovemaking. She still hadn't had time to adapt to the discovery that there was yet another side to Tarl she had never seen. How many more "Tarls" were hidden away behind those fine-cut features and dark brown eyes?

"My uncle put it there," Tarl said. At her start of surprise, he added, "Actually, it's the second one he had placed on the transport. Joeffrey's people found the first, which wasn't so carefully hidden."

"But . . . why?"

"To kill us. And after that, to break the pact your people have signed with the Sherl and the Burnarii. It—"

"What pact? What are you talking about? The Zeyn Elders wouldn't work with those Families. They've invaded our territory, threatened our people—"

"Political leaders tend to forget little details like that when it's more convenient not to remember.'' Tarl cocked his head, watching her. ''It seems your father and the Zeyn Elders have very flexible memories when it suits them.''

''I don't believe it.'' Anger mixed with shock, denial with a very real fear that Tarl was telling her the truth.

Tarl shrugged, then rose to his feet and stretched. ''You don't have to. You can ask your father. Or you can ask the Elders of the other two Families, since we're going to see them first.'' He pulled the hold door back into place and made sure it was properly sealed and locked, then picked up the bag of tools at his feet and turned back to the main transport door.

''Wait!'' Marna scrambled to her feet. ''You said this was the second bomb. Why didn't Joeffrey's people find this one, too? And how did you know it was there?''

The corner of Tarl's mouth curled upward, but it wasn't with amusement. ''They didn't find the second one because they stopped looking when they found the first. And I didn't know it was there, but I guessed it might be. When the pilot turned onto the direct course toward the Diloran desert instead of the new coordinates Joeffrey had given him, I was pretty sure I was right.''

Marna frowned. ''I don't understand.''

Tarl's eyes fixed on her with a somber, questioning look Marna had never seen there before. For an uncomfortable minute he simply studied her, as if seeking an answer to a question she couldn't even guess at.

At last he said, ''All along, Marott's tactics have been to turn the Families and the states against each other, let them spend their energies fighting among themselves instead of against him. What faster, easier way to break up this new alliance between your people and their long-term rivals—an alliance whose sole purpose is to depose Marott and take over his power—than to stage an 'accident' that looks suspiciously like deliberate sabotage? Given the pilot's new course, the accident would probably have occurred in airspace that's claimed by all three Families. With you dead, your father would be forced to break the agreement. With me dead, Marott would have the ideal excuse to bring down three Old Families, and none of the other Families or independent states would have any choice except to support him. Your people played right into Marott's hands.''

Marna winced at the anger in his voice. ''What about the pilot? Is he one of Marott's men, or Joeffrey's?''

''Marott's, probably.'' Tarl shrugged. ''Not that it matters. He would have been killed along with us. Just one more innocent bystander caught in somebody else's ambitions.''

There were a hundred more questions Marna wanted to ask, but she wasn't sure where to start, and she *was* sure Tarl wouldn't take the time to answer them, anyway. She followed Tarl into the transport, then watched, uncertain what to do next, as he stored the bag of tools, then slung the unconscious pilot over his shoulder and carried him outside to lay him down under a thick clump of bushes at one side of the clearing.

At Tarl's direction, Marna put together a small bag of emergency rations, water, compass, and protective rain sheet for the pilot when he awoke, while Tarl ran one last test of the transport's systems, checking for any other possible problems. They took off a few minutes later, heading on a slightly different course from the one the pilot had followed earlier.

All Tarl would reveal was that he intended to speak with the leaders of the Sherl first, then the Burnarii, then the Zeyn. The choice was made on the basis of geography, not politics—the Sherl was closer—but Marna couldn't help feeling a twinge of suspicion and more than a few doubts.

Between the Sherl and the Burnarii, the Sherl had always been the more difficult to deal with, at least from the perspective of the Zeyn. Old enmities and old enemies weren't easily set aside, and Marna had to struggle against the mistrust that rose in her at the thought of contact with the Sherl. How could her father and the Elders have forgotten the past so easily?

Marna sat in the narrow jump seat she'd pulled down from the rear wall of the cockpit and stared out the transport's front viewscreen, watching the brilliant green of the central lands gradually fade beneath them as they crossed into the vast area of the Diloran desert that was claimed by the Sherl, the Burnarii, and the Zeyn.

Tarl kept his attention on the transport's controls and his own thoughts, but his silence didn't bother her as much as it might have otherwise. She had more than enough to keep her mind occupied.

What else didn't she know about her father's and the Elders' plans? Marna wondered. How many lies had they told her all those weeks ago? What was she to do now?

What was Tarl going to do? Whether he'd wanted it or not, he was being forced into the role of peacemaker, just as his ancestors had been before him. What would he do if he learned that she had intended to kill him?

She hadn't found answers to any of her questions when an alarm suddenly sounded in the narrow cockpit. Tarl cursed and threw the transport into a steep, climbing curve that pressed Marna back against her seat. He just had time to yell a warning before something exploded against the side of the transport.

Chapter Eighteen

The explosion rocked the transport, but Tarl was already pulling up and away. Another explosion near the rear and a third at the side of the ship made the transport buck and threw Marna against the restraints of her safety belt. She grabbed the handles set in the cockpit walls and grimly held on while Tarl fought the ship around. They were almost out of range when a fourth projectile struck the underside of the transport near the cockpit.

Tarl cursed as the transport spun out of control. Lights all across the command panel flashed urgent red warnings. The muscles in Tarl's back and shoulders bunched as he fought to drag the transport's nose up and regain level flight. The ship wheeled and rocked, refusing to obey, and there was nothing Marna could do except watch helplessly as they spun down toward the desert beneath them.

At the last minute, the transport groaned and belched and somehow straightened. Tarl ran a quick check on the ship's instruments, then slowly brought the craft up to the minimum altitude for cruising. The transport wobbled sickeningly, preferring an erratic path that veered from side to side to its usual direct course, but at least it was still flying.

The question was, for how long would it continue to do so?

Marna watched tensely, hands still tightly wrapped around the handholds, as Tarl tried to bring the transport around to head back the way they'd come, before they'd drawn fire from the camouflaged military outpost they'd unwittingly overflown. The craft wasn't responding to his demands. The instant he passed a certain point in a curve to either right or left, the transport threatened to break out of control. Only when Tarl brought it back to the course they were already on did the ship settle back into unsteady, but still manageable, flight.

Even though she knew she shouldn't, Marna unfastened her safety belt and moved forward to kneel beside Tarl's seat. She put her hand on his arm and realized as she did so that the touch was more to comfort her than to attract his attention.

He glanced down at her and the hard lines of his face softened. "Are you all right?"

Marna nodded. "A bit shaken. How's your shoulder?"

"Not quite ready for this kind of exercise, but I'll live."

"What's wrong with the ship?"

"That last hit damaged navigational controls and stabilizers, and the computerized repair systems can't fix them. Right at the moment, we're headed straight into the middle of the Diloran desert, and there doesn't seem to be anything I can do about it, unless you want to put down within range of the folks who fired on us in the first place." His eyes locked on hers, dark with a challenge Marna couldn't interpret.

Marna ignored the challenge. "I don't know who fired on us, but I don't think it was my people. I've never heard of any of our patrols shooting at any transport.''

She turned to stare out the front viewscreen, then frowned and shook her head. ''The main caverns are too far to the west. Unless you can turn . . .'' Marna let the comment die. Tarl couldn't turn. She'd already seen ample proof of that unpleasant fact.

''There's one small settlement that might serve,'' she said after a moment's thought. ''Ouadi Caverns. They'll have a few ground skimmers, at least. Someone could take us to the main caverns from there. If we can reach it,'' she added doubtfully.

Tarl pointed to a navigational screen set in the command panel. ''Unless this settlement is located somewhere other than where it's shown on the maps, I don't think we'll make it. I can't turn this thing enough to come close. We'll have to put down in the desert and ask your people to come get us.''

He was right. The navigational computer had projected several possible flight paths onto the map shown, but every one left them at least two days' walk from the settlement. Marna rose to her feet, suddenly grateful she'd chosen to wear her traditional Zeyn robes rather than the lighter, more colorful robes she'd worn in Diloran Central.

''If you'll get us as close as you can,'' she said, ''I'll get us the rest of the way, whether my people reach us or not. But alert them, anyway. It will be a lot easier for you if we have a skimmer.''

Tarl's left eyebrow cocked upward at her estimation of his ability to survive in the desert. She ignored it and turned to leave the cockpit, but Tarl grabbed her sleeve to stop her. ''Where are you going?''

''I'm going to gather some emergency supplies,'' Marna said. ''It looks like we're going to need them.''

Tarl managed to establish contact with the Ouadi Cavern settlement, but he didn't manage to get the transport as close as he'd hoped. The ship's systems were becoming more unstable the farther they flew into the desert, until it was clear they'd have to abandon ship sooner than he'd thought.

Marna was ready. She'd already fastened two laden packs to safety grips beside the cockpit's escape hatch, then strapped herself into the jump seat behind Tarl. If he had to crash-land in the desert, Tarl thought grimly, at least he'd been clever enough to bring along an expert at desert survival.

Tarl could feel her silently watching him. He could almost believe he heard the soft sounds of her breathing and of her heart beating.

The muscles of his back and shoulders tensed at the thought. He'd be better off ignoring her. She was certainly ignoring him. Except for that brief moment when she'd knelt and touched his arm, Marna had maintained her distance from him, as if she'd already forgotten what had passed between them.

He ought to forget it, as well. Forget and focus all his energies on the already difficult task of keeping alive long enough to fulfill his promise to the Tevah.

But once Marott was gone from Diloran . . .

He lifted his head to stare out the viewscreen at the vast red-gold desert that swept endlessly before them, changeless and ever changing. It was a harsh, unforgiving world that awaited them out there, yet it was home to Marna and her people. Home and family, their past and their future, the source of their strength and the heart of their lives.

Marna was going home and he . . . where was he going? Tarl wondered.

Behind him, Marna shifted in her seat. The slight sounds of her movement roused him from his unwelcome thoughts, reminding him there were more urgent concerns facing them than his future. Assuming, of course, he lived long enough to have one.

Warning lights flashed on the command panel, alerting Tarl to another system failure. As if the transport had been waiting for a sign, a series of red lights lit in rapid succession as one system after the other started to fail. With regret, Tarl abandoned any hope of getting closer to the settlement. He'd have to land the transport now, before it fell out of the sky.

He just had time to shout ''Hang on!'' before the task of bringing the transport down in one piece claimed all his attention. Tarl pulled on the control yoke, desperately fighting against the ship's destructive plunge.

Tarl got the nose up just before they hit. The awkward angle forced the transport into a wild, careening ride across the sand until it plowed into an inconveniently placed dune. The front end bent upward. The back, carried by its forward momentum, dug into the heart of the massive dune. With a deafening ripping and tearing, the ship broke apart.

The section with the cockpit, specially constructed to survive all but the most violent crashes, tilted up and back with the twisted front half of the transport that held it, then tore free and rolled down the side of the dune. Tarl braced himself against the violent, tumbling motion, wondering wildly if the safety belt would cut him in half before the ship blew up. The section stopped with a neck-wrenching jerk, canted at an awkward angle against the side of the dune.

Tarl lunged out of his seat an instant later. ''Let's go! Before the fuel explodes!''

Marna staggered out of her seat two seconds behind him. While he fought the hand controls of the escape hatch, which had jammed into its frame with the impact of landing, she freed the packs from their moorings.

Battered and bruised, they tumbled out the hatch when it finally opened, grabbed the packs, and ran like sand hares with a pack of hungry jackals after them. They rounded the end of the dune just as the transport's ruptured fuel tanks exploded. Tarl threw himself at Marna, dragging her down into the sand and covering her body with his as protection against the concussive force of the explosion.

Marna dug her fingers into the hot sand, fighting to regain the breath Tarl had knocked out of her. The red-gold granules spilled away from her, refusing to provide a solid hand hold.

The minute Tarl rolled off her, Marna shoved herself upright. She staggered a bit as the sand once more shifted beneath her feet; then her body automatically adapted to the unstable but familiar surface, compensating for the sand's drag without her having to give much thought to the process. It was just as well her body knew what to do. All her attention was focused on the vivid, red-orange flower of fire that had suddenly blossomed on the other side of the dune.

Another explosion spat a huge ball of fire into the air, like a trickster entertaining the crowds. Marna ducked and threw up her arm to shield her face against the intense heat. Tarl stood a step behind her, grimly staring at the smoking fireball, his sculpted features set in hard, unforgiving lines. The implacable ferocity of his expression made her shudder.

Shaken, Marna turned away from him and hastily retraced their steps through the heavy sand, driven by a sudden, compelling need to see for herself the destruction the fireball had wrought.

Raging heat engulfed her the instant she came around the end of the towering dune. In the space of a few minutes, the once gleaming transport had been transformed into a blackened skeleton only partially visible in the red-hot tongues of fire that consumed it. It sang its death song in the popping, cracking, and groaning of metal twisting under the stress of the intense heat.

Marna staggered back, shaken by the magnitude of the conflagration. If she'd had any hope of retrieving anything from the ship, it was gone. Everything was gone, including her battered wooden chest that had been strapped against a bulkhead at the back of the passenger area. She'd opened it to retrieve her disruptor and an extra robe when she was preparing their packs, but she'd been so focused on her task that she hadn't thought about it then.

She thought about it now as she watched the ravenous flames devour the ship. The only thing she owned, and it was gone forever.

Marna swayed, shaken by an almost overwhelming sense of loss. She shoved her hands up the full sleeves of her robe and hugged her arms tight across her midriff, fighting for control.

How foolish to be so upset. It was an old chest, nothing more, worn and battered and of no value to anyone but her. Replacing it wouldn't be difficult, for its only purpose had been to hold her few clothes and her weapons. She was a Zeyn, after all, and the Zeyn did not tie themselves to possessions.

Sensible, rational, reasonable observations every one, and they did absolutely nothing to comfort her. She'd clung to that old chest her first night in Diloran Central, grateful for its solid, comforting familiarity. She mourned its loss now, as if a part of her, a part of who she was, had died with it in the flames.

"Marna?"

The soft query startled Marna out of her thoughts, bringing her around with a jerk, her disruptor in her hand.

Tarl backed up a step, as startled as she was. "Where do you keep that thing?" he demanded. "I thought, after all that time in the Palace, you were beginning to forget about it."

Marna sighed, forcing out the tension that held her, and returned the disruptor to the sheath strapped to the inside of her arm, deep within the full sleeve of her robe. "I'm sorry. You surprised me."

"I didn't mean to." He frowned and gently laid his hand

on her shoulder, clearly worried by her reaction to the fire. "Don't think about it, Marna. We escaped. That's all that matters. Don't *ever* think about what might have happened, because it *didn't.*"

"That's not . . ." Marna let her words trail off. She didn't want to explain, and she didn't want his concern. Not now, not when she was defenseless against it. "It doesn't matter."

She twisted to look back—no, to look ahead, she told herself firmly. More than just her old chest had perished in the fire. With the attack on the ship and the attempt against Tarl's life by his own uncle, whatever hope she'd had that there might be an easy resolution to the conflicts that surrounded them had died, too.

Better not think of that now. Her steps dragging, Marna returned to where they'd abandoned their packs on the far side of the dune. Tarl came with her, his movements clumsy in the heavy, shifting sand.

As she slipped the pack's straps over her shoulders, Marna scanned the sun-bleached sky, once more conscious of the intense desert heat, which was normal for afternoon, but augmented now by the heat of the fire and the hot wind it generated.

"We'd best get moving," she said. "The people in the settlement will find us, but they can't reach us until tomorrow, at the earliest. It will be safer to make our camp for the night in one of the caves on the Koradi Ridge. It lies between us and the settlement, but close enough that we can reach it by nightfall."

Tarl squinted against the sun as he studied the dunes rolling endlessly away from them. A puff of dry wind along the crest of the dune they stood on lifted a skiff of sand and sent it whirling down the slope. The fine grains shushed across the surface, like faint voices whispering secrets, audible even over the hungry roar of the fire that was destroying the transport.

"There wasn't any portable map projector, but I managed to find a pocket compass," he said, abandoning his study of the desert to fumble in one of the numerous pockets of his uniform. He dragged out a small, metal-encased compass and extended it to her. "It's not much, but it will help."

Marna couldn't help smiling as she touched a finger to the metal case. "I don't need this. I know where we are."

"Yes, but—"

At the doubt in his voice, her smile faded. "I may not know how to swim, Tarl Grisaan, and I may not have traveled the galaxy like you, but I can find my way across the desert. I don't need your compass or your maps."

Something of her hurt must have shown in her face, because he instantly pocketed the compass. "I'm sorry. I didn't mean to question your ability. It's just . . ."

He stopped, then turned and stared out across the dune toward the distant horizon whose edges were lost in a blur of heat and sky. "I've trained on desert worlds, actually fought in a campaign on one, but they all look alike to me. They all seem so . . . empty. So dead and uncaring."

Marna let her gaze follow his. "It's not empty, you know," she said softly. "And it's not dead, not even here. This land is very much alive. You just have to let yourself see what is already there."

"Here?" Tarl's right eyebrow rose in disbelief.

"Of course. There is life all around us. Do you see that small ridge of sand? There, at the base of the dune. You see it? It was left by a desert serpent. And just beyond are the half-buried tracks of the sand rat it was hunting."

As she spoke, Marna could feel the eagerness growing within her. She was home. She *belonged* here. This was her world, to treasure and to know and to share with this man who still had so very much to learn about belonging.

"And on the other side of that chain of small connected dunes will be a shelf of rock," she added, turning to point out the dunes she meant. "Plants can grow in the crevices of those rocks, where they're protected from the sand and where the rock will hold little pockets of water after a rainstorm." She turned back to find Tarl watching her, rather than looking where she indicated.

"You love this land, don't you?" There was puzzlement in his voice, and understanding, too.

An odd combination, Marna thought. A disturbing combination, especially now. "Of course," she said. "It is my home. I belong here." For right now, anyway, Marna reminded herself. She couldn't afford to let her relief at being back in a world she knew make her forget everything she'd learned over the past few weeks.

Tarl's gaze flicked to the fire and the black smoke rising from the other side of the dune. For an instant Marna could see the flames reflected in his eyes, flames that would have devoured him along with the ship if he hadn't outmaneuvered both his murderous uncle and whoever had shot at them.

The thought reminded her of her own guilt and her own equally murderous intentions. Ashamed, Marna dropped her gaze to the open collar of Tarl's shirt, unable to meet his eyes.

It didn't help, for the sight reminded her all too vividly of how he'd looked that morning after the bout of lovemaking with which they'd greeted the day. The skin at the base of Tarl's throat glistened with a fine coating of sweat, just as it had then.

Marna pulled her eyes away and fixed her gaze on the dune instead, desperately trying to ignore the thrumming of her blood in her veins.

"We'd best be going," she said, forcing the words past a throat suddenly grown tight. "The Koradi Ridge is still three to four hours away. We'll be lucky to make it before sunset."

* * *

"Strange that a fire can be so comforting after hours in that hell of sand." Tarl stretched his hands to the small fire he'd built near the back of the cave. The heat reflected off the dark stone walls, warming the narrow space Marna had chosen for their camp.

Distracted from her intent contemplation of the crackling flames, Marna raised her head to stare at him across the fire. The firelight made her dusky skin glow, outlining the curve of her cheek and jaw and throat in liquid gold and setting sparks dancing in her dark eyes.

They'd reached the Koradi Ridge and the cave shortly after dark. After a quick search for dead branches from the tough, scrubby bushes that clung so precariously to the interstices in the rocks, Tarl had set up their meager camp while Marna fixed a simple meal from the emergency rations she'd taken from the transport.

Conversation had, of necessity, been limited during their trek across the hot, shifting sands. Tarl had found himself struggling to keep up with Marna, floundering and cursing as the heavy sand sucked at his every step while she seemed to sail across it, as though she drew energy from her contact with that most basic element of her world. She'd spoken even less once they'd found the cave, retreating into herself like a sand turtle into its shell.

For a while, Tarl hadn't minded too much. His legs and hips were stiff from the hours of fighting against the sand; his injured shoulder ached from the dragging weight of the pack. The quiet and the meal and the chance to rest had all been welcome, but now the silence hung heavy, and Marna's withdrawal worried him.

"What are you thinking of?" he asked now, before she could turn her attention back to the fire.

She blinked and shifted her position slightly, as if his words had stirred her to life. "So many things. Nothing." She shook her head, as though she were irritated by her own vagueness. "It doesn't matter."

Tarl picked up a dried twig near his feet and carefully broke it into three tiny pieces, then tossed it on the fire. Perhaps he was reading too much into her tone of voice and the haunted look in her eyes, but perhaps not. With sudden decision, he said, "You don't have to stay, you know. If you find it's too . . . unpleasant."

"Unpleasant?"

"If your father blames you because I'm still alive."

His words hit her with the force of a physical blow. Marna drew in a sharp breath, hunched her shoulders, and wrapped her arms around her middle, as if protecting herself against another assault. "How did you find out?"

Tarl shrugged and tossed a second twig into the fire, then watched as the hungry flames instantly curled around the scrap of wood. He leaned forward to pick up another. "I always assumed it was a possibility. Joeffrey confirmed it this morning."

"And yet you chose to let me on the transport with you? Ate with me? *Slept* with me?" Her eyes widened in disbelief.

The twig in Tarl's fingers snapped as his hand abruptly clenched into a fist at the thought of Marna's warm body trembling in ecstasy beneath his.

Suddenly, he wanted to tell her that it wasn't a matter of choosing, one way or another. He wanted to tell her that he dreamt of her, waking and sleeping. That he'd brought her on this trip with him because he couldn't bear to let her go, because she'd become a part of him, whether he'd wanted her to or not. He didn't have the courage to give voice to any of it.

He wanted to tell her he loved her.

That abrupt realization made his soul shake.

Tarl struggled to get his voice under control. He couldn't say what he wanted to say, and he didn't want her to misinterpret the silence he'd allowed to stretch between them.

"You've had any number of opportunities to kill me, yet you saved my life instead. Hardly the work of a competent assassin."

"I . . . couldn't." Her anguish and shame were almost tangible things burning in the fire between them.

"I know that." A hard, hot knot was forming somewhere just under Tarl's breastbone, squeezing his lungs until each breath cost him an effort. He wanted to take her in his arms and comfort her. He wanted to say that it didn't matter and that everything would somehow work out all right, but that would be a lie. He wasn't sure anything would—or even could—work out all right.

"How can you? Know that I wouldn't kill you, I mean?" she demanded.

What could he say to that? *I know by the way you laugh. By the fire in you, and by the pain. I know . . .*

Tarl shrugged and reached for another twig. "I just know." He frowned as he twirled the twig in his fingers. "What will you do when we reach the main caverns of your people? What will you tell your father and the Elders?"

Behind his questions lay another, more important question he couldn't ask. Would she stay, or return with him? He wouldn't ask where her loyalties lay because he already knew the doubts that tore at her. The same ones had ripped at him for far longer without his ever having found an answer.

The questions and the doubts were like the twigs he burned, tiny, fragile things that shattered in his hands, leaving him with nothing.

When Marna didn't answer, Tarl raised his eyes to find her staring at him, head high, breast rising and falling unsteadily with the force of her emotions.

"I won't let them harm you. I swear it," she said fiercely.

The passion in her drove out the gloom in him, as the fire drove out the cold of the desert night. Tarl smiled, and this time when he reached out it was to her, not to the scattered twigs on the ground around him.

''Come sit beside me, Marna,'' he said softly. ''It's warmer here, and tomorrow is still hours away.''

Marna hesitated, stunned by his smile and his outstretched hand. Then she rose and scooped up the emergency blanket she'd salvaged from the ship, laid it beside the blanket Tarl sat on, and gratefully sank into the welcoming comfort of his outstretched arms.

Tarl had already propped his pack against a rock so it was easy for him to lean back against it, stretch his feet to the fire, and pull her head down to lie on his uninjured shoulder.

As Marna settled into his warmth, she fought against the temptation to worry and to press Tarl for answers she knew he didn't have to questions she didn't want to ask. He was right, after all. Tomorrow was hours away. Until her people found them, there was nothing either of them could do about any of the problems that lay ahead.

The warmth and the soft, comforting crackle of the fire made it impossible to worry for long. Marna's eyes grew heavy. The tension and tiredness in her muscles were beginning to ooze away when Tarl's hand started gently stroking along her arm. She stirred, pulled from the edges of sleep by the slow heat his touch generated in her, then remembered a question she'd forgotten to ask.

''Tarl?''

''Hmm?'' He didn't stop his slow stroking, but Marna could hear the sleepy note in his voice.

''What about Joeffrey? Is he safe? Does your uncle know? About the Tevah, I mean. And you.''

''Mmm.'' He sounded, Marna thought, as if he were pleased she'd asked. ''Joeffrey's safe. We made plans, just in case. And Marott is probably too busy with the Tevah right now to care much about Joeffrey, anyway.''

"That's good." Marna yawned, then shifted to press even closer against Tarl.

He pressed her head to his shoulder and settled more comfortably against the pack. "Go to sleep, Marna," he said softly. "Go to sleep."

She couldn't see the sunrise, since the Koradi Ridge stood with its back to the morning, but she could see the sands painted first pink, then purple, then brilliant gold as the day dawned.

Marna stood on the shelf of wind-carved stone outside the cave, watching the transformation. For the first time in her life, the sight brought no pleasure. She wasn't ready to face the day or the problems it would bring.

This morning she had awakened in Tarl's arms, warm and content with his closeness. Tomorrow she would awaken in the caverns of her people, and there would be a dozen others to share that awakening with her.

She could hear Tarl emerging from the cave behind her, but Marna didn't turn to look at him. Without speaking, he placed his hands on her shoulders and drew her back against him. Marna grabbed hold of his fingers and hung on, grateful for his presence.

"It's beautiful, isn't it?" he said at last, very softly.

"Yes."

His grip on her shoulders tightened. He bent and rubbed his cheek against the side of her head where strands of hair had worked lose from her braid. Marna felt his breath, warm on her exposed neck, then his tongue, lightly tracing the arc of her ear and the curve of her jaw.

Her hands clamped around his and fire shot through her as the muscles of her lower belly contracted in a sudden spasm. "Don't," she whimpered. "Please don't." They were the hardest words she'd ever spoken.

Tarl froze, then slowly released his hold on her. "You're

right.'' He pulled back, but instead of walking away, he turned her around to face him. For a long, long moment his eyes fixed on her face, as if he were memorizing every detail; then his gaze dropped and he fumbled in one of the numerous pockets of his uniform.

Marna watched, puzzled, as he drew out a small leather pouch. He opened the pouch and shook out two bright gold objects that made a sweet, metallic ching as they tumbled into his palm.

''They're for you,'' Tarl said with an odd catch in his voice. ''The gold earrings from that first tour of the city. You remember?''

She remembered. Troubled, Marna looked up to meet his dark gaze. ''Among my people, such things are . . . frowned on.''

''I know, but it would be . . .'' Tarl stopped abruptly, frowning with the effort to find the words he wanted. ''I would like to think of you wearing them.''

So she could remember him when he was gone. Marna shut her eyes against the thought, willing away the hot tears that suddenly pricked the back of her eyelids.

She didn't open her eyes when she felt the soft brush of his fingers against the side of her face, the gentle fumbling as he set first one earring, then the other, in place.

She didn't open them when he said, ''They're beautiful, you know, but not nearly as beautiful as you are, Marna of Jiandu.''

His lips brushed hers in a sweet, fleeting kiss; then he was gone, back into the cave behind her, and Marna opened her eyes to look out on an empty world of sand and sun that seemed to go on forever.

Two men from the Ouadi Caverns settlement appeared at the mouth of the cave shortly after breakfast. They'd camped on the sands late the night before, they said, then started out again before daybreak. A third man was waiting with the skimmer at the base of the ridge.

"Our orders are to take you directly to the main caverns," the tallest of the two said to Marna. He glanced at Tarl, then added, as if in an afterthought, "You and Kiri Grisaan."

Marna nodded and picked up her pack. "We're ready."

Tarl reluctantly followed her out of the cave, his own pack slung over his almost healed left shoulder, leaving his right hand free. He wasn't expecting any trouble—at least not yet—but he wasn't going to take any chances he didn't have to, either.

The taller Zeyn, who had introduced himself as Kelbar, led the way off the rocky ridge toward a travel-worn skimmer parked on the wind-flattened sand below them. The shorter man, who hadn't spoken and hadn't seemed perturbed when Kelbar neglected to introduce him, followed behind. Despite the roughness of the stone, Tarl noticed that he scarcely made any sound as he walked. It wasn't a skill Tarl appreciated in any stranger who was armed and walking behind him.

They reached the base of the ridge without incident. As they drew nearer the skimmer, its door opened and a third man emerged, his face stretched by a wide, wide grin, his arms open in enthusiastic welcome.

"Marna!"

"Dorn!" With an exuberant laugh, Marna raced forward and flung herself into the man's open arms. "It's so good to see you!"

"And you!" Dorn said, releasing her and holding her away from him so he could look her over closely.

Much too closely, Tarl decided, glaring.

"How long has it been?" Marna asked, still laughing.

"Two years. No! Three!"

"Surely not that long," Marna protested. "Where is Caithra? Is she with you?"

Dorn's grin widened, a feat that Tarl would have sworn was impossible. "She's in the main caverns. She's going to have a baby. Our first!"

A baby! Tarl smiled and relaxed. He approved of babies, especially other people's babies.

"Perhaps you could tell her about the baby in the skimmer, Dorn," Kelbar suggested, a faint hint of disapproval in his voice. "I will serve as pilot if you two would prefer to talk."

Marna and Dorn clearly preferred to talk. Tarl settled into a seat across from them, one which, so he told himself, gave him an excellent view out the skimmer's front viewscreen.

It also gave him an excellent view of Marna as she listened, eyes sparkling, to Dorn's recitation of news, including the complications his companion had suffered with her pregnancy, and how Caithra had been sent to the main caverns for medical care, and the plans they had for the coming child. They talked of friends and friends of friends, of what was happening in the new settlements, and of how the old settlements were changing. They scarcely noticed anyone else, too immersed in their conversation to care, knowing there were long hours of travel still ahead of them and nothing to pass the time but talk.

Tarl listened to it all, and as he listened to the words, he heard all the other emotions that lay beneath them. He heard the passionate caring in Marna, her love and her soul-deep concern for those around her, as if her people were as much a part of her as her hair and hands and eyes.

Perhaps they were. Who was he to say?

Tarl shifted to stare out the skimmer's front viewscreen as Kelbar skillfully guided them through the towering, constantly changing dunes. It seemed strange that this should be his first visit to the vast desert that claimed the heart of Diloran's major continent.

In his years of growing up, Tarl had traveled across most of Diloran. He'd learned to love the vast, diverse world that was his birthplace and its even more diverse people, but he'd never really *belonged* anywhere. He'd studied Diloran's history and the history of its people, but he'd always known that his own past lay outside the normal course of the lives around him, as if he were a part of everything and nothing, all at the same time.

Everything changed once he'd left Diloran. Among the Marines, he'd fit in because he was as much a stranger as everyone else. What mattered was what he did, not who he was or who his parents had been. No one cared that he didn't belong because he never stayed long enough for anyone to notice.

The thought troubled Tarl, but before he could pursue it, Marna laughed. The sweet, light sound caught his attention, drawing him out of his thoughts.

He turned his head in time to catch her as she carelessly tucked some loose strands of hair behind her ear. With the slight tilt of her head, light caught the gold of her earring, making it flash bright yellow, like a drop of sun against her cheek.

A quick flash of desire shot through him, immediately followed by a hungry longing that burned even hotter than the desire. His fingertips tingled with the remembered feel of her skin, of how soft and warm it had been when he'd fitted the earring in place.

He'd come so close to asking her to leave Diloran with him, just as he'd asked her once before. Something had held him back. He'd thought then it was fear, but now he realized it was the sure knowledge that he couldn't ask Marna to leave her world behind. She was a part of this world; she belonged here and he could not—*would* not—ask her to give it up. Especially not when there was nothing he could offer her in exchange. He had nothing to give—no world, no roots, no people, no place. No future on Diloran save the future that others had chosen for him; no future elsewhere save exile and the wild uncertainty that was the daily lot of the companion of a Galactic Marine.

Marna laughed again and leaned forward to lightly touch Dorn's arm, murmuring something Tarl couldn't hear. There was nothing sexual or suggestive in her actions, just the casual intimacy of one friend to another, yet Tarl was conscious of a sudden rush of jealousy.

Marna was home. Among her people. Among friends. And he, Tarl Grisaan, heir to the greatest position of power in all of Diloran, watched from a distance, knowing that he would never, ever, be able to offer her anything to replace the richness she already owned in such full measure.

Chapter Nineteen

They reached the main caverns long after dark, tired, cramped, and impatient after so many hours in the utilitarian skimmer. Tarl followed Marna out of the skimmer and into the harsh white glare of security lights that illuminated the open area between the skimmer staging area and the protected entrance of the caverns.

The entrance itself had clearly been shaped out of what had once been a natural opening in the intimidating wall of black rock that loomed up out of the desert sands and stretched away from them into the dark on either side. A massive plas-steel door slid open at their approach, just far enough to allow one person at a time to pass through. Though the entrance was easily defensible, Tarl suspected the arrangement was designed more for protection against the often violent desert sandstorms than against enemy attack.

That thought didn't stop the hairs at the back of Tarl's

neck from prickling, however, or his shoulders from tensing as he passed the four silent, hooded guards posted beside the entrance. He couldn't see their faces in the shadowed depths of their hoods, but Tarl knew they were watching him the way desert hawks watched their prey. Although he still carried the needler he'd used to disable the transport pilot, it was a weapon of stealth and surprise, not direct confrontation, and would be useless against the guards' energy rifles. If he'd made a mistake in his assumption that neither Eileak nor the other Zeyn Elders would risk an attempt on his life in their own territory, he'd know soon enough.

Nothing happened, but Tarl could feel the guards' eyes following them as he and Marna passed through the entrance and into the more dimly lit stone passageway beyond. Behind them, the outer door slid shut with the solid finality of a prison gate. Tarl frowned, irritated by the grim thought, and concentrated on studying his surroundings instead.

In contrast to the harsh security lights outside, the lights set in grooves in the corridor's ceiling provided a soft, natural illumination that warmed the gray-black of the stone walls. Gray conduits carrying communications and electrical cables ran beside the lighting panels, almost invisible against the stone. The ceiling and upper walls of the corridor still bore some of the original unevenness of the natural stone, but the base of the walls and the level floor had clearly been cut out to provide easy passage to the caverns' inhabitants.

The inhabitants themselves were nowhere in sight. They weren't even audible. The only sound in the corridor was the soft, almost imperceptible shush of fans circulating fresh air and the sharp ring of his and Marna's footsteps on the rock.

As though sensing his thoughts, Marna stopped and turned back to face him, her body suddenly stiff and awkward with her own doubts. "We're in a side entrance that leads to the caves the Elders use as offices. Since Kelbar brought us here,

I'm assuming that my father or the Elders want to speak with us first.''

They'll want to know why I haven't killed you yet.

Marna didn't have to say the words. Tarl knew what she was thinking by the worry lines around her eyes and the tension he could feel thrumming inside her. He repressed a sharp urge to take her in his arms and kiss away her doubts. But holding her—kissing her—would only make it harder for them to deal with whatever lay ahead. Including their inevitable separation.

Despite that grim thought, Tarl couldn't resist the temptation to lightly touch a finger to her lips. ''You should smile,'' he said gently, laying aside his own worries as he forced his mouth into the rough semblance of a smile. ''There are more important things to think about than your father. Like dinner, for example.''

The corner of Marna's mouth quivered, then twitched upward. ''We'll have to hurry, then. There's probably only one more scheduled serving. If we don't make that, we won't get anything to eat until morning.''

Tarl's smile widened. ''Now *that's* a frightening thought. Maybe we ought to skip our chat with your father altogether and just go eat.''

Marna smiled in response. It was a weak little smile, but it was a smile nonetheless. ''I'd like to see you explaining *that* to the Elders.''

As it turned out, skipping the chat with her father proved to be easy. Only one of the Elders—a lean, middle-aged woman—awaited them in the little warren of caves they found at the end of the corridor.

The woman calmly laid aside whatever she'd been working on, then rose to her feet, tucked her hands into the full sleeves of her robe, and stood watching them cross to her.

''Kiria Parra,'' Marna said, nodding respectfully.

Parra gave a slight nod in return. "Marna. And you, I suppose, are Tarl Grisaan," she added, making no effort to disguise her cool-eyed appraisal of him.

Tarl bowed, a little lower than necessary, but not so far that anyone could openly object to his mockery. "I'm afraid you're correct. But I am also a beggar, stranded in the desert and come to claim some of the hospitality of the Zeyn." He gave her a sweet smile that told her he knew exactly what she and the other Elders had plotted.

"Yes," Parra said. "Well."

When she didn't say anything else, Marna said sharply, "I'd expected my father and at least some of the other Elders to be here, Kiria. Especially since Kiri Tarl and I were shot down over Zeyn territory. I expected them to be . . . concerned."

Parra's already thin lips thinned even further, until they almost disappeared from her face. "Grebnar is in the caverns, as are Wylen and Strogal. The rest, including your father, have been called to some of the border settlements. On top of everything else, it seems there have been some . . . misunderstandings with the Sherl and the Burnarii. Your father is expected back tomorrow morning."

Tarl could see the relief in Marna's face at the news that she wouldn't be forced to face her father quite yet. "May I ask what these 'misunderstandings' were?"

For a minute, he didn't think Parra was going to answer; then she grimaced, as if reluctantly coming to an unpalatable decision, and said, "We had a . . . political agreement with our neighbors, an agreement which is no longer viable due to the rather . . . dramatic events in Diloran Central."

Tarl stiffened. "Dramatic? What do you mean?"

Parra's eyes widened. "Surely you know?"

"Know what, Kiria?" Tarl asked softly. He could easily guess, but guesses could be wrong.

"Why, that the Tevah has finally made its move against

the central government—and your uncle.'' At Marna's soft gasp of shock, Parra frowned, suddenly unsure of herself. Her glance flicked from Tarl to Marna, then back again. ''Isn't that why you're here? Because you were running from the fighting?''

''What fighting? What are you talking about? Tell me!'' Anger mixed with sudden anxiety threaded Marna's voice. She took a step toward Parra, her hands clenched as if she intended to pull the information out of the older woman by sheer force, if necessary.

It wasn't necessary. ''The Tevah are trying to oust Marott Grisaan and take over the government,'' Parra admitted, clearly amazed by their ignorance. ''There's been fighting in Diloran Central and at some of the key military outposts, but according to the information we've received so far, they seem to be winning.''

Once more Parra's gaze flicked between them, as if she couldn't quite believe the evidence of her own eyes and ears. ''Surely you knew that?''

Marna's mouth, which had dropped open at Parra's revelation, suddenly closed with a snap. She shook her head. ''No. No, I didn't. Did you?'' she demanded, turning to Tarl.

''No. They weren't planning to act until I returned.''

''Planning to—Do you mean you're a member of the Tevah?'' Parra demanded, clearly stunned by the unexpected revelation.

Tarl's eyebrows rose. There was no sense in lying now, and less chance of anyone trying to kill him if they knew he was allied with what appeared to be the winning side in the conflict. ''I don't care for my uncle any more than you do, Kiria,'' he said, ''and killing me wouldn't have accomplished anything except to cause more trouble for everyone, especially the Zeyn.''

''How did—? You told him!'' Parra protested, turning on Marna.

"Marna didn't tell me anything. She didn't have to. It was your own clandestine agreement with the Sherl and Burnarii that gave it away. Besides," he added, "given Eileak's rather obvious ploy to have Marna pledged as my companion, we'd always assumed that assassination was a possibility."

"We? How many others know of—of our plans?" Parra could barely get the words out.

"Quite a few. Me. The leaders of the Tevah. Marott and his followers." At Parra's expression of stunned disbelief, Tarl added gently, "Did you really think that no one would wonder about your intentions, especially after your people have insisted on maintaining their distance from everyone else for so many years?"

Parra's hands dropped helplessly to her sides. She suddenly looked ten years older than she had a moment before. "What were we to do? Years of quarreling with our neighbors have drained our resources. Most of the Zeyn don't know that, but it's true. Your uncle has blocked every attempt we've made to resolve the problems. He's actually *encouraged* the Sherl and the Burnarii in our quarrel. We couldn't go on as we had. We *couldn't.*"

Tarl shrugged. He couldn't feel much sympathy for her. "It doesn't much matter now. What does matter is what's happening in Diloran Central. What exactly have you heard?"

Parra abruptly sat back down at her desk. "Nothing more than what I've told you. We—we don't have very good sources, I'm afraid. Not even for monitoring public communications. As you pointed out, we've kept our distance from everyone, and now . . ." She breathed deeply, then tried again. "Eileak and the others are at the settlements along the borders or meeting with the Sherl and the Burnarii, trying to get more information."

She tilted her head up so she could look directly into Tarl's eyes. "If you are with the Tevah and they triumph . . . Well, perhaps we will be glad that Marna did not carry out her task after all.'' Parra blinked. ''Or perhaps not.''

Tarl's mouth twisted in wry acknowledgment of her dilemma. The Zeyn leaders were going to have a hard time explaining their intentions to the Tevah, but that wasn't his worry.

At least he could be grateful that the Tevah's attack against Marott had occurred when he wasn't there to help. Without him as titular leader, they would be less inclined to look to him for guidance later. Their success ought to be seen as more than adequate proof that Diloran, at long last, could govern itself without a Grisaan at its head.

All that could wait, however. Marna was staring at Parra as if she'd never seen the older woman before and would prefer not to see her again. Now that he knew there wouldn't be any unpleasant confrontation with Eileak tonight, Tarl's stomach was rumbling. He lightly touched Marna's shoulder, drawing her attention. ''Didn't you say there was only one more chance for dinner tonight?''

Marna gave him a weak smile, clearly relieved at the prosaic distraction. ''Yes. I suppose we'd best get moving.'' She nodded politely in Parra's direction. ''Kiria. If you'll excuse us.''

Parra dismissed them with a vague flip of her hand. ''Of course.'' Before they were halfway across the small cave, she called out behind them, ''Marna!'' When they stopped and turned back to face her, she said simply, ''I am glad you have come back to us safely.''

Marna bowed slightly in acknowledgement, but that was all. Then she turned and left the area and Tarl followed after.

The closer they got to the main dining cavern in this sector of the caverns, the more crowded the passageways became. For the first time in her life, Marna found it difficult to obey the conventions of courtesy and acknowledge the people streaming past her. To her surprise, she even caught herself longing for the cool, impersonal distance to which she'd objected so strongly in Diloran Central—that and the silence of a private space where she could think over Parra's revelations and her own jumbled feelings about returning to her people.

Tarl kept close on her heels and tried to blend in, but with his pale skin and Galactic Marine uniform, his presence inevitably drew attention. Marna suspected that the only thing that kept some of the passersby from stopping him and asking rude questions was the rigid Zeyn rule that one could not ask about the affairs of another, especially a stranger, unless invited to do so.

To Marna's relief, they not only had time to fill their plates from the serving center, but Dorn and Caithra were seated on cushions set around a low table where there would be room for her and Tarl, as well.

Her friends greeted them enthusiastically. As she settled onto her cushion, Marna was conscious of a comfortable sense of belonging that was a welcome antidote to her worries and the odd, disconnected feeling she'd been fighting ever since she'd entered the caverns.

The food was simple—roast cavral with steamed grains and spices—but tasty, and Marna quickly discovered she was a great deal hungrier than she'd thought. Once she'd had a chance to take the edge off her hunger, she and Caithra launched into a happy discussion about everything Dorn had forgotten to cover earlier. The two men sat and listened, clearly bemused by their feminine fascination with preparations for the coming baby, while Tarl industriously worked his way through the substantial servings of food he'd put on his plate.

Once Tarl finished and Marna and Caithra's animated discussion slowed somewhat, Dorn shoved his own plate to the side, propped his forearms on the table, and said, "Well, Tarl, what do you think of the main caverns so far?"

Tarl glanced over at her. Marna could see the mischievous twinkle in his eyes, reminding her of her own comments on society in Diloran Central, which she'd announced with such disdain at that first meal they'd shared.

Tarl cleared his throat and looked around the wide, low-ceilinged area with its clusters of people seated on brightly colored cushions scattered around low tables like theirs, as if he wanted to study it one last time before passing judgment.

"It's a lot more crowded than anyplace I'm used to, but everyone is so courteous you don't notice the crowding quite as much as you would otherwise," he said, carefully not meeting Marna's eye. "I think I'd find it difficult to be shut away from the sky and the sun every day, but I like the way you've used bright colors on these cushions and tables to lighten the gray of the rock. Makes it seem . . . cheerier, I guess."

Caithra laughed, a sweet, delicate laugh that went well with her delicate, feminine features. "Cheerier. I like that." She stretched out her legs and leaned back against her willing companion, her movements awkward because of the huge belly even her full robes couldn't hide. "Ah, that's much more comfortable."

Dorn smiled down at her protectively and began to massage Caithra's shoulders, all pretense of interest in Tarl's impressions forgotten in his love and concern for his companion.

"It won't be long now, my love," he said, gently placing his hands over her belly and tracing its smooth curve. His arms enclosed her, as though even here he would do whatever he could to shelter the woman he loved from the harsh world around them.

Marna's heart gave a little lurch at the sight. She'd never

really thought about raising a child, or entering into a relationship as bound companion, but now, watching her friends, she suddenly longed for the same simple joy they shared. She wanted to be the center of someone else's world instead of just one person among the many who filled these caverns.

What would it be like to be bound to Tarl just as Dorn and Caithra were bound to each other, by law and love and a shared commitment to a future together? What if she could lean back against Tarl and feel his arms around her, just as Dorn's were around Caithra? What if she could be sure that she was the center of his universe, just as Caithra was the center of Dorn's?

Tarl was so near. She could *feel* him, even though she was fighting to keep her attention focused on the happy couple across from her. She could hear him and hear the soft rustle of his clothes as he moved. If she tried, Marna was willing to bet she could hear the soft in–out sigh of his breathing.

Foolish thoughts. Foolish longings. And she had never been a fool.

Forcing a smile to her face, Marna leaned toward her friends and said, "Looking at you, I can't believe your baby's waited this long to pop out, Caithra. I'd swear you're carrying twins, as big as you've gotten."

Caithra's smile faded. She dropped her gaze to her swelling stomach, then protectively placed her hands on top of Dorn's. "This baby's given me enough trouble for twins. I've already miscarried twice, you know, and this pregnancy . . ." Her voice trailed off. She bit her lip, as if by refusing to give voice to the fears that plagued her, she could somehow ensure the safety of her longed-for child.

"Now hush," Dorn said, forcing a lightheartedness into his voice that Marna could see he was far from feeling. He'd told her about his worries in the skimmer earlier, but she hadn't realized just how great those worries were until now. "The healers said you should be fine, that the baby will be coming any day. They said there's nothing to worry about now that you've come this far."

Caithra gave a small, uncertain laugh. "I know. I'm being silly, aren't I? I guess I've gotten so used to worrying that I don't know what else to do."

"What you should probably do is go to bed," Marna said briskly. "Dorn hasn't seen you for weeks, and here we are keeping you up." She forced a grin, for Caithra's sake. "Now that I think about it, I'm worn out, too, and it's all Dorn's fault. He talked about you and the baby all the way from the Koradi Ridge."

"That's not true!" Dorn protested. "I swear there must have been at least five minutes when I talked about something else. Maybe even ten!"

Marna could swear their combined laughter echoed from even the farthest corners of the big dining area.

"You're right about getting to bed," Caithra admitted as soon as the laughter died down. "I'm always tired these days, and I don't imagine it will get much better once the baby comes." She awkwardly shoved herself into a sitting position with Dorn's help; then, with Dorn on one side and Marna on the other, she staggered to her feet, grunting at the effort.

Once Caithra was standing, she glanced over at Tarl, an unmistakable blush on her cheeks. "You must think I'm awful, grunting and groaning and complaining."

Tarl smiled. "On the contrary," he said softly, "I think you're beautiful, and I have no doubt you will be even more beautiful once your baby is born."

The smile and the warm glow in Tarl's eyes were enough to set Marna's heart thudding hard in her chest. She ducked her head, hoping none of her confusion showed in her face.

"Oh!" Caithra's blush deepened, but it was clear she was pleased, nonetheless. "What a nice thing to say."

Dorn gave a mock growl. "I'm not sure I agree. That it

was a nice thing to say, I mean!'' he added hastily as Caithra playfully hit him. ''I absolutely agree with the sentiments. Honest! Ow!''

''We'd best go or we'll run the risk of being called on as witnesses when Caithra's charged with battering poor Dorn,'' Marna said, forcing a light note into her voice with effort. Her palms were sweating, her pulse pounding, and her body aching—and all because of a casual glance and a few even more casual words that hadn't been intended for her. ''I'll see you tomorrow,'' she said to Caithra. ''Sleep well.''

Marna waited as Tarl murmured his good-byes, then picked her way through the still crowded tables where people lingered over their late meal or relaxed in conversation with friends and acquaintances. She was almost out the arched door on the far side of the cavern when Tarl pulled her to a halt with a firm tug on her sleeve.

''Would you mind telling me what you're planning next?'' he asked. ''Just so I know?'' '

Marna reluctantly looked up to find his brown eyes firmly fixed on her face. He still hadn't let go of her sleeve.

To her chagrin, Marna started to blush. ''I thought we'd take a bath and go to bed,'' she said.

Tarl had to concentrate on putting one foot firmly down in front of the other as he followed Marna through the interconnected caves and stone passageways of the complex. It wouldn't do to be seen staggering after her, but his legs were so wobbly that it required a real effort of will to keep upright.

Take a bath and go to bed, she'd said. He'd be the last to deny he needed a bath—two days in the desert didn't do much for one's masculine dignity—and a comfortable bed sounded immensely appealing after a night spent sleeping on a rock floor followed by a day in a cramped skimmer. But simply bathing and sleeping weren't what he had in mind when it came to Marna.

All through the meal he'd watched Marna's friends, Dorn and Caithra. He'd seen the little intimacies, the fleeting glances they'd exchanged. He'd studied Caithra's impossibly rounded belly, but instead of thinking of the coming baby, he'd found himself imagining how Marna would look if she were pregnant with *his* child.

Loving Marna was dangerous enough. Dreaming of her with his child was . . . outrageous. It was mad. Absurd. Insane.

It was tempting.

It made his legs go weak and his head spin and his stomach flutter like an adolescent's in the painful throes of first love.

If he had a gram of sense, he wouldn't let himself think of it, even for a moment. Having a child was making a commitment to the future, a commitment he didn't dare make. It was roots and responsibilities and a belief, not only in tomorrow, but in all the days after that.

Hard enough, even if you belonged somewhere. Impossible for someone like him, who belonged nowhere at all.

To Tarl's relief, the disturbing trend of his thoughts was broken by their arrival at the outer chamber of the steam caves which served as communal baths for the Zeyn. He didn't need Marna's quick gesture toward one of the two diverging passageways to see that men and women had separate entrances. Before he could ask Marna when and where they would meet afterward, she was gone and he was left to venture in alone.

The passage was short and opened into a broad, low-ceilinged chamber that was divided into different areas for the hygienic facilities and for bathing. A wizened old man took Tarl's clothes for cleaning and gave him soap and a small basin filled with warm water in exchange.

After a quick glance at the other bathers to figure out the proper protocol, Tarl carried the basin and soap to an open spot near one of the channels cut in the stone floor. He set the basin on the floor, then squatted beside it and proceeded to wash himself as best he could. The result was less than perfect, but better than nothing at all. Following the lead of the other bathers, Tarl finished his ablutions by sluicing the water remaining in the basin over his head and down his back, then traded the empty basin to the attendant for a heavy towel that he immediately slung over his shoulder.

He'd known the Zeyn steam caves were used by all the Zeyn, regardless of age or gender, but the experience of walking into a host of strangers clad only in a towel tossed over his shoulder was a great deal more disconcerting than he'd expected. For a moment, Tarl hovered near the exit from the men's bathing area, trying not to stare and hoping no one would notice just how uncomfortable he really was.

The dense mist rising from the subterranean hot springs quickly soaked him, disguising his sweaty brow and palms. His worst fear—that he would humiliate himself by an uncontrollable physical display of desire—mercifully proved unfounded. His body behaved with due decorum even when Marna emerged from the women's bathing area with a towel wrapped around her hair and nothing else in the way of clothing.

Of course, the two naked old women studying him with such beady-eyed interest from their perch on an outcropping of rock at the entrance to the first steam cave might have had something to do with his physical restraint. The presence of the small, naked boy who stood avidly watching him helped, as well.

Striving for an air of nonchalance, Tarl started to cross to Marna, only to be brought up short when the boy darted forward to stand in front of him.

After a frowning and totally unabashed study of Tarl's hip and groin, the child, who couldn't have been more than three, four at the most, tilted his head back, looked up at Tarl, and demanded, "Have you *always* been like that?"

The mist might have hidden his sweaty palms, but Tarl knew it couldn't disguise the hot flush that instantly blossomed on his face.

There was no mistaking the source of the boy's wonderment. What fate had denied Tarl in the way of great height and massive physique, it had more than made up in endowing him with impressive masculine equipment.

Never, until now, had he regretted the arrangement.

The two old women giggled.

"Umm . . ." Tarl said. He cleared his throat.

Marna snickered.

"Betan! Don't be rude." A woman whose sole adornment was a towel around her hair rushed up. She grabbed the boy's hand and tried to pull him away. "I'm very sorry," she muttered to Tarl, her own blush visible even under her dusky skin.

"But look, Mother!" Betan persisted, pulling free of his mother's grip and pointing at Tarl. "He's white and pink, not brown like us!"

Tarl's blush deepened, but he couldn't stop the embarrassed grin that insisted on breaking out. Nothing like a small child to put a person in his place.

"Where I come from," he said, meeting the boy's stare without flinching, "a lot of people are white—err, white and pink. Like me."

Betan frowned, clearly dubious about so outrageous a claim. Before he could ask another question, his mother grabbed his hand and, with a muttered apology to Tarl, dragged her curious offspring away.

"The little fellow has a point, but what I want to know is, do all those people have quite so *much* pink?" Marna asked, all sweet innocence.

The two old women, who had followed the conversation with interest, chortled wickedly. When Tarl turned to glare at them, they calmly got up and walked away, still chuckling.

Tarl turned back to glare at Marna. She tried to stifle her laughter and produced an undignified snort instead. Since speech was impossible, she gestured for him to follow her, then led him into a labyrinth of small, steam-heated caves that opened onto one another like interlocking pieces in a child's puzzle.

Once safely into the more dimly lit caves, Tarl's blush faded. The mist and the low light provided slightly more privacy, despite the large numbers of bathers sitting and lying around on shelves cut from the living rock. Naturally heated mineral waters from a number of hidden springs flowed in channels cut into the floors of the linked caves. The steam was the densest and hottest closest to the pools, but even the more distant caves were warm. The air was so fogged that Tarl could feel minute water droplets floating into his lungs with every breath he took.

Marna chose a quiet corner in a cave where the slow drip of condensation from the stone and the soft gurgle of the steaming mineral waters running through their channel dampened the murmur of nearby voices. Tarl settled on a stone shelf across from Marna and casually, he hoped, draped his towel across his lap, suddenly wary. So much lay between them, spoken and unspoken, yet so little lay ahead.

The trouble was, he hadn't the slightest idea what to say or do to keep the few precious hours remaining to them from slipping away too fast. Everything that occurred to him, every comment he felt tempted to make, was either absurdly inane or led inexorably back to all the things neither of them wanted to discuss.

Desperate for any safe conversational gambit, however trivial, Tarl ventured into what he hoped would be safe territory. "Tell me," he said with as casual an air as he could manage, "does anyone ever get lost in the caverns? I'd have trouble finding my way back out, and I was trying to pay attention."

Marna laughed, an awkward, breathy little laugh that told him she was as uncomfortable as he. "Children are always getting mislaid, and even adults can go astray if they aren't paying attention."

"Why don't you put up signs or guides, something to help people find their way?"

"Why? There aren't any signs in the Controllor's Palace in Diloran Central, are there? This is our home, after all. We belong here. We all learn our way around sooner or later."

Tarl's stomach squeezed suddenly and his mouth felt dry, as if he'd just eaten something bitter. *This is our home.* She might as well have said, this is *my* home.

"You're glad to be back." It wasn't a question, and Tarl didn't really want to hear her response, but he couldn't help himself. It was like picking at a scab, this constant need to remind himself of the vast gulf that lay between them.

Marna ducked her head, as if unwilling to meet his eye. "Yes. Yes, I suppose I am."

As a response, it was notably less enthusiastic than he'd expected. As a hint that perhaps she, too, was dreading the coming parting, it was a welcome and oddly terrifying relief. Maybe this conversation hadn't been such a mistake, after all. "I never asked. What is it you do here?"

"Me? I'm a tracker. A guide for any work group that needs to go out into the desert, especially in the areas we don't visit very frequently."

Tarl winced in sudden embarrassment. "My offer of the compass was more than a little insulting, wasn't it? I'm sorry. I didn't realize . . ."

Her mouth tilted in a wry smile as shook her head. "You didn't mean to be rude, I know, but I could have brought us all the way back to the main caverns on foot, if it came to that."

"I'm glad it didn't."

"So am I." The light died in her eyes and her smile faded away. "Strange, isn't it? I can find my way across the desert but other times . . . when it really matters, it's not easy to know which way to go." She hesitated, frowning at some unspoken thought. "It isn't easy at all," she murmured at last, as if to herself.

"No, I don't suppose it is," Tarl said, suddenly uncertain about the drift of the conversation.

He didn't know whether to be heartened or frightened that Marna was no more sure of the path she would take than he was of his. Two confused souls blundering about blindly could cause untold damage, to themselves as well as each other. He wanted to say something wise and comforting, but he didn't feel at all wise and he couldn't think of anything comforting that wasn't at least a little dishonest. Neither of them needed lies right now, not even well-intentioned ones.

Silence hung between them, heavy on the humid, misty air.

"I have to admit, I hadn't realized quite how pleasant these steam caves can be," Tarl said with forced casualness, settling back against the warm, damp wall of rock behind him.

Marna leaned back, too. "Not the same as your baths and pools, are they?" she said to the opposite wall, which was half hidden in the drifting mist.

"No, not the same."

When Marna abruptly broke off their useless conversation and rose to leave, Tarl willingly followed.

As he pulled on his now clean clothes in the dressing area, he couldn't help thinking that, naked or not, they'd both managed to hide behind the trivial conversation and the heavy mists.

But what were they really hiding, and who were they hiding it from? Themselves, or each other?

Chapter Twenty

Marna lay flat on her back and glared into the dark, grimly fighting against an intense and very much unwelcome longing for her private room in Diloran Central.

The sleeping chamber allotted to visitors in the main caverns was crowded as usual, and she and Tarl had been unappreciated additions. Since all the more favored spots against a wall had already been claimed, they'd been forced to throw their pallets down in the middle of the open area where they were at the mercy of clumsy latecomers—and where they received the full benefit of the other occupants' vocal talents.

Regular, sharp grunts issued from the right. High whistles, interrupted every now and then by a loud, snorting gasp, echoed off the rock wall on the left. Someone lying behind Marna boasted a snore like rocks rattling in a jug, while another, uncomfortably close by, muttered and argued in her sleep.

The worst was the young couple who had chosen to lay their pallets near the wall farthest from the entrance. Safely hidden in the dark and with the rousing chorus around them to partially drown out the sounds of their lovemaking, they'd rapidly progressed from giggling kisses to the rhythmic slap of flesh against flesh. Their low, unintelligible cries of pleasure were clearly discernible, even this far away.

Marna thought the sound of them would drive her mad. She lay staring at nothing, fighting against a hunger she couldn't appease as she tried to shut out the tuneless chorus around her.

Beside her, Tarl lay on his side on his pallet, deep asleep. He'd fallen asleep easily, as if he were accustomed to the close quarters and the lack of privacy.

It bothered her that he should be so comfortably at home while she lay awake, too unsettled by the noise and the press of sleeping bodies around her to sleep. This wasn't the comfortable, familiar sleeping chamber allotted to the children of the Zeyn Elders that she'd always known, but it was no more crowded or noisy. The only real difference was that now she didn't know any of the people with whom she was sharing it. None, that was, except Tarl.

Perhaps, Marna tried to tell herself, she was simply overexcited by her return and anxious about the coming confrontation with her father and the Elders. That had to be the reason—it was such a sensible explanation. She refused to believe she'd somehow changed in these past few weeks, drifted away from her people and her world so she no longer fit in.

Yet *something* had changed. The familiar caverns she'd missed so much in Diloran Central now seemed crowded and noisy instead of friendly and comfortingly close. She'd been pleased to see her friends, even if only in passing, yet she'd also seen the questioning look in their eyes and their slight withdrawal from her, as if she were a stranger come among them and not quite to be trusted. Now, in a sleeping chamber that was not really so very different from the one she'd occupied before, she found she couldn't sleep even though her body ached with the accumulated stresses and exertions of the past few days.

Marna angrily rolled onto her side, trying to will away her unwelcome thoughts so sleep would come.

The move was a mistake. Just enough light crept into the chamber from a far-off corridor to reveal Tarl's sleeping form beside her, a darker mound in the darkness—and much closer to her than she'd thought. She only had to move her hand a few centimeters to touch him.

Marna longed to wake him so they could make love. She craved the warmth of his touch, the comfort of his strength and his teasing laughter. Even more, she craved the temporary forgetfulness his lovemaking would grant her.

She was afraid to move, not because of the people around them, but because she didn't dare risk lowering her guard against the love for him that had crept in so gradually she wasn't even sure when she'd first realized it was there. She didn't want to be in love with a man who would soon leave Diloran and its problems far behind him.

Marna flopped onto her other side, but even in the dark she was conscious of Tarl's nearness. She sighed and grimly forced her eyes shut, to no avail.

Sleep, no matter how much she longed for it, was not going to come any time soon.

Resigned, Marna sat up and threw back the light covers, then slipped the heavy outer robe that she'd left neatly folded at the foot of her pallet over the simple under-robe she still wore. A walk through the semi-darkened passageways of the cavern ought to work off her restlessness—enough, at any rate, so she could sleep.

She made every effort to be quiet; her movements, she

thought, were safely covered by the din of the sleepers around them. It didn't matter. Tarl stirred and rolled onto his back. The whites of his eyes betrayed him, even in the dark.

Marna drew in her breath sharply, suddenly oblivious to the raucous sleepers surrounding them. Tarl was awake and watching her, and her body automatically responded to his awareness with a growing heat and a hot, sharp beat of desire, deep and low down.

She was already on her knees. Marna knotted her hands in the full skirts of her robe against the temptation to touch him, then leaned forward to whisper in his ear, "Go back to sleep. I won't be gone long."

As she drew back, Tarl's hands came up to cup her face, capturing her before she could flee. His head shifted slightly on the pillow as he drew her down to him; their lips met, and all Marna's stern resolve to keep her distance melted away as if it had never been.

The faint stubble of his beard rasped against her lips, teasing her. Marna ran her tongue across the roughness, savoring the taste and texture of him, helpless to resist temptation as a sharp bolt of desire shot through her. She bent her head and placed a wet, tugging kiss on his throat, just at its juncture with his jaw where the flesh was most sensitive.

Tarl groaned—a soft, long, low groan of pleasure. He tilted his head back, inviting more kisses, and threaded his fingers through her hair, loosening the crude braid she'd plaited after her bath.

How far she might have yielded to the promptings of her body and the urgent entreaty of Tarl's response, Marna didn't know. She was brought back to a sharp awareness of their surroundings when a nearby sleeper whose existence she'd momentarily forgotten gave a deep, wracking snort that shivered its way up the scale, then broke off with a loud gasp. An even deeper, louder snort finished off the performance.

Marna froze, head up, senses alert for any indication that

their neighbors were aware of what had passed between her and Tarl. Her face and throat burned with a heat that was only partly embarrassment.

The racket in the sleeping chamber continued unabated. The chamber's occupants slumbered on, untroubled by even so momentous an event as the kisses she'd just shared with Tarl.

Beneath Marna's hand, Tarl's chest shook. The sound of a stifled laugh broke through Marna's tension. She bent her head to study him, but he was still little more than a black shadow in the dark. Only her hand on his chest and her achingly acute awareness of him told her he was watching her, and that he knew what she was thinking.

Marna shoved away from him at that, torn between wanting to laugh with him and wanting to forget their surroundings and take up where they'd left off so abruptly. She did neither. Her first impulse had been the right one, after all—to seek some privacy and a chance to think, without Tarl's presence to distract her.

Resolved, Marna once more bent to whisper in his ear, "I'll be back. I promise."

She rocked back on her heels and gathered the skirts of her robe, but before she could rise to her feet, Tarl sat up and grasped her arm, drawing her close.

"Will you be all right?" he demanded, keeping his voice to the level of a whisper, just as she had. Even that wasn't enough to disguise the concern she could hear in his words.

Marna nodded, then, realizing he might not be able to see that slight motion in the darkness, said, "Yes. I just—" She hesitated. "I just need some time to myself."

His hand dropped away at that, releasing her. Beneath the heavy sleeve of her robe, Marna's skin pricked into cold bumps. She felt . . . abandoned. Bereft. Alone as she had not expected to be alone even in the desert beyond the caverns.

Without another word, she tugged her robe free and rose

to her feet. At the foot of her pallet, she bent to retrieve the soft-soled shoes she'd chosen to replace the sturdy desert boots she'd worn from Diloran Central. Shoes in hand, her robe carefully gathered so she wouldn't brush against someone, Marna crept out of the sleeping chamber and into the darkened passageway beyond.

She dropped the skirts of her robe then, but kept her shoes tightly clutched in one hand as she carefully felt her way along the passage with the other. The stone floor was cool against her bare feet, reassuringly solid. She felt an inner surge of gratitude for that solidity; her head was whirling too rapidly for her to be able to concentrate on anything but the difficult task of moving forward, knowing Tarl remained behind.

Once safely away from the sleeping area, Marna knelt to pull on the shoes she'd brought, then set off down the semi-lit passage to her left, for no reason other than that she was already facing that way. She rambled without direction or goal, avoiding the darkened passages that led to sleeping areas just as she avoided the brightly lit ones where those whose work kept them up at this late hour would still be abroad. The maze of shadowy passageways and public caverns seemed as cold and unfriendly as the Government Palace in Diloran Central had a few short weeks before.

An hour passed, perhaps more, and still Marna wandered, distracted, unwilling to force herself into the light, unable to drag herself back into the dark and to sleep. Once she ventured out into the night, past the guards posted at each access door and the small pools of gold cast by the security lights, far enough so it seemed she was alone under the stars. She hastily retreated when all she found out there was emptiness and the mournful keening of the wind across the sand.

All the while she carried the memory of Tarl for company, of his low moan of pleasure when she'd kissed his neck, of the scrape of his new beard across her lips, the warmth of his skin, and the way he'd laughed at her, silently, with the laughter bottled up in his solid chest like bubbles in a jug of sweet spring wine.

None of it brought her comfort. Nothing reassured her. She felt like a stranger blundering about in a world where she didn't belong, chasing answers that eluded her at every turning no matter how hard she tried to catch them.

At last, weariness dragging at her heels, Marna stumbled upon the small service area that was kept open through the night to provide meals for the night workers. She couldn't ask for food, but she ought to be able to convince the attendant to give her something warm and soothing to drink that would help her sleep.

The area, a replica in miniature of the larger dining and meeting area where she and Tarl had eaten earlier, stood empty. Several tables bore the odd crumbs and splotches of spilled liquids that indicated a few late diners had recently come and gone, but that was all. No one was in sight.

Marna settled at a clean table in an out-of-the-way corner. A few minutes later a young woman, who seemed to be about her own age, emerged from the service area. Head down, oblivious to her surroundings and Marna's presence, she thumped the basket of cleaning supplies she carried down on the nearest dirty table and listlessly began scrubbing the tabletop one-handed.

Irritated, Marna watched her inept performance for a minute or two in silence before saying, "Excuse me. Would it be possible to get something hot to drink?"

The woman jumped and whirled about, startled out of her dull reverie. Only then could Marna see why she'd been working one-handed—her left arm dangled uselessly at her side, so twisted and shriveled that only the tips of her fingers peeked out of her sleeve.

Marna blinked and swallowed uncomfortably, ashamed of

her earlier irritation. "I'm sorry. I didn't mean to frighten you."

"There usually isn't anyone here at this hour," the woman said, resentment clear in her voice. After her first startled glance, she carefully avoided meeting Marna's gaze and sullenly turned to finish her task.

"I couldn't sleep, so I thought . . . If it's too much trouble . . ."

"I'll get you something, but I have to finish here first." There was no trace of conciliation in the woman's voice, but her hostility wasn't so overt that she risked a reprimand, either. She gave the table a few more half-hearted swipes, then gathered up her basket with an officious clatter and carried it to the kitchen. A few minutes later she returned bearing a steaming mug. Without a word, she set the mug in front of Marna, then turned back toward the kitchen.

She hadn't even glanced up when Marna murmured her thanks. Was it to avoid being forced to see the residue of shock and pity Marna knew must still show in her face?

Memories of another woman came pouring in. Marna's fingers tightened around the cup she held. Where was Sesha? What was she doing? Was everything going well for her, or was she sorry she'd chosen to stay among strangers? Would she, Marna wondered, ever know the answers to all her questions?

The serving woman interrupted the train of Marna's thoughts when she once more emerged from the kitchen with the basket dangling from her good hand. Without a word, she chose a table as far from Marna as possible, then bent to her task. As she worked, she took care to keep her good side to Marna and her crippled arm pressed tight against her body, safely out of sight. After a moment's hesitation, Marna picked up her mug and crossed to the other woman, who glanced up in surprise.

"Kiria?"

"My name is Marna," Marna ventured. "What is yours?"

The woman's eyes narrowed in suspicion. "My name?"

"Yes. I don't believe I've ever met you before."

The silence stretched before the woman reluctantly said, "Hanmel, Kiria. My name is Hanmel."

She started to turn away, but Marna grabbed hold of her right sleeve—the sleeve that covered her good arm—to stop her.

"Kiria?" Hanmel said warily, clearly surprised at the contact.

"I wondered . . . Hanmel, what happened to your arm?" The question burst from Marna before she'd had time to think about it.

"My arm?" Hanmel flinched and reflexively pressed her crippled limb against her side, as if to protect it. Or hide it. "A skimmer accident, Kiria," she said at last, reluctantly. "A long time ago."

Hanmel would have retreated then, but Marna continued to cling to her sleeve. "What were you trained for, Hanmel? What did you do, what were you before the accident?" she persisted.

The serving woman hunched her shoulder and looked away. "I was a child, Kiria," she muttered. "I never had a chance to be anything."

Marna stiffened and let her hand fall from the woman's sleeve, too shaken to maintain her grip. *I never had a chance.*

Hanmel backed up a step, intent on retreating. Before she could leave, Marna, desperate to find words to cover her shock, lifted the mug she held as if in salute and said, "Thank you, Kiria."

She might as well have slapped the serving woman. Hanmel recoiled, then anxiously scanned Marna's face, unmistakably upset by the simple, yet unexpected courtesy. Before

Marna could gather her wits to explain, Hanmel scuttled away.

Marna waited for more than a quarter hour for Hanmel to reappear before she gave up her futile vigil and returned, feet dragging with weariness, to the sleeping chambers . . . and to Tarl.

She'd found no peace in her wanderings, and no answers. Perhaps she never would. Perhaps she'd simply spend the rest of her life like Tarl, a stranger among her own people crying out in useless protest against what she could never change.

Marna stopped abruptly, shaking with the cold that had shivered down her spine at the thought. She glanced back along the passageway behind her. Empty. She forced herself into motion and headed back to the dark, crowded sleeping chamber where Tarl lay waiting for her. At the thought of him, she walked faster.

At mid-morning, a messenger summoned them to appear before Eileak and the Elders.

A more urgent summons had reached them two hours earlier when Dorn, wide-eyed and sweating with nerves, found them and announced that Caithra had gone into labor shortly before dawn. Marna had clapped her hands and crowed in delight, but Dorn hadn't been in any mood to be reassured.

"She's having a hard time of it," he said grimly. "We're gathering now, but it may be hours before the child appears."

"Of course it will. This is a first baby," Marna chided, carefully sidestepping the question of Caithra's two miscarriages. "First babies are always difficult."

Dorn wasn't so easily comforted. The lines of tension around his eyes deepened until they looked as if they'd been indelibly sculpted into his flesh. "But what if the proctors . . . ?" He choked, and his mouth twisted as if he'd swallowed acid. "What if the baby's deformed and the proctors won't allow it to live? Vergat's child was completely normal except for being albino, yet it was taken out into the sands. What if the miscarriages—?"

"Don't think about them!" Marna spoke more sharply than she'd intended because of her own horror at Dorn's mention of the proctors, the men and women who inspected all newborns and judged which would be allowed to live, and which, because of some physical imperfection, some congenital defect, would be taken out into the desert and abandoned.

"Don't think about them," she said again, more gently this time. "Think about Caithra and how happy you'll both be when you can hold your child in your arms. You have to be strong now. For Caithra's sake."

Marna wrapped her arm around Dorn's shoulders and led him back to the gathering area where, by tradition, friends and family members were assembling to await news of the birth. Tarl followed silently, his expression a mixture of grim misgiving and masculine helplessness.

The messenger from the Elders found her and Tarl in the gathering area two hours later, still anxiously waiting along with everyone else for news of Caithra and the baby.

"Kiria," the messenger said, nodding with cool, distant politeness. "The Elders will speak with you now." She glanced at Tarl. "You and Kiri Grisaan." Only when she said "Grisaan" did she display any emotion—a quick flare of hostility that disappeared as quickly as it came, but left no doubt of her personal feelings.

Marna bit down on the sharp reprimand that rose to her lips and glanced at Tarl. He seemed oblivious to the messenger's reaction, but he would never have missed anything so obvious. Whatever changes might follow Marott Grisaan's overthrow, resentment for his treatment of the Zeyn clearly would not be soon forgotten—and that meant one more item added to Tarl's long list of reasons for not remaining on Diloran.

Eyes downcast so that no one would see the sudden bleakness within her, Marna followed Tarl and the messenger through the now crowded corridors, back to the complex of caves that served as offices for the Elders. The messenger led them directly to the council chamber, then left them standing there, silently facing the seven age-lined faces that studied them with icy dispassion from the other side of the council table.

Among the Elders, only Marna's father gave any hint of his feelings. His dark eyes had fixed on her the moment they entered the chamber; the corners of his mouth pulled down, and his lower lip thinned to near invisibility with repressed anger. He looked, Marna thought, much as he'd looked in Marott Grisaan's office, pitiless and rock hard in his uncompromising determination to have his way.

Behind the anger, Marna knew, would be shame for her failure and even greater shame for his responsibility in having entrusted her with the Elders' plans in the first place.

Anger and shame. It was a dangerous combination, and it made her father a dangerous enemy.

Marna shuddered inwardly. The word "enemy" had a harsh ring to it, but she knew her father saw *her* that way, a traitor to him and the Zeyn. The proof of her broken vows was standing beside her, undeniably alive and almost insolently relaxed as he coolly assessed the five men and two women across from them.

Tarl's confidence comforted her. Without intending it or thinking about what it might mean, Marna took a step closer to him. As she moved, her gaze locked with her father's. Undisguised fury sparked in Eileak's dark eyes. Her defiance of his orders was one thing, openly siding with the enemy quite another. That one short step divided her and her father just as the massive table divided them physically.

It was too late to wish she hadn't set down the challenge.

Marna wasn't even sure she regretted it, whatever the outcome. In the end, it wouldn't matter, if she could only find the words to make them—make *all* of them—understand what she had to say.

Surreptitiously, Marna rubbed her damp palms against her robe, fighting to calm the nervous knotting of her stomach and wishing she could appear as calm and unruffled as Tarl did.

Although the Elders remained seated, they made no effort to offer their visitors a chair. Marna hadn't expected them to. Tarl clearly wasn't going to put up with being forced into a position of weakness, however. He turned and, with an imperious gesture that reminded Marna of his uncle, said, "We need two chairs here, please," to the attendant posted beside the chamber door.

The attendant blinked and straightened in surprise, then nervously glanced at the Elders for guidance.

Eileak scowled, but reluctantly nodded his assent. "Do it."

Once the attendant had placed the chairs to Tarl's satisfaction—directly across from Eileak—he hastily retreated to his post out of the way of the coming fireworks.

Marna took her seat, back rigidly straight, gaze fixed on her hands where they lay clasped tightly together in her lap. Tarl leaned back in his chair and casually crossed his legs, ankle to knee. His posture spoke of careless indifference, but his hard gaze fixed unflinchingly on Eileak, as though warning her father that he was prepared for a fight if someone forced it on him.

The Elders began cautiously. Sour, mistrustful old Yethan spoke first. "We had not expected to see you here, Kiria Marna. Especially not accompanied by Kiri Grisaan."

He's supposed to be dead and you should still be in Di-

loran Central, as you were instructed. The unspoken message came through as clearly as if Yethan had said the words out loud.

Marna defiantly raised her chin. "Marott Grisaan sent us. He wished to warn you of a plot against the Zeyn." She'd meant to keep all trace of her thoughts off her face, but she could feel her eyes narrowing and her lips drawing tight in a hard, angry line. Well, her father would give her no credit for restraint. What could she lose by speaking plainly? "It seems our efforts were wasted. I have learned that the conspiracy of the Sherl and the Burnarii was not against the Zeyn."

She paused, then looked her father square in the face. "Not *against* the Zeyn," she repeated, "but *with* them, in spite of every rule of honor we have ever been taught. In spite of our own past."

Eileak's dark brows drew together in a ferocious scowl. Before he could speak, thin, dyspeptic Strogal spoke up. "It is not your position to question the decision of the Elders. You know nothing of the matter."

"I know enough to realize that there is nothing to be gained by squandering our people and our resources, or by plunging into an alliance with Families who have earned our enmity, not our trust. I know—*now*—that our willful refusal to associate with the rest of Diloran has held us bound to traditions and values that no longer serve us well. I know—"

"Enough!" Eileak slammed his palms against the table and half rose to his feet. With his baleful glare and his head thrust forward between hunched shoulders, he looked like a desert scavenger eyeing his prey and trying to decide how best to rend it limb from limb. "We did not bring you here to discuss your foolish notions, but to hear what news you bring of this turmoil in Diloran Central."

Marna stiffened. "We told Parra everything we know yesterday. I knew nothing of it and Tarl did not expect the Tevah to move against his uncle until he'd returned to Diloran Central. What more is there to say?"

Eileak shoved away from the desk and slowly straightened to his full height. His hard, unblinking gaze never wavered from her face.

Bile rose in Marna's throat. Did he think she could tell him more, but wouldn't? Or did he think she was lying, deliberately concealing the truth from him for reasons of her own? Impossible to know. Either way, the gulf that had always lain between them now gaped wider and deeper and darker, until she thought she might be swallowed up in the void.

"Suppose, instead of demanding information we don't have, you tell us what *you* know?" Tarl's cool, even tones muted the tension in the room like a hand touched to a vibrating string. Eight heads, including Marna's, turned to look at him. He uncrossed his legs and leaned forward, elbows on knees, hands loosely clasped before him, seemingly as relaxed as if he were among old friends instead of facing people who had actively plotted his destruction.

Perhaps it was that unexpected calm, or simply the compelling power of his gaze, but Marna and the six Elders waited, unmoving, to hear what Eileak would say in response, each of them sure somehow that he *would* respond.

A tense moment passed, then two. Eileak stood as if cast in stone, staring at Tarl. Only the line of taut muscle visible at the corner of his jaw betrayed his inner struggle.

Just when Marna thought her lungs would burst from the breath she held, Eileak spoke.

"I know that I risked everything—the honor of the Zeyn, our future, our lives, perhaps—on the mistaken belief that my daughter would carry out the task she was sworn to. Her failure may have condemned us all."

The emotionless wall her father had always kept between himself and the rest of the world fell suddenly, shattered by the bleak, self-condemning despair Marna could now see so clearly in his eyes.

Her heart stopped. The world spun around her. Yet still she heard his next words.

"Marott Grisaan lives. He lives, and he is winning, in spite of all the Tevah's careful planning. And once he has conquered the Tevah, he has sworn to destroy all the Families who have moved against him."

Eileak's grim, haunted gaze turned on Marna accusingly. "All of them," he said. "Including the Zeyn."

Chapter Twenty-one

Tarl watched helplessly as Marna, seated across from him in the almost empty dining area, clutched a cup of hot kava and stared bleakly into nothingness. Her eyes, wide and round and glassy, looked out of a face gone white with shock.

Nothing he'd said, either in the council chamber or afterwards, had penetrated the guilt and self-doubt that had taken hold of her soul when her father all but accused her of destroying the Zeyn. She hadn't heeded the pandemonium that had broken out among the Elders in the council chamber at Eileak's announcement. Instead, she'd just sat and stared at her father, clearly incapable of seeing that he was the one responsible for whatever threatened the Zeyn now, not her. Her father and the Elders and the xenophobic traditions they'd so adamantly refused to put aside.

She couldn't see it now, either. All of Tarl's arguments fell on deaf ears, no matter how often or how passionately he repeated them. He was growing desperate.

Tarl frowned, thinking of what Eileak had told them. He

didn't believe Marott had taken control of the fighting and was driving everything before him as Eileak said, but Tarl *did* fear the Tevah had risked too much too quickly and had ended up overextending their resources.

Beginning a fight was one thing, continuing it quite another. After three hundred years of relative peace—a peace, Tarl wryly admitted, for which his family could claim a large part of the credit—there were few on Diloran who understood the often horrifying twists of armed conflict, fewer still who had the experience to cope with them. And he was one of those few.

He had to return to Diloran Central. Immediately. He was needed and he dared not risk Diloran's future—or his—by lingering in the Zeyn caverns.

Getting away wasn't the problem. He'd already identified several routes out of the caverns, and from scraps of conversation he'd caught, he knew where the Zeyn kept their transports and long-range skimmers.

The problem was, he couldn't leave Marna. Not here. Not like this. But did he have the right to take her with him?

Tarl's fists clenched on the hard tabletop. They closed around nothing. Marna didn't notice, too lost in her private hell to acknowledge anything that was happening around her.

With a sigh, Tarl dropped his gaze, then forced his hands to open, flexing his long fingers to ease the strain in his arms and shoulders. It would be so much easier if only there were something he could do to help her. Action, even dangerous action, was always easier to deal with than inaction.

Tarl ached to take her away with him, someplace far away where no one had ever heard of Diloran or the Zeyn, where no one cared who they were or what they had been. Someplace they would be free to live their lives as they chose, not as others wanted. He longed to make love to her until the pain in her was replaced by wonder and that fierce joy he could spend a lifetime sharing.

A lifetime . . .

The thought made a mockery of the present.

Gently Tarl enfolded her hand in his and drew it across the table toward him. Until Marna was ready to say what she wanted and what she would do next, he would stay here with her, and he would wait.

The minutes trickled past. Tarl could see her gradually returning to him. She sighed once, then again. Eventually she blinked and shifted on her chair, and her eyes slowly focused on the world around her.

Her gaze slid to his hands where they were carefully folded over hers. For one brief moment, Tarl saw a flicker of hope in her dark eyes, but it died away as quickly as it had come.

Her hand turned within his grasp until her fingers laced with his. "You have to return to the city," she said, hesitating over the words.

"Yes." He clasped her hand more tightly between his own, desperately wishing there were something he could say to comfort her.

"I . . ." She stopped, then said, very carefully, "I can't go with you. There's nothing I can do here, not now. But I can't leave, either. I *can't.*"

A pain twisted inside Tarl, sharp and hot. He swallowed the sudden burning in his throat and said, "I understand." Gently, he drew her other hand into his clasp.

The tall, gray-haired man who came seeking Marna a quarter of an hour later found them seated across the low table from each other, their fingers twined together, their eyes locked on each other's as if they never wanted to look away. They hadn't said a word since Tarl had claimed both of Marna's hands.

"Kiria Marna?" the man said, obviously uncomfortable at the intrusion, and just as obviously determined to deliver whatever message it was he carried.

Marna jumped and slid her hands free of Tarl's. "Yes?"

"It is Dorn. He is asking for you. The baby has just been born and the proctors—"

He didn't have to say more. Marna was on her feet and running. Tarl had to race to catch up with her.

The gathering area was even more crowded than when Eileak's messenger had called them away earlier. At their entrance, an eager rustle went up as the crowd turned to them anxiously, only to turn away again an instant later with a murmur of disappointment.

In that brief moment when everyone was facing Tarl's way, the drab, sand-colored robes of the Zeyn seemed to blend with the pale gray of the chamber's walls until he had the disorienting impression that he was looking at a mass of disembodied dark faces floating in a sea of sand and stone. On each face, old or young, male or female, he could read clearly the strain of waiting for news of the child.

Tarl hadn't had much experience with babies or birthing, but even that little wouldn't have led him to expect the kind of hushed, electric tension that gripped these people now.

What had Dorn said earlier? Something about what if the baby was deformed and the proctors wouldn't allow it to live? He'd spoken of another child, a child that had been "taken out into the sands."

Tarl's stomach twisted, and he tasted bile as the meaning of Dorn's words sank in.

How long would an otherwise healthy newborn live if it were deliberately abandoned in the desert? An hour? Two? Assuming, of course, that the scavengers didn't find it first.

He thought of Sesha and her resigned acceptance of her injury and understood at last, *truly* understood, what she had faced. Tarl turned, but Marna had already slipped away from him. He spotted her halfway across the chamber, slowly making her way toward Dorn and scarcely stopping to acknowledge the greetings and comments of the people she passed.

He also spotted Parra, strangely alone in the crowd that pressed around Dorn. She didn't seem to notice her isolation, however, for her attention was firmly fixed on Marna. At this distance Tarl couldn't read the Elder's expression. He wasn't sure he'd be able to decipher it even if he were closer, but there was something . . . watchful, almost questioning, about the way she studied the younger woman as Marna bent to speak with Dorn.

More latecomers pushed through the entrance, looking for space in the already crowded gathering area. Forced to move, Tarl reluctantly worked his way along the wall to a spot that left him out of the way, yet able to see and hear whatever might happen next. After that first glance when he and Marna entered, everyone had turned away from him, no longer interested.

Being excluded didn't bother Tarl; being parted from Marna did.

At the thought, Tarl set his jaw and pressed his shoulders against the cool stone wall behind him. He was going to have to get used to the idea. In fact, now might be the best time to slip away, when he wouldn't have to say good-bye and when Marna's attention was turned elsewhere.

One glance revealed it was already too late for escape. He'd made a mistake by letting the new arrivals push him into this back corner of the chamber. If he tried to leave now, everyone would turn to see who it was at the entrance, and one thing he didn't need was to draw attention to himself or his movements.

Resigned, Tarl leaned back against the wall and tried to concentrate on making plans for his return to Diloran Central. It wasn't easy. His recalcitrant mind preferred to watch Marna and think about impossibilities, instead. And watching Marna simply made him more aware of the rising tension in the chamber and the worry that was showing more and more clearly in the eyes of the people around him.

The sudden appearance of three somber, gray-robed proctors was greeted with something very like a sigh of relief from the gathered crowd, as though the stomach-wrenching strain of waiting was worse than whatever they might have to hear.

Worse, that was, until a fourth proctor, a woman, appeared in the entranceway, a twitching bundle shrouded in drab, dark gray in her arms. At sight of the bundle, the people gathered in the chamber grew still and hushed. Tarl heard a faint whimper of protest from someone in the crowd, then Dorn surged to his feet, his eyes wild and his face twisted in disbelieving agony.

"No! You can't do this! You *can't!* Caithraaaa!" He plunged forward, only to be grabbed by a half-dozen friends, who dragged him back. Tarl could hear the hiss of their urgent, whispered warnings even from his position at the far side of the gathering.

The woman who held the bundle stood unmoving and unmoved, waiting for the anguished murmurings from the crowd to die away. Her hard, black eyes fixed on Dorn. "Your companion lives," she said at last. "The child, however, is deformed. The proctors are agreed. For the good of our people, it cannot be permitted to survive."

A low moan filled the chamber, but Tarl didn't turn to see who had made it. His gaze was riveted on the gray-robed woman as she slowly unwrapped the newborn child she held, then held it up above the crowd.

"You see?" she cried defiantly. "You see?"

The tiny babe, its skin still reddened from the trauma of birth, kicked at the sudden liberation from its covers. With each feeble kick, its twisted leg and misshapen club foot waved in the air, clearly visible to everyone in the chamber.

No sound broke the shocked stillness of the crowd. Dorn, eyes screwed shut and head thrown back, stood frozen in agony, an animal impaled on the merciless lance of its hunter.

No emotion showed in the face of the woman who held the child—not triumph, not anger, and certainly not pity. Slowly she lowered her small burden, then drew the ends of the grim little blanket over it, neatly tucking in the corners as if such careful attention to detail were all her job demanded of her.

And perhaps it was, Tarl thought, fighting against a wave of nausea and an overwhelming recognition of his own impotence. He staggered as the people in front and to the side pressed back against him, hemming him in as they shrank away from the grim tableau in the entranceway.

An instant later a loud shot of "No!" startled him and everyone else in the chamber out of the helpless resignation that had claimed them. Tarl felt his heart skip a beat at the sudden wild surge of hope that raced through him. He shifted position to gain a clearer view of the chamber and immediately spotted Marna pushing her way toward the entrance and the woman who held Dorn's firstborn child.

Anger flashed from Marna's eyes like bolts of lightning. Her jaw looked set with steel. Her lips had thinned to a hard line, revealing the clenched teeth behind.

One glance at her, and the people in front of Marna scrambled to let her through. Only the proctors in the entranceway appeared unimpressed by the storm headed their way. The three who had entered first moved to stand in front of the woman who held the baby. Each of them held a small but deadly disruptor in his hand, and each of them pointed it squarely at Marna.

Their threatening stance didn't faze her, though it did stop her forward movement. She came to an abrupt halt, then swung around to face the astounded crowd that now watched her nervously, clearly uncertain what would happen next.

"You can't do this!" Marna said. She didn't shout, but her voice rang against the hard stone walls. "*We* can't do this. It's wrong and it's time we stopped clinging to a tradition that has long since outlived its purpose . . . if it ever had any."

No one moved. Not even a whisper sounded in the hushed, expectant silence.

Marna swept the crowd with her unflinching gaze. A few

who met that gaze shrank back, shaken by its power. The rest glanced at the gray-shrouded bundle the proctor held, then at the three disruptors pointed so unwaveringly at Marna's back. Then they leaned forward to hear what else she had to say.

Once sure of her audience, Marna continued in a voice of scarcely restrained passion, "There are specialists in Diloran Central who could help the child, perhaps cure him. We can't do it, but *they* can, if only we ask for their help."

She paused, as though gauging the emotions of her audience, then stretched out a hand to point at the gray-wrapped baby and said, "We can't continue to throw our future away like this, as if it didn't matter. Even this one small life is worth protecting."

Still the crowd stood unmoving, clearly undecided how to react to this unexpected challenge. Yet Tarl could see that Marna's words were having an effect. He studied the faces before him, waiting, like them, for what Marna would say next.

"Some of you know Sesha," she said, more quietly now. "She was called my servant, but she was more like a mother to me than the mother I scarcely remember."

A few heads nodded. Several people frowned, clearly wondering what Marna was leading up to, and one of the proctors let his disruptor wobble slightly in his hand, too caught up in Marna's plea to notice. When the companion on his right nudged him, the man started, then took a tighter grip on his weapon as an angry flush darkened his skin.

"Sesha was crippled in a hunting accident years ago," Marna continued, her voice lower now, more restrained, but no less passionate. "The specialists say that she could have walked normally, if only she'd had the proper treatment in time. *She could have been healed!*" A dozen people jumped, startled by Marna's sudden shout. "This child might have a chance to be healed, as well, but our traditions say he can't have that chance. Well, our traditions are wrong. *Wrong!* We can't destroy this child. We can't abandon him to the desert as if his life didn't matter. We *can't!*''

Marna stopped and blinked back the tears that threatened to blind her. ''Give the child a chance,'' she pleaded. ''We can take him to Diloran Central, to the specialists who—''

The middle proctor, the one whose grip on his disruptor had wavered slightly, cut short whatever else she was going to say by bringing the butt of his weapon crashing down on the back of her head.

With a grunt of pain that Tarl could hear halfway across the chamber, Marna crumpled to the floor, unconscious.

Somehow, Marna was aware of the harsh glare of overhead lights and the unyielding hardness of stone beneath her, but that awareness was peripheral to the sharp, incessant pounding of a hundred men with rock drills who were hard at work inside her head.

''She's coming around.''

The low voice added a dozen more men to the rock-breaking crew. Marna repressed a heartfelt curse and resolutely forced her eyes open.

She immediately wished she hadn't. The lights sent needle-sharp bursts of pain shooting past the rock drillers. She blinked, and from somewhere close by she heard a low moan.

''Marna?''

Marna slammed her eyes shut. The moaner, she realized suddenly, was her. She wondered if anyone else wanted to claim the drillers. ''Marna's not here,'' she said sourly at last. ''Come back later.'' Her mouth felt as dry as if she'd swallowed a bucket of sand.

''At least you'll live.''

There was a note of amusement in the voice. ''Not if I have any say in the matter.''

She kept her eyes shut, but forced herself to sit up. A

strong arm slid behind her back, helping her. She was conscious of a solid, masculine chest and shoulder that were firmly attached to the arm. With another groan, she gratefully leaned her head against the chest. "Tarl?"

"I'm here." He placed the cool edge of a cup to her lips. "Drink this. They say it will help with the headache."

Marna drank. The cold, slightly tart liquid slid down easily, soothing the dryness in her mouth and throat. She gratefully licked the last drop from her lips; then, eyes still firmly shut, she leaned once more against the welcome solidity of Tarl's chest.

Whatever drug the liquid contained worked quickly. As the pain receded, memory returned. Marna sat up with a jerk, and instantly regretted her haste. She clapped a hand to her aching temple, but forced her head to stop spinning and her eyes to focus on the familiar face so close to hers.

"They've taken the child," she said. There was no lingering dryness in her throat to account for the tightness in her voice. She could feel the tears burning behind her eyelids, unshed.

A shadow darkened the soft brown in Tarl's eyes, turning them hard and cold. "Yes."

"And Dorn?"

"He's gone to Caithra. He tried to help you, but the proctors kept him back. Once they left and he saw you would be all right, he went to her. I was sure you'd want him to."

Marna didn't try to nod—her head was still too imperfectly settled on her shoulders for that—but she ventured a small, half-hearted smile of thanks; then, carefully and with Tarl's help, she climbed to her feet. She didn't protest when he kept hold of her arm.

The gathering area, so crowded only a short while ago, now stood empty save for one grim-faced young man who appeared to be about her age. He watched her, expressionless, yet every line of his body betrayed the tension that held him in its grip.

"The proctors assigned him to guard us," Tarl explained, his voice carefully expressionless. "They asked if he knew you, and he said no. He hasn't told me his name. Someone else, someone I haven't seen before, brought the drink for your headache, but she didn't stay."

Not even a flicker of emotion showed in the man's eyes at Tarl's words. He watched her, waiting for what she would do next. Challenging her, perhaps?

Marna wasn't sure where that mad idea had come from. It didn't matter. All her doubts and uncertainties had burned away in the hot rage that had claimed her when that gray-robed horror had held Dorn and Caithra's child aloft and said, "You see?"

In that instant, Marna had seen. Seen and, at last, known without a doubt what it was she had to do.

"I'm going after that baby," she said, and felt a brief surge of satisfaction at the steadiness of her voice. Tarl didn't move, didn't by even a slight intake of breath betray surprise at her words. Had he known what she would do? Known even before she had? Marna shook aside the thought.

"I'm going after that baby," she said again, firmly fixing her gaze on the young man opposite, "and I will not permit anyone to stop me. Do you understand?"

Marna wasn't sure what she'd expected, but she certainly wasn't prepared for the overwhelming relief that washed across his face. His body quivered with an eagerness he no longer tried to repress. "What can I do to help?"

Either she was still too befuddled from the proctor's blow to think straight, or Tarl had somehow expected exactly that response, too, because he was speaking before she even opened her mouth.

"Escort us to an exit. Somewhere close to where the long distance transports or shuttles are parked. You have your disruptor, don't you?"

Their guard's head snapped up at the unexpected question,

but he instantly pulled the hidden disruptor out of his sleeve with the quick, practiced motion of one trained for the desert. "I'll shoot anyone who tries to stop you."

Marna gaped. An ally? She'd expected grim opposition. To suddenly find that their guard was willing to become their protector left her feeling as if she were standing on unstable ground.

"I hope that won't be necessary." The irrepressible note of amusement was back in Tarl's voice. It seemed nothing could keep it down for long. "I hope you won't have to pull it at all. But if anyone tries to stop us, you'll have to make it look like you're escorting us under orders from one of the Elders. Can you do that?"

Understanding dawned in the young man's eyes. With a slight grimace that might have been embarrassment, he slid the disruptor back up his sleeve. "Of course I can. I'll even guide you—" He stopped, then added deferentially, "But Kiria Marna can do that, of course. I have heard of her skills as a tracker."

"Why?" Marna demanded, still dazed at the sudden change in their condition. "Why would you go against the Elders to help us? You don't even know me."

His mouth thinned and there was no mistaking the look of mingled anger and pain in his eyes. "No, but I know Caithra. I know how much she and Dorn have wanted a child." He hesitated, as if he was trying to decide if he should say more or not.

"I was an only child," he added at last, choosing his words with care. "My parents had a second child, a girl, when I was seven. Her arms were stunted and some of her fingers and toes were webbed, but she . . ." He stopped, swallowed hard, then continued slowly, "She was one of the most beautiful babies I've ever seen. And she was taken out into the desert to die, just as they've taken Caithra's son."

His dark eyes met Marna's. In them she read a steely determination that startled her.

"I've never forgotten my sister," he said, "and I will do whatever I can to help you now."

Before Marna could reply, Tarl had once more taken charge. "Let's go, then. The sooner, the better, before anyone decides to come looking for us. Don't forget," he added on a somber note of warning, "that Elder Parra was in the gathering, too. She saw Marna's defiance of the proctors. It probably won't be long before the other Elders hear of it and order Marna detained. And me as well."

Yet despite his warning, and despite the interested gaze of their nameless guard who had suddenly become a friend, Tarl didn't make any effort to get started. Instead, he let go of Marna's arm, but only for the time it took to draw her into his embrace.

"Don't worry," he said softly an instant before his lips claimed hers. "We'll find the child and get away before anyone remembers we were here."

And then he kissed her—a deep, lingering kiss that drove out the shadows. He murmured her name, so low she could scarcely hear it, yet with a hungry longing that struck deep in her soul, then kissed her again.

In that moment Marna knew with a sureness beyond all wondering that rescuing Caithra's child was only the first of the tasks that lay before her. The second was to restore to Tarl a sense of belonging in the world to which he was born, and the third was to hold him by her side for all the years that lay ahead, no matter what.

When Tarl let her go at last, reluctantly, Marna stepped back, shaken by the vision of what lay ahead. She wanted to laugh and cry and she wanted to go on kissing this man who had so quickly become a part of her, but now was not the time and this was not the place. For now, she would have to be content simply to know that the path ahead of her at last lay clear and straight. She refused to think of the many obstacles that still might block her way along it.

At Tarl's direction, Marna chose their route through the twisting corridors, deliberately selecting the less frequented ones where there'd be fewer chances of running into someone who knew of her encounter with the proctors. Tarl followed her, and their guard, who had introduced himself as Wergan, trailed after Tarl.

They'd been more than fortunate in Wergan's support, for he proved to have a quick mind and a skill for dissembling that might, with practice, have rivaled Tarl's. Twice, when some of his acquaintances stopped him in the passageways, he'd smoothly brushed them off with a muttered explanation that Marna doubted any heard clearly, or would have understood if they had.

To Marna's relief, no one they passed recognized her, and though she detected a few curious glances thrown their way, no one tried to stop them.

Marna tried to tell herself it was far too early to celebrate their escape, but she couldn't keep down a little burst of eager confidence as she rounded the last turn in the passageway leading to the seldom-used exit she sought. She was half a meter past the turn when she stopped abruptly in midstride. Tarl and Wergan, hard on her heels, almost ran over her before she could warn them.

The bottom dropped out of Marna's stomach. Her heart suddenly felt as if it had lodged halfway up her throat.

In the narrow corridor ahead of them, Elder Parra stood like a cold and stony judge, silently awaiting them. The two guards on either side of her had their stunners drawn, and both were pointed straight at Marna.

Chapter Twenty-two

"I'm glad to see my estimation of your intentions was accurate, Kiria Marna," Parra said coolly.

Before Marna could respond, Wergan shoved himself in front of her, weapon drawn. Tension had strung the cords in his neck in rigid lines, but his grip on his disruptor was as unwavering as Parra's two guards' were on theirs. "You can't stop them, Elder Parra," he said with grim determination. "I won't let you."

Marna swallowed, forcing her heart firmly back into her chest where it belonged, and stepped in front of Wergan's disruptor. Their uneventful progress to this point had made her overconfident; it was her fault they'd walked into this trap and her responsibility to get them out.

From the corner of her eye, she spotted Tarl taking up a position to her right. He moved with the same easy languor that had deceived her for so long. If they were lucky, it would deceive Parra and her guards, as well. If they were very lucky, they would get past the three in front of them and out onto the sands without any violence whatsoever.

She didn't expect to be that lucky.

"I didn't realize my intentions were of any interest to you, Kiria Parra," Marna said with perfect courtesy, despite the tension thrumming in every muscle of her own body.

Parra ignored her weak attempt at evading the issue. "It is against Zeyn law to defy the proctors' decisions regarding malformed children, Kiria," she said. "It is also forbidden to take any transport that belongs to the people without proper authorization."

Before Marna could respond to the blatant challenge, Parra reached into a pocket of her robe and pulled out a small disk of dull gray metal. She extended the disk to Marna. "That's why I have brought you an authorization key. It will give you access to whatever vehicle you need and allow you safe passage over any checkpoint between here and the Zeyn borders."

Marna gulped and stared at the gray circle that lay in Parra's outstretched palm, too stunned by this unexpected turn of events to respond. Dimly, she heard a sharp gasp from behind her, but couldn't tell if it had come from Wergan or Tarl. The former, she supposed, then dismissed the thought. She lifted her gaze and focused on Parra's face, which was still as coolly expressionless as ever.

"I'm afraid there's nothing I can do about the proctors," Parra continued when Marna didn't speak. "At least, not now. But I can tell you there is a small, fast transport parked at the far edge of the ridge. It's equipped for the desert and convenient for . . . where you are going . . . and what you have to do."

The slight breaks in the older woman's voice were the first signs of emotion Marna had seen in the Elder. Parra clearly wasn't pleased with even that small self-revelation, for she immediately drew herself rigidly erect, head high, her features once more schooled in an expression of icy detachment. She stretched her hand out further. The disk she offered gleamed dully in the overhead light. "Take it," she said. "You'll have enough to deal with as it is."

Without speaking, Marna took the proffered disk and slipped it deep in her pocket. That was one problem out of the way, at least. She never took her eyes off the woman in front of her, but she sensed the sudden release of tension in Wergan and heard the sound of his disruptor as it slid back into its sheath. A moment later, Parra's two guards lowered their weapons, as well.

"A sandstorm is moving in," Parra continued. "A bad one. The proctors won't go far, given the conditions, but you will have to move quickly if you are to succeed."

"And the guards outside?" Tarl's question startled Marna. Trust him to think of the details, even now.

Parra didn't blink, but she didn't look as if she appreciated the interruption, either. "I could do nothing about them. I have no direct jurisdiction over their activities and any interference on my part would only draw attention to you. At least the storm will hinder them as much as it will hinder you."

She hesitated, then turned and gestured to one of her guards, who immediately sheathed his weapon and bent to pick up two bundles lying on the floor behind him. As he offered the first bundle to Tarl, Parra said stiffly, "It's a Zeyn robe. Take it. You'll need it. Your Marine uniform will only attract attention, and it can't provide the protection the robe can. Not in a storm."

The second bundle was for Marna. "It's food and supplies for the baby," Parra said, deliberately ignoring Marna's start of surprise.

She pointed at Wergan. "You. Go with my men and make sure no one is posted anywhere near the entrance to the sands." As Wergan started to move past her, she added,

"Then come see me in an hour or two. I can use someone like you."

Wergan didn't reply, but his eyes narrowed warily as they met Parra's. After one quick glance to make sure Marna had no objections, he slipped away after Parra's guards, who were already at the far end of the passage, where the controls for the outer door were located.

"Tell me, Kiria Parra. How did you know what we would do?" Marna demanded as Tarl quickly slid the heavy robe he'd been given over his head. "Did you have spies posted near the gathering area?"

Parra shook her head. "No spies. It was too short notice and I wasn't sure whom to trust, under the circumstances. But this route made the most sense. I could only hope you would act on what you said, there in the gathering area."

Marna fought against the dizzying sensation of once more finding her world turned topsy-turvy. This woman was risking everything she'd spent her life to obtain—position, influence, power—and all for the sake of a crippled newborn. Yet Parra had willingly joined in the plotting against the Grisaans and the Diloran Central government without once revealing any concern for all the lives that might have been lost—that might still be lost—as a result.

"Why are you helping me now?" Marna demanded. "What about the—mission you and the other Elders gave me?"

Parra glanced at Tarl, then back at Marna. Her lips thinned into a hard, uncompromising line. "Our plans to destroy the Grisaans, you mean." She didn't wait for Marna's nodded confirmation. "I would do the same again, if I could. It's one thing to admit we need to . . . reconsider some of the customs we have always lived by, but the Grisaans . . ."

Anger sparked in Parra's dark eyes. The look she turned on Tarl dripped pure poison. "Your family has caused my people untold grief for generations. They betrayed their responsibilities and used their power for their own benefit, not ours. It's long past time they—*you*—were removed, Tevah or no."

"By murder?" The scorn in Tarl's voice stung like acid. "Is that how you want to solve your problems? By ignoring every tenet of your precious Zeyn honor and asking Marna to turn spy and assassin?"

Parra's chin snapped up as if he'd hit her. "What else *could* we do?"

Tarl snorted in disgust. "What you should have done years ago—openly worked to limit the power of the controllorship. Built a political force strong enough to offer an alternative to the people of Diloran."

In the space of a heartbeat, Tarl's pretense of calm detachment had disappeared, consumed by his flaring anger. Parra had unwittingly struck at the core of his own disillusionment, Marna realized, shattering his control and letting loose the frustration and fury that must have smoldered within him for years. And he was more than willing to loose that fury on Parra.

"You—all of you—are responsible for the future of your people," he snarled. "By leaving everything in the hands of my family, you abdicated that responsibility and left yourselves vulnerable to their abuses. You didn't protect your people by confining them here in the desert, you condemned them to a marginal existence at the edge of Diloran society. And do you know why?"

He didn't give Parra a chance to tell him if she did or not. "I'll tell you why. Because you didn't want to admit that there are no easy answers and never will be. Because you and the people who came before you wanted somebody else to do the dirty work, somebody else to take the blame. You still do. That's why you and the other Elders sent Marna to carry out your cowardly schemes. But she was too decent to give in to the pressure you put on her, just as she's too decent to sit back and ignore your obscene custom of abandoning crippled babies to the desert.''

Tarl's words lashed at Parra with the ferocity of a desert storm, but the Elder endured his tirade without flinching. Only the flexing of the muscle at the side of her jaw and the rapid rise and fall of her breast betrayed her. She was choking on the truth she'd chosen to ignore for so long, struggling to swallow in one huge lump what she'd spent a lifetime avoiding.

Head high and hands clenched, Parra put her back to the solid stone wall of the passageway. ''Go. Now,'' she said, spitting the words out as if they were sharp-pointed darts, each once aimed straight at Tarl.

For an instant, Tarl wavered, clearly torn between the angry urge to challenge her further and the far more pressing need to get away while they still had a chance. Marna watched his inner struggle and bit back the words of warning that trembled on the tip of her tongue. He knew as well as she did that Eileak and the other Elders would soon hear of her challenge to the proctors. When they heard, they would act. There wasn't much time left.

Yet when Tarl drew an unsteady breath, then another, and reluctantly turned to follow Wergan, Marna hesitated.

''He's right, you know,'' she said to Parra, heedless of the note of pleading in her voice. ''There are so many things we've missed out on, so much we don't know and haven't tried to learn. And all because we're afraid we won't measure up.''

Marna's last words succeeded in piercing Parra's emotional armor where Tarl's had not. The Elder raised her chin defiantly higher. ''That's not true!'' she protested. ''You know that's not true!'' But even as she spoke, her eyes grew wide and she pressed her back against the wall behind her as if she hoped it would swallow her up.

In that moment, Marna understood what it was that had driven her father and the other Elders. It wasn't anger, as she'd sometimes thought. It wasn't a desire for justice, nor even the need for revenge for past injustices. It was fear. Fear that somehow the Zeyn couldn't measure up to the rest of Diloran, that the world they'd always known was being passed by and that the Zeyn and their traditions were irrelevant to everyone else on Diloran, including the Grisaans.

Whether they had realized it or not, Eileak and Parra and all the rest had been more afraid of being forgotten than of being destroyed, and they had let their fear and their ignorance guide them, regardless of the price their people might have had to pay—and might still have to pay.

The unwelcome insight pressed on Marna like a suffocating avalanche of sand. With an effort, she wrenched her gaze away from Parra and glanced toward the end of the passage where Wergan stood at the half-open door, his body outlined by the dull light pouring in from outside, waiting. Tarl was already out of sight.

She turned back to Parra. "We have to go." The Elder didn't move. She still hadn't moved when Marna called out, "Thank you," an instant before Wergan swung the outer door shut behind her.

Parra had been right about the coming storm. Marna hunched her shoulders and turned her back to the stinging onslaught of air-borne sand.

Tarl suddenly materialized out of the rising storm. "Parra's people have temporarily drawn off the guards who were posted at this entrance," he shouted over the whine of the wind. "They said the transport was over that way, at the end." He gestured along the towering ridge of rock that sheltered the caverns and that was quickly disappearing in the swirling clouds of sand.

"Tarl and I will grab the transport," Marna said to Wergan. "You stay here and guard our backs."

He nodded. His dark eyes burned. "Go quickly," he said.

"Then bring the child back to us again, whole. For my sister's sake."

Before Marna could thank him, he turned away and strode into the teeth of the wind.

Marna led the way along the base of the ridge. Even that massive wall of stone could do nothing to dampen the ferocity of the wind. The sun peered balefully down at them through a curtain of swirling sand like the malevolent, dull-yellow eye of a one-eyed monster. Transports and skimmers loomed, dark ghosts in a world that was rapidly growing darker, then disappeared after she and Tarl had passed, consumed by the rising storm.

The transport Parra had suggested wasn't easy to find; its squat lines and tan body blended with the encroaching desert. Marna, half blinded, fumbled for the door controls. As the door slid back, she and Tarl tumbled in, then quickly keyed the door to close behind them. Even then they weren't fast enough. A film of dull-gold sand already covered the floor of the small transport.

Marna tossed the bundle Parra had given her into one of the two passenger seats, then settled into the cramped pilot's position and started the sequence of commands that would get the transport moving. She shoved the authorization key into its slot, and gave a small gasp of relief when the transport's computers acknowledged her control. She could have overridden the computers if necessary, but it would have taken a great deal longer.

Tarl, meanwhile, was checking out the transport's arrangements, including the weapons cabinet.

"Nothing here that's of any use," he said as he settled in the one remaining seat. "That is, unless you want to crash this one, too. I found a fair stock of emergency rations."

Marna glanced over at him as the transport's engines warmed up. A grin broke out on her face, despite the tension that held her. There was nothing left of the carefully groomed man she'd first met. Grains of sand coated Tarl's skin and clung to his eyebrows and lashes. A darker ring of sand circled his neck where the close collar of the robe had trapped it. He looked, she thought, exactly like one of the raffish desert sprites that filled Zeyn folklore. "I take it no one ever gave you a lesson in the proper use of a Zeyn hood."

Tarl's right eyebrow quirked upward, spilling more sand over his lashes and down his cheek. "You need to learn how to pull a hood over your head?"

"For a Zeyn hood, you do. There's a special liner that blocks out most of the sand—if you use it right."

The corner of his mouth twitched, but he managed to keep a straight face as he said, "I'll look forward to a personal lesson."

A metallic beep from the console interrupted Marna's reply. The transport was ready to fly. Her stomach muscles tightened, but she quickly broke the ship free of the sand that was beginning to pile up around it, then pointed its nose into what seemed a solid wall of howling wind and sand.

They were on their way.

If he'd been piloting the transport, Tarl knew his eyes would have been glued to the navigational screen. Marna scarcely glanced at it. Her gaze was fixed on the transport's viewscreen, but Tarl couldn't figure out what she saw to guide her. Other than an occasional vague shape that briefly materialized out of the storm, then vanished, he'd seen nothing but endless, indecipherable sheets of storm-driven sand. Yet Marna didn't falter once as she carefully steered the bucking, protesting transport through the maelstrom.

Less than ten minutes after taking off, Marna set the transport down in the middle of what looked like nothing. Nothing but sand, at any rate. Tarl couldn't even tell where the horizon was.

"They left the child here?" he demanded, stunned anew at the barbarity of the custom.

Marna was already out of her seat and adjusting her hood. "Not here," she said. "On a stone outcrop not too far from here."

Tarl swore softly and once more glanced out the viewscreen. "How are we going to find him, then? We already turned off all the communications and navigation equipment so we wouldn't alert the others to our presence. We don't dare turn them back on. So how will we—"

"Not we. Me."

"You can't go out in that storm alone!"

Her dark eyes met his. Even at this distance Tarl could read the determination in them. "It's safer that way. I know what I'm doing and where I'm going. You don't. I don't want to run the risk of alerting the proctors in case they're still out there."

Tarl opened his mouth to protest. He shut it again without speaking. She was right. Her own people clearly recognized her abilities as a tracker. Who was he to question their judgment?

It was a reasonable question, but watching Marna vanish into the storm without following her was one of the hardest things he'd ever done. He forced the door shut, fighting against the urge to charge out after her. To give himself something useful to do, he checked the disruptor he'd pulled out of the weapons cabinet to ensure that it was properly charged; then he made a small pack out of emergency supplies in case they needed it.

He glanced at the chronometer set in the ship's console. She'd been gone a little less than three minutes.

He verified that the ship's systems were still functioning normally, ran a quick test on the outer door's seal, made sure the outer lock would open smoothly when Marna returned, then started pacing in the narrow aisle. An eternity later, he checked the chronometer again. She'd been gone a little more than five minutes.

Tarl bent to peer out the viewscreen, but this time there was more to see than just sand. A shrouded figure briefly emerged from the storm, then vanished, only to be followed by a second figure, which disappeared as quickly as the first.

The proctors, returning from their grim mission.

An instant later, Tarl was at the transport door. Only the realization that the sound of the door opening might draw unwanted attention stopped him. Frustrated, he leaned against the door, his mind racing.

The two individuals he'd seen didn't appear to have spotted the ship, but that didn't mean someone else wouldn't. On the other hand, there was no reason to suppose that anyone else would be more alert, either. They hadn't expected to be followed, after all, and the small transport would be easy to miss in the sand storm if they weren't looking for it.

But Marna was out there somewhere, one woman against who knew how many armed Zeyn. Worse, if she'd found the child and was on her way back to the ship, she'd be burdened where the others were not.

His mind made up, Tarl doused the interior lights of the transport, pulled up his hood, and used the quieter manual controls instead of the electric to open the door just wide enough so he could slip through. He warily poked his head out, senses straining to detect any sign that others were nearby.

There was nothing to hear except the howl of the wind, nothing to see except the madly blowing sand. Even the front and back ends of the transport seemed to have disappeared, swallowed up by the desert itself.

Fighting against the wind and the driven sand, Tarl stepped out, stunner in hand, then dragged the door closed. He paused again. Still no sign that either he or the ship had been detected.

He started off in the direction Marna had gone earlier. He hadn't gone fifty meters before he realized that he couldn't help Marna. Not this time. The transport had disappeared behind him. He couldn't see anything in front of him. He didn't know where he was going, he was beginning to lose his sense of direction, and he ran the very real risk of becoming lost if he ventured any farther. Marna might be able to find the stone where the child would have been abandoned, but she'd have a much harder time finding him if he was blindly blundering about—and that was assuming she could take the time to try.

Reluctantly, Tarl retreated to the ship. The wind roared in his ears like a maddened monster, hungry for prey; the sand clutched at his feet as if trying to drag him under. He was deaf, blind, and battered, and he was cursing with every breath he took.

It was the longest fifty meters he'd ever traversed.

He was almost on top of the ship before he realized it was there. With a choked sigh of relief, he slumped against the transport's door, fighting to regain his breath. Even here in the lee of the ship the storm tore and ripped at him.

He'd been trapped in desert storms a time or two during his years with the Marines, but never had he experienced anything like this. At least he and his fighting companions had had special protective shelters, hand-held direction guides in case they got lost, desert suits with masks and air filters, and a host of other, more sophisticated equipment to make their sojourn marginally endurable.

If the Zeyn hadn't established their home here centuries ago, he would have said it was impossible for humans to survive in such a brutal, unforgiving place. Yet Marna had gone out into the storm with nothing but her own instincts to guide her.

Huddled against the violence of the storm, Tarl began to understand the necessity that must have driven the Zeyn to adopt the appalling custom of abandoning deformed children so long ago. When the first Zeyn had come to Diloran, they'd had nothing but a few caves in the rocks for shelter and no resources except what little they'd brought with them in their ships. They were desert people, and they had made their home in one of the most unforgiving wastelands in the galaxy. The crippled, the weak, and the infirm would not have survived under such brutal conditions, and so the people must have decided that, given their limited resources, only the babies who had a chance of surviving to adulthood could be saved.

It had been a horrible choice, but perhaps, all those centuries ago, it had been the only choice they could make.

Tarl staggered as a particularly violent gust of wind half knocked him off his feet. He planted his feet more firmly in the rapidly drifting sand and clung to the recessed hand grip on the door, cursing the storm.

Marna was out there, risking her life in an effort to change the world she knew. One woman, alone, and yet . . .

Tarl thought of Wergan, who risked his life because Marna had given him the courage to fight against a system he hated, yet had accepted because he didn't know any other. Tarl thought of Parra, grimly determined to help Marna, regardless of the consequences, and the two guards who could have refused to assist the Elder, but had chosen to support her instead. Because of what Marna had done. Because of what she was trying to do.

Marna. She was only one woman, alone, yet by her actions she was reshaping the world she had known. Because she cared. And because she believed.

One woman.

Tarl's grip on the handle tightened.

He was one man. Just one. And yet—

Marna materialized out of the storm, head bent, her shoulders hunched to provide some small bit of shelter for the tiny, gray-wrapped bundle she carried.

Tarl jerked on the manual controls and dragged the door open. She swept past him and into the transport as though blown by the wind. With one last glance to be sure no one had followed her, Tarl leaped into the transport behind her and slammed the door shut.

It was like plunging from scalding heat into the sweet, cool water of a shaded pond. Outside, the storm continued to vent its fury, but inside the air was soft and the sound of the wind seemed nothing more than a dull, distant susurration.

Tarl's only interest was in Marna. She sat slumped in the nearest seat, desperately clutching the small bundle in her lap. What little Tarl could see of her face beneath the hood was pale, coated with gritty sand, and drawn in lines of strain. He felt a sharp stab of pain deep in his chest, as if her pain had suddenly become his.

He dropped to one knee beside her and gently touched her arm. "Marna?"

She stirred at that and looked up with eyes that were pinched and hollow-looking. "He hasn't moved, Tarl. Not once since I picked him up." She hardly spoke above a whisper, but her voice had a rough, raw edge.

Tarl's fingers curled around her arm. "They swaddled him too tightly. Or perhaps he's too hot."

Her hold on the bundle tightened. "Do you think?"

For answer, Tarl tugged at the edge of the blanket. Before he could pull it free, Marna was ripping at the sand-encrusted folds of cloth, her fingers flying with her desperation.

A moment later, a small pink face emerged, then two small fists, curled tight. The baby's eyes were shut, its tiny, perfect mouth half open. He lay in Marna's lap, unmoving and silent.

Marna was just as still, just as silent, yet Tarl could feel her grief, like a physical presence filling the transport. Her lips trembled. She pressed them closed. Tears formed in her eyes. She squeezed her eyes shut, but still one tear escaped to carve a crooked path down her cheek.

Unable to look upon her pain, Tarl ducked his head to study the sweet face framed by its shoddy gray shroud. He gently brushed his finger over a little fist, then traced the soft, round chin and cheek, marveling . . . and mourning.

The child pouted, then blinked and glared up at the rash stranger who had disturbed his sleep. One look at Tarl was evidently enough, for he immediately screwed his eyes shut, twisted up his mouth, and let out a lusty wail of protest.

Marna gasped. Her chin dropped and her eyes flew open, then widened until they couldn't grow any wider.

Caithra's child kicked feebly, too tightly wrapped to do more. Now that he'd been wakened, the restrictions to his movements clearly infuriated him. The wailing increased in pitch and volume until his outrage echoed in the transport.

Tarl laughed and blinked back the tears that were threatening to betray him. ''He's a desert child, right enough,'' he said, choking a little on his relief. ''Only a Zeyn could sleep through a storm like this one.''

''Oh, Tarl!'' Laughing and sobbing, Marna bent into Tarl's embrace, pressing her cheek against his until it would have been impossible to tell which tears belonged to whom.

Not that it would have mattered. Only the baby protested the arrangement.

The storm eased an hour later, reluctantly subsiding into a muttering freak incapable of anything more than scratching at the transport with its sandy claws.

The babe had been changed and washed and fed and now lay peacefully sleeping, safely strapped into the cradle they'd made out of a passenger seat. Marna and Tarl had washed off the worst of their accumulated grime, then made a meal out of emergency supplies stored on the transport.

Now Tarl, strapped into the pilot's seat, carefully eased the ship out of the sandy blanket that held it. Red-gold sand cascaded down the viewscreen in a slithering rush; then they were free and rising fast. A few minutes later, they were well above the last remnants of the storm, on autopilot and headed in the direction of Diloran Central, half a world away.

Once clear, Marna abandoned her seat to claim the small open space beside Tarl.

He watched without speaking as she knelt and peered out the viewscreen at the desert below them. Her hair had worked loose from the tight knot she'd worn earlier until it hung about her face in a tangled mass of curls and undone braid, obscuring her profile.

Obscuring it, but not hiding it completely. Tarl could see her inner tension in the taut line of her neck and the tilt of her chin. He could see the sudden compression of her lips and the swift dip and flutter of her lashes as she blinked back the tears she wouldn't permit herself to shed. She hesitantly brushed the transparent surface of the viewscreen with her fingertips, then stretched her fingers wide in a futile effort to touch once more the home and land she was leaving behind, perhaps forever.

He turned away, painfully conscious of an ache somewhere deep inside his own heart, and focused on the view that Marna was studying with such intensity. Below them, the desert seemed to flow on forever, its harsh contours softened now by distance and the gentler light of a lowering, late-afternoon sun. It was a grim land, grim and forbidding and dangerous. A land without softness and yet, strangely, not without its own raw beauty.

What had Marna said once? Something about how the desert had always seemed to go on and on forever . . . until she'd discovered that it didn't. Her voice had had a catch in it then. Right now, he didn't think she'd be able to speak if she tried.

She didn't try, and he didn't try to make her. His hands ached to touch her. His arms trembled with wanting to enfold her. And his heart . . . Ah!

Tarl wrapped his hands around the steering mechanism and hung on for dear life. He fixed his gaze on the far horizon and kept it pinned there. Below them lay Marna's world. Ahead—somewhere beyond the horizon—lay his.

But where?

He glanced over at Marna, still so intent on the desert slipping away below them. She was so delicate, yet so strong. Alone now and caught in a struggle that was not of her choosing, yet somehow not afraid.

A woman. Alone.

Tarl gritted his teeth and turned his gaze back to the horizon—a horizon that, even from this altitude, looked as if it lay at the end of existence.

One woman and the power to bring about change.

He'd thought about that while he'd cowered under the lash of the storm, waiting for Marna to return with Caithra's child.

He was one man. Just one.

Did he dare even consider the possibilities? Where would Marna fit in it all? He'd talked of taking her away with him when he left Diloran forever, but she'd never go. Not now.

He couldn't bear the thought of leaving her behind and he wasn't sure what lay ahead if he stayed. If he couldn't be sure of his own future, how could he ask her to share it with him?

Tarl once more glanced over at Marna. She'd moved away from the viewscreen and was kneeling beside his seat, her eyes wide with concern and fixed on him.

He forced a smile onto his lips. It must have reassured her, at least a little, for she gave him an uncertain smile in return.

Since he didn't have the courage to ask any of the questions he wanted to ask, Tarl said, "Tell me, how could you possibly have found your way through that storm, then back to the ship? I tried to follow you and gave up."

Her smile turned from uncertainty to unmistakable amusement. "I am of the Zeyn, remember? I was born to the desert."

The corner of Tarl's mouth twitched in automatic response. "That's scarcely an explanation."

Marna's brows scrunched into a frown as she considered how to answer him. Tarl repressed the urge to trace the tiny valleys the frown made along her brow. Touching her now, when he felt so adrift, wouldn't be a wise thing to do. Not when he ached to gather her in his arms and hold her forever.

"I don't know if there *is* a better explanation," she said at last. "No one of the Zeyn is allowed out of the caverns unsupervised unless they have at least some ability to find their way without help. And people like me, the trackers . . . I guess you'd say we have a special sense that guides us."

She hesitated. "They say . . ." She stopped. Her frown deepened suddenly.

"What do they say?" Tarl asked gently when it appeared she wasn't going to continue.

Marna took a deep breath. The frown disappeared and her eyes widened as they locked on his. "They say that all you have to do is follow your heart."

Tarl's hand curled convulsively around the armrest of his seat as he fought against the urge—no, the *need*—to claim her.

She must have read his thoughts, for she gently pried his hand loose, then twined her fingers with his and hung on. "I wasn't worried, out there in the storm," she said. "I knew I could always return because I could follow my heart back to you."

He let go, then. Let go of the past and the future he'd thought he wanted. Let go of everything except his hold on Marna.

As he drew her into his arms, Tarl knew he'd been wrong, back there in the storm. It wasn't a matter of one person alone at all.

It was simply of matter of letting go and following his heart.

It always had been, if only he'd known.

Chapter Twenty-three

Tarl brought the armored transport down with care, senses alert for any threat the ship's systems hadn't spotted. He could see a number of Zeyn guards posted along the top of the ridge and more on the sands near the main entrance to the caverns. None of them carried long-range weapons, but there was no way of telling what armaments the ones he *couldn't* see were carrying.

Even though he didn't think it would be necessary, Tarl ordered the co-pilot to remain alert, with engines running and controls set for a speedy departure, just in case. Much had changed in the four months since he and Marna had fled the caverns. In all that time they'd had no contact with the Zeyn, and Tarl had finally been forced to send a messenger—suitably armed and escorted—to arrange this meeting.

At least Eileak, the Elders, and the others whose presence Tarl had requested had decided to meet him partway. They were waiting near the cavern entrance in a gesture of courtesy that Tarl hadn't dared hope for, but was profoundly grateful to see since it boded well for the discussions to come.

Eileak stood motionless at the front of the small group. He didn't move even when six armed Diloran soldiers clambered out of the transport right behind Tarl, but Tarl could see his hands curl into fists at his side, as if he were restraining himself by sheer force of will.

After a quick glance to verify that the soldiers had taken the places assigned to them and that the special unloading ramp was sliding into place, Tarl strode across the packed sand toward the silent group awaiting him.

"Eileak. Honored Elders," he said, acknowledging the Zeyn leaders with a curt nod. He scanned the still, silent faces in front of him, trying to judge the emotions hidden behind them. He saw fear, sullen anger, curiosity, distrust, and doubt. Most of all, he saw hope, and that hope nourished his own.

"We received your message, as you see," Eileak said reluctantly. "You are to be congratulated on your victory."

Tarl met the man's hostile gaze squarely. "Not my victory, Eileak. That belongs to the Tevah, to the people who fought for it."

Eileak's eyebrow arched upward in an insulting display of disbelief. "Perhaps the victory is not yours, but you will use it for your own purposes, will you not, Grisaan?"

Tarl grinned. He couldn't help himself. "I will indeed. I already have, in fact." He turned and gestured to one of the soldiers near the transport's door.

The soldier nodded, then disappeared into the craft's shadowed interior. She reappeared a moment later, closely followed by Joeffrey Baland, who irritably waved aside her offer of assistance. Leaning heavily on his cane to balance the weight of his hump, Joeffrey slowly picked his way down the sloping ramp.

Tarl heard the collective gasp of shock from the assembled Zeyn, but he kept his gaze fixed on Joeffrey so Eileak and the Elders could have a moment to adjust to the sight of the crippled old man shambling across the sands toward them. They'd need that moment of adjustment because there were even bigger shocks in store for them. Shocks he would enjoy seeing delivered.

Joeffrey came to a halt at Tarl's side. He planted his cane firmly in front of him and leaned on it while he studied the Zeyn leaders from under his heavy, wrinkled eyelids.

Tarl didn't give either side much of a chance to study the other. He gestured to Joeffrey and said, "Respected Elders, Eileak, this is Kiri Joeffrey Baland, Chief of the new Council of Leaders of Diloran."

"Chief—What do you mean?" Eileak demanded suspiciously. He eyed Joeffrey in appalled fascination, as if he expected the old man to suddenly grow fangs and devour him.

"He means that I'm the head of the new central government of Diloran," Joeffrey snapped. "If you hadn't severed your outside relations after Tarl left you, if you'd bothered to establish decent communications systems and a regular presence in the capital like every other Family on the planet, you would know that already."

"Know what?" The question erupted out of Eileak with explosive force.

"Know what!" Joeffrey's exclamation was just as explosive. "Why, man, that we've restructured the government! There is no controllorship, no all-powerful individual with total authority. Not any more. We've done what we should have done long ago. We've taken the responsibility for our government into our own hands."

As Tarl listened to Joeffrey's quick explanation of the changes that had taken place in Diloran Central during the past four months, he found the corner of his mouth twitching in spite of his best efforts to maintain a respectful demeanor. The old saying that there was no true believer half as fanatical about his faith as one who had converted was certainly true in Joeffrey's case.

Tarl had thought Joeffrey would never come around. Even as he'd grappled with the problems created by Marott Grisaan's abrupt removal from office, Tarl had worked to persuade the Tevah leaders to consider his proposals. He'd argued until he was hoarse before the others had finally come to accept his ideas. Now there wasn't one of them who didn't admit that this new way of working might actually serve them better in the long run, despite its inherent problems and challenges.

Joeffrey had been the hardest to convince, but once convinced, he'd become one of the most vehement advocates of the new order. The man who had once fought to defend Tarl's inherited power now insisted that the office of Council Chief should not be held by any one individual for more than three years. If they were going to have more participative government, he'd grumbled, then they'd better make sure that no one could ever gain too much power or hold it for too long.

It had taken a great deal longer to convince Joeffrey that he was the best man to lead the new Council as they confronted the daunting tasks that lay before them. Bringing the Zeyn into the new government was one of those tasks, and one that Tarl was more than happy to leave in Joeffrey's hands. Judging from the looks of mingled interest and bewilderment on the faces of Joeffrey's audience, the task might not be as difficult as he'd feared.

Whatever the other Elders might think of Joeffrey's recital, Eileak apparently had other concerns to distract him. He kept glancing at the half-open door of the shuttle as if trying to catch sight of someone who remained hidden behind the craft's reflective windows. Tarl thought he detected a hint of longing, or perhaps of desperation, in Eileak's eyes, but he couldn't be sure. He could hope, though. For Marna's sake.

As Joeffrey's clipped explanation of the past months' events ended, Eileak reluctantly turned his attention back to the new leader of the Diloran government. "That is all very well, but what does that have to do with us?"

At his hard, dismissive words, the others in the group stirred restlessly, clearly uncomfortable with his challenge.

Joeffrey wasn't impressed. "Absolutely nothing," he snapped. His gnarled hands tightened around the head of his cane as if he could barely restrain himself from striking out against such obstinate blindness. "Nothing, since you want to be the only Family excluded from a say in the new government. Nothing, since you're not interested in maintaining the economic ties that are essential to your people's future. And I dropped in because you were just around the corner and I felt like a little chat."

Eileak's jaw hardened at the scornful sarcasm.

"Don't be a fool, man!" Joeffrey snarled. "You're the leader of your people. You're responsible for their future. Act as if you care! As if you had some common sense! Join with us on the Council—for the good of Diloran *and* the Zeyn." Joeffrey punctuated his insults by poking his cane at Eileak's chest.

It was an arrogant, foolhardy gesture. Eileak, who was clearly growing more and more enraged, could easily have grabbed the cane and pulled it out of Joeffrey's grasp. If he'd tried, Joeffrey probably would have fallen on his face. Eileak didn't try.

Instead, he drew himself up to his full height, turned on his heel, and started to walk away. Tarl waited, his breath trapped in his throat, to see if the other Zeyn would follow him. Two, old Yethan and the stoop-shouldered Grebnar, hesitated only a heartbeat before turning to follow in their leader's tracks. Three of the Elders wavered, clearly uncertain. The remaining Zeyn, with Parra at their head, planted their feet and stood firm.

Tarl took a deep breath. That clarified where each of them stood, but he couldn't let it go any further. If Eileak wasn't stopped, not only would their plans to bring the Zeyn into the new government fail, but rifts would form within the Zeyn leadership that might take years to heal. He started to speak. A firm, clear voice from the transport behind him spoke first.

"Wait! Don't walk away until you know what you are walking away from."

As if jerked by one string, everyone but Eileak turned toward this new speaker who dared issue a command to the Elder of the Zeyn.

Eyes flashing and head as proudly high as her father's, Marna stood on the transport ramp, staring at her father's back.

Eileak had frozen in his tracks at the sound of his daughter's voice. His back stiffened, but he made no move to turn around. He looked, Tarl thought, like a hunted animal testing the wind for scent of its hunter, uncertain which way to turn because it wasn't quite sure where the real danger lay.

Marna scanned the small gathering before her, unflinching even in the face her father's hostility. "You can't reject Kiri Baland's offer. Not without thinking about what it can mean for our people. For our future."

Her hair was dressed in the same complex arrangement Tarl remembered so vividly from her first appearance in the Great Hall of the Palace, but this time she'd woven a delicate gold chain in among the dark strands of hair. Instead of the traditional drab robe of the Zeyn, she wore a robe that was common in Diloran Central, but scorned among her people. Made of brilliant, multi-colored silk that shimmered in the desert light, the robe draped into delicate folds that hinted at the soft curves beneath, including the slight rounding of her belly where their child was beginning to grow.

Their child. Tarl's breath caught in his throat. Somewhere deep in his chest he could feel the tightness, the excitement that the mere sight of her always aroused in him. She was his future and his soul, and in the four months that had passed since their formal ceremony of bonding, he had learned to wonder at the miracle that had brought her into his life.

But she was more than his future. She was her people's future, too. If they rejected what she had brought them—if her *father* rejected what she had brought *him*—Tarl knew it would be very difficult indeed to convince the Zeyn to join the new world government they were all fighting so hard to build.

With the easy grace that so distinguished her, Marna strode down the transport ramp and toward her father, heedless of the taut attention focused on her. She stopped beside Tarl, clearly arraying herself with the forces of change even as she pleaded for her father and the others to listen.

"Don't walk away from this, Father," she said. "Not now. We've gone too far and the world has changed too much for us to hide in the past, no matter how much we might want to."

Eileak whirled about, fists clenched and teeth bared, but he made no effort to move toward her. "How dare you return to the caverns, dressed like a—like a *stranger*"—he spat the word out as if it were bitter poison—"and tell me what I must do. You lost your right to speak as a Zeyn the moment you challenged our traditions and betrayed your sworn word. And as if that were not enough, you . . . you . . ." He pointed at her belly, choking on the words he could not bring himself to speak.

Marna's chin snapped up as if he'd hit her, but she didn't give ground. Tarl moved protectively closer to her, but all her attention was focused on her father.

"I have carried out my pledge," she said proudly. "I said I would do everything within my power to help free my people from the chains that bound them, and that is what I have done. The only difference is, those chains weren't forged by the Grisaans or any of the Families who have opposed us for so long. They were forged by *us,* one heavy link at a time."

"You lie!" Her father was shouting, but even his anger couldn't drive out the wild, lost look in his eyes. "You—"

"Let her speak!"

Eileak jerked, startled by the peremptory command, and spun to confront this new challenge.

Parra stepped forward. Her cold gaze fixed on Eileak. "Let her speak, I say. It is long past time for us to listen to new voices and new ideas. The world has changed, whether we will it or no. It will keep on changing in spite of anything we do to stop it. I, for one, believe we must change with it . . . or die."

The remaining Elders, including the two who had been so ready to follow Eileak back into the caverns, stirred restlessly, clearly uncertain how to react to this unexpected turn of events.

Parra swept them with her steely gaze, then turned to face Marna. "Well?" she demanded in the same harsh tones with which she'd challenged Eileak. "What kind of tools have you brought to cut these chains you talk about?"

Instead of replying, Marna darted back to the transport and up the ramp. She emerged a moment later, closely followed by her former maid, Sesha.

No one around Tarl moved. He would almost swear no one had breathed since Parra had uttered her challenge. Even Joeffrey, who knew what to expect, hung over his cane, watching the two women expectantly.

Tarl smiled. He'd never realized Marna had such a well-developed sense of showmanship. Always, she surprised him. He supposed she always would.

The proud, gaily dressed Sesha limping down the ramp was a far different person from the grim-faced woman Tarl had encountered in the palace garden months before. She held her head high, and her wrinkled face glowed with the radiance of her smile. The startling change in her was so great that it took the watching crowd several seconds to realize that she carried a brightly wrapped bundle in her arms. The bundle squirmed, and Sesha shifted it in her arms as she came to a halt in front of the waiting Zeyn.

"I haven't brought any tools to cut our chains, Elder Parra," Marna said. She made no effort to raise her voice, but it rang clearly in the expectant hush that held them all. "What I've brought is the proof that the tools can be made. That they *should* be made."

As Marna spoke, Sesha was carefully unwrapping her bundle to reveal a squirming, bright-eyed baby boy. He sat in her arms and stared back at the strange faces staring at him, totally unimpressed by all the attention.

Marna turned to the couple who had remained at the far edge of the group, watching all that went on in silent bewilderment. "Do you recognize him?" she asked quietly, smiling in spite of the tears that were beginning to course down her cheeks. "You had him for such a very short time."

"My . . . my son?" Caithra's words were little more than a whisper. She stared at the chubby baby in Sesha's arms like a blind woman who has suddenly been given the gift of sight, awed and wondering and filled with hope, but clearly not yet able to believe what she saw.

Dorn didn't move. He'd drawn Caithra safely against him when Joeffrey first appeared in the transport doorway and hadn't let her go since. His eyes were wide, dark wells of disbelief. His hands trembled on Caithra's shoulders.

Since neither Caithra nor Dorn seemed capable of moving,

Sesha brought their child to them. Her crippled leg cut a trail through the sand as she dragged it behind her, but she might as well have been an Elder of the Zeyn, so grand did she seem.

"Your son," she said, holding out the eagerly kicking baby.

Caithra stared at the chubby legs with their fat little feet. "His leg . . . His foot . . ." She looked around wildly, as if daring anyone to challenge the proof of her own eyes. "Do you see?" she demanded, caught between a sob and a cry of joy. "His leg's all right. It's all right!"

"Of course it's all right." Sesha's grin threatened to split her face in two. "The specialists in Diloran Central are used to dealing with things like this. I'll show you how to exercise his legs so they both grow strong and straight. You'll need to work with his foot, too, give him special massages, but he'll be walking as well as any other child in a year or so."

Tentatively, one hand clinging to Dorn, Caithra touched the perfect little foot waving in front of her. The child kicked free of her fingers, then blew a few disrespectful bubbles and stared at this odd adult who seemed to be making such a fuss over nothing.

Once more Sesha offered her the child, and this time Caithra grabbed him up, laughing and crying and babbling incoherently, all at the same time. "Do you see, Dorn? Our son. Our son!"

Dorn leaned over his offspring, who obligingly booted his father in the jaw. "He's beautiful," the proud father cried, half choking on his tears, half shouting for joy.

If either Caithra or Dorn said anything else, it was lost in the laughter and the tears and the excited babble of the other Zeyn who clustered around them, as awed by this small miracle as his parents were.

Tarl ignored the tears that dampened his own face and

gathered Marna in his arms. He didn't try to speak. He wasn't sure he could.

Not that it mattered. Words weren't necessary when Marna was in his arms. He drew her closer still and gently clasped his hand over the curve of her belly. She leaned against him and laid her hands over his, so that they were three, together as Dorn and Caithra and their child were once more together, safely bound within the compass of their embrace.

A soft, almost imperceptible moan broke the moment. Marna turned in Tarl's embrace until she could see her father, the only one among the Zeyn who had not rushed to view the wonder she had brought them. Eileak seemed unaware of his daughter's scrutiny. His dark eyes stared blankly, fixed on something far beyond the present that only he could see.

Whatever he saw, it didn't please him. His jaw tightened once in anger, then slowly dropped as if in despair. The hard lines of his face sagged until he looked old—old, and tired, and beaten. His hands opened, then fisted closed, then opened, again and again, as if he were trying to hold on to something that was slipping away from him.

Joeffrey, too, remained silent, his attention fixed on the sand in front of him. His hands lay folded over the head of his cane and he leaned on them heavily, clearly tiring under the strain of remaining standing for so long. But unlike Eileak, Joeffrey smiled.

It wasn't a smile of triumph, Tarl thought, but of wry sympathy. If anyone could understand what Eileak was thinking and feeling right now, it was Joeffrey. The future his old mentor had worked for was not the future he'd found, but he had adapted nonetheless. Because he had to. Because he'd been willing to learn and grow and change. He'd raged at Tarl's adamant refusal to accept any position except that of advisor to the new Council, and then he'd listened, and nodded, and made what he could of what he had. For the sake of what he'd always fought for—the people of Diloran.

Tarl's arms tightened around Marna, and when she glanced up at him in surprise, he bent and kissed her. Hard. Savoring the sweet wonder that she never ceased to stir in him.

How different his life was from what he'd expected only a few months before—and how much richer! None of them—not Marna, not Joeffrey, not Marott, and certainly not Tarl—had achieved what they'd started after, but only Marott and his followers, who had just completed their third month on the inhospitable colony world of Jeralan IV, had lost anything in the bargain. And who knew? Perhaps Marott, too, would learn to be grateful for the new life he led. Someday. Maybe.

Tarl stole one last kiss. Then, still holding Marna tight against him, he glanced over at Eileak. The Zeyn leader was the only one who had not yet come to terms with this future he had not expected. Judging from the awed excitement of the Zeyn around Caithra and Dorn, he would have to soon, whether he wanted to or not.

The small group split apart suddenly as Caithra and Dorn, faces radiant with happiness, broke free and came toward Marna.

"I . . . I don't know what to say." A tearful, smiling Caithra clung to her squirming son, who had managed to drool down the front of her robe.

"There isn't much we can say—except, thank you." The traces of tears lingered on Dorn's cheeks, but he made no effort to wipe them away.

Behind them, a grinning Wergan loomed protectively, clearly awed by this unexpected result of his defiance.

Marna laughed, but made no effort to pull free of Tarl's embrace. "You don't have to say anything, so long as you let me cuddle him once in a while.''

''I don't know if we can bear to let go of him long enough for that, but we'll try!'' Dorn tried to say more, but choked on the words as tears of happiness once more threatened to claim him. He wrapped his arm protectively around Caithra and his son, and led them toward the cavern entrance.

The rest of the assembled Zeyn trailed after them, still babbling excitedly. A couple glanced at Eileak, clearly uncertain how he would react to their defection, but most appeared to have forgotten about him. Only Parra remained behind.

As soon as the last straggler had disappeared, she turned her steady gaze on Marna. A tiny tear glimmered in the corner of her eye, but she ignored it, too proud to give in to so common a weakness. ''You were right about the child, it seems, Kiria. I suspect you may be right about a great deal more.''

Marna's grip on Tarl's hands tightened. ''Come to Diloran Central,'' she said quietly. ''It would make a good beginning.''

''Perhaps.'' Parra frowned, as if searching for what to say next. She glanced at Eileak, then back at Marna. ''Give us time. You can't remake a world in a week.'' Her frown deepened. ''I take it your Sesha has decided to return, after all. If she has come back—''

''She's come back, but not to stay,'' Marna cut in sharply. ''Sesha's training to become a therapist for crippled children. She's very good at it. She came with us only because someone had to show Caithra and Dorn what to do, and she'll go back with us when we leave.''

''I see.'' Parra's dark eyes shifted to meet Tarl's. ''And you, Kiri Grisaan? What will you do?''

Tarl glanced at Joeffrey and grinned. ''I'm an advisor to the new Council Chief. Joeffrey spent a lot of time telling me what to do over the years. Now I'm enjoying telling *him* what to do for a change.''

''Hummph!'' Joeffrey shifted his grip on his cane. ''Well, you'll just have to wait on that, because I'm tired of standing here in this heat talking. I see they've managed to unload my cart, so if Elder Parra would be so kind as to offer me a cup of kava . . . ?''

Their departure left Tarl and Marna and Eileak alone on the sands. Even the guards had retreated.

Marna pulled free of Tarl's arms and crossed to Eileak. ''Father?''

She gently touched her father's sleeve. It was surely too light a touch for Eileak to feel it through the heavy cloth of the robe, yet he flinched as if with pain.

He breathed deeply, then let the air out of his lungs slowly. ''That's not their son,'' he said at last. ''Their child was born a cripple. The proctors told me. They had no reason to lie, and our traditions—''

''That child *is* their son,'' Marna cut in sharply, ''no matter what you think. Changed, yes, healed as we could not heal him and with a future we could not give him, but still their son.''

Eileak turned his head from her, refusing to listen.

Marna blinked, fighting back tears. ''He is their son, Father, just as I am your daughter. Nothing can ever change that. You have to believe that, even if you refuse to believe everything else.''

Tarl watched, and waited, and listened to the faint skitter of sand blown along the ground by the dry wind. When the silence stretched, he crossed to Marna and gently laid his hand on her shoulder. She twined her fingers in his, but didn't take her steady gaze off her father.

''We thought we'd name your granddaughter Jesera, after your wife, Marna's mother,'' Tarl said at last when neither Eileak nor Marna spoke.

Eileak turned his head back to stare, first at Tarl, then at Marna. His eyes were wide and dark and hollow-looking. "Jesera."

Marna's hold on Tarl's fingers tightened. "Jesera of Diloran."

Eileak's mouth twisted in sad acknowledgment. "But not Jesera of the Zeyn."

"No. She will have a world to choose from . . . if she wants. A universe." Marna took a deep breath. "I thought . . . that is, Tarl and I thought . . . I hoped, when she was old enough, that you would teach her the ways of the desert, just as you taught me."

Eileak's breath caught. His eyes suddenly glowed with remembering and his mouth twisted again, this time in a wry smile. "You were always so determined to do things your way. You disappeared once or twice, in spite of all my watching. I was so frightened that I'd never find you again, but . . ." His smile disappeared. He blinked once or twice, as though fighting back tears, and said softly, "But you always found your way back, even when I didn't think you would."

"And I always will," Marna said just as softly. "Always."

Eileak nodded, once, twice. His gaze shifted from Marna to Tarl, and back again. "There are many paths in the desert . . ." His voice trailed off.

"And many ways to follow them," Tarl added softly.

"Yes." Eileak nodded slowly. "Many ways." He stepped back, then hesitantly gestured to the open cavern entrance. "Perhaps we should join the others now. There are . . ." He paused. "There are many things we need to talk about."

Side by side, Marna and Tarl followed Eileak to the open doorway into the rock. Just before the guard closed the door behind them, Marna stopped, then turned to stare out at the golden sand and the bright desert sky.

Tarl turned to see what had caught her attention. ''Is anything wrong?''

''No,'' she said. ''Nothing's wrong.'' She smiled, her eyes bright with unshed tears, and slipped her hand in his. ''Absolutely nothing at all.''

AUTHOR'S NOTE

Dear Reader:

I seem to be working backwards these days.

Hidden Heart was set on a world in the distant future. My next story is centered around one of the marvels of the present day—electronic communications and the ways in which it can bring two very different people together.

In "Dance on the Edge," a story in the *Lovescape* anthology to be released by Leisure Books in August 1996, architect Jack Martin and interior designer Marlis Jones thought that communicating by e-mail would allow them to keep their working relationship cool, distant, and professional. They never imagined that it would lead them to reveal the deepest secrets of their own hearts.

In December, Michael Ryan and Hetty Malone journey to 1890s Colorado in *The Snow Queen*, a story based on the fairy tale by Hans Christian Andersen. A medical doctor, Michael has dedicated himself to a quest for a cure for tuberculosis, but it is Hetty who will teach him that the power of the human heart is greater than the power of science.

I very much enjoy hearing from readers. My address is P.O. Box 62533, Colorado Springs, CO, 80962-2533. A self-addressed, stamped envelope would be much appreciated.

Sincerely,
Anne Avery